QUEST OF THE
CHOSEN
— THE JOURNEY BEGINS —

BRUCE CAMPELIA

BOOK I
LIGHT PASSERS CHRONICLES

This book is dedicated to Morningstar, Zack, Kai Li, and Liyah, who brought out the best in me, and took me on a journey of a lifetime—into their lives and the lives of those who came before them.

"The center of the universe is everywhere."

- Black Elk

Acknowledgments

A debut novel requires an unyieldingly strong foundation of support. This one, eight years in the making, is no exception. For a usually confident person, my self-doubt reared its ugly head more times than I care to remember during this arduous process. Those times when I found myself lacking, I turned to others of greater strength who believed in me to provide that foundation.

So, here I have an opportunity to openly thank a few of the many people who have given me support along the way: Elizabeth Littlefield, my better half, artist, and sometimes editor, for her never wavering encouragement and belief in me and the important messages delivered in this book, and who cleared the path so I might finally complete what I started so long ago; Darlene Grove, who always encouraged me to write and believed in my ability to put a story forth in a creative way, one that would be meaningful to others; Paul Campelia, my older brother, who assisted me financially to make this happen; Kelly, Alexis, and Gina, my three lovely daughters who blessedly love me unconditionally as I do them, who try constantly to pull their dad back to earth (a tough task), and whose lives define and inspire me; and Joseph Lack, whose overwhelming enthusiasm for this book and true friendship helped carry me to the finish line.

And of course, a big acknowledgment to my very special publishing team at NOW Publishing and the many others who helped me through this oftentimes overwhelming endeavor. You all know who you are. Thank you.

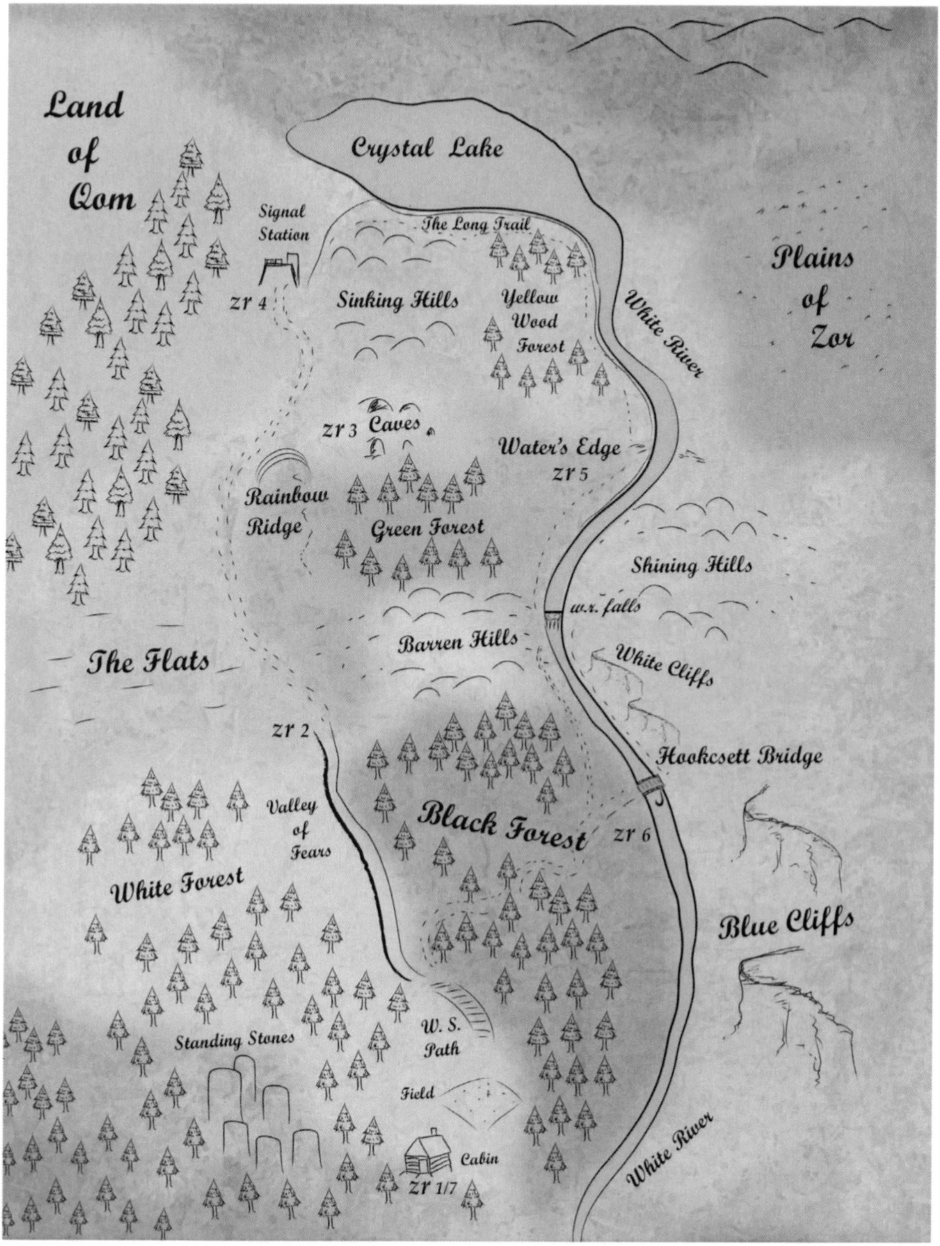
Land of Qom
Crystal Lake
Signal Station
The Long Trail
Sinking Hills
Yellow Wood Forest
White River
Plains of Zor
zr 4
zr 3
Caves
Water's Edge
zr 5
Rainbow Ridge
Green Forest
Shining Hills
w.r. falls
Barren Hills
White Cliffs
The Flats
zr 2
Hookcsett Bridge
Valley of Fears
Black Forest
zr 6
White Forest
Blue Cliffs
W. S. Path
Standing Stones
Field
Cabin
zr 1/7
White River

ONE

———

Badlands, South Dakota

THE WINDS AND howling ceased, replaced by an eerie silence. The darkness remained for a moment, then it too receded, slowly giving back control to the dawning sun. Light began to pour into a world of . . . *nothing.*

Sarah Morningstar uncovered her ears, grabbed the sides of the bathtub, and raised herself up. How much time had gone by? Seconds? Hours? She couldn't remember time at all—she could only remember her grandfather shoving her in there and shouting at her to cover her head. She had made herself as small as possible, holding tight to her shins and kissing her knees, her eyes clamped shut. All the while an earsplitting roaring sound shook the house on its foundation.

She stumbled out of the bathroom, which was now only a space with no walls and no floor, just the concrete slab where her home had rested. No couch, no kitchen, no refrigerator. Only the tub remained. The rest of the trailer home was missing too, her whole world flattened and scattered about, like the compacted trash on top of the landfill she and her grandfather had just been to over the weekend.

She gazed out beyond the trailer but could see nothing except debris scattered about: no houses left standing—just their foundations. No mailboxes, no irritating loud yipping from little Button the French poodle that belonged to the Stantons, her closest neighbors, and no giant oak tree between her house and theirs. No cars, no furniture, no people.

Nothing.

Morningstar sat down on the concrete slab, wearing the only clothes she had left: her jeans, her blue beaded moccasins, and her traditional Native American tunic, dark tan with its brown suede fringe and red, yellow, and white sequins. She had been dressing up for a special school gathering. Before she could make the final adjustments of exchanging her jeans for dress pants, and her red bandana for her woven Lakota headband, the blackness and wind came calling.

"Hurry up, Sweetie," her grandfather, her *lala*, had urged her just before her world collapsed, "you don't want to be late for your big day."

Then the air had sparked, and the roaring had begun. One quick glance out the kitchen window, and her grandfather had grabbed her hand and bolted toward the bathroom. It was the last thing she remembered clearly; him grabbing her, his frightened eyes, his instructions. And now everything was gone. Was it even possible? Was she dreaming?

Morningstar stood back up, cupped her hands around her mouth to magnify the sound, then called out into the morning air, first quietly, then louder.

"Lala! Lala? Are you there?"

No answer, only dead silence. The entire park was gone—the place where she had lived for the past five years, since fire had claimed her parents. That disaster, now this. It couldn't be happening, again! Could it? Her eyes must be lying. Lala must still be here somewhere. He would never leave her, ever.

She moved out toward the yard, first walking then running throughout what was left of the park, screeching the Lakota name for grandfather. Down the street she dashed, hurdling past clumps of debris, past what remained of the Stanton's house, past the Lamberts', and over to the bus stop. She circled 'round then headed back, all the time yelling out, "Lala! Lala!"

Tears poured down her face as a fist of fear threatened to choke her. She searched the distance, the vast nothingness in front of her. Where was he? Was he dead? And why was she spared? She could imagine his kind eyes looking into hers, eyes she might never see again. Had the tornado swept him up? Should she go and look once more for him? But where? There was no place left to look. Everything was simply gone.

Nothing made any sense at all right now. Weak and tired, she dropped onto the concrete steps that once led up to the front door of the house. They seemed so very odd standing there by themselves, leading to nowhere—no door, no wall, no home to go to. Her scattered, frightened mind dropped into a darkness of another kind.

"Breathe," Lala would say. "Breathe and calm your mind, focus on something else."

Sarah drew a lazy circle in the dirt with her moccasin, watching the blue beaded toe box swirl in the dusty earth. *This* was real. This earth. This shoe. But if that was so, how could everything else be real too?

A shadow whispered across the desolation. A few black storm clouds lingered, and the sun broke through between them, illuminating random patches of ground as the remaining clouds permitted. One of the patches hovered lazily over the debris. *How odd,* she thought. It was as if the sun was silent and searching too, stunned by the peacefulness of the place, the finality of it all. It was all here just a short time ago, but now everything was gone. There wasn't even the rustle of a piece of paper wandering down the road blown by the spring wind, or the flap of curtains across an open window. No bird song or buzzing of lawn mowers, no sound at all, just the quiet push of her breathing.

Out of the corner of her eye, she caught a glimpse of a fuzzy cone of light moving perpendicular to the rolling, sunlit patches. The light appeared to kiss the ground with the small end of its funnel, but silently, not like the vicious black funnel of that tornado: no sign of the deafening, freight train roar brought on by the ferocious wind that ripped through her life at dawn, spewing chaos across the landscape.

The light within the funnel moved in upward waves, the same way heat radiated off the tar road in the summer—on those days so hot Sarah's science teacher would try to fry an egg on the road just to make a point. The air around her had a heaviness and power about it, which was strange, because she knew air weighed nothing, but as the funnel came closer, the weight pressed on her chest, tightening her breaths.

A hundred feet away.

The light moved slowly but steadily toward her, and she couldn't look away or think. With no place to go, all she could do was sit still and stare at it. Just a few years ago she'd ridden out a hurricane when visiting Florida with her lala—*but where is he now, why isn't he here?* This was like that moment in the eye when the air stilled into a heavy calmness.

Anticipation built inside her, a sort of ominous and thick wariness—*what is going on here?* She squinted to get a better fix on this thing moving toward her, but she could see nothing but the swirling light.

Her grandfather had positioned their trailer at the far edge of the small, spread-out neighborhood to provide the feeling of an even more spacious yard. A very short distance to the north was the land known as the Badlands, a cavernous, rocky and unlivable area. Around her were the remains of the neighbor's homes, and beyond those homes lay the poverty-stricken Pine Ridge Reservation that was still the home of many Lakota. She kept her eye on the funnel as it made its way from the edge of the Badlands, closer to her.

The funnel dipped and then rose over the nearest knoll, crossing the field where she and her friend Mica played soccer together only yesterday. The light grew wider, brighter, and ever nearer.

The air around her had thickened, and a sweat broke out on her brow. All she could sense was a deathly stillness; the hair on her arms stood up, as if charged with static electricity.

Suddenly, it was upon her.

She tried to scream. Tried to stand so she could back away. But there was nothing there, nowhere to go. Everything—everyone—was gone.

Multicolored prisms of light rose from nowhere, swirling faster and faster, a tornado of pure energy. It was almost mesmerizing in its beauty and perfection.

Sarah tensed and gasped for breath just as she was engulfed. Her short life flashed before her eyes: her mom, her dad, the fire, clutching her stuffed bear as her grandfather rescued her in his arms, then his eyes as he told her of their death. She wondered oddly what had been the point in even getting excited about the special event she was to star in this morning if this was to be her final ending, or if maybe the ending had already happened? Then there was no more time to think, no time to worry.

The swirling colors flashed and streamed about her like a funhouse on steroids. A soothing warmth bubbled inside her then radiated outward, seeping through her skin. She tried to fight, tried to move, but the light held her as if she were wound up in a rope. A moment later her muscles softened, her eyes relaxed, and her breathing steadied. She could feel herself giving in, letting go.

She felt as if she were falling into a dream, growing weightless. The light now passed right through her because she too was part of the funnel, but she couldn't see the other side, couldn't see anything anymore. She sensed the very molecules of her body diffusing into the air.

She was fading faster now; becoming part of the ether about her, becoming one with the tempest of light. *So this must be death*, she thought just before a high whining sound radiated from the center, swelled quickly to a deafening volume, then cut off with a sudden flash of intense white light.

POP!

A few dried leaves and bits of debris swirled above the concrete stoop then settled back down, but Sarah was gone. She had vanished into the thinness of the light.

Two

Kowloon, Hong Kong

THE MOON WAS dimming in the twilight sky and would soon give way to a rising sun. A sliver of light found its way through the window above the shade, striking a bright line on the floor. The moon's trajectory moved the line across the floor, then the bed, then over Kai Li's fingers, along his arm and onto his shoulder. It slid up the side of his face, flowed along his neck and crested over his cheekbone, illuminating the corner of his eye.

Kai Li lay silent in the light for as long as he could before patting along the side of the mattress for his cell phone. He stared at the time: 6:05 AM. It was late, and now he would have to hurry. No time to linger in the warm bed.

He threw off the covers and got to his feet. If he was late, he knew they'd give his job away in a nanosecond. His mother had cautioned him time and time again, warning of the consequences of being irresponsible. "At least think of your father if not yourself," she would admonish. The fear of letting his father down always pulled at him, even though Kai Li knew it was too late to make his father proud. Too late for everything.

He grabbed his black cuffed pants from the back of the chair, jumped into them, zipped the fly. Yanking his dress white, long sleeve jersey down over his head, he thought he saw a flash of light. He pushed the sleeves up to just below his elbows, then pulled the shade aside and glanced up at the predawn sky. Nothing. He jammed the tail of the shirt into the top of the pants. He never allowed himself a moment to think what normal teenagers in other parts of the world did. Kai Li was far from normal, and so was his life.

It's good to have this job, he thought, as he threaded the black belt through the pant loops. In this poor part of town, kids his age who worked were accountable for every minute they were there. High stress, high pressure, high expectations. Often with no break. Kai Li's work worries had shifted in new ways once he received the promotion to "gopher," the English word he'd learned for running all over the lower city getting last minute supplies, taking shipping papers to the pier, or doing a host of other errands. Going for this and going for that—whatever anyone needed to keep the factory running at optimum pace. Still high stress, high pressure, and high expectations, but at least he could take a deep breath now and then. And far better than spending hours inside the stifling, sweaty, stinking factory.

Any resentment Kai Li felt about his life evaporated when he reminded himself that his mom worked even harder, cleaning hotel rooms during the day and sewing in a local sweatshop sometimes in the evening. The two of them lived their lives day to day, hour by hour, saving the odd dollar for his education. Someday he'd have enough to go to college in America. His "ticket out," his mother called it. His way of becoming *more*.

Kai Li slipped his feet into a pair of white socks, then into his high-top white sneakers, lacing them up. He made his way quickly into the bathroom that separated his bedroom from the small living area where his mother slept. The worn porcelain handle of the cold-water faucet squeaked as he turned it on. A rush of water splashed into the green-stained basin. As he bent his head forward, he squinted into the mirror in front of him; a tired young boy stared back. It was an image of long hard days and short nights. His fine black hair stood straight up in the back. He grabbed the comb from the side of the sink and dragged it across his head, brushed his teeth, then slipped on a pair of black-rimmed tortoiseshell spectacles with wide lenses. They often skated along the bridge of his flat nose forcing him to push them back up, irritating him to no end.

In the living room, his mother lay on her side, curled up with her face turned toward the only other window in the apartment. The yellowed shade was pulled down to block the view of the brick wall across the alley and cast a jaundiced color over his mother's face.

Each morning he followed the same routine. And each time, just before he bent down to kiss her, he thought about how much he loved her, how she had sacrificed so much for him. Almost ten years ago, after the trouble with the Chinese authorities on the mainland, they had moved to Hong Kong, at the southernmost tip of China, and settled into this small apartment on the Kowloon Peninsula, starting over with just a suitcase and a handful of cash.

These were the times he missed his father. When he resented him for dying, and the authorities for lying about it.

He kissed the top of her head. She stirred ever so slightly, enough to acknowledge his presence but not so much as to fully wake. In the kitchen, he grabbed a soda from the fridge then one of the two house keys hanging on the wall next to the door. Slowly and silently, he unlatched the dead bolt, removed the chain lock on the door, and slipped out into the hallway. He relocked the door before hurrying down the hall, his sneakers squeaking along the epoxy-coated concrete corridor. Ignoring the staircase, he headed straight to the fire escape.

Faster and more direct, the fire escape route was also the safest route out; it dumped him a ways up from the drunks and thugs who loitered at the corner of the building. Just as he took his first step onto the rusted wrought iron platform, another flash came from somewhere behind him. He spun around. Nothing. Maybe a streetlight burning itself out in the darkness. He clambered down three floors, the fire escape clanging and swaying under his weight. Jumping from the bottom rung, he landed in the alley with a heavy thud.

The full moon was quickly turning into a ghost but could still be seen in the dim morning sky, and the sun now began to rise. He headed off toward Hoi Yuen Road; he would have to go about five blocks before cutting over toward the factory, where they made stuffed animals of all kinds to be shipped to America, Europe, and other destinations.

He hustled down the street, making his way under the Kwun Tong Road Overpass, then finally over to the normally busy Hoi Yuen Road, which was still sleepy at this hour. Aside from a few lonely cars and the odd person hustling silently along the sidewalk, the only real evidence of activity were the signs atop and protruding from the sides of the buildings, flooding the main street with their blinking and buzzing, shouting out messages like city roosters crowing at the coming of dawn.

Suddenly a bright flash of orange light flared over a rooftop ahead of him. It stopped him in his tracks. He stared hard at where he thought it originated, trying to figure out what had happened. There was nothing. Just the neon lights talking to each other. He spun around, gazing nervously in all directions. What was happening? Was he losing his mind?

Collecting himself, he stepped up his pace, following Hoi Yuen Road a few more blocks. He began to turn onto the street the factory was on; from there he only had to cross one more street and Chi Sun Exports would then just be a half block away. As he completed the turn, he took his phone out of his pocket and checked the time. It would be tight. Why had he paused so many times along the way? Why did he feel so spooked?

He began to cross the last street. As he got to the other side, a sign above him started sputtering loud electrical noises. He thrust his eyes upward. Bursts of red, white, and blue light startled him. Sparks started to pour from the sign, a shower of tiny flames.

He darted quickly to his right, away from the shower of sparks and into the street, heading toward the factory. His stomach churned. He glanced down at the can of soda, debated taking a swig but knew he would need it for lunch. As he looked toward Kowloon Bay, he caught a glimpse of the sun rising over the water, its light shining right between the buildings. It appeared like a reddish-yellow ball, caught between two thin layers of clouds.

Behind him, Kai Li could hear the last sputters of the sign. Ahead of him, workers were pouring into the factory, heads down, attention on their hurried steps. Only a few turned their heads, briefly distracted by the commotion.

The sun was inching toward the tops of the buildings, gaining greater intensity by the second; his eyes were fixated on it. Then a streetlight to his right suddenly flared up. Disoriented, he felt captive between night and day, yet he couldn't seem to break the spell of the sun.

Fear again began to wedge its way into Kai Li's thoughts. His stomach knotted and a lump lodged in his throat. A jerk and a flash, and then the blazing sun shot directly toward him, like a meteor on fire. He froze. His eyes widened in terror. His phone fell from his hand and crashed on the street. Before Kai Li could call out, the ball of light was upon him.

Flash!

The workers continued to pile into Chi Sun Exports, and first traffic of the day broke upon the quiet morning streets. Kai Li's solitary green ginger ale can spun slowly to a stop, finally coming to a rest against the curb. Kai Li was nowhere to be found.

THREE

———————

Beit Lahia, Gaza Strip

THINGS WERE BUZZING inside the two-story sandstone house on the small, narrow street. Guests would be arriving any minute to celebrate her father's birthday. Pungent, sweet smells filled every inch of the house.

Liyah stood in front of the mirror in her best outfit: her favorite dark-blue jacket and light dress pants. Her cousin's friend Ahmad had been invited. Every time she saw his dark eyes and shy smile, she prayed he would notice her. It was a secret she told no one, especially not her mother, who was a traditional Muslim and believed any formal "relationship" introductions should be made by her. Ahmad had worked last summer for her dad, when Liyah first saw him, when she thought her father could surely hear her heart beating when Ahmad would walk by. How could she confess this? Especially to her mother. She knew there was no way she could ever be alone with him. Her life as a dutiful Muslim daughter seemed so small and inescapable. She felt there was no room for *her*, that she was disappearing. That she couldn't breathe.

Liyah smoothed her hair and was adjusting the hijab around her head when her mother stepped into the bedroom and frowned.

"Why are you not downstairs? Everyone will be here soon, and I need your help in the kitchen." She turned away, fully expecting Liyah to follow. "And where is your brother?"

Liyah stole a last glance at the mirror. "Khalib?"

"What other brother do you have?" Her mother's voice rose with impatience.

She hurried to keep up with her mother's quick steps down the hall. "He said he was going to the square to meet up with his friends and would be back in time for the dinner."

"That boy will be the death of your father! He told Khalib not to go anywhere today. You'll have to go find him and bring him back before your father finds out."

Liyah knew she might miss Ahmad if she left. Boys like to eat, but they don't like to hang out with the family.

"But—"

"No buts. Get moving! And be careful. I hear there's another protest in the square." Her mother turned away to stir the lamb stew.

Liyah sighed then exchanged her dress shoes for a pair of more comfortable sandals. Why did she always have to keep track of her younger brother? It was hot, and the dust from the streets would surely ruin her clothes.

As she picked up her pace on the half-mile walk to the main square, she tried calling Khalib from her cell. No answer. As usual. She slowed as she texted him and waited for the "read" notation. Nothing. She called again, this time leaving a message: "Where are you, Khalib? Mom's pissed. Call me when you get this."

The blazing sun bore down. Not a cloud above to block it. A light-headedness overcame her as she looked for her brother and brushed by people on the sidewalk. Turning the corner, she saw the out-of-control throng pushing past the mosque, heading toward the police barricade.

Tensions between the Israelis and Palestinians had risen again. *Typical.* There would be a flicker of peace, followed by a bombing of a hospital or school, and an uprising of some radicals in Beit Lahia. Then retaliations again from both sides. *When would this stupidity ever end? So useless.*

The men and boys lingered after praying at the mosque and were easily pulled into the angry demonstration, trying to solve a problem that began even before her grandparents were born, and it was just getting worse. It was impossible to unravel it. It all just seemed dumb.

The sun baked the landscape and fueled the discomfort of the crowd. Voices of peaceful protesters quickly gave way to shouting, and the crowd began to transform into a mob.

To Liyah Al-Rahim it was hard to say when or how any of this all started, but it didn't matter. She was sixteen and this had been going on for as long as she could remember. It was the same old anger, the same old hatred, the same tired old scene. Liyah wished she could close her eyes and be somewhere, anywhere, other than here. How was that ever going to happen? How was she ever going to have *a life?*

She wandered into the square searching the faces for Khalib. A few years younger than her and as thin as a stick, he'd gotten so much taller this past year, almost as tall as her. Undoubtedly, he was part of this rumbling throng. Total idiocy in Liyah's eyes. Only a week ago three people had been killed in a disturbance on the other side of town, all Palestinians, including a boy in her class. She'd heard her parents say the promise of a recent peace seemed to now be blowing away with the rising swirls of the sand and wind.

As Liyah drew closer to the group, a tightness gripped her stomach. Something was not right at all. The crowd was approaching the police barricade and it looked like they weren't going to stop. Signs carrying the messages "Destroy Israel!" and "America the Great Satan!" bobbed up and down as angry voices shouted in unison, "Death to the infidels!"

The officers in the front began to press their shields into the crowd, pushing anyone who resisted away from the area near the government buildings. In response, the crowd surged forward. The police swung their batons, and then the first stone was thrown. Chaos ensued. Liyah, now caught in the melee, tried to shove her way through the sea of angry men, still searching.

"Khalib! Khalib!" Liyah stumbled amidst the wave of bodies. Their crushing weight pressed against her until she could hardly breathe. For a second, she was nine once more, pinned under the dusty rubble after a bomb destroyed her home. Stifling, suffocated, terrified.

"Let me out! Khalib! Where are you?" She kept stumbling forward, pressing against the stronger, bigger bodies of the men. Panic rose in her throat.

Then, finally, she caught a glimpse of the thin frame and curly black mop-top head of her brother, just ahead of her.

"Khalib! Khalib! Khalib!" she screamed at the top of her lungs.

He turned around and tried to fight his way to her, but like her, could barely make headway against the angry, storming masses pushing into him. Khalib went down. Liyah screamed, reaching out a desperate, futile hand toward him. She bent low, scurrying past legs and arms until she was able to grab onto Khalib's arm. "Come on!"

Holding each other tight, they slid to the right, careening off bodies, but weren't fast enough. The barricades, the police, the batons loomed closer, only a few feet away. A stocky policeman is his dark-blue uniform and black helmet brought his club over her head. Khalib yanked her out of the way just in time. They broke free, just as an angry roar filled the square.

"Run, Khalib! We must run!"

Her brother, younger and faster, flew ahead. Liyah tried to keep up but tripped over a man on the ground and tumbled to the dirt-packed street. The world seemed to slow, then go silent, as she lay on her back. Above her, narrow rays of light pierced the blue sky, the wavy haze of confusion around her.

Two bright beams of light flashed into Liyah's eyes. She closed them tight, but when she reopened them, all she could see was the mesmerizing light. Was it Paradise?

The light brightened, began to pulse, slowly, then faster. A high-pitched whining accompanied the light, and started winding up, louder and louder. The crowd covered their ears, dropped to their knees, wailing against the pain inflicted by the sound.

Liyah, too, covered her ears, tried to close her eyes. A sudden flash, then . . .

SNAP!

And she was gone.

The square in front of the mosque fell silent. The last of the dust squalls settled. People began to stand up cautiously, confused.

Khalib stopped running and turned around. "Liyah?"

She was nowhere to be seen. The crowd began to disperse, drifting toward their homes, the protest forgotten, the world calm.

Four

Detroit, Michigan

A LATE MAY breeze trickled through the open window, doing nothing to quell the heat of the cramped third-floor apartment. In the living room, Zack Owens made a quick detour around Elijah, who was sparring with Jayden over the remote. Elijah, wiry and tall at fourteen, was faster than shorter and younger Jayden. "Guys, cut it out," rang their mother's stern voice from the kitchen. Neither of them listened.

Zack dumped his dishes from dinner in the sink before his mother could remind him, then grabbed a few French fries from the remainders cooling on a cookie sheet atop the stove. His mother reached over and swatted his hand.

"You got enough. Leave 'em for your sisters."

At the table, Kiara had her head buried in a book while nine-year-old Angel was pushing her dinner around on the plate. Mom hovered between the hot stove and the unsteady table. Ketchup and hamburger grease spotted her wrinkled apron. Her graying hair was up in a messy ponytail, and her mouth turned down in its familiar, perpetual frown. She shot Angel a look of disapproval. "Eat your dinner. I don't work all day for you to waste that food."

Angel made a face. "I don't like peas."

"Be grateful you have any." Mom yanked Kiara's book out of her hands. "You too."

Elijah raised the remote in a victory wave, darted into the kitchen, and sank into his chair, glancing back at Jayden, who was behind him, sulking. "Loser."

"Mom!" Jayden blurted out, frustrated. "He called me a loser!" Elijah shrugged as he flipped stations on the small TV that sat in the corner of the kitchen counter, a gratified grin on his face.

Their mother sighed and shook her head. "It's too hot for you all to be annoyin' me. Just eat your dinner and quit your fighting." She cast a sharp look at Zack when he tried to duck out of the kitchen. "Where *you* goin'?"

"Upstairs." *Anywhere but here,* he thought. The noise, the heat, the cramped quarters sometimes felt suffocating to him. Jayden started kicking the bottom of Kiara's chair with a steady *thump, thump.* Their mother ignored it.

"Dishes?" Mom questioned.

"It's Jayden's turn." His brother began another protest, but Zack ignored him and left the room. He headed down the hall to the bedroom he shared with both his brothers. For five minutes, maybe, he'd be alone. He kicked the door shut behind him and flopped onto his bed, the sagging twin mattress bouncing under his weight and the old springs letting out protesting squeaks.

Zack grabbed a paperback from the small stack next to his bed: James Baldwin's *The Fire Next Time.* It was a favorite of his dad's and had become his favorite, too, even though it sometimes conjured up his anger towards him. The worn cover was soft, the edges ragged. He'd read it so many times, he knew every word; he could flip to any page and recite a passage from memory. His dad had left it behind when he moved to Boston four years ago. Said he'd be back. *So much for that.*

Zack rubbed the edge with his thumb, flipping it open at the bookmark. He propped one arm behind his head, his tight braids pressing into his scalp. He could hear the sounds of his brothers fighting again, their voices barely muffled by the hollow wooden door, and Mom losing what patience she had, screaming at them to stop.

He read the page before him, read it over and over, until the biting family squabbles disappeared, and the words of the book took their place. As the familiar story settled into one part of his mind, another part, finally untethered, drifted to his day at school, to the chaos at home, to thinking about his dad. So often to his dad. Years ago, no, ages ago, he sat on this very bed and read Zack stories every night. Hadn't he? Or was Zack adjusting the memory, creating a better one, and losing track of the reality?

A weariness crept through his mind like a green fog. He brought the book to his chest, clutching it as if it could be a way out of the prison he lived in. As the oldest, Zack had become the one his mother leaned on the most, the one the other kids looked at as the boss, the one everyone expected to be strong and smart and a million things Zack knew he wasn't.

In these rare quiet moments in his room, he could finally shut it all out. Could avoid the streets that were filled with gangs, drugs, and violence; a world that called to him like the sirens did to Odysseus, that dude he'd read about in English. Calling to him, loud and insistent, as tempting an escape as coke or smack. The loudest voices belonged to the gangs. Always lookin' for tender meat they could put to use and spit out later.

His brothers came thundering down the hall and tumbled into the room, fighting again. Zack swung out of bed, grabbed his phone out of his pants pocket and texted his best friend, Tommy.

Hey dude, what up? Dyin' here. Mom's up my ass per usual. Thought we'd hang.

The reply was immediate.

OK bro. Got to be here tho.

Deal. OMW.

Zack paused for a second at the side of his bed, staring down at the phone in his hand. Since the first day in kindergarten when Zack was lost and Tommy knew the way to the classroom, Tommy had been there for him. Why did his other so-called "friends," all Black like him, let him down or leave? *He might as well be White, too,* he thought. *No way he fits with anything here.*

Zack grabbed something from behind the books and tucked it in his hoodie. He slipped the phone back into his pocket and stepped over his brothers. "Headin' out."

He had almost reached the door to the outside hall before he heard her. "Where you think you goin' now?"

Zack pivoted back. Mom stood in the hall, hands on hips, frustration on her face.

"Tommy's."

"On a school night?"

Like his mother cared if he did well in school. She barely noticed him. "I'm up every morning for school . . . on time. Get off my back."

She looked hard at him and shook her head. "You gettin' mo' and mo' like him every day."

"Him" was his father, the man his mother hated more than anyone in the world. There had been a day when Zack would have been pleased to hear those words. But the way his mother almost spat them at him made his stomach sour.

His sisters had turned up the volume on the show they were watching in the tiny living room, and the high-pitched sound of some mindless animated absurdity echoed along the walls. "Turn that damn thing down!" His mother spun on her heel and kept yelling as she went back down the hall. "The whole neighborhood can hear it."

Zack took the opportunity to slip down the hall and out the door to the main hallway of the apartment building. Just as he began descending the stairs to the outside door, to freedom, his mother caught back up with him. He braced himself for another lecture, but instead she pressed a jacket into his hands.

"Wear this. S'posed to get cool."

It was about as much of an olive branch as he was going to get. "Thanks." He shrugged into the lined, navy denim jacket and hurried down the stairs to the outside door and out to the street. He made his way down the dimly lit sidewalk. He drew in a deep breath, free again, even if the streets really did have that smell of the inner city, of bad air from bus exhaust, trash, and urine.

A few blocks away from home, Zack reached into the pocket of his hoodie and removed a leather sheath that carried the small knife he'd retrieved from the hiding place behind his books. He bent down and strapped it to the side of his calf where it would rest under his pants, but still be easy to access. Even so, a knife wasn't much protection these days. He knew it. Real gangs used handguns, even shotguns. But it was better than nothing.

Zack moved briskly, past the other run-down brick project-style apartment buildings similar to his own. A few big old dilapidated triple-decker houses were mixed in along the way, sporting peeled paint, broken wooden stairs, and yellowed railings leading up to their porches. He glanced up at a streetlight as he passed by, noting the shot-out lamp at its crown. *Didn't used to be this way,* he thought. *Maybe it wasn't so great back then, back when I was little, when Pops was here. But it sure was a whole lot nicer than this.* Or was he kidding himself again? He remembered playing street hockey with anyone who wanted to join in until he couldn't stand up any longer, and his mom and the other moms yelling down the street that it was way late, and for them to come home, now. The few friends he had, all except Tommy, had either joined gangs or moved away, their dads—if they still had one at home—were off trying to find work, just like his.

A sudden gust of wind spawned dust eddies that swirled and danced down the street, sending a plastic bag skittering ahead of him, and blowing bits of paper and other debris across Zack's path. He looked up at the sky. Storm clouds were racing toward the full moon. He flipped up the collar of his jacket and zipped the front up halfway, then pulled his hood up over his head.

Before he knew it, the crumbling brick façade of Gates Middle School appeared out of the shadows. Looming tall and imposing, it could have been the ghost of an ancient castle. Tommy's house was in the neighborhood behind it.

Zack took his phone from his pocket and texted him.

Near the school. There in a few.

He approached the far end of the giant structure then angled through the yard and across the macadam basketball courts, which took up the better part of the side of the building. Most summers he used to play here. Now cracked and lightless, no one used them. It used to be that you could play day or night—pickup games with whoever was around— but no one was around anymore; the lights had been shot out here too, and the courts were now used as a place to buy drugs or settle scores.

The light of the moon bounced off weeds struggling to break through the tar, spilling over the broken chunks that rose up like frost heaves on a winter road. One of the backboards bent toward the faded paint of the foul lines, its rim twisted and rusted. The chain net missing entirely. Broken, crappy, and useless. Pretty much his own life lately.

Zack glanced up again, the moon slid behind a cloud leaving him surrounded in darkness. A shiver chased up his spine, catching him by surprise. *Chill in the air,* he figured. But it really wasn't that cold. Nerves, maybe? Something felt a bit off. It was still early in the evening, though, so less chance for trouble. Probably nothing at all. Besides, the hole in the fence to Tommy's was just on the other side of the school.

As he turned the corner, a flash of lightning startled him, pursued by a hard clap of thunder. Then a clanging sound rang in the eerie darkness, making Zack jump a little. He brushed it off as a rope on a forgotten flagpole, or a neglected door left open.

Then he heard the sound again and saw a side door to the school, propped open with a piece of wood. Someone was in there, sleeping, stealing, dealing—didn't matter. If he was smart, he'd keep going, but . . .

Slipping cautiously past the door, he stepped into a darkened hallway, passed several classrooms, and approached the central part of the building where the main hallways intersected. Patches of light filtered in from upstairs through un-boarded holes in the windows. Chipped and broken wall tiles lined the hallway floor, graffiti covered the walls, and busted light fixtures hung overhead. He moved in the direction of the stairwell.

Multiple flashes of lightning poured in through the windowless holes above him. The room across from him lit up for an instant, illuminating rusted lathes and drill presses, some lying tipped over on their sides. It felt like he was witnessing a graveyard of machines, waiting for someone to push the big green power button to jolt them to life again. So that it would be as it was . . . before.

He moved along down the hall, stopping briefly one last time to peer into his old homeroom as he made his way out of the school. Outside, another huge bolt lit up the sky, blasting a bright light into the room. It flashed across a huge whiteboard, imprinted with an unfamiliar blood-red insignia. Some gang he didn't know, or maybe the scrawled signature of a wannabe gangbanger.

Muffled voices stopped him in his tracks. He turned away, taking one step as he did, trying to get out of the room before—

His foot landed on some loose plaster. *Crack!*

A thin, tall frame rose up against the whiteboard, a shadow in the dim room. "Who the hell are you?"

Two other boys stood up on either side of the first.

Zack was stunned. How had he not seen them? He'd been so distracted by the symbol on the whiteboard, he'd missed the most important thing. His throat tightened. His tongue tripped in response. "I l-live 'round here," he stammered.

Another flash of lightning, brighter than the others, jerked the boys' attention to the windows. Zack wasted no time. He bolted back into the dark hallway. Pulling open the stairwell door, he flew down the stairs toward the back exit, one floor below. There were three bends in the stairwell before it ended on the bottom floor, then a short distance to the outside exit. The stairwell was pitch black. Halfway down the stairs he heard the slamming of feet on the steps just above him.

At the bottom of the stairs, Zack spun off the railing and headed down the short hall. He moved as fast as he could, touching the wall ahead with his left hand, keeping it close. When he hit the end he stopped, feeling for the door, searching for the handle. He heard the boys come off the stairs and land on the floor, closing in.

The big door swung open, and Zack ran out onto the grass. The moon was sliding behind the clouds. Lightning flashed again. A rumble of thunder roared. He took a hard right and headed back up toward the main gate—the fastest way out.

Suddenly, the ground dipped before him. He tripped, falling head over heels and onto his back. They were upon him instantly, hovering, looking down. He tried to reach for the knife, but one of the boys stepped closer, pinning his sneakers against Zack's calf. "Where ya goin'?"

A double flash of lightning rocketed across the sky, immediately followed by two deafening bursts of thunder, light so bright it turned the night into day. A third bolt. The ground trembled beneath them.

And just like that, Zack had disappeared with the flash of the lightning.

FIVE

————·————

AS TWILIGHT YIELDED to dawn, a soft green mist crept
through the forest, swirled among the trees, then silently
drifted up and away. The sun nudged its way into the sky,
washing into the grassy clearing in the woods, and peeked under the
eyelids of the young boy lying near its center.

Kai Li stirred, then blinked, like he was coming out of a dream, his
mind gradually taking back its consciousness. *Something*, he thought,
is very, very wrong. He scrambled to his feet. The grass beneath his
sneakers was thick and lush, a deeper green than he had ever seen
before. In front of him sat a dark, dense forest, the kind that seemed
to be straight out of a fairy tale or something.

Is this real?

Maybe he was having a nightmare again or some weird-as-hell
dream. He touched his face, felt the warmth of his cheek, and listened
to the push of his breath going in and out. *No. Not a dream.*

Where was his mom? The factory? His life? This place with its
dark secrets and towering trees was not his. He didn't belong here.

He held his breath and listened. For a bird, a squirrel, a car, but
there was total silence. He wanted to call out, to ask for help, but it
almost seemed wrong somehow.

Don't panic. Don't panic. He scanned his surroundings once more. Nothing but woods in all directions, except for a bunch of huge gravestone-like rocks, upright in the grass, about ten feet tall and forming a circle.

Kai Li took a tentative step forward. His heart pounded against his rib cage so hard he thought it might break right through. He inched toward the closest stone. His stomach tightened into a knot, and his steps faltered when he noticed a small pale lump resting at the base of the stone, partially tucked behind it. He shifted left, peering around the rock. Arms. Legs. Dark hair braided in pigtails. A girl, maybe his age, curled up in a ball. Dead? *God. I hope not.* He'd never seen a dead body and didn't want this to be his first.

He gently tapped the toe of his sneaker against the girl's thigh. No response. Was she breathing? He couldn't tell and didn't want to touch her to find out.

Kai Li sucked in a breath and let it out slowly, then bent closer. His entire arm trembled as he reached forward. *Please don't be dead, you.* Then, just as he was about to poke her shoulder, she stirred.

Kai Li scrambled back, kicking up dirt and stones in his haste, the rocks sputtering against her. She winced, rolled over, and pushed herself up into a sitting position. When she opened her eyes, the deep brown color of them reminded him of his mother's strong coffee. Of home.

Her skin was more red-brown than yellow-brown, and her eyes had an almond shape. Where had she come from?

Kai Li mustered up some courage, and mumbled in Chinese, asking if she was okay.

She gave him a blank look. "Do you speak English?"

"Y-Yes" Kai Li stuttered, caught off guard by her voice, the request, the strangeness of it all. "My n-name, Kai Li."

"I'm Sarah . . . Morningstar. My friends call me Morningstar."

"Y-you know this p-place?"

Morningstar rose to her feet, glanced at the field, the trees encircling it, then at the nearby stones. Kai Li studied her as she her knitted her brow. She must see what he did: the stones, and not a hint of civilization.

"No. Where am I?"

Kai Li shrugged. Some secret part of him wished he could protect her. Like he could reach out his arm and be one of those guys in the movies who make everything better. Be the hero he'd always wanted to be, or maybe could never be.

"Not s-sure," he said, painfully aware of the words stumbling out of his mouth. What hero stutters? "We m-must be l-lost."

She nodded. "Guess we both got caught up in the storm."

Was that it? He recalled lights flashing, buzzing noises, his head spinning, the world turning inside out. A sudden flash. Then, nothing. Is that what she's talking about? "I . . . I guess s-so."

Morningstar turned and patted her back pockets, then her front. She scanned the grass around the stone. "Can you call someone? I think I lost my phone."

He shook his head, trying to ward off a feeling of shame creeping over him. *I can't even help with that.* How could he be so unprepared for . . . well, everything. "I . . . I . . . l-lost mine too," he managed, finally.

He saw her attempt a smile, but her chin only wobbled. Her face was splotchy with dried dirt and a film of dust dulled the brightness of her clothes and stifled the twinkle from the many sequins studding her jacket. Shadows lurked in her eyes. For a brief moment, Kai Li wanted to reach out, to tell her he felt the same way. Sad. Adrift. Clueless.

Instead, he turned his head away. Maybe it was wrong for him to see her like that? To make assumptions. Why did his own fear keep him wrapped in chains? "Well," he said softly, "somethin' f-funny happenin', no?"

"Something funny happenin', *yes*," Morningstar replied to him, like she was now returning a serve.

She seemed confident—where he wasn't. He imagined he must look like a black and white photo to her: black hair, black-rimmed glasses, black pants, white shirt, white socks, white sneakers. No color at all. No red like in her bandana, or the blue of her jeans, or the bright colored beads on her moccasins.

Indigenous American. That's what she was.

Morningstar propped her fists on her hips. "Okay, guess we better look around. Find someone to help us."

Why hadn't he thought of that? "Yeah. Good." He started to lead the way—to where he had no idea—but she grabbed his arm, stopping him. He jerked back a step, and her touch dropped away.

"Look. Over there, at the top of those trees," she said, pointing. "Smoke."

Kai Li's eyes followed the command of her finger. A fine, wispy cloud, slightly darker than the others, snaked between the treetops. "S-smoke mean p-people."

He cursed his stutter, the way it always made him sound even more unsure. This beautiful, smart girl must already be doubting him, questioning his ability to lead. What use would she have for him? *Men are supposed to be strong. Why can't I be?*

"I bet it's a house," Morningstar said. "Maybe they'll let us use their phone? Let's check it out."

"M-maybe wait." An adventure into unknown woods? Or any woods for that matter. Foreign turf was never a good place to be. Hadn't his father told him that a dozen times? *Stick to what you know, Kai Li.* At home, pavement ruled. Gigantic buildings towered over the city streets as cranes lowered pallets onto ships at the many docks. That was familiar. This was very scary. The closest thing to a forest at home were the neatly groomed, small grassy areas between the steel structures, with their nicely spaced trees and curvy cement walkways. *Anything* could be in these woods. "We could get l-l-lost."

"We're *already* lost. Look, there's nothing to be afraid of. I have no idea what's going on, either. But there's no point in staying here." Morningstar shrugged. "It's just some trees. C'mon."

She charged forward and Kai Li became her shadow, keeping close to her as they headed toward the forest on the other side of the stones—all thick, tall, crystal-like granite structures. He'd seen something like them before. Maybe in a geology or history book? Or maybe in that movie about the aliens? He wanted to reach out and touch them, to see if they were real or part of some Hollywood set, but then Morningstar stopped abruptly and Kai Li collided with her back.

A boy stood near the edge of the woods, not more than a few hundred feet away. "Who is that?" Kai Li whispered.

Morningstar waved her hands and moved toward him. "Hey, hey you. Over here."

The boy came into clearer view. He was tall, taller than both of them, with dark skin shadowed by a red hooded sweatshirt, braids peeking out of the hood; he wore matching red running shoes, and Kai Li could see the glint of a gold earring in one ear.

"Who are you?" asked Morningstar.

"Who am *I*? Who are you?" he shot back, then turned to Kai Li. "And who are you?"

"Kai L-li." He moved closer to Morningstar, as if he could shield her from this angry boy. "Who are y-you?"

The boy ignored him, shifting his weight toward Morningstar. "What's your name? And what's with the Halloween costume?"

"Morningstar. And it's not a costume." She raised her chin. "I'm a Lakota Sioux."

"Whatever," he replied. "I'm Zack. What are you two doing here?"

"I was about to ask you the same thing," she replied. "There doesn't seem to be anyone here at all, except us."

Zack's eyes bounced back and forth between Kai Li and Morningstar. "Well. . .that's not exactly true. Someone else is here."

"What do you mean?" asked Morningstar.

"I mean 'zactly that, girl. Someone else is here. Behind that big tombstone, or whatever the Christ those things are over there. Hasn't stopped crying since I found her. Couldn't get much out of her. Real basket case."

He led them back to the opposite side of the giant circle where Kai Li had found Morningstar. Sitting there on the ground with her back against the cold stone slab, head in hands, sobbing, was a young girl. "We got guests," Zack said to her, matter of fact.

The girl's head jolted from her hands. She craned her neck to see their faces, her eyes red and floating in puddles. Black mascara had gathered in gobs along her eyelashes and smudged the tops of her cheeks. But she was none the less striking to Kai Li. Her eyes were a beautiful brown, like Morningstar's. Their deep color broke easily through the wells of water that surrounded them and were bordered by heavy sculpted eyebrows. It looked like she was dressed for a party. She wore a pantsuit, a shiny blue, lightly coated with a fine dust. A powder-blue scarf covered her head, one end sweeping across her chin, hiding much of her tan face. Gold loops hung from her ears.

Kai Li placed his hands on his knees and bent down, tilting his head nearly level with hers to give her some words of encouragement, but in doing so his glasses slid forward to the end of his nose. Flustered, his courage trashed, he pushed them back up hurriedly, trying to gather himself together again. "My n-name is Kai Li. You okay?" he asked.

The girl studied Kai Li. Her sobbing had morphed into a light sniffling. She wiped away the tears from her cheeks using the edge of her scarf, the bangles along her wrist clinking. In-between sniffles, she spoke in a shy, tired voice. "I must have gotten lost somehow. Can you tell me where this is?"

"N-no. We l-lost too."

"Now there's an understatement," Zack mocked. "Makes four of us."

"How long have you been here?" Morningstar asked.

"An hour maybe? Don't really know. I found her here behind this stone a little while ago, after I left you two," Zack added. "Not much I could do, so I just started lookin' around the place."

"What do you mean 'when you left us?'" Morningstar questioned.

"You guys were asleep or something. Thought maybe you were dead. I was tryin' to remember how I got here but couldn't. Last thing I knew I was headin' over to my friend's house. Thought if I scouted the place, I might figure out what the hell was goin' on. Or find someone who could tell me." His eyes shifted between Kai Li and Morningstar. "Obviously, you two weren't gonna be of much use, so I kept lookin', an' came across *her*."

"What's your name?" Morningstar asked, reaching out her hand and helping her to her feet.

"Liyah," she said, her sniffling subsiding. "Yours?"

"Zack," Zack replied, intercepting the question. "This is Morningstar . . . and he's Kim Lee."

"Kai L-li." he reminded.

"Sorry. Kai L-li." Zack chuckled a bit, the corners of his mouth turning a half smile.

Kai Li's eyes flashed. He was unsure of what to make of Zack and these random jabs. *Why is it so hard for me to read people sometimes?* And why did new people make him so nervous? He never knew what to say, and when he did, it always came out wrong, in a stutter, which just made him even more nervous. His mother, who was usually on top of him to study so he would get to go to college in America, would even say to him, "Why don't you get your nose out of that book Kai Li and call up a friend? Pretty soon you won't have any friends at all."

Kai Li looked over at Morningstar who was staring at Zack, her lips taut, eyes narrowed. Maybe he wasn't the only one who wasn't thrilled about this guy? At least someone seemed to be on his side.

Zack just grinned at both of them.

"Where f-from?" Kai Li asked Liyah, trying to restore a little pride.

"Palestine. I was—"

"Sorry, but for now we need to make best use of our time," Morningstar pressed. "Find out where we are. How to get home."

"And that means . . . like . . . what?" Zack asked stiffly. He pulled his phone out from his pocket waving it at her. "I tried this. But there's no signal here."

"I don't know. Like, follow the signs."

"Signs?" Zack smiled wryly at her. "You think maybe there's some road sign nearby? Like telling us to take Exit 5 for Detroit?"

A puzzled look came over Liyah. "Detroit? America?"

"Jeez," Zack moaned, shaking his head at Liyah. "Do any of you have a clue about anything?"

Kai Li glanced over at Zack and frowned, then quickly shifted his eyes as he glanced back.

"We can't waste time," Morningstar insisted.

"And the signs?" Zack harped, his mouth forming a bit of a smirk.

"Signs can appear in all kinds of ways, if you pay attention. Like the smoke rising in the woods, that tells us there must be a house nearby."

Zack's eyes moved quickly through the sky above the treetops, but a nearby stand of tall trees obscured the smoke from where they were all standing. "What the Christ you talkin' 'bout, girl? Where? I don't see nothin'."

Morningstar started off towards the edge of the field. "This way," she called out, motioning with her arm. "I think I saw a path into the woods."

Liyah pulled herself together and was the first to comply.

"What the . . .?" Zack protested, flashing a dumbfounded look at Kai Li, who then turned away and ran to catch up to the girls.

"What's the point?" Zack shouted after them. "You guys have no clue. Why are you trusting her, anyway?" Then, as if not to be left alone, he set out as well, calling ahead to Morningstar. "Who appointed you leader?"

Morningstar halted at the beginning of a narrow dirt path. She turned to face Zack as he joined them. "If you have a better suggestion, I'm happy to listen."

"No, but I ain't gonna follow *you*," Zack replied, brushing solidly against her as he passed by. Morningstar lost her balance, tripping backwards several steps. Then they all watched as he followed the trail, snaking in and out of the trees, until he disappeared completely.

Six

———†———

THE BRIGHT MORNING sun did little to illuminate the dense woods. The trees closed in like a cloak, deathly dark and foreboding. If she looked straight up, Liyah would have caught a sliver of a blue sky with the patchwork of white clouds. She took in a deep breath, paused briefly, then stepped cautiously along the dirt path, following behind Kai Li and Morningstar.

She had never been in such a place, swallowed up by everything, all sides closing in, thick darkness like an envelope, and only a narrow light above to remind her there was more here than these woods.

No. Not true. Her thoughts sputtered in her head—back to home, the square, Khalib, the suffocating mass of humanity congealing around her, and suddenly that other light. Then the flashback passed as quickly as it had arrived, like the wind, too ethereal for her mind to catch.

She refocused her thoughts on the uneven path beneath her feet. She'd gotten distracted and fallen behind, so she sped up her pace, trying to close the gap with the others. But not as close as Kai Li was with Morningstar. *He was like a puppy, wasn't he?* Like her little Sasha back home, who stumbled over her awkward oversized feet to keep up with her longer strides. She could just see Sasha's head bobbing this way and that, eyes wide, clearly frightened to be left behind.

A flash of home again. Then it was gone. Why couldn't she hold onto these thoughts? Her memory seemed like a computer with a virus: crashing, rebooting, then crashing again.

Liyah's gaze darted from side to side as she stumbled down the shadowed path, on guard for anything that might pop out of the darkness and snatch her up. These trees, packed tightly together like giant marching soldiers, made her feel small, and frightened her. Beit Lahia had no woods like this, only open streets and alleyways, with small homes sitting side by side, dust-blown from the desert-like surroundings.

But more than dark shadows and odd noises, there was something a whole lot scarier: the not knowing. Not knowing where she was, how she got here, where her family was, if she was living in a nightmare.

The narrow dirt path wound through the thick woods, slithering in and out of the trees like a serpent. Zack's long strides had already carried him out of sight. She hurried to catch up, but her sandals were no help. They had no substance. The smallest rocks felt like sharp knives, stabbing into her, and the roots poked into the openings between the straps and scratched at her ankles. As the gap between her and group widened, she began to panic. *I am going to be left behind.*

As if she had heard Liyah's anguished thoughts, Morningstar suddenly halted and turned to look back. Kai Li stumbled to a stop behind her.

"You okay, Liyah?" Morningstar called to her, then didn't wait for an answer. She waived at a small clearing in the trees. "We'll stop here and rest for a minute."

Liyah hurried to join the rest of them. "Thanks for waiting. It's a bit scary here, isn't it?" Her words tumbled out of her, rushed and staccato, as anxious as her breaths.

"It'll be okay. We just need to stick together." Morningstar glanced down the path and frowned. "Zack apparently disagrees."

Liyah studied Morningstar. Never had she seen anyone like her before. The sequined tunic over her faded jeans, the dark braids stretching down from under her red and white bandana, and the beaded moccasins. The bandana framed Morningstar's jet-black hair and light-caramel face, like a crown.

She carries herself with such quiet confidence, while I disgrace my family with my crying. Oh Allah, where am I? Get me out of here. Take me home. Her thoughts traveled to the adobe house where she had been just moments ago it seemed, then the image faded again.

Her tears threatened to pour out of her and betray her for the coward she felt she was. Liyah turned away and pointed at the trail. "We should probably try to catch up to him. Maybe he's waiting for us?"

Kai Li grumbled a bit as they got to their feet and set out again. Liyah tried to keep pace, but it was no use. The continual smattering of twisted roots and broken branches forced her to concentrate on her footing, and every time she looked up, the gap between her and the others widened.

A second later, Morningstar and Kai Li rounded a sharp turn in the trail and disappeared from view. The muscles in her neck squeezed like a clamp around her windpipe, and her breaths shortened into rapid-fire bursts. *They're gone.*

The woods closed in. She heard a twig snap. Then another noise. She spun left, then right, and tried to move forward, but it seemed like the overhanging branches were reaching down to grab her.

"Kai Li! Morningstar! Wait!" she screamed as she tried to run, stumbling, tripping over the roots and loose rocks. She rounded the turn in a panic and collided at full speed right into her companions.

"Whoa there, sista!" Zack grabbed her and held her back. "Get your crap together."

Liyah gathered her breath. "I just didn't want to lose track of you all," she managed, as calmly as possible. Her feet ached and were swelling up like fat sausages, spilling between the laces of her sandals. She could feel blisters forming. Surely they would only slow her even more.

"Well, keep up. We're not your babysitters," Zack said as he turned back to the fork in the path that had stopped him. He looked at Morningstar. "Guess someone stole that sign you were talking about. So, now what, Einstein?"

"Let's take the one to the right," Morningstar said. "I'm not sure, but it seems like that will be the best direction to get to the house."

Zack scoffed. "And what are you gonna do if we get lost, huh? It's not like we have GPS out here."

Morningstar picked up a small rock, crossed to the closest tree, and used its sharp, jagged edge like a knife to carve an upside down *V* into the bark. "There, now we have a mark, so we can find our way back."

Zack shook his head. "Yeah, that's *exactly* what I wanna do. Come back to this place. Thought we're tryin' to get the hell outta here."

"We might have to if this path turns out to be wrong," Morningstar said. "Then we can come back and try the other one."

Zack shrugged, then started up the path Morningstar had suggested. "What's the point?" he grumbled as he walked away. "Not coming back, anyway. Nothin' here."

As they marched along, Liyah noticed Kai Li nervously scanning the woods on both sides every few minutes as if something or someone was about to launch an attack at any moment. She paused and waited while he caught up. "Everything okay, Kai Li?"

"N-not sure 'bout this p-place, an' n-not know why Zack angry. Bother m-me."

"Maybe because it's hard on all of us. I know I'm not holding up so well myself." That was an understatement. She ached for home, for something familiar, for a road, a building, a bird, anything she knew—anything she could hold onto.

How did they all end up here? And where was here anyway? They needed a plane or a helicopter or a time machine or something to get them back home, and if there was one thing Liyah wanted right now, it was home.

They continued through the woods for a short time, Morningstar stopping occasionally to carve her mark into the bark of other trees.

Kai Li broke a long silence. "How w-we know we not lost?"

Zack laughed. "Seriously, Mr. Li? Like, where you been? We been lost since the second we got here."

"I think we're going in the right general direction," Morningstar said. "I haven't seen the smoke in a while, but these trees are just so thick and—"

"Seems to me we've been walkin' in *every* direction," Zack grabbed a leaf from a low-hanging branch, shredded it to pieces, then let them flutter to the ground. "Why should we trust that you know everything anyway?"

"My grandfather taught me a lot about hiking. He told me the forest talks to you, and if you pay attention, it can help you find your way."

Zack let out a short laugh. "The forest talks? C'mon, girl, don't be crazy."

"Yeah. It does," Morningstar continued, firm and quiet. "The wind has been blowing toward us from up the path. There is moss on that side of the trees." She pointed. "The cool side. Which means we are going a bit southeast. If we watch the wind and the trees, we can know which direction we are going. Hikers who get lost can just follow the movement of the leaves and branches to adjust their direction, keeping the wind at one side."

She took a step forward, waving at the small circle of light above them. "The clouds, too, move along in one direction, 'at the wishes of a higher wind,' as my grandfather would say. They serve as another reference point. The sun speaks too, telling the trees to remind you of the time of day and the direction of his path, by the shadows that he sends down. And other signs, like how trees bend to drink in the sunlight."

She stopped talking and her voice lowered into a sad, lonely range that echoed the hole in Liyah's heart. "Anyway, that's how my grandfather would talk about the earth and the world and it just . . . well, it made me feel safe."

Her words were like a magical broom to Liyah, sweeping out her immediate worries, brushing away the dust of despair, clearing her mind so a single ray of hope could enter in. Morningstar had a way about her that made this all seem possible somehow. That they would find their way and end up home again with the people they loved.

"Work for me," Kai Li said, as he passed by Zack.

As they rounded another in the seemingly endless bends in the path, Liyah's throat dried, her tongue felt like sandpaper. How long had she been without water? Food?

I'm going to die here. And where was "here," after all? She thought of Khalib, of the worry that would be on his face. She remembered the square, a whining sound, and a flash like a lightbulb. Was he running all over, looking for her? Or had that light come for him too, and he was somewhere in these very woods, scared and alone?

Maybe I'm already dead. Maybe we're all dead.

But the pain in her feet told her otherwise. The stones stabbed at her arches, and her toes stubbed against immovable rocks jutting up from the hard-packed dirt below. She wanted to quit. To sit down. To never take another step. Suddenly Morningstar broke through her worries.

"We're close."

"What makes you so sure?" Zack snorted. "You get a sign from heaven or something?"

"I smell smoke," Morningstar replied. "And—"

"I don't smell anything." Zack shifted left, right, then shrugged. Morningstar parked her fists on her hips. "Whenever I interrupted my grandfather he would say, 'Speaking blocks your ears, Morningstar.' Maybe you need to listen more and complain less."

"L-look! House!" Kai Li pointed up and to their right.

"Shut up, dude!" Zack hissed. "Someone could hear you."

"Don't we want that?" Liyah would kill for a chair to sit down on. A glass of water. A bite of something. Hopefully, whoever was in that house was nice.

"Christ, Liyah. Don't be stupid. Haven't you ever watched a single horror movie?"

"I agree," Morningstar said softly. "We need to be cautious. We don't know where we are or . . . what's here."

Their ragtag group approached slowly, crouching down behind some large rocks, and there, resting at the bottom of a slight incline, dark smoke rose from a stubby stone chimney atop a small wooden house. A faded wood door marked the entrance, bordered by single windows on either side. No signs of life anywhere; no road nearby, no driveway, no car. It was just sitting there, all by itself. *More like a cabin than a house*, Liyah thought . . . *in the middle of nowhere.*

"This is where I know what to do," Zack said. "And I don't need no grandfather to tell me not to be stupid." He took the lead, slipping out of their hiding space, and hurried down the small hill towards the cabin. As he got closer, he ducked down and positioned himself between one of the windows and the door. He remained crouched for a minute, then inched his way toward the window. He paused, Liyah held her breath, then he waved them to come down the hill.

The three of them stayed low, moving fast and certain down the hill. Kai Li's eyes flashed like a scared rabbit. Liyah latched onto the sleeve of Morningstar's tunic.

"Looks like no one's here," Zack whispered.

Morningstar rose and peeked inside beside him. Liyah screwed up her courage and did the same, still holding tight to Morningstar's sleeve and willing herself not to scream.

Nothing moved inside.

The light from the sun was now barely visible. The long shadows setting in around them made the inside of the cabin dim. But Liyah could see a splash of light on the far wall, its source blocked from her view by the back of a what looked like a sofa and a couple of stuffed chairs. That was all she could see.

"I'm going to check the other side," Zack said, then circled the house, returning a few moments later.

"No one's here."

Morningstar nodded. "Okay, we should try—"

Zack brushed by her, springing onto the stone stoop. Morningstar gaped at him, shook her head, then joined him. He grabbed a hold of the doorknob, twisted it, then nudged the door.

The hinges creaked open like a crypt in a horror movie. The sound sent ripples up Liyah's spine, and fear ricocheted like a bullet through her brain.

Kai Li was behind Liyah's shoulder, Morningstar just ahead of her. The three of them paused behind Zack, who put a finger to his lips then pushed the door open the rest of the way.

They crept ahead silently, one almost on top of the other, entering into a single spacious room. The smell of burning wood filled Liyah's nostrils. Before she could even adjust to the darkened interior, she could hear the fire crackle, feel its warmth against her skin, making her realize how cool it had gotten outside. The room filtered into view—plain walls, made of unpainted wood planks, large hand-hewn beams supporting the ceiling, a bare, clean wooden floor.

The only light in the room came from the small flames hopping across the tops of the logs in the fireplace, casting flickering shadows around the room. Either someone had just left, or someone was waiting for them to get here.

SEVEN

———·———

MORNINGSTAR FELT THE blood throb in her ears as she entered the room. Why was she suddenly feeling scared? In this cabin was the reality—or unreality—of it all just now sinking in? Her eyes darted about, taking careful notes of the details of her surroundings: three doors against the back wall; a simple two-seat sofa and coffee table sat in front of the fireplace bordered by two small side tables, each with a short, fat candle sitting atop, unlit; no upstairs, no basement, just this one big room.

She made her way slowly, hesitantly, toward the fireplace, halting as she neared. It was a large stone structure with a raised hearth. A mantle made from a thick rough-hewn beam jutted out from above it. Inside, a few large slow-burning logs bridged two long, narrow, rectangular stones. Red, blue, and yellow flames hopped along the logs, lapping at the darkness above. The heat felt good to Morningstar, and the ashy scent filled her nostrils, reminding her of the many times she had camped with her grandfather. Her heart rate slowed. She watched as a trail of black smoke escaped upward through the chimney and into the cool outside air.

Kai Li, Liyah, and Zack separately circled the room, stepping lightly, scanning, and then finally joining together again by the sofa where Morningstar now stood. With her eyes now better adjusted to the dim light and supported by the glow from the fire, she could make out additional details. The sofa was drab green. The coffee table was the length of the sofa, made of a dark wood, with a grey slate-like top. The stuffed chairs facing each other on either side were plain, worn, and burnt orange in color. In the center of the coffee table was a decorative wooden box, the dimensions of a small notebook.

Kai Li's whisper called them to attention. "If owner c-come, we in big t-trouble."

"We're already in big trouble, Mr. Kai. Or hadn't you noticed?" Zack brushed by him and slumped into one of the chairs. "Maybe whoever owns this place might be able to show us how to get home. But then we probably can't trust them, either."

Liyah took a seat on the sofa. "We'll have to trust someone, don't you think?"

"No. I don't."

Morningstar eyed Zack as she plunked herself down next to Liyah. "She does have a point, you know. We've got to figure out what happened to us and what to do next. We can't be wasting time arguing."

Zack frowned. "Fine. I s'pose I have to put up with all this 'til we get out of here. Doesn't mean I have to like it."

Kai Li remained standing, looking down at the wooden box. As he bent forward to study it more closely, his glasses slid to the tip of his nose. He grabbed the box with one hand while pushing his glasses back in place with the other, twitching his nose and furrowing his forehead as he did.

Morningstar studied the box as Kai Li turned it in a circle between his hands. It was made from a yellowish wood unfamiliar to her and buffed to a high polish. The lid was inlaid with beautiful multicolored jewels. On its sides were intricately carved, swirling designs. There were two shiny metal hinges connecting the base to the lid. A small latch with a keyhole secured the lid to the base.

Although larger, the box reminded her of the one her parents gave her when she was little, the one where if you popped the lid open, three pretty little ballet dancers in braids and sequined tutus rose up, twirling around on a spinning disk. But that was gone now, probably splintered into a zillion pieces and blown away with the wind with her lala. Both taken out of her life without warning, like her parents before them. And where was she now? Maybe dead too? Her eyes stared blankly at the box in Kai Li's hands, as he spun it slowly back and forth. Sadness filled her thoughts. *I miss you, my lala.*

"Odd, n-no?" Kai Li asked, snapping her back into the present.

"W-what?" Morningstar replied.

"Box."

"What about it?" asked Liyah.

"Mean f-fancy. Not p-plain like other things."

Zack reached over, snatched the box from Kai Li, and studied it. "So? What's so odd about that?" He handed it back to Kai Li.

Kai Li concentrated on the box again, like he was pondering a math problem. "Not logical. No f-fit."

"So what if it doesn't fit. Who cares?" Zack shot back, impatiently.

Kai Li tried unsuccessfully to open the lid. He moved his fingers along the top, over the inlaid stones that rose slightly above its surface, and then over the finely carved designs. As he continued to study the box, Zack slumped further down in his chair. "Ain't no one here. There's no food, no water . . . nothin'. We have to move on." He glanced again over at Kai Li. "Are you listening, Kai-bo? I was saying, man—"

"Well, there is the fire," Morningstar countered. "Someone had to start it. And then there are the backpacks."

"Backpacks?" Zack asked, lifting his eyebrows.

"The ones behind the sofa."

"Huh?" replied Zack and Liyah simultaneously.

Liyah craned her neck as she leaned over the back of the sofa. "You're right. How'd we miss those?"

"Easy. Most people don't notice much, especially anything right under their feet. I only noticed them myself when my eyes adjusted."

Kai Li, not listening, just shook his head. "Can't open," he complained, turning the box on its side and exposing the bottom.

"What's that?" Liyah asked, pointing.

Kai Li turned the box upside down. Something was fixed to the underside. Grasping the object between his thumb and index finger, he tore it free. "K-key!" he said, holding it up. He held the small, gold object for only an instant before placing the box on the table and inserting the key into the keyhole of its latch—a perfect fit. Morningstar and Liyah edged closer. Even Zack's eyes were now glued on the box as Kai Li turned the key and lifted the lid.

The inside of the box was lined with a rich, emerald green felt-like material. Resting at the bottom was a single envelope. Kai Li retrieved it using both hands, as if it were a fragile, ancient treasure. He turned to the others. "S-should open?"

Zack chortled. "You've gone this far, Mr. Kai. Doubt we could get in much more trouble, anyway."

Kai Li opened the unsealed envelope and stared in at its contents.

"Well, hurry up! Tell us what we've won," Zack joked.

Kai Li's hand trembled as he removed two pieces of paper from the envelope. He then double-checked the inside of the envelope. Nothing else. They all watched him closely as his eyes scanned over the top sheet. He slid the bottom one on top, scanning it similarly. Zack's wide eyes betrayed any attempt to act aloof. Liyah was transfixed.

Kai-Li finally spoke, grounding the electricity in the air. "There letter an' m-map."

"Well, what's it say?" Zack questioned, abruptly.

"I th-th . . ."

Morningstar reached out, taking the pieces of paper and envelope from his hands. "No worries, Kai Li. Let me see. I'll read it for us." Kai Li let go, not making even the slightest effort to resist, his eyes turned downward.

"No worries," Liyah echoed softly, reaching out, gently touching his knee.

On the front of a powder-blue envelope, in bold script, was the word *Welcome*, written in steel-blue ink. Morningstar put the envelope aside, shifting her attention to the letter, made of a white parchment-like paper. The print matched that on the envelope, the letters smaller but in similar script. She looked around at the spellbound faces of the others, then began to read, calmly, evenly, deliberately:.

> Welcome, my friends. You have arrived at a place far from your homes. It is not important how you came to be here, only that you were chosen to be part of an important mission. Your success in this mission will

depend on the support you give each other. You must locate the lessons of the book known as the Zah-re, the Book of Universal Truths. Your task is to find these and then return here—together. You cannot leave this place until your task is completed.

This map will act as your guide. You will recognize the locations of documents by their markings. Each carry the inscription 'zr.' There are seven, representing the seven states of being of the Zah-re. Follow the path of the white stones. It begins at the wood's edge and is the safest place to be during your journey. Stay close to it. You will find the water safe to drink. Share everything.

If your journey is successful, I will meet you all here and help you return home.

Morningstar lifted her eyes from the letter. Kai Li was staring at her, his eyes locked on hers, his large black pupils magnified even more through the lenses. Liyah's jaw had become unhinged, like she had seen a ghost but was unable to scream.

"This is some kind of a joke," Zack exclaimed, his anger bursting forth. "What the hell is going on? I mean, *come on*. What is this?" His eyes shot to Liyah, then Morningstar, then over at Kai Li. "You all in this together?"

"Huh?" Kai Li replied, a quizzical look on his face.

Morningstar's eyes met Zack's. Her tone was measured, steady.

"What do you mean, Zack? Kai Li and Liyah are upset about being here, wherever we are. Pretty clear, no?"

"Let me see that map!" he demanded, ripping it from her hands.

The map was hand drawn. At the bottom left was a blank area marked "Standing Stones." Moving up the page on the right, above the cabin, there was a group of trees and the words "Black Forest." Further to the right was a river, which either began or ended at the top of the page where it met with a body of water labeled "Crystal Lake." On the far-left side of the river was a path, beginning at the cabin, that twisted its way through a series of hills, plains, and forests, also ending at the top of the page at the lake. The path continued back down toward the cabin, remaining close to the river, forming a big loop. Surrounding the lake to the north, east, and west were mountains. On the upper left part of the map was a section marked "Land of Qom," and on far the right side appeared the notation "Land of Zor."

Zack handed the map back. "Who says this was meant for us?"

"Who else f- for?" Kai Li replied.

"Anyone. We did break in here, you know."

"Not exactly," said Morningstar. "The door wasn't locked. And it doesn't appear anyone is close by. The smoke was a clear sign . . . and no one else was in the clearing besides us."

Liyah took the pages from Morningstar's hands, glancing briefly at them. "Don't you think it's also kind of strange that there is nothing in this house except this box and those backpacks?" She looked over at Zack.

"Yeah, well this whole thing is more than freakin' strange if you ask me. It's like some kind of bizarre scavenger hunt. No matter who it's for."

"What difference does it make?" Liyah replied, timidly. "I mean, maybe it's not meant for us. And maybe it's a game, as you say. But we need to try *something* to get home, don't we?"

"Not sure," Kai Li replied. "S-strange. Like Zack s-say."

"Liyah's right," said Morningstar. "At least if we follow the instructions, we might meet the person who wrote the letter. We have no other option right now, no other way to know where we are or how to get home. We've got to take this chance." She turned toward the windows. "Night is setting in. We need to stay here, set out in the morning."

Morningstar took Zack's silence as a sign of resignation, although his narrowed eyes indicated otherwise. He probably knew she was right about spending the night there. What choice did they really have, anyway? Tramping off into woods in the dark really didn't make any sense at all.

Kai Li pulled one of the backpacks out from behind the sofa and began unzipping the pockets and examining their contents. Liyah slid her sore, blistered feet out of her sandals and dragged her tongue across her parched, cracked lips. "I'm so thirsty; aren't you guys?"

"Definitely," Zack replied, frustration dissipating from his voice. "My mouth's like a desert."

Morningstar pointed across the room. "Maybe there's something behind one of those doors." She made her way over to the opposite side of the room, opened the closest door, and peered inside.

"What do you see?" Liyah asked, catching up to her.

"It's a bedroom. Two small beds. Nothing else."

"But better than sleeping on the ground in the woods," Liyah replied. "For sure."

They moved to the next door. Liyah opened it. It was a small, simple bathroom with a metal sink set on a high wooden base. Next to the sink was a small hand pump for water, to its right a small window, and next to that a toilet. Above the toilet was a large container with a chain device attached to a handle. Morningstar remembered seeing something like that one time in an old house of one of her friends.

"How does that work?" asked Liyah.

"If you pull the chain the water in the tank flushes down. Better than an outhouse, but maybe only good for a few flushes. Then you need to refill it." She located a full refill bucket next to the sink and pointed it out to Liyah. "You have to . . ."

"I see," Liyah said, smiling. "Never seen that before. But I get it. Most of the toilets where I live, in Palestine, are like the ones you have in America. Although there are still many of the old style where you just squat over a hole in the floor."

Morningstar tilted her head. "Really? Gross! More like what you have to do when you're on a hike in the woods and can't hold it."

Liyah laughed. "Guess you could say that. But they've been around for a long time in our culture. Let's check out the other room."

The last room was identical to the first. They returned to the boys. Kai Li was sitting cross-legged on the floor with the packs. Zack was slouched back in his chair, staring at the ceiling.

"What's in the pack?" asked Morningstar.

Kai Li grinned up at her. "Lotta s-stuff." He had already removed most of the items from one pack and laid them out on the floor. Morningstar took inventory in her head: two thin rolled-up gray blankets, two small plastic cups and bowls, a pouch to hold water, several protective pieces of plastic sheeting, a super light tent wound around springy posts, three long cords with carabiner-style clamps attached on either end, a few loose hooks, a small flashlight, plastic tent stakes, and some small towels.

Reaching into another zippered compartment, he hauled out several large packets—a collection of food items. Morningstar bent down and examined them, opening a few. "Looks like a ton of dried fruit and snack bars."

"What about the other pack?" Liyah asked.

Kai Li leaned over, yanked it closer to him, started pulling things out of the pockets, then stopped abruptly. "Look same."

Liyah sighed heavily. "Looks like we're going on a scavenger hunt after all."

"Well, let's make sure we know exactly what's in these packs and then repack them," Morningstar instructed. "Can you also leave a bar out for each of us for tonight, Kai Li?"

Kai Li smiled. "Yup. Guess w-we means m-me."

"And cups for now, please," Morningstar added, reaching out her hand. Once he had placed them in her possession, she headed back across the room.

Back again in the bathroom, Morningstar bent down to fill the cups from the bucket of water sitting beside the sink. As her face neared the water, the dirty, splotched face of a tired girl took form, staring back at her. A torrent of wild visions stormed into her head. The plastic cups fell from her hands, rattling across the floor. Her mind flashed to her home in the Badlands, to the time just before she blacked out, when the wind roared like a freight train and the whole trailer rattled like a metal lid on a pot of boiling water. She gasped, clamped her eyes down tight to block the images, covered her ears, and held her breath.

After a moment, her thoughts returned to a safer place. Cupping her hands, she reached into the bucket and retrieved some water. She splashed it to her face, then rubbed the heels of her hands into her eyes, hoping that when she removed them, she might be awake. *Can this really be real?* She gathered in a deep breath, paused briefly, then opened her eyes. She stared back down into the water. It was still her. She was still there, staring back.

Using the sleeve of her tunic, Morningstar dabbed her face dry, filled the two cups, and made her way back to the others.

Kai Li was already repacking the bags, minus the other two cups and snacks, which he had placed on the table. Liyah had returned to the sofa. Still brooding, Zack hadn't moved an inch. Morningstar sat down beside Liyah, handing her and Zack each a cup. "You guys can go first," she said. "Just share. Then we can each get as much as we need from the bucket in the bathroom. There's a pump in there too."

Zack picked up one of the cups, chugged half of it, then handed it back to Morningstar. He grabbed a bar and sank back into the chair, biting off half before he finished unwrapping it. Liyah passed Kai Li her cup as he joined them. They ate the bars in silence, darkness falling, the fire warming, exhaustion setting in.

"How w-we all get here?" Kai Li asked, finally.

Morningstar looked around. No one seemed willing to replay the events. Or maybe they just didn't remember? *It's an innocent-enough question,* she thought. Certainly one that needed to be answered. But it dredged up those feelings lurking just below the surface of her thoughts. Once more the image of her face in the bucket rose foremost in her mind. She fought back her fears and her tears as a deep, suffocating sadness overtook her. *Who will be strong if I am not? But why must it always be me, and me alone, again?*

Morningstar paused briefly on each of their faces as she spoke. "I live in a small trailer in South Dakota. There was a storm. A tornado. It was night. Nothing was left in the morning when I woke up. No one moving. No one there. I was sitting and wondering what to do . . . then there was a bright light—that much I know. Kai Li woke me up, I guess, near the big stones. That's it. That's all I remember, except some flashing pictures in my head at times that I can't make out." She looked back over at Kai Li.

"I w-was goin' to w-work," he said, taking the cue. "See light t-too, and buzzing s-sound. I get dizzy. Wake up by s-stones, then see you."

Morningstar turned to Liyah. "And how about you?"

Liyah sighed, almost imperceptibly, delaying her reply. She had a lost look in her eyes. Morningstar sensed she was trying to avoid falling apart yet again. Then she spoke quietly, her voice quivering slightly. "I was in the square in Beit Lahia, my Palestinian hometown, looking for my brother. There was some trouble. I remember falling down, but nothing after that, except pain in my ears . . . and . . . and I saw a light too."

"Zack?" Morningstar caught him fidgeting with the ties on his hoodie. He shifted his eyes to her but didn't answer right away. *Not like him*, she thought. *What is in that moody mind of his?*

Zack shrugged. "What you all lookin' at? What the hell you want from me? What can I tell you? There was some thunder. Maybe a light. Don't remember nothin' else. This can't be real anyway."

"You think maybe you're making this up in your sleep?" Liyah asked.

"Right, girl. You got it."

"We're real, Zack," Morningstar assured him.

"Yeah? Well, how do you know that for sure? When mornin' comes I bet none of us will be here. You'll see."

Morningstar scanned them. "Okay. I guess no point in continuing this tonight. Time to get to bed and rest up. We need to be strong in the morning. Liyah, why don't you and I take the first bedroom, and the boys the other one." On her way to their room, Morningstar stopped and added a couple of logs to the fire from the small stack next to the hearth, out of habit to keep warm through the night and any animals at bay.

———

In the boys' room, Zack was on his side facing the wall. Kai Li lay on his back, staring at the ceiling, his glasses next to him on the floor. "Think we be ok?" he asked in a whisper.

No response.

Kai Li repeated his question.

Zack rolled over. "Look man, how should I know? My guess is you won't even be here when I open my eyes. So everything will be okay for me, won't it? If you're real, then I guess we'll have to deal with that in the morning." He rolled back to the wall, yanked his red hoodie over his head, and closed his eyes.

Kai Li lay quietly, continuing to stare up at the ceiling. Morning seemed like a long time away. He took a deep breath in, letting it out slowly. The air gently hissed through his nose. He repeated this several times until, finally succumbing to fatigue and the night, he drifted off.

———

In the girls' room, Liyah lay on her side. She had removed her hijab and pulled the blanket securely up over her nose, slowly running her fingers along its silky border. Morningstar lay on her stomach, her head resting on her arm. She felt exhausted, too tired to even worry about getting home, about her grandfather. She stared at the back of Liyah's head. It was a hard day, especially for Liyah. *What could she be thinking?*

"Goodnight, Morningstar," Liyah whispered.

Morningstar closed her eyes. "Goodnight, Liyah."

In no time they were both out, like two porch lights.

EIGHT

———⁘———

MUFFLED NOISES FILTERED into the boys' bedroom. Kai Li yanked the blanket up over his head, snuggling in deeper, his back against the noise. Zack sat up with a start, head turned to the door. He strained to interpret the sounds. Voices? He rubbed his eyes, then glanced over at the lump on the bed next to him.

Crap!

He slipped out of bed, pulled down his hoodie, and swung the door open. Closing the door behind him, he made his way into the main room. Morningstar and Liyah were sitting next to each other on the sofa, talking.

Liyah smiled up at him as he neared. "Guess this is real, huh?"

"I don't believe it."

"Morning, Zack," said Morningstar. "Sit down. Join us. I went out early this morning and found some berries nearby." She handed him a cup. "Have some."

Zack shook a couple into his hand as he studied her. "Sure they're not poisonous?"

"Saw a few birds eating them," she reassured him.

Zack popped them into his mouth, plunked himself down into *his* chair, and proceeded to finish off the rest in short order. He set the cup on the end table, looking over at Morningstar, then Liyah. His eyes lingered on her. He noticed the dust had been brushed from her clothes. Her hijab was clean, and loosely guarded her face. The redness was gone from her eyes—large, deep brown and accentuated by her long black lashes. She smiled at him.

Why hadn't he noticed before how striking she was? She seemed like a different person. More together, or something. A twinge of guilt crept into his mind. Maybe he should have helped her out more yesterday? *She probably hates me.*

"You okay?" asked Morningstar. "Looks like you're in a daze. You should wake up Kai Li so we can get going."

Zack snapped out of his stare. "Taking charge already, girl? Why look at me?"

"Because it's better you go in than us."

"Why's that?"

Morningstar stared at him blankly. He turned away and began fidgeting with the gold cross dangling from his earlobe. *A little early to be picking a fight, anyway*, he considered. He stood back up and headed for the bedroom, his deep voice boomed out as he opened the door. "Rise and shine, Kai-bo!" His task completed, he headed back to the girls.

Kai Li let out a dull moan in protest. Finally dragging himself out of bed, he retrieved his glasses then made his way to the others. He sunk into the chair opposite Zack.

"Nice hair," Zack chuckled. "You look like a rooster."

Kai Li drowsily felt the crown of his head. The uncooperative cowlick was standing up, at full attention. He licked his fingers and patted it down, unsuccessfully.

"Eat some fruit, Kai Li," said Liyah. "Morningstar thinks we should get going as soon as possible."

"What's the hurry?" Zack responded. "It's not like we have to be somewhere or anything."

"It's always good to get an early start, don't you think?" Liyah asked. "It gives you more options for the day."

"Options?" Zack questioned.

"Yes," Morningstar answered. "In case things don't go well, or we need more time to find a place to stay for the night."

Zack continued looking at her. She seemed sure of herself and the situation. Why was he letting this girl with the red bandana and Lakota clothes take charge of the situation again? He felt the muscles in his jaw tense up, but this momentary frustration quickly passed. He sank deeper into the chair. What was the point?

Kai Li eyed the charred logs and white-gray cinders that remained in the fireplace, then picked the map up from the table and began studying it while he ate some berries. He then leaned over and picked up the letter that had accompanied it. He looked again at the map, then back to the letter.

Zack smiled over at him. "You get really fixated on stuff, don't you?"

"See something?" asked Morningstar.

"Yah. M-markers numbered . . . in order . . . on m-map."

"So?" Zack challenged, nonchalantly shrugging his shoulders.

"S-so. F-first one here."

"Here, where?" asked Liyah.

"Here. In house." Kai Li placed the map on the table and pointed to the square that was labeled "cabin." "See?"

Morningstar and Liyah leaned in for closer look. In the corner of the square that represented the cabin was written "zr1."

Morningstar took the map from him. "I didn't see anything in our bedroom this morning. I'd have noticed it. Kai Li, can you check your bedroom? I'll look again in ours just in case. Liyah, the bathroom? And Zack, can you see if there's something anywhere in this room?"

"Yes, ma'am!" Zack quipped, saluting briefly as she walked past.

Zack began looking around the main room, starting over by the fireplace. Nothing there but a few logs and a box of kindling next to the hearth. He checked under the sofa and chairs. Nothing there either. Walking along the far end of the room, he made his way along the main wall, ending at the door where they had come in. Next to the door, chest height, was a narrow wooden box with a flip-top lid. For mail? But how could that be? Mailbox? Here? In the cabin? He opened the lid and looked inside. Spotting a large envelope, he reached in and removed it. On the front, in dark-blue ink, was the marking *zr1. Damn if Kai Li wasn't right.* That same sense of guilt and regret seeped into his mind once more. Why was he being so hard on them? Nothing here is their fault. Not like it was with his dad. It was all his fault after all, wasn't it? *He just stopped calling one day. He knew I was mad, didn't he? Couldn't face me anymore. Could he? Chicken shit.*

The others returned to the table empty handed. Zack joined them, holding the envelope up in front of him like a trophy.

Liyah held out her hand. "What you got there?"

"He was right," Zack admitted, sending a half smile over at Kai Li, then placing the envelope in her hand. "Here ya go."

"Kn-knew it," Kai Li exclaimed, grinning ear to ear. "R-read it, Liyah."

Zack followed Liyah's eyes as she searched for support from each of them. What was she waiting for? So timid. But so beautiful. "Well, gonna open it? Or do we have to guess what's inside?"

Liyah put her finger inside the flap, sliding it along gently, then lifting it open. She withdrew a letter, glanced at it for a moment, then looked up.

"What s-say?" asked Kai Li, removing his glasses and anxiously rubbing the lenses clean against his shirt sleeve.

"On the envelope it says: *Surrendering,*" Liyah replied.

"Surrender?" questioned Zack. "We have to surrender to someone? Shit. I knew it. I thought the worst case was we're s'posed to go off on a dumb scavenger hunt."

"It's just one of the markers. One of the things we need to collect," Morningstar replied. "Remember?"

Zack cast her a doubtful look.

"R-read it." Kai Li urged, excited, the tone of his voice rising, sounding almost like a child's to Zack.

Liyah sat down on the sofa, while the others grabbed their standard seats. When they were all settled, her eyes shifted briefly to each in return. Then she began.

"Surrendering," she said, pausing, looking up again at the others, then back down at the page. "The first step in becoming is surrendering. Without surrender it is not possible to find one's true self."

Zack raised his eyebrows. "I told you."

"Zack," cautioned Morningstar, holding her index finger to her lips.

Liyah continued:

When we are very young children, we are in touch with our inner nature. We are in awe of life and open to all that is possible. But as we go along in our lives, we lose that child within us. It is an imperceptible process, occurring so slowly that we don't sense that it is going on at all. This happens because we begin to use our mind to create the picture we have of ourselves. We begin to let fears filter in and take emotional injuries personally. We diminish our spirit by giving false status to our own physical or intellectual limitations. We let others define who we are.

Think back. Back to when you were really little. Did you not have a trusting nature? Were you not wildly curious about all things? Did your eyes not search for the light? Were you not amazed at the brush of your mother's kiss on your cheek or the touch of your father's hand? And did your heart not crave love? Were you not a true child of this universe?

"Oh, come on," Zack complained. He rose up, then started pacing back and forth in front of them. "What's this all about? I mean, really. What the hell."

"Zack," Morningstar insisted. "Let her finish it."

Liyah went on:

Even at your young ages now, if you can imagine that child in the mirror, can you see how you have changed? Where did you go? When did you become so fearful, so lost? How did you come by the notion you have of yourself, at this very minute? Why do you now judge others when that child inside you had no such notions?

Some fears are useful to us. We experience physical pain in order to protect us from danger—real danger—danger that might harm us physically. But there are other fears that we simply make up, and when we give them weight, they then become part of a false identity.

Think back when you could first remember things. What were your thoughts about who you were? Perhaps they were of your mother whispering in your ear and telling you how special you are; or maybe they were of someone yelling at you and telling you "No!" or "Don't do that!" Was it the tone? Did you feel loved—or judged? These experiences are not only recorded by your brain but embedded in the very cells of your body and felt by your spirit—the real you.

In your short lives you have already gone through an uncountable number of these experiences. You incorporate them, then assemble them in a movie loop of sorts. And this movie becomes the story you tell yourself in the back of your head, over and over again—the false story of who you are. And then you bring this false you forward into all your encounters with others.

Liyah paused as she turned the page. Zack had stopped pacing and was looking down at her. She seemed deeply in thought to him. He felt anxious. What was making him so uncomfortable? Then she looked up at him.

"What ya lookin' at?" Zack blurted out, his words scorching the air between them. "Like we need this, right? It's ridiculous."

Liyah flinched, then looked over at the others. Kai Li nodded his assurance for her to continue.

Others want to simplify things. They want to put you in a slot: to categorize you in terms of coordination, speed, strength, and talent. Even your friends may send you messages—like you are too heavy, or too thin, or unattractive. Too short. Too tall. That you just don't measure up.

It is a false ruler, this physical body. It is not you.

Similar measures are applied to your intellectual ability. You receive information from tests at school, or comments from others who may not think the way you do, making you feel measured again, against standards created by those who do not know you, on topics that confine you, for subjects of which you have no interest. It happens to all of us. Once we are measured, we are judged, and that judgment settles into our minds. It then puts chains on our choices as we move through the years of our lives.

Do not believe these projections. They do not reflect the real you. Disregard the rulers! Measure only how much of your light you let shine into the world.

Who are these people who would send you such messages? Everyone. They cannot help it. They are your parents, your brothers and sisters, your relatives, your friends, your teachers, your coaches, and everyday people you meet on the street, and as you get older, they are your colleagues and even spouses—the people who we love and trust—all of them limited by their

> *own false understanding of themselves, and who have long since forgotten their own child-state. They dangle precariously on an ultra-thin gossamer of hope. They live in fear.*

"Christ, this is too much for me." Zack said, interrupting her. "What's the point?"

"I don't know," Morningstar replied, "but it seems this is part of the book we need to bring back. Or it has something to do with it."

"Well, why would they leave it here and then ask us to find it. Seems stupid. The whole thing is some kind of joke."

"It very s-strange, yes," agreed Kai Li. "But I s-sort of get what say."

Zack grew more impatient, flashing Kai Li a distrusting glance.

"Go ahead, Liyah. Continue," said Morningstar. "I think we're all supposed to know this for some reason."

Liyah brought her eyes back down, turned the next page, and continued:

> *The judgments of others expose their own weaknesses and insecurities, but they don't see this. We only see our reflection in the mirror and listen to the others as they bombard us with suggestions on how to improve ourselves—as if we weren't actually perfect to begin with. But our brain incorporates all this information and creates a picture. This picture is then reinforced by our societies and through our cultures, which have been built upon layers and layers of these untruths. And so we begin to believe it. It becomes our story—our notion of who we are.*
>
> *But it is a lie.*
>
> *Your true self is born of the very essence of the universe, and of which you are a special and necessary*

part. It can be found easily in the child. You can get a sense of this when you look in the mirror and look past the image of the physical you. Stand before that mirror with a calm mind. You will see that there are two of you: the one in the mirror and the one observing the one in the mirror. The one in the mirror is just a reflection of the physical you. The observer is the real you.

The false self, the one that is created by your mind—this is your ego.

The ego may appear helpful at times because it can help drive you forward or protect you from danger. But the ego gains power at the expense of your true self. As your mind fills with this false sense of identity, your true voice is crowded out. Perhaps you know this as 'that still, small voice within?' It is what you must listen to because it comes from the universe itself and belongs only to the child-observer within you.

So, the surrendering I speak of is the giving up of your ego—your false self, the movie you have created, the story in your mind. It is the process by which your observer voice, your true voice, becomes the dominant force in your life, and the babble of the ego is silenced. Success in achieving this state will bring the greatest joy to your life, and to all the lives you touch during your journey through this world.

This is the first truth you must learn. It is of great importance because it is required to fully understand the others. Surrender is the primary, foundational state of being. You will come to understand this.

When you learn all the seven states of truth of the Zah-re and express their wisdom through your everyday actions, you will become one with your true nature. Your spirit will soar. And you will discover joy.

Be kind to yourselves, and each other. You are the hope of the universe.

Safe journey.

Liyah placed the pages in her lap. Everyone remained quiet, even Zack. He was familiar with "the still, small voice" the letter spoke of, having learned about it from a priest when he was just a young boy. Somewhere deep inside him he knew the meaning of this message. Maybe Morningstar was right? Maybe he should pay more attention to what was being said in the letter? But he didn't like it.

"What do you think of that?" Morningstar asked quietly to everyone.

"Well," Liyah replied. "I guess I understand because in my religion we are asked to surrender to Allah. The idea is you are surrendering to something greater than yourself. You accept what is in this life and rely on the spirit within you. And for me that is also with Allah himself, the highest spirit. That's what I've been taught."

"Buddhist s'render t-too," added Kai Li. "Ease mind."

Zack's thoughts had drifted to the bizarre situation he found himself in. He finally broke his silence. "I don't get it! We're told to find and bring back this dumb book, whatever it is. And they, whoever they are, leave part of it in the same cabin where we start from. I mean, c'mon! What the hell are we s'posed to make of that?"

Morningstar stood up. "Well, no time to worry about it now anyway. We can't stay here."

"What should we do with it?" Liyah asked, picking up the pages.

"Bring the letter with us," Morningstar replied. "We were told to return with the book. Sounds like it has something to do with it. Maybe we have to reassemble it later with the rest of the book, or something. And besides, if we leave it here, someone might take it. Why don't you put it in one of the pockets of the backpack? We can't take any chances. We should do exactly as we're told if we expect to get out of here."

"Wherever 'here' is," Zack replied sarcastically.

"Why don't you and I each take one of the packs for now?"

"Yah, guess so," Zack said, begrudgingly, as he headed off toward the bedroom. "Just need to grab my jacket."

Liyah folded the letter into the envelope and stuck it in one of the backpacks. Morningstar turned to Kai Li. "Can you take charge of the map, please?" Kai Li accepted with a nod and a smile, took the map from the table, folded it neatly, and stuck it into his pocket.

When Zack returned, Morningstar suggested they all use the bathroom one last time before heading out. "We may be using the woods from here on depending upon where the trail takes us."

Kai Li scrunched up his face. "Gross!"

Nine

———†———

ORNINGSTAR REPACKED THE cups in the packs. When
they were all back together, she handed one of the packs
to Zack. Kai Li helped him get it situated on his back,
while Liyah assisted Morningstar with the other.

"Not exactly light, are they?" Zack observed, pulling the straps
tighter on his shoulders, and clipping the waist strap. "Sure you can
carry yours?" he asked Morningstar, grinning playfully at the others.

Morningstar tried to ignore him. "I'm used to it," she replied, in
her quiet, expressionless tone. "Thanks anyway."

They stood for a moment, communing in silence. Morningstar
opened the door, letting the others out ahead of her. As she turned
to close it, she glanced around the big room one last time. She could
sense the presence of spirits. Maybe the spirits of her people's legends?
Or maybe, just maybe, she was already in the land of the Great Spirit.

———

The path was easy to find—a narrow trail lined on either side with
small white stones spaced a short distance apart. The four made their

way along in the cool morning air, under a clear sky, finally arriving at a point where the trail split. Both paths were bordered by the white stones. Morningstar retrieved the map from Kai Li and traced the paths with her finger. Zack and Kai Li peered over her shoulder, Liyah crowding in behind them. "What can you tell?" she asked, anxiously.

"We should take this one," Morningstar replied, pointing over to the left fork.

"Why?" Zack prodded.

"Because if we take the path to the right, we come to the sixth marker first. The second marker, the one we need to find next, is on *this* path."

"S-same path," Kai Li added. "One b-big loop."

"Okay. Guess so," Zack begrudged, taking a step back. He then turned away and, without delay, started up the trail.

They marched on at a steady pace, Kai Li close behind Zack, stumbling now and again over small rocks, roots, and ruts, each time pushing his glasses more securely back over the bridge of his nose. Liyah fought to stay as close to Morningstar as possible, keeping her eyes glued to the trail right in front of her next step, carefully placing her feet between the same obstacles Kai Li was trying to negotiate, and occasionally snatching her pant legs out of the grasp of the small thorny shrubs that lined the way.

Their first stop to rest was by a cold stream that splashed and gurgled as it made its way down the hill past them. They sat down quietly along the embankment, sharing some snacks from the packs, looking quietly at the water bubbling over the small rocks.

Liyah adjusted her sandals and splashed some water over the scratches between the straps. She glanced over at Morningstar. "What do you think of the *Surrender* letter?" she asked timidly.

Morningstar paused briefly to consider the question, then her eyes met Liyah's. "Well, I think I kind of understand what it's trying to say. It reminds me of a ceremony in our tribe called *Hanbleceya*. Most people know it as a vision quest."

"I know quest," Kai Li replied. "Big m-med'tation."

"Yes, that's right, Kai Li. How do you know that?"

"Native American th-think like Buddhist, teacher tell me."

Zack chuckled. "You're full of surprises, Kai-bo."

Liyah's scrunched her face up at Zack. "Go on, Morningstar."

She took another sip of water, then looked around at her companions. "*Hembleciya* is usually for someone who is coming of age, mostly boys who are becoming men, but it's not always the case. The idea is that the person who seeks to know their true path in life—the one they must follow—is sent out alone into the wild for several days. During this journey they fast and become close to nature. It's said this helps them locate the spirit world, so they can receive a dream—a vision. The vision is treated as a signpost to help lead them to their true path in life. In this way he abandons his childish ways and overcomes the ideas others have of who he is."

"It does sound sort of like the message in the letter," Liyah agreed.

Morningstar noticed Kai Li was still staring down at the stream, watching it flow and swirl in whirlpools about the rocks jutting up from below the surface. "Do you have something like this?" she asked.

"Kai Li?" she repeated when he didn't respond.

Kai Li lifted his head and stared at her blankly for an instant, as if he was coming out of a dream. "Uh . . . Well. Not 'zactly, but si-sim'lar. Yes. W-we give up belief we s-separate. Cuz not. We p-part of all things. An' nothing stay, all d-die. When you know this, not l-live on expec-t-t-tations; mind f-free to accept truth. Give up old s-self. When mind calm, s-spirit at peace. This what the letter say to me."

"Zack?" Liyah asked. "How about you?"

"You in charge of this exercise?"

"It's not an 'exercise.' I'm just curious, since we are talking about it, what do you think?"

"I think, like I said, it's all stupid."

"Why?" asked Kai Li.

"Cuz I don't see what this gets us," Zack replied, rigidly. "We don't need to know this stuff. We just have to find some freakin' book and return it. But if you have to have an answer so that we can get on with things, then I say because surrender is not something anyone should do. They should stand up 'n' fight for what they believe, not bow down. Not to no one. You surrender, you lose. That's just the way it is."

Morningstar looked over at him. She sensed an almost anger in his voice. "It's not a battle," she offered.

Kai Li smiled. "It m-mean win back s-self. L-like letter."

"Whatever you say, Mr. Kai," Zack replied, cutting the discussion short. "Let's get moving."

Morningstar retrieved the map from Kai Li, studied it, then handed it back to him. "Not much detail on this map so it's hard to tell exactly where we are, but at some point, we pass through a place called 'Valley of Fears.' Maybe we can make it there by the end of the day."

The path continued meandering through the woods, crossing several small streams, maintaining a slight upward slope. After a while they made it to the crest of a steep hill. There the trail entered into a small field, passing several logs sitting off to one side. They rested again, sitting on a dead log at the side of the trail. Morningstar tilted her head up at the sky and felt the gentle, warm breeze kiss her face. She studied the golden rays of the sun as they poured down between the trees, noting the sun beginning its downward arc through the afternoon sky.

Zack got up without saying a word and approached a high outcropping of rocks just to their right. Morningstar watched as he made his way up over them, scrambling easily to the top on all fours. She could hear the faint squeaking of his sneakers along its granite-like surface. She could see him gripping at the crevices, his strong arms pulling and guiding him up. She decided to join him.

Although hiking was second nature to her, the steep rocks were clearly more suited to someone taller, someone with long arms and legs to push and hoist themselves up, like Zack. He had easily ascended to the very top. But she found she couldn't reach the last crack in the large boulder where he stood; she needed help to lift herself the rest of the way up. Perched precariously halfway up its surface, she craned her neck, staring up at him.

"Give me a hand, Zack."

"And suppose I don't?"

"Then I'll have to go back down," she replied, matter of fact. "Your choice."

She watched as Zack shook his head at her, turned sideways, and slid one foot down so it was closer to her. He rested it against a ridge in the rock's surface then reached out with his hand and grabbed onto her arm. With a sudden burst of great force, he pulled her up to him, while she hop stepped lightly, skipping along the smooth surface of the boulder, only her toes touching its surface, like a ballerina flitting across the stage. When she was safely beside him at the top, he let go of her arm.

"You're no fun, you know that?" Zack teased.

Morningstar scanned the horizon, her level palm shielding her eyes from the sun. Far away, across a wide range of evergreen-like trees, was a series of large reddish mounds. Over to the left, a section of multicolored trees blanketed the undulating land, and behind her was the sloping dark forest which they had just come through. Looking directly ahead, she could see an expansive valley, lush with bright yellow-green trees, their leaves shimmering in the sunlight. Beyond the valley was a wide bluish-gray strip she couldn't quite make out, ending at the horizon.

She glanced at Zack. "Mother Nature. She's beautiful, isn't she?"

"I guess I have to give that one to you," Zack agreed. "It's nice up here for sure. Not like home. Not like Detroit. No one is nagging me here, no one crowding me. But the rest of the world's not like this, Morningstar. And even Mother Nature can be a bitch. Who knows what's in store for us out there?" He pointed to the rust-colored hills in the far distance. "What you s'pose makes those hills red?"

She studied them for a moment. "No idea. Could be rocks like the ones in the Painted Desert in Arizona. Hard to tell from here." She gazed down the valley where she knew they would be going.

"I think we can make it to the valley tonight. Maybe two or three hours from here."

"Whatever you say, Ms. Star."

She turned to face him. He was looking straight out at the horizon, the corners of his mouth curled up just a touch. She had never met anyone like him before. *He's a handful, for sure,* she thought.

The two slid on their butts much of the way down the big rocks, finally joining up with Kai Li and Liyah at the base. "We need to move as quickly as possible along the path toward the valley," Morningstar advised. "When the sun sinks into the treetops, we should begin looking for a place to spend the night."

They followed the path's meandering turns, its dips and rises and sometimes rocky footing. The sun began to sink lower, finally kissing the tops of the highest trees.

"Time to start looking for a place to stay," announced Morningstar.

"Where you think that might be?" Zack asked. "I don't see any hotels along the boulevard."

Kai Li snickered, then shrunk shyly into himself as Liyah caught his attention. "Don't play into it, Kai Li," she said quietly.

Zack laughed. "I heard that you know."

Liyah turned to Morningstar. "What should we look for?"

"We need to find a place that can shelter us from the wind and weather, since we don't have the right clothing to keep the heat in and the rain out. Hopefully near a stream."

"Not much to ask for, since we have no idea where we are, where the wind might come from, or if there's even a stream anywhere within fifty miles," Zack replied. "Maybe we can find an electric blanket, too?"

Morningstar kept her back to him as she continued. "But no one should go looking alone. We go in pairs along either side of the path, keeping the path in sight and staying within calling distance of each other. That way we don't get lost. There's no way we'll be able find each other out here if we don't pay attention to those simple rules. Kai Li, you come with me. We'll stay to the left of the path. Zack, you and Liyah—"

"Yeah, yeah," Zack groaned. "We'll be on the other side. I got it."

Morningstar and Kai Li came to a flat area where the trees were farther apart. She turned to him. "This will do. Why don't you call the others?"

Kai Li's face lit up with excitement. He yelled out loudly, cupping his hands by the sides of his mouth. "Zack . . . L-liyah . . . Come back!"

Morningstar removed her pack and set it on the ground against the base of a large tree. After a few more calls back and forth, Zack and Liyah appeared near the path. A few minutes later they joined Kai Li and Morningstar.

"Is this the place you have in mind?" Liyah asked.

"It's clear enough to have a fire, and those big rocks can block the wind and provide some shelter from the weather, if needed. Yes, we can make camp here. I think it may be the best we'll find." Morningstar gazed up at the sky. The shadows from the trees had closed ranks and blended into the twilight sky. "It's getting too dark, so we can't go on. We'll have to make do. There's a stream nearby too. We can take turns freshening up there and refill the water pouches."

Morningstar reached out to Liyah, taking her by the wrist, tugging gently. "Come on. Let's go wash up at the stream."

"Sure," Liyah replied, her eyes lighting up, a big smile broadening across her face.

As they passed in front of the boys, Morningstar turned to them. "Can you two gather some kindling and small branches for the fire? When we get back, we'll set up camp while you take your turn at the stream. You guys good with that?"

"Guess we have no choice," Zack quipped. "Thanks for asking anyway."

"Yup," Kai Li added.

The girls made their way to the stream, about a hundred yards away at the bottom of a shallow embankment. Liyah took off her sandals, wincing as the straps brushed across the scratches and small blisters, then set them on the embankment. She rolled her silky dress pants up to her knees, waded a few feet in, and turned to look back at Morningstar. "Wow! It's so cold. Like ice."

Morningstar removed her moccasins, folded the bottoms of her jeans up, and joined Liyah. She bent down, drew up some water in her cupped hands, and splashed her face. She repeated the ritual several times, finally dousing the back of her neck. Liyah followed suit, pulling her hijab down around her neck then splashing her face.

"Not taking off your scarf? The cold water will feel good on your head?"

"Hijab," Liyah reminded her. "In public it's frowned upon by my family. My mom likes me to stay pretty covered up, even though the rules in Palestine aren't as harsh as they are for some other Muslims."

Morningstar didn't really know much about Muslims, or their religion, only what the pictures she'd seen in her schoolbooks and the little she had read in the papers her grandfather would buy when they would go into town. *In public? This isn't really in public.* "So I guess that bathing would be out of the question, then?"

Liyah grinned. "Yes, you could say that."

"Well, this is refreshing, but I think I need to rinse off completely," Morningstar replied. "We're not in a big rush, anyway." She waded back to the bank, stripped down, dumped her clothes next to her moccasins, and reentered the water. Liyah eyes stayed latched on her for a moment, then she turned her head quickly, shifting her eyes downward.

"Sorry, Liyah, but I have to get this dirt off me so I can sleep. Sure you don't want to change your mind? There's no one here."

"I'll be okay. Just the water on my face, and especially my feet, feels great. I can brush off my clothes. Hopefully, we'll find someone soon and get out of here."

Morningstar shot her a bewildered glance. "Well, I wouldn't count on *that*."

Liyah swished back though the stream to where she left her sandals. "There's always hope."

Morningstar soon joined her at the embankment. She retrieved her clothes, beat the dirt and dust off with the heel of her palm, then put them back on over her wet body.

The two walked along the stream, searching for berries without success, then headed back to the campsite. When they arrived, the boys were sitting down next to a pile of sticks and twigs they had gathered. Morningstar stared down at them. Zack had his knife in his hand and was whittling a small stick. "Thanks guys," said Morningstar. "Your turn. Maybe on the way back you can bring a couple more branches—something bigger to keep the fire going while we sleep."

Zack nodded, smiled, and saluted. "Sure thing, Captain."

As Zack and Kai Li left, Morningstar began digging a hole for the fire using a pointed rock and one of the cups from the back packs, then looked up at Liyah. "If you get me the two nylon tents out of the packs along with the ropes, plastic stakes, and poles, we can set them up."

Liyah was back in no time with the items requested. She placed them where Morningstar indicated, then sat and watched her. Morningstar could almost feel Liyah's intense concentration. When the hole for the fire was completed, she found a few stones the size of her fist, placing them at the bottom of the pit.

"What are those for?" asked Liyah.

"They'll provide air to the bottom of the pile, so that the fire will start easier and grow faster. Fire needs air to burn wood. This will help bring it up to the wood. Same reason fireplaces need grates."

"We don't have a fireplace," Liyah replied. "It's warm most of the year. When it gets cool, we just bundle up. And besides, there isn't a lot of wood to go around for burning."

Morningstar busily placed a handful of twigs in alternating directions across the stones. "How hot does it get there?"

"Often into the 30s."

"That's pretty cold. You mean winter."

"No, that's summer . . . degrees Celsius."

"Oh. I don't know what that is."

"I think that's about mid-90s Fahrenheit," Liyah replied.

Morningstar moved over to where Liyah had placed the tents. "Well, we have some of those days too in South Dakota," she said. "Here, I'll show you how this works."

Morningstar fit the curved pieces of the support sections of one of the tents into the base, attached the nylon ropes to the tent, and placed the stakes through the loops at the other end of the rope. Once completed, she went back to the fire area and picked up one of the larger stones she had not used for the pit, then pounded the stakes firmly into the ground.

"There we go! Think you can help me with the other one?"

"Sure. I guess so," Liyah replied, excitedly.

———

The boys showed back up at camp as the girls were completing the construction of the second tent, Kai Li dragging behind him several large branches while Zack carried a few dead logs in his arms.

They dumped their haul at Morningstar's feet.

"Well, that was quick," Morningstar said.

"Not wash yet. We d-do this first." Kai Li replied, eyeing the tents. "Look great!"

"Thank you, Kai Li," Liyah acknowledged. "I was able to help Morningstar. She's really good at this."

Morningstar couldn't help but notice a change in Liyah's demeanor; gone were her tears, and although she still seemed to be generally unsure of herself, she was gaining some confidence. "Great job to you two as well," Morningstar returned. "We should be good for the evening."

Morningstar then asked Liyah to pass out the food for their dinner, telling them it was best to start the fire later in order to conserve the wood. "Dinner," if it could be called that, consisted of a similar fare as the night before: an energy bar for each of them, some dried fruit, and water. After they ate, Liyah and Morningstar stayed at camp while Zack and Kai Li went down by the river to clean up. The sun had disappeared below the horizon. Darkness began to set in.

Zack and Kai Li returned shortly and joined the girls, sitting by the fire pit, talking quietly. As they approached, Morningstar looked up at them.

"Zack, I need your knife."

"What for?"

"To notch some sticks to start the fire.

Zack handed the knife over to her slowly and carefully. She sensed a distrustful, protective measure in Zack's motion and his eyes, as if he might pull it back as she reached out for it. But he didn't. Maybe it was just her? Something only in her mind. Maybe it was she who had become distrustful of him?

She flipped it back and forth between her hands, trying unsuccessfully to get the blade out. Zack reached over and retrieved it. Holding it out in front of him, he cupped it tightly in his hand, his thumb against its side, pointed at her. Then, he flicked his wrist with a jolt. The blade flew out toward her with a loud metallic snap, just like she had seen in a knife fight one time in a movie. She jerked her head back and ducked away.

Zack roared with laughter, then twirled the knife between his fingers like a majorette's baton, handing it back to her handle first. "Switchblade," he said calmly.

Morningstar didn't smile at all. She eyed him, finally regaining her composure. "Why don't you and Kai Li have a seat?"

Still sitting cross-legged, Morningstar placed the knife on the ground in front of her and reached into the pile of sticks, picking out two. She set the larger flatter one down next to her, then picked the knife back up. She began scraping the bark from the lower part of the longer narrower one in her hand, finally rounding off the bottom. She then cut an indentation into the middle of the larger stick. Moving to her knees, she positioned herself in front of the pit. She placed the rounded end of the narrower stick in the groove she had cut into the flat one and began alternately spinning the stick, first clockwise then counterclockwise, using the palms of her hands.

With great patience, Morningstar rapidly spun the stick until the friction generated heat on the end of the spinning stick. When a thin stream of smoke began to appear at the end of the stick, she sped up the pace of spinning. Looking up at Kai Li she nodded to him. "Put a small handful of pine needles at the base of the stick where the smoke is, please."

Kai Li did as told. As the temperature of the stick hit the kindling point, a tiny orange flame peaked through.

"More, please."

Kai Li complied. In a few seconds, the small pile ignited. Morningstar moved the small clump of burning needles to the bottom of the pile of twigs just above the stones. Leaning close, she then blew gently at the patch of fire. The flame attached itself and moved jerkily along several twigs, flickering, gasping for life. Suddenly it burst up through the twigs—the fire had come alive.

Morningstar piled larger sticks onto the flames until the fire had grown big enough to fend off any wind. Zack stared at the flames as they made their way between the sticks and lapped at the air, and Liyah loosened her hijab and drew the end that covered her chin to the side, then pulled up the cuffs of her pant legs, exposing the tops of the sandals that had been her only protection against the rough terrain. She gingerly removed the sandals from her feet and set them to one side. Having released her aching feet from their bindings, she gently caressed them with her hands.

The flames poured up through the pile of sticks, crackling with confidence, shooting sparks up into the early evening sky. Morningstar watched the others, each one captivated by the fire's glow, smokey smell, and radiating warmth. She sensed that Liyah had begun to fall deep under its spell. "What are you thinking about, Liyah?" she asked quietly.

Liyah stared into the fire for another moment, then addressed her. "Home," she said, with a sigh. "But not my house, really. I was imagining what it must be like for the Bedouin sheep herders of my country, some still living now as in ages past, as it was even before the coming of the great prophet Muhammad. They sat like we do right now, wrapped in the chill of the evening air. They watched mindfully over the silent movement of the lambs under a starlit sky, the fire keeping them warm and the wolves at bay. I really never thought of them much. Until now. It's like I'm getting to know them for the first time, and I can see the past and present together. As if time itself has stopped."

Morningstar gazed into the fire, her thoughts reflected in Liyah's words. *Perhaps it had.*

"I'm going to be really pissed if this turns out to be some joke," Zack said.

Even though his words were familiar, Morningstar noted the calm, tamed tone of his voice this time. She knew it had been long day for everyone. She removed his knife from the sash at the hip of her jacket where she had tucked it and tossed it on the ground next to him. It was enough to draw his attention from the fire. "I wouldn't dwell on that too much, Zack," she said. "No point in worrying over things we can't control."

Zack picked up the knife, then looked over at her and gave her a weak smile. "Okay, Mom."

"We at v-valley?" Kai Li asked.

"Yes, I think this is it," Morningstar replied.

"Why do you think it's called the Valley of Fears?" asked Liyah.

"I don't know."

"I think we're gonna find out," Zack added.

The darkness grew blacker, caving in around them, the fire the only light. Weariness returned them to silence for a while. Morningstar then got up and moved to the pile of sticks and branches. She threw a few of the medium-sized ones onto the fire and watched the smoke rise up above the flames. Her eyes followed the swirling clouds, which dissipated quickly as they rose up into the darkness. She was now looking straight up into the night. Twilight was long gone, and a patchwork of stars had appeared in the sky. She remembered the words of her grandfather, how he used to tell her that all the people of the earth were connected by the stars, that you could be with your loved ones wherever you were simply by knowing that they were looking up at the same sky. He told her that her blessings would bounce off the stars and fall upon the ears of those she missed. Then thoughts of him being swept up in the tornado and vanishing from her life suddenly flashed like lightning in her mind. How could her blessings find him if he was no longer alive? "I miss you," she quietly whispered anyway to the stars. Then she closed her eyes and imagined her grandfather's face, sadness rising in her throat.

She sat back down by the fire and stared blankly at the flames. She had been in front of many campfires in her short life, but never had she been so empty. Her mother and father had died when she was very little, and although she was told many wonderful stories about them, they seemed more like characters in a book to her than her parents. Her grandfather was the one who had raised her. He often apologized that he couldn't provide her the part that a mom or dad could, and now she regretted that she had never told him out loud that he had. And that she loved him.

Morningstar studied Zack as he glanced across the top of the flames at Liyah. Her head was tilted slightly downward as she gazed into the fire. With her hijab pulled away, he could see her entire face clearly. The orange light of the fire washed her features in a soft glow, painting her light-brown skin with a mellow hue. The flames danced in her dark eyes, and there were no signs of the many tears cried earlier. She looked at peace with the world.

Liyah lifted her eyes, briefly meeting Zack's stare, then quickly brought them back down to the fire. Zack appeared caught off guard and averted his stare as well, directing his eyes to the left, to Kai Li. But Kai Li remained fixated on the fire. He returned to studying Liyah. "What's with the outfit?" he asked, awkwardly.

Liyah looked back up at him, surprised. "What?"

"What's with the outfit?" he repeated. "You know . . . the suit . . . the headgear."

"This is how we dress where I come from. And this 'headgear,' as you refer to it, is called a hijab," she replied, serving him back a little of his own tone.

"Okay, okay," Zack said apologetically, laughing and raising his hands in front of his face as if she was going to throw something at him. "I didn't mean anything by it . . . just curious. Where in the Middle East did you say that was?"

"Palestine."

Zack continued, still looking at her. "So, I mean, is it a uniform or somethin'?"

Liyah studied him briefly before speaking. "No, but I think I know what you mean." She glanced over at Morningstar and Kai Li then back to Zack. "Most women wear something similar on their head and a dress. This jacket and pants are more formal for me because we were having a gathering of family. It's not a uniform. Just the traditional clothes of our community and religion."

"What religion is that?" asked Morningstar.

"Islam."

"I know Islam," said Kai Li. "You M-muslim?"

"Yes, I am."

Kai Li then turned to Zack. "What 'bout you?"

"Nothin'," Zack replied, pausing for an instant then continuing. "I mean, I was brought up Catholic, but I don't go to church anymore. I didn't like the formality of everythin' at the church. It seemed whether I was home, at school, or at the church, everyone wanted to tell me what to do. I liked being there, though, when no one else was. Somethin' about it."

"Place of s-spirits," Kai Li responded. "Huh?"

"Ya, I guess so."

"Why the cross then as your earring?" Liyah questioned.

"J-Jesus," Kai Li inserted. "Zack not l-like religion, jus' f-founder."

"Is that right, Zack?" asked Morningstar.

He kept silent, but she had her answer nonetheless.

Zack stood up and made his way over to the tents. "It's getting late," he mumbled. "Which one of these is for me?"

"Either one, they're both the same. You and Kai Li can share, and there's a blanket for each of us," Morningstar replied. She turned to Liyah and Kai Li. "It *is* getting late; we should all turn in. Help me restoke the fire before we call it a day, okay? It will keep us protected for a while."

Midway through the night, Morningstar awoke, as if by an imaginary alarm clock. She got up, leaving the tent, and made her way to the pile of branches. She knew the fire would need tending at least once during the night in order to keep it going. She was right; the flame was out, but the coals still bright red. She dragged the remaining logs over and set them on the coals. She stood over the fire for a few minutes, poking at the embers and raising the flames; when she thought it would carry on without her, she headed back to her tent.

Just before arriving at the entrance to the tent, Morningstar noticed her shadow on the ground; it was split in an odd way. She turned and looked up into the night sky. To her surprise, she saw not one moon responsible for the shadow, but two. One was a quarter of the way up the sky above the horizon, the other directly overhead. She was stunned. *Why hadn't I noticed this on my way to the fire?* She studied the sky further, noting the stars and their positions; she blinked several times trying to get a fix on the constellations she knew. Finding none, she suddenly realized: *This was not a place on Earth.* Turning her gaze from the sky, she entered the tent, closed the flap door behind her, and crawled back under her blanket.

TEN

As the night air cooled, the four wrapped themselves tight in their blankets. The fresh air and the weariness of their bodies propelled them into a deep sleep. Their bodies drank in the rest they needed for replenishment; pleasant dreams sailed through their minds.

Before the sun's light could rise to dim the stars, those dreams took a different path, morphing into dark visions and fearful thoughts; Zack's whole body twitched, Kai Li's legs jerked as if he were trying to run, Liyah's mouth stretched wide open but emitted no sound, and Morningstar's eyes bugged out into an eerie stare.

Zack's dreams began with him going home, then drifted to seeing friends at school and finally to remembering his dad taking him on a trip to Niagara Falls when he was little. He found himself standing at the Falls watching the flood of water crash into rocks at the bottom of the giant ledge, sending great misty plumes into the air all around him; he was laughing; his dad had a hold of his hand and was smiling.

But then suddenly he was no longer beside him. He searched for his dad's hand, it had been replaced by the hand of a gang member . . . and then other gang members approached, laughing like clowns; they surrounded him. His mind seized. *Daddy, where are you? Don't leave me.* But he was gone, Zack left to the groping grasps of the gang. They grabbed him and dragged him to the safety rail on the walkway. Holding him by his feet they dangled him over the side. Through the mist he could see the jagged rocks below; they let go of one leg. Panic set in. *What's going on? Stop! Daddy! Daddy!* He screamed and screamed. *You know I don't like heights! Where are you? Save me. Save me! Where are you?*

———

Kai Li's dream brought him back to the factory. His boss asked him to help package up a large order of stuffed animals that were being sent to America. He was part of a team, and they were all working hard to get the order out; the others were telling him what a good job he was doing, that he was going to get a promotion. His face broke into a grin, but then the faces of his coworkers melted into the faces of scary figures with huge green heads and yellow teeth; their bloodshot eyes stuck out, and their huge tongues wagged; their bodies flashed different colors. He could see right through them. The ghouls laughed and laughed as they flew at his head. Then the stuffed animals came alive—the lions and dinosaurs, the cows and pigs, they lunged at him and bit him all over with their sharp little teeth. He tried to run away, churning his legs faster and faster, but he was getting nowhere—like he was caught up in a slow-motion movie. The ghouls and the animals laughed as they closed in on him.

———

For Liyah, her dream started out at home, at the party. Everyone was happy, laughing, chatting. She handed out hors d'oeuvres with tiny napkins. Everyone told her how pretty she looked. But her mother then appeared from the kitchen, a scowl across her face, wanting to know why she hadn't brought her brother back. Liyah protested, pointing into his room. *In there, Mom.* Her mother told her she was lying, that she and her father were angry and disappointed with her. Her dad joined in. "Bring him back! Bring him back!" they both yelled. Khalib then dashed out of his room and into the hall closet; she chased after him. The closet opened into a room she had never seen before. She left her parents and followed him down a carpeted ramp that turned into a wide spiral corridor, where the corridor spun round and round, getting narrower and narrower. Her brother got smaller and smaller, and so did Liyah, until they were just two tiny people headed into a dark place. As her parents' voices began to fade away, she turned to look; she tried to call out to them but tripped. She began sliding down and down in the dark until the space got so small, she got wedged into the narrowing, twisting, funnel end. She was choking with fright, *I'm here in the dark! I can't breathe! Help me!* But she heard only a distant, faint reply: "We told you to bring back your brother."

———

Morningstar was dreaming of being with her parents. She conjured up the picture of them that she had pinned to the wall of her bedroom in the trailer; they became real. They took her to a picnic spot in a park with them; there were many flowers and honeybees, and they were lying on their backs on a blanket on top of lush green grass. The sun was shining, and they were having a contest to see who saw the craziest shapes in the puffy white clouds drifting across the sky; she had never been happier. But in an instant, the clouds blackened, sporting angry faces, moving toward her—their eyes wide, mouths open, snorting hail from their nostrils. She spun her head to the side to avoid them, looking over at the trees, but the treetops burst into flames and fell to the ground about her, then ignited the blanket and the grass. Her parents tried to run but were trapped by the flames; they yelled out to her then turned back into the picture in her hand. The picture began melting, its edges turning brown and curling; then it ignited, their faces transformed into black soot, disappearing before her eyes. Morningstar stood shocked, frozen, unable to help them. Then the flames closed in on her.

All four were simultaneously witnessing their darkest fears, in bold colors. At the moment when the nightmares spiked at their worst, the rising sun cast its rays between the trees, enveloping the two tents and snapping them awake. Bewildered at first, they settled back into the reality of their present situation. As they joined each other outside the tents, nothing was said about their dreams. Morningstar and Zack showed no signs of being upset, while Kai Li fought off lingering images. Only Liyah had a stricken appearance, but not knowing each other well enough, her appearance was not unusual enough to catch the others' attention. They began to get ready for the day ahead, first taking turns at the stream.

After refreshing at the stream, they ate a few pieces of dried fruit, packed up the gear, and headed back out along the path. The weather continued in their favor, the sun shining brightly in a cloudless sky, warming the morning air. A while later, resting and replenishing by the side of the trail, Morningstar reached out to Kai Li.

"Map?"

Kai Li removed it from his pocket and handed it to her as he chewed on some dried fruit. Morningstar studied it, Liyah peering over her shoulder. Then her hands dropped to her lap as visions of the previous night's dream flared in her mind, stealing her thoughts.

"Something the matter?" whispered Liyah.

"We should try to get to the other side of the valley before nightfall," Morningstar replied, as she stared blankly out along the path then slowly raised the map back up, collecting herself.

"It looks like there is another one of those markers," Liyah added. "There, next to the path . . . at the far side of the valley."

Morningstar looked closer, finally noticing the small "zr2" with a circle around it. "Okay, let's keep an eye out for it when we get near," she replied, catching Zack out of the corner of her eye trying to sneak another bar from his pack.

"We should save those for lunch," Morningstar admonished.

"I'm starving!" Zack complained. "No one can eat like this and live. Not even you."

"If we don't conserve our food and water, we'll be starving worse in a few days." She watched him as he slid it back into the pocket of the pack then zipped it shut.

"Fine," he said, offering up a disgruntled stare. "Just fine."

Halfway across the valley, as they followed a sweeping bend in the path, they entered into the midst of a grove of fruit trees. They rested among the trees, eating the fruit and storing some in their packs. As Morningstar grabbed her pack and headed toward the path, Kai Li called out from behind her. "Why Valley of F-fear? M-make me nervous."

"I was wondering that myself," Liyah chimed in, forgetting about her dream. "It's so beautiful here."

"It's just part of the mind game someone is playing on us," Zack responded, glancing back at them.

"Maybe you're right, Zack" Liyah replied, sighing deeply.

Morningstar felt the resignation in Liyah's voice and was also reminded, again, of her own nightmare.

"Well," Zack replied, "the sooner we get that book and bring it back, the sooner we find out who's effin' with us, the sooner we get outta here."

They made their way to the other side of the valley. Soon the beginning of a wide flat plain became visible through the trees a short distance ahead. The sun was dropping fast.

They stopped to rest at the edge of the plain, sitting in a line upon the dead trunk of one of the trees that had fallen down along the path. In front of them was a vast stretch of what appeared to be a kind of short prairie grass—a woven mat of gold, red, and purple hues, lit up by the late afternoon sun and flowing in waves from the push of the wind.

"So, this is the end of the valley, I guess," Morningstar sighed in relief, munching on a piece of fruit and looking out over the flatness in front of them, her feet with beaded moccasins dangling down below her jeans. She turned to face Liyah. "But I don't see the marker that was on the map."

"Oh, I forgot about that," Liyah replied. "Sorry."

"M-maybe p-pass it?" Kai Li posed.

"Why don't you and Liyah go back up the path just a little, no farther than the stream we passed a bit ago, and see if you can find anything there," Morningstar suggested. "Maybe we missed it."

Kai Li was off the log almost before Morningstar finished her sentence, his boyish eyes dancing. "C'mon, L-liyah!"

Morningstar watched as Liyah followed Kai Li back along the path, struggling to keep up, then both disappearing into the woods. She turned to Zack. "Even if things go well for us," she said, "looks like many more days to complete this. I'm pretty sure of it. It'll be difficult on those two."

Zack poked at the ground with a stick he had picked up along the way, not answering right away. Morningstar studied him, certain that by now he must have settled into that possibility himself, that they might not be getting out of there anytime soon. "Why so concerned about *them*?" he asked. "What makes you think *we'll* be okay?" Morningstar sensed a tiredness in his voice.

"Kai Li seems very smart, but he doesn't have any survival skills, not for out here anyway. And Liyah . . . she's a kind one. She cares for others, you can tell, but she can't help *herself.* She can barely hold herself together."

Zack kept poking at the ground, widening a small hole. "Okay, girl. Can't disagree. So?"

"So, you, Zack. You're strong. You're what my lala calls a survivor. Somebody who digs in, fights back. Even though you hide your feelings for those two, I know you would watch out for them, wouldn't you?"

His eyes met hers. He said nothing for a moment. She backed off. Maybe she had crossed a line? He finally spoke, quietly, turning his eyes back to the ground, jabbing again at the dirt. "I don't know them. I don't know you, either. I mean, we only just met. Sometimes I think you're more like an old man than a girl. And sometimes I wonder if you've ever been angry in your life. Don't you ever just want to let loose?"

Morningstar raised her guard. Her eyes grew wide, her brows lifted, her forehead furrowed. "This isn't about me . . ."

"Not tryin' to make it that way . . . just sayin'. Look, I don't hate people, if that's what's on your mind. Although, you shouldn't trust anyone, either. They always let you down."

Morningstar looked out across the field. "Not always."

Zack tilted his head toward her and stopped digging. "Always."

Morningstar kept her gaze on the distant horizon, but she could feel him staring.

"Anyway," Zack added, "what am I s'posed to do about it?"

She turned to him. "Just watch out for them, Zack. Watch their backs."

Zack got off the log and stood looking out over the same field. Morningstar took a sip of water from the backpack and sat quietly contemplating what to do about the coming evening.

It wasn't long before Morningstar heard Kai Li's voice as he and Liyah emerged from the woods, moving toward her along the path. As they got closer, she noticed he had something in his hand. He ran the last fifty yards waving it above his head. "We f-find it!" he shouted.

Zack turned around to see what the commotion was about. Kai Li joined Morningstar at the log then waited for Liyah to catch up. He handed an envelope to Morningstar; on the front was written "zr2." Morningstar opened it and removed the contents—another letter.

"Where was it?" Morningstar asked Liyah.

"There were several of the white stones in a circle where the path crosses the stream back there; 'zr2' was scratched on one of them in big letters. I can't believe we missed it. The envelope was under that stone. I wonder if all those markers on the map are letters?"

"Read n-now?" Kai Li asked.

"On the envelope it says *Fearing*," Morningstar said. She looked at the two of them, then over at Zack, back to the letter. She unfolded it and then began to read, loud enough so that she knew even Zack could hear her:

Fearing is the second state of truth found in the Zah-re. Some refer to it as one of the untruths, since in some ways it's not a natural truth. Fear, itself, sits in your mind. It is learned. Babies, when they are born, do not naturally fear fire or drowning. They scream not out of fear but as a signal that something is wrong; they are hungry, or perhaps sick. They are requesting help. They begin to develop fear by touching hot objects or falling down and getting hurt. They learn fear as a way to remember to avoid those situations. Even wild animals in the place you come from do not naturally fear people; it is something they learn from the behavior of man.

"What the hell is this guy talking about?" Zack blurted out. "And who is he anyway? It's like we're on another planet or something."

The image of the two moons flashed in Morningstar's head. *They're going to notice at some point. Maybe he's accidentally right? Or, maybe we're are really dead and in the land of the Great Spirit.* That seemed more likely.

"Must be part of the *Zah-re* it refers to," Liyah replied. "Still, it's strange that these letters seem to be speaking to us at the same time. Maybe when we find the book it will become clear."

Morningstar continued:

> Fear of physical harm is learned through observation and experience, sometimes gained from our own curiosity and exploration and sometimes from the hurt we receive from others. While we are not born with this fear, we learn it as a way to manage our physical life.
>
> The mind creates another fear that is different from this physical fear, and it is deeper. It is a fear that begins much earlier than fears relating to pain. It begins shortly after birth; it is a fear that has to do with the very nature of 'being.' It is born from the mind's struggle to understand itself relative to its greater self.
>
> When you were conceived, much of your physical nature was determined by both your mother's and your father's genes: the part of them passed on to you by each of them and to them by all the generations that came before. As you grow within your mother's womb, you rely on her body, and the food she eats, as your source of nourishment; you are, in effect, an extension of her.
>
> When you are born you are cast from this safe place and become your individual self. But to your young

mind, you are still a part of her. This forced separation creates a pull, like gravity: a need to remain close to your mom. This need to be close is like the need to be safe from pain, except it goes to the very sense of what 'being' actually means to you—far beyond the concern about physical pain.

Zack grew impatient. "Jeez. C'mon."

"*Sssh!*" Liyah hissed. Morningstar read on, shifting the pages:

The time unavoidably comes when you realize that your mother is not there and cannot be found—when you are laid to sleep in a separate place and wake up without her near. There is, at that very moment, a sense of great loss: part of you has been taken away. The fear that rises is a basic one, born of that sense of loss—the fear of loss of your very self. It is not a loss the young brain can understand, so it calls out in pain. You call out in fear, to bring your mother back, so you can be whole again.

A related fear arises later, as your mind develops and you come to understand you are actually a separate person from your mother. Your own personality emerges as part of the reflection of the true self inside you. As you get a little older, this sense of separateness strengthens, and your life focus swings in that direction. This creates a sense of need to break away— of cutting the strings that tie you to something or someone else. There is a feeling of suffocation that comes with wanting to break away faster than you are allowed. Unwanted hugs can also create this sensation of suffocation because they represent the physical side of restraining you, even if they may be given with love. Anything that now represents a force against the freeness of your individual self is perceived as a threat.

The fear of your mother's continued absence is based, at first, in abandonment; someone has left you. It is the earliest point at which your brain understands your relation to 'other,' and its need to retrieve that other in order to be truly whole. The screams of the baby are a cry for oneness to return. The fear of suffocation, on the other hand, is the cry for your separate identity—to protect the person within. All other fears, with the exception of physical pain, arise out of these two primary ones, whether it be the fear of heights, small places, drowning, or anything else. This is because they all carry the same message: loss of self.

You cannot hold your mother to blame for abandonment, because it had to happen at some point: she had to let you sleep by yourself when you were a child—she could not avoid it, and you could not avoid waking up to find her gone.

In a similar way, our physical selves must die someday and abandon those we love. It is a reminder of how special we all are to each other—that our time together is relative, brief, and precious. The fear of abandonment and the fear of suffocation are really two sides of the most basic fear of all: the 'fear of not *being,' not existing. When you finally understand that your mind, your ego if you recall, and your body are not you, you realize that you are connected to all things and, therefore, an indispensable part of the universe. Only then will you fully conquer your demons. Only then will we live in peace, without fear.*

Morningstar let the letter rest on her lap. She looked up to see the faces of her fellow travelers. Liyah and Kai Li seemed deep in thought. Zack, who Morningstar knew had settled into listening rather intently himself, coughed then looked away, pretending to be disinterested as she caught his eye. "So, what are we supposed to do with this?" he asked.

"Keep it with the other one, I guess," Morningstar replied.

Liyah reached out to take the letter from her lap. "Is it the same writing?"

"Look like it," Kai Li replied, as he slipped the letter from her grasp, placing it back in the envelope, then placed the envelope with the other letter inside the pack next to them. He glanced back at Liyah and smiled his big smile. "Jez k-keep it s-safe."

Zack was unable to let it rest. "It seems pretty stupid for this guy to ask us to go on this scavenger hunt to bring back that book, while at the same time giving us pieces along the way. Why wouldn't he just go get it himself if he knows where it is?"

"Maybe it is like you say," said Liyah. "He's playing with us. It's part of a test we have to pass before we can get home."

"Yeah, well the whole thing is just too weird."

Knowing they should not chance going any farther, risking getting stuck in what appeared to be called "The Flats" on the map, Morningstar led them back along the path, close to the stream, where they made camp. The boys scrounged for firewood, while Liyah replenished the water supply for the packs. Morningstar started the fire.

They spoke very little about the note on fearing before retiring, even though it dredged up thoughts about their own personal fears and the nightmares of the previous evening. They talked only of their tired legs and the long days that might be ahead, turning in for sleep before the moons had a chance to rise.

Later, in her tent, Morningstar found it difficult to fall asleep. Were they really out of the Valley of Fears? Maybe it was just about the nightmares and the letter. It was possible. But something still bothered her. She felt an uneasiness in the pit of her stomach. Would the morning quell her fear? Or was it tomorrow she needed to watch out for?

ELEVEN

The sun inched its way into the morning sky, hanging like a red jewel around the neck of the horizon; a few puffy clouds drifted high above in the early pale-blue light. Before long, bright yellow rays lit up the tents, signaling the official start of a new day.

Munching on the fresh fruit from the packs, Kai Li and Morningstar checked the map before heading out across The Flats. Once back on the trail, the four followed the white stone path as it cut through the open fields. The journey was less arduous than navigating the twisting rolling hills through the forest; Kai Li and Liyah were able to take their turns carrying the backpacks, sharing the burden; Liyah's feet still hurt, but the blisters were subsiding a bit, making it easier to negotiate the trail. Every few hours they rested and refreshed by the side of the path. By mid-afternoon, a few scattered trees in the distance made their crowns viewable, and before long they entered new terrain.

The path veered to their right and headed on a gentle downward slope; bright red, blue, and white flowers blanketed the hill; their sweet fragrance filled the noses of the four as they sat in the grass, snacking and resting. Kai Li bent down and picked one white one shaped like a tulip and presented it to Liyah, then a blue star-shaped one for Morningstar. Zack watched as Liyah fawned over him, then glanced over at Morningstar. Could that be a hint of a smile? He chuckled, calling out Kai Li. "Suck-up."

Kai Li grinned at him, pushing his glasses back up along the bridge of his nose.

In the late afternoon, fields of flowers ceded to a grove of small trees, bearing olive-like fruit. They gathered as much as they could, stuffing them in the packs. The olive trees gave way to fir-like ones, and before long they came to a wide, rapidly flowing stream. Upstream along the path, shrubs punctuated large stretches of grass.

As the afternoon wore on, the warmth of the unrelenting sun began taking its toll on all of them. Zack turned around to check on the others and noticed that Kai Li and Liyah, weighed down by the packs, had begun falling behind.

"We should call it a day soon," he said, as Morningstar caught up to him.

"Good idea. We're losing them."

Zack slowed the pace, and before long they came across a bend in the trail, where the path moved slightly inland from the river. There they found what they were looking for: a wide flat area surrounded by what appeared to be pine trees; brown needles covered the ground around them, keeping back the weeds and providing a level, soft area to set camp. Across from this clearing, on the other side of the path, the ground dipped down slightly, ending at the base of a small hill. They set up the tents on the edge of the clearing, near a row of trees that could provide some shelter from the wind.

With the sun finally disappearing into the woods, darkness began quickly infiltrating the camp. Zack and Kai Li scavenged for wood to get the fire going and keep it alive through the night. Morningstar and Liyah prepared the campsite, dug a firepit, and scooped up handfuls of dry pine needles to help ignite the fire.

Liyah laid out a meal of olives, dried fruit, and pieces of the bars. Zack gobbled his share as the others were only beginning to eat theirs. He leaned back on his elbows, scanning the others, wondering how much longer he would have to put up with this. "There are people in prison, you know, who eat like kings compared to this," he grumbled. "And they don't have to sit on the ground like a frontiersman, either."

"We don't have much choice, do we?" asked Liyah, swallowing a bite.

Zack stood without answering and stretched his legs side to side, like he was about to run in a race, then made his way over to a shallow depression he had noticed in the side of a small hill across the way; he returned a few minutes later.

"Find anything interesting?" Morningstar asked.

"There's a big hole in the side of the hill over there. Probably enough room for all of us to sleep inside if we want."

"Is it damp?"

"Didn't notice."

"I think we're better off where we are," Morningstar replied. "The trees can give us a little shelter, and the ground is soft and dry. But at least we know it's there in case a storm should come our way."

They all stared wearily into the fire, without speaking. Finally, looking around at the others, spellbound by the bouncing flames, Morningstar broke the silence. "It's nice, isn't it?"

"What?" asked Liyah.

"The light of a campfire."

"Very n-nice," agreed Kai Li, his voice almost a whisper. He poked at the fire with a long stick, sending sparks up into the night sky.

Zack remained silent, watching the fire dance, casting a flickering orange glow on the faces of the others; he felt the warmth of its energy. His mind grew calm. For the first time in a long time, if only for an instant, he felt a connection so profound that it was impossible to deny. The nightmarish uneasiness he sensed since he arrived here, wherever here was, seemed to be thawing. Even though he wanted to be back in Detroit with his family and Tommy, it wasn't all good there, was it? It sort of vibrated there—the fast pace with few breaks, the suffocation that he felt sometimes between the craziness in the house, the demands from school, and the danger of the streets. There was danger here, too, he suspected. And also the unknowing of it all. But here, by this fire, with these others, there was something . . . something else, something that made him feel different—maybe safe? Or free? But something definitely different.

Kai Li poked again at the fire. "So why Valley of F-fear? Name give me bad d-dream."

"You too?" exclaimed Liyah. "I had an awful one too."

"Actually, me too," admitted Morningstar, "but maybe the name is about the fear in the letter . . . although something still bothers me. Like the dream was a warning, or something. How about you, Zack?"

The question dragged him out of his quiet moment. He looked over at Morningstar. "Don't have any idea what you mean by warning. It was all very weird."

"What think of 1-letters?' Kai Li asked Morningstar.

"For me," Morningstar replied, "I think it's about that we are connected to all things, past and future, in the universe and that we shouldn't let other people tell us who we are . . . that we are really one with the Great Spirit. And that is our real nature. My grandfather used to say that to me all the time."

"Uh huh.," replied Liyah, nodding. "I think I see that."

"An' fearing?" Kai Li continued, turning to Liyah.

"Well, I kinda get it, at least in my mind, about how we develop fear. But I'm not sure what we can do about it. I mean, what can anybody really do about their fear of heights or the dark?"

"M-message say put ego away, cuz it create f-fears. It mean think of s-something m-more 'portant than you."

"But how?" Liyah asked, her eyes bouncing between Kai Li and Morningstar, as if pleading for the answer.

"All fears are not the same," Zack replied, creating a look of surprise on Liyah's face.

"What do you mean?"

"I mean that there's something you can do about being afraid of another person . . . like a bully . . . or someone trying to hurt you. You can stand up and fight, you can make 'em stop. But if you are afraid, say, of heights . . . who do you fight?"

Morningstar turned to him. "Some people can't stand up to bullies, Zack. They don't have enough self-confidence to do that . . . like you do."

Zack studied her, the muscles in his face tightening a bit. "Yeah, well it's not that hard when you finally get it that living in fear is worse than being killed by some jerk."

"Maybe that's one of the keys, Zack," Liyah replied. "That if you are actually willing to die, you can also break some of the chains that your ego has locked around you. It sounds similar to what was in the letter."

"Maybe," Zack replied, "but still not easy to do if the thing you fear is in your mind. Not some smart-ass bully."

"I think Kai Li is right, though," Morningstar added. "If you're concentrating on someone else, or something else, you can also overcome your fear this way."

"Yes, well maybe so," said Liyah. "At least I hope so . . . that would be good."

Zack got quiet again. He studied his new friends across the campfire. *Morningstar definitely knows more about nature than any of us,* he thought, *and she has an awful lot of confidence for her age. And Liyah seems to be the more compassionate one—at least I see that in how she helps everyone and doesn't judge us, even though she is clearly afraid of just about everything. And then there is Kai Li, so quiet most of the time . . . maybe because of his stutter? Although there is a lot going on in that brain of his.*

"Time to turn in," Morningstar announced. "Zack, let's you and me find some more wood to hold the fire for as long as possible."

Zack grumbled but finally rose and joined her in the search, both staying close to the camp.

Once the fire was set and they had retired to the tents, Morningstar lay on her back under her blanket, her hands behind her head. She looked out through the open flap at the stars; the first of the two moons had poked its head above the horizon; she knew that shortly the second one would do so as well, as they both began their twin flight across the evening sky. *When would the others notice this?* She could see clouds closing in above the treetops. *Probably not tonight.*

By the middle of the night the clouds had taken over the sky, and the wind picked up. Kai Li and Liyah wrapped themselves tighter in their blankets; Zack was dead to the world. A distant roll of thunder echoed across the camp.

Just after dawn the storm reached the camp; a lightning bolt split the heavens, and thunder ripped loudly over their heads. They woke with a start, Kai Li jumping up first. Liyah reached out for Morningstar's hand. Zack dragged himself to his feet, still groggy, and Morningstar sat up. She looked out at the sky through the flap then turned to Liyah. "It's going to storm any second. We'll be safer from the lightning in the shelter of the hill, Liyah. Zack can show us the way."

They knocked down the two tents, repacked the backpacks, and followed Zack to the shelter.

"This should work, Zack," Morningstar confirmed. "It's protected and large enough for all of us to weather the storm here."

They stood there for some time, huddled together, looking out from their hole in the land, wrapped in their blankets. The wind began picking up more steadily; gusts sent the trees swaying wildly, and lightning split the night air right behind them. Liyah latched onto Zack's arm, while Morningstar tried to calm her with words of assurance, but they were half-hearted words—her mind was elsewhere. She sensed an evil presence, like when they went through the Valley of Fears. She worried about the lightning hitting the dry needles.

Flashes quickly peppered the sky, and the thunder shook the ground around them. The hair on Morningstar's arms stood up; she could sense the static electricity in the air. Suddenly, a giant bolt pierced the sky, followed immediately by a deafening *crack* of thunder and a piercing creaking sound, then a loud *thud* not too far away.

Morningstar strained her eyes in the direction of the sound. She had heard that sound once before, on a camping trip with her grandfather: the sound of a tree falling in the woods. A lump of fear lodged in her throat. She kept staring and staring in the same direction. Then they appeared: *flames.*

"L-look! Over there!" Kai Li shouted, pointing to where Morningstar was looking. "F-fire!"

They watched as the fire spread out along a line parallel to them but still a safe distance away. It grew wider and higher, attacking trees and shrubs in its path. Then all of a sudden, the wind changed direction, setting the fire on a new course—directly toward them. Another lightning bolt split the sky, striking just off to their right, sending a tree crashing down in front of them, a large branch blocking part of the entrance. The top of the tree landed in the middle of the campfire across the way, scattering hot coals onto the dry needles. The needles on the ground ignited, like a match in gasoline.

Fear set in when the wind shifted again, blowing straight into the hole, bringing dense smoke from the fire with it. The larger fire burning in the distance headed toward them as well, fanning out as it crept along. The shelter was now surrounded by fire.

The fire came within thirty feet of them then suddenly halted, having no more needles to fuel it, but its heat was intense, and the wind continued to blow smoke directly at them.

Liyah shrieked. She, Kai Li, and Zack backed up until they were pressed against the inside wall. Morningstar remained at the edge of the hole staring into the fire, her mind racing.

The spiking flames sent her thoughts back to a time when she was little, back to when she was with her parents on a trip to the Pine Ridge Reservation to see her grandparents: They had come for a visit when she and her parents lived in Rapid City—where her father had a good job as a mechanic. Her grandparents still lived on the "Res" in a small dilapidated ranch-style house. She remembered waking in the middle of the night from smoke and crying for help, the flames blocking her way out. She'd hid under her bed. The room had gotten so hot she could feel the skin on her face and arms baking and the heavy black smoke choking her. Then she remembered something else: being scooped up in someone's arms. She had opened her eyes to see her grandfather, wrapping her in wet towels then stepping back through the flames. An investigation later revealed it had been a gas leak that had been ignited by a burning candle. Her grandfather had been the one who broke the news to her that her parents and grandmother were gone. As those words had departed her grandfather's lips, she recalled feeling a suffocating, sinking, sadness seep into her bones.

She stood there mesmerized. *It's this same fire. It has returned.*

"Get back here, Morningstar!" yelled Zack. "What are you doing?"

"It's here again," she said half out loud.

Zack called again to her, "What? What are you saying?"

She remained like a statue, staring out at the fire.

The others just looked at each other, confused. Zack reached out and grabbed her arm, pulling her back to where they were huddled, away from the intense heat. The smoke was beginning to build up in the hole; Kai Li was yelling in between coughs. "What we do? What we do?"

Liyah was holding onto Kai Li and pleading for Zack to do something, but Zack was frozen. He stared out at the fire then over to Morningstar for a clue of what to do. She was still mesmerized by the fire. Zack grasped her by her shoulders and shook her.

"Morningstar! Morningstar! What the hell? Snap out of it!"

Morningstar finally turned to him, her mind questioning how much time had passed since the fire stole her thoughts away. She gazed back out at the fire again, except now she was frightened. It was the first time she felt fear since she was that little girl in the house that was on fire. It was happening again. *It was happening all over again.*

Zack looked stricken. "What do we do, Morningstar? If you lose it, there isn't much hope for the rest of us."

Morningstar stared into his eyes, suddenly remembering their talk about fear; fear was holding her captive. She realized it was up to her. Only she could help the others. She gazed again out at the fire, but it was hard to see through the smoke; she could only catch glimpses of the path between the flames and swirling plumes.

She looked over at Kai Li and Liyah, huddled together, then back at Zack. *Forget the fire. Forget yourself. Do something. Do something for them.*

In the next instant, she raised her blanket up, covering her head and shoulders. She grabbed another blanket from Liyah, holding it in her other hand. "I'll be back!" she shouted then turned and stepped into the fire.

"Morningstar!" Zack shouted at the top of his lungs as she disappeared into the smoke and flames. "Oh my God!"

"What's she doing, Zack?" Liyah cried out in desperation.

Zack began to cough. "I don't know. We might suffocate here, but at least we have a chance. There is no chance out there."

Liyah began to cry hysterically. "I just want to be home," she begged. "Allah, Allah. What have I done?"

Morningstar felt the heat building against the blanket and on her face. She kept her head down, eyes forward scanning the ground, trying to locate the path; if she could find it, she might be able to follow it back the way they had come—toward the stream. *The fire cannot get me there.*

The edge of the blanket was already singed. The heat and smoke were unbearable; she began coughing. *Where is it? Where is the path?*

A few steps more and suddenly there it was. She stayed low, keeping along the path and quickening her pace. Finally, away from the camp, with no trees or dry needles to feed it, the fire and smoke thinned. She ran hard, turning to her left, knowing that the water could not be far away. In a matter of seconds, she found the stream, running straight into it.

There was very little brush around the rocky banks of the stream, so Morningstar found safety there. She was standing in the middle with the water up to her knees. *No time to rest. I have to get back.* She submerged both blankets in the water; she had known she wouldn't be able to carry all four heavy, wet blankets back. She quickly wrapped one around her and up over her head, picked the other one out of the stream, and without hesitation climbed back onto the bank and headed back toward the fire.

She found the path quickly, but the smoke was now heavy again, her coughing worse. Taking a corner of the blanket she was holding in her hands, she covered her mouth; her eyes burned from the smoke, but she had to keep them trained on the path. She counted the seconds: sixteen, seventeen. It was now about the same time she had spent on her way to the stream; she began looking for the others. Unable to see anything more than a few feet in front of her, she called out to them as loud as she could. Nothing. She called again. And again.

"Over here! Over here!" came the voices, muffled by the roar of the wind and crackle of the fire.

She left the path, running as fast as she could, weighed down by the heavy blankets. She thought back to when her grandfather had swept her up and carried her to safety. *It must have been like this for him . . . saving me . . . not knowing, not knowing if he would make it out. He was daring the fire: 'Try if you want, but you will not take her.' I must find that courage. Fear cannot have me. I must be strong for them. They must get out.*

They all kept calling to her. She homed in on their voices. She strained to see them, her eyes burning. A handful more steps. Then out of the smoke and fire, they appeared. She ran into the hole. She ran to save them.

"Are you insane?" admonished Zack, in between coughs. "You're freakin' crazy. What were you thinking?"

"Where did you go?" Liyah cried.

"To the stream. I have two wet blankets." She coughed several times. "If we go by twos, we can get out of here. We can make it to the stream and wait out the fire." She let out a huge, raspy cough then continued, "Zack, you take one and cover yourself and Liyah. Kai Li, you come with me." There was a method to her directive; she knew it would be easier for her to take care of Kai Li because he was about her height; she wouldn't have to reach up, and he wouldn't have to crouch low; Liyah was taller and a better match for Zack.

She picked up the backpacks and handed one to Zack, keeping the other. They each put them on, then Liyah went over to Zack, and he wrapped the blanket around both of them; Morningstar covered herself and Kai Li; she then used one hand to secure the blanket around her and Kai Li, then reached out to Zack with the other. "Hold on so I don't lose you!" she yelled.

Zack took hold of Morningstar's hand then made sure he had a strong hold of the blanket around himself and Liyah. He nodded to Morningstar. In his eyes she saw only trust, and it gave her strength. She gazed out at the fire then over to Kai Li. "Let's go!" Into the blaze they all went.

The intensity of the fire had increased, and the dense white smoke from the burning needles made it almost impossible to see now. Morningstar kept her eyes glued to the ground, looking for the path again, but it was even harder to see now. The smoke was so thick it clung to Kai Li's glasses, and he was soon unable to see to help her; he began staggering, trying to follow her steps.

They finally stumbled over the path. Morningstar didn't see right away, but her foot caught the edge of it. She made a slight adjustment to their course then crouched as low as she could in order to remain on it, still moving forward as fast as possible. She could feel the heat on the hand that held Zack's; she knew he must be getting the worst of it since his hand covered most of hers. She was in an oven, and every breath was filled with smoke; she was suffocating. She began gasping, wheezing, and coughing as if she would lose her lungs. She could hear Zack coughing too. Liyah and Kai Li were spared, able to breathe through the blankets which filtered out the smoke.

Morningstar was still counting the seconds in her head again as they moved along the path: sixteen, seventeen. She let a little extra time go by because they were going slower than when she had come back by herself. When she thought she was at the point that was closest to the stream, she turned off the trail—just guessing, but she had no choice. The heat was brutal now; she felt she might pass out. She yanked the hand that Zack was holding onto, signaling him to move faster.

She pulled him forward as hard as she could, the ground uneven and invisible. She lurched along, staggering and tripping with every step.

Just when she was about to give up, she and Kai Li burst into the fire-free space next to the stream, pulling Zack and Liyah with them. The ground fell off suddenly, and she careened forward over the rocks along the bank of the stream, landing face first in the water and dragging in Kai Li, Zack, and Liyah with her. They struggled in the water, falling over each other, coughing, trying to stand up.

Liyah and Kai Li caught their breath first. They looked over at Zack who remained bent over, gasping for air, then tried to help Morningstar; she was lying in the middle of the stream, her body pinned down by the weight of the pack. She was fighting, unsuccessfully, to keep her head out of the water, and Kai Li was unable to raise her.

Zack's breathing had returned to the point where he was able to stand. He saw the struggle Kai Li was having with Morningstar and went over to them. He removed his pack and handed it to Kai Li; bending down, he pulled Morningstar up from behind, his arms under her shoulders. As he raised her up, he turned her around then lifted her over his head, placing her waist against his back. He then brought one leg and arm in front of him, like the fireman's carry he had learned from his dad when his dad was a volunteer fireman. Liyah and Kai Li appeared stunned at the ease with which he did this.

Zack carried Morningstar over to the far bank of the stream, more protected from the fire, and set her down against a rock. Morningstar's head dangled down as she sat there choking, coughing out smoke and water. Finally, she was able to steady herself. Zack bent over and kissed the top of her head; tears collected under his eyes.

After making sure Morningstar was okay, he removed her backpack and set it on the bank behind her. Clearing his eyes with the backs of his hands, he turned around to Kai Li and Liyah.

"You guys okay?"

"Oh, Zack. Thank you!" Liyah gushed, tears pouring down.

"Yeah. Great j-job," Kai Li added.

"Don't thank me," Zack insisted. "Thank her." He motioned over at Morningstar. "We would have been in big trouble without her, man. We wouldn't have made it."

The three of them stared at the raging fire from where they had come. They could feel its heat even in the stream. Zack turned to them.

"We'll rest here for a while. When Morningstar is stronger, we'll move downstream, farther away from all this." He bent his head down, shaking it back and forth. "We're lucky. We're so very lucky."

The first drops of rain began to fall, each one creating concentric ripples in the stream.

TWELVE

A RECOVERED MORNINGSTAR and her companions moved
along the bank of the stream, away from the campsite—
away from the inferno. The air sagged with humidity, and
the fluctuating wind blew intermittent swirls of smoke their way, once
again stinging their eyes and infiltrating their lungs. A light, misty
rain accompanied them.

Kai Li studied the sky. This was all too familiar: the humidity, the
shifting wind, the eerie yellow sky, the sinking air pressure that swelled
his joints. *Monsoon season at home,* he thought. *Maybe we are near there?*
A picture of his mother slipped into his mind, then quickly disappeared.
He stopped, held out a cupped hand, then rotated it like a weather
instrument. "N-not know, guys," he said, loud enough for all to hear.

"Not know what, Kai-bo?" Zack teased.

"Bad f-feeling."

"About what?" asked Liyah.

"Storm. We sh-should get safe."

"You might be right, Kai Li," Morningstar replied, eyes scanning
the skies. "It does kind of feel that way. Maybe we should find a
place . . . get something to eat."

That instant, the heavens opened up; a deluge poured down from above. They scrambled along the edge of the water, keeping the trail in site. In a short distance they came upon an outcropping of rocks that formed a wall. Near the bottom it formed a ledge that provided shelter from the rain. They huddled together, wrapped in the two blankets that hadn't been dunked into the stream. The water continued to pour down like a waterfall, just a handful of feet in front of them.

The downpour lasted over an hour, providing time to rest and reenergize. It was near noontime when it finally ceased, and patches of sunlight could be seen between the clouds. The heavy smoke was gone. Only a mixture of black, gray, and white trails could be seen rising from the charred, smoldering embers of the once living bushes and trees.

Morningstar checked the map with Kai Li. She pointed at the words "Signal Station" near the top. "With some luck we could make it all the way to *here* today. Maybe we'll find someone there to help us?"

Kai Li repacked the bags, splitting the two wet blankets between them to even out the weight, then secured them. Zack lifted one onto his back then assisted Kai Li with the other. They left the shelter, finally making their way back onto the white stone path. Scorched trees studding the landscape gave way to an area of open plain, untouched by the fire. By mid-afternoon they had reached the far side of the Green Forest. There, the terrain began an uphill slope toward Crystal Lake.

At their next break, Kai Li dragged out the map again. Liyah bent down alongside him. "We have to locate 'zr3,'" she reminded him.

"Here," Kai Li said, pointing. "It c-close to 'zr4.'"

Zack gazed over at them. "If we could rent a car, we could get all seven today then get the hell outta here!"

Liyah smiled. "One step at a time, Zack."

They headed back on the trail. By late afternoon they had covered a lot of ground, and high hills appeared in the distance. The steepness of the path increased as they neared them; their pace slowed.

Zack stopped to let the others catch up. "I don't think we're gonna make it to the station," advised Morningstar as she joined him. "We should look soon for a place to spend the night."

"There's plenty of daylight left. I'd rather keep pushing on," Zack replied with halfhearted conviction, as the other two joined them. Kai Li consulted the map.

"M-must be close to r-ridge . . . m-marker there."

"We'll keep our eyes open when we get there," Liyah assured.

"Okay," Morningstar replied. "I guess we do have time to try to get to that point."

The pace of the sinking sun accelerated as it headed to meet the horizon, and it soon sat like a big orange ball just above the hills, framed above and below by two layers of thin clouds. Kai Li's mind flashed back for an instant; it was an eerily familiar scene, but he couldn't quite put his finger on it. *Maybe from a recent dream?*

As they approached the base of the hills, rounding a bend in the trail, Rainbow Ridge sprung into view: a gigantic rainbow-colored cliff rising sharply into the sky, its jagged face a red-orange hue at the base, turning bluish green in the middle, then deep purple near the top.

"Wow! Look at that!" Liyah gasped. "Beautiful!"

Zack turned to Morningstar. "This is what we must have been looking at when we were up on the big rock . . . that you said was like a desert."

"The Painted Desert," she replied, "near the home of the Navajo and Hopi tribes in the Southwest."

The path dumped them at the far end of the ridge. Kai Li studied it as they walked closer, estimating it to be about a quarter mile across. Its colorful face rose straight up at almost a ninety-degree angle; between the base and the white stone path was a dried-up riverbed. Along its front was a low wall; two rows of cavern-like holes sat atop.

Zack stepped up on the wall and entered the closest cavern, disappearing into the darkness. His loud voice echoed from within. "People must have lived here at some point. There's stuff here . . . like wood tables or something and broken pots."

Morningstar joined him. "Wow, it's just like the home of Pueblo Indians. Some of these holes are interconnected, and there are steps over there that go up to another level."

Kai Li jumped up on the wall then climbed the stone stairs to the second floor, catching up with Morningstar. Peering through the big open archway, he cupped his hands around his mouth and yelled down to Liyah. "Ha-l-l-looooo!"

Zack moved back outside and looked up at him. He chuckled then yelled back. "Haloooo yourself, Kai-bo!"

"Halloo!" Liyah shouted. She then laughed as she made her way up to Kai Li and Morningstar.

"This may be fun and games," Morningstar said, "but we have to think about making camp."

"Yes, Mom," Zack kidded sarcastically, making his way up the stairs.

"Very funny, Zack" Morningstar replied, straight-faced.

Moving back down below, the four sat along the wall. Morningstar removed a plastic bag she found in an obscure side pocket of Zack's pack. She turned to Liyah. "The path appears to go along this dried-up stream. We can follow it ahead and see if there's a clearing where there might be some food we can gather. We can make camp here and set up the tents in one of the rooms. It might not be as comfortable, but it'll be safer . . . and more protected."

"Yes, Captain," Zack replied, extracting a smile from Kai Li.

Morningstar ignored him. "C'mon, Liyah. Let's go."

"Don't be late with dinner, girls," Zack called to them, as they disappeared in the bend of the path.

Ten minutes out, Morningstar and Liyah came upon a slow-moving stream, maybe twenty feet across. Following the stream, they made their way to a small clearing where they found a few patches of red berries, and a few tuber-like plants that could serve as vegetables. Liyah placed them in the bag, and they continued along the edge of the field searching for more, keeping within view of the stream.

Morningstar gazed ahead, toward the source of the stream, her eyes stopping on a very small hill covered in bushes. "There might be some more berries up there, Liyah. What do ya think? Let's go check it out."

Liyah balked. "I don't know. We're getting a little far away from the camp, aren't we?"

"Not too far. We can follow the stream back."

"I don't like being too far from the path," Liyah complained, in a timid tone. "What if we get lost?"

"We'll be okay, Liyah," said Morningstar. "Really."

They approached the bottom of the hill. Morningstar spotted a few bushes bearing orange-yellow fruit. She made her way over, picked a sample, and took a small bite. She handed it to Liyah. "Tastes kinda like a pear."

They picked a number of ripe ones, working their way up the hill. As Morningstar started working her way up the steeper part, Liyah tugged on her sleeve. "I think we have enough for now."

"I suppose," Morningstar replied, scouting the area one more time. Just as she was turning around, she caught a glimpse of an opening in the rocks at the top of the hill. She turned to Liyah.

"That looks like a cave up there, doesn't it?"

"Where?"

"Up there. See it? Right above where you lose the stream."

Liyah squinted to get a better look. "Oh, yes. I see it. You have good eyes."

"'Eagle eyes,' my grandfather would say. Let's go check it out."

"Oh, I don't think that's a good idea," Liyah replied, haltingly, her words tripping out. "We should go back now."

"We'll be all right," Morningstar assured her. "Let's go see!"

"I don't know. We're supposed to stay near the path. And the boys will be waiting."

"Don't worry. I promise we'll just check it out quickly and then return to camp. Besides, we're still following the stream."

The sun was setting, and the diminished light added to Liyah's apprehension. But she also didn't want to disappoint Morningstar. What was wrong with her anyway? She wasn't like this at home. She was much stronger there—taking care of her brother, being a leader at school. *Maybe it's just this place?*

"Well . . . as long as you promise, Morningstar."

"Promise."

They scrambled up the short distance; the stream took a turn to the right just before they arrived at the top, hooking around the side, up and out of sight. The opening of the cave was fairly large; it was easy for several people to enter side by side without having to duck. The sun was still above the horizon and sat directly across from the opening, providing plenty of light. They entered together.

The walls of the cave were dry, and there didn't appear to be anything unusual about it to Liyah, except for perhaps a group of stones that formed a circle in front of them. She took a few steps toward the stones. *No signs of any recent activity*, she observed; no bones that may have been left if some animal had used it as a temporary home. *Wow, I think Morningstar is getting in my head.* She stopped in front of the stones.

"Looks like maybe someone made a place for a fire," Liyah observed.

Morningstar bent down and picked one of the stones up in her hand. "No. No fire here. No black marks on the stones, and no ashes. I don't know. It would certainly be unusual for these rocks to form a perfect circle by chance. And there aren't others anywhere nearby. They must have been placed here by someone."

Liyah looked down at her. "Why?"

Morningstar set the stone back in it its place, stood up, and brushed the sand from her hands. "No idea." A little beyond the other side of the circle, near the back of the cave, she spotted a tunnel entrance. She stepped around the stones and approached it.

"Look at this Liyah. I wonder where it leads?"

"Let's get out of here, Morningstar. It's creepy. And I don't like little spaces like this."

"I'll just go a little way in."

"No, Morningstar," Liyah insisted. "I don't like this. I want to go back."

"Well, wait there while I check it out."

"Don't leave me alone here, Morningstar," Liyah replied, alarmed.

"Don't worry! I'll only be a minute." She bent her head down slightly to accommodate the narrowing of the tunnel and moved into it.

"Wait," Liyah implored, moving toward her. She stepped across the edge of the stone circle, her right foot landing just inside the circle, sinking slightly into the sand.

———

Zack and Kai Li piled the firewood from their scavenging inside one of the stone rooms strung along the ridge, then sat on the wall in front of the opening, awaiting the imminent arrival of Morningstar and Liyah. Zack removed his knife from its holster and broke a small stick from a branch. Facing away, he began stripping the bark from its end, now and again shifting his eyes up, looking down the path.

Kai Li was soothed by a warm breeze that blew through the archways of the ancient stone homes that were cut into the side of the cliff. The only sounds he could hear were the gentle rustling of the leaves in the trees across from them and the scraping of the knife's blade against the bark of the stick. He closed his eyes and began breathing rhythmically, slowly, deeply, something he did often to slow his racing mind. Meditating like this was his way of taking control of his thoughts, away from the day's crazy pace and his worries. It also helped him ease his stutter; when he got nervous or excited, he always stuttered more.

He rested his wrists on his knees, palms facing up, his index fingers and thumbs touching ever so lightly. He remained in this position for several minutes before opening his eyes again. When he did, he noticed Zack had stopped whittling and was staring at him.

"Thought you were going to start snoring any minute," Zack joked.

"No s-sleeping."

"No sleeping? Really?"

"Meh-tating."

"Meditating?" Zack questioned, raising an eyebrow.

"Y-yes."

"So, what do you think about when you meditate?"

"No think."

"What d'ya mean?"

"Mean mind can m-make you crazy."

"Crazy?"

"Yeah, it take over . . . you r-react 'stead of be in control."

"Well, aren't you in control if you're thinking? I don't get it, man."

"No. T-to be in c-control must be calm . . . must be 'ware all r-round you . . . be mindful."

"So, what you thinkin' of?"

"Idea is *no* think . . . obs-s-serve . . . like letter say."

"Observe what?"

"F-focus on breath . . . th-then notice thoughts."

"Like this," Kai Li took a few deep breaths, closing his eyes and slowly exhaling each time. "Relax body, observe m-mind." He opened his eyes. "Do like me."

Kai Li read the skepticism in Zack's eyes as they met his.

"Hmmm," Zack returned. "Well, what the hell. I'll give it a go."

Kai Li led him through a meditation exercise, watching him, keeping him relaxed, eyes closed, focused on his breathing, and encouraging him to concentrate—to observe how his mind bounced around from one thing to another.

Zack began thinking of what Kai Li was trying to accomplish with this mediation thing, then he switched to thinking about how he met Kai Li, then to how they were going to get home, to the last thing he remembered before he found himself in this place: *Where was Tommy? Was that lightning that hit him?* Back to Kai Li, then finally to how to stop his mind from thinking all these thoughts. His whole body tensed with anxiety when he realized he couldn't stop his mind from wandering. But as he breathed and listened to Kai Li, his mind seemed to slow down, let go.

He listened to the creaking of the trees and the voice of the wind through its leaves, felt the breeze kiss his face. He breathed more slowly, deeply. The tension in the muscles of his shoulders and back began to dissipate; he could sense the heavy energy flowing out of his body. The sweet night air filled his nose; he relaxed some more.

Other images soon popped into his mind. He thought about the camp where he and Kai Li were right now, then of Morningstar and Liyah. *Where were they?* He noticed his mind beginning to wander again; he brought it back, focusing on his breathing again. He started thinking about time: *How much time had gone by? A few minutes? An hour?*

Kai Li tapped him gently on his shoulder. "Okay. You open eyes n-now."

Zack's eyelids lifted up. Kai Li was smiling broadly at him.

"N-no easy, eh?"

Zack laughed. "Yup. Not so easy."

"Mind race, no?"

"Yup."

"What y-you think of?"

"All kinds of stuff. I see it's very hard to think about nothin'."

"You do it m-more . . . get easier. N-not so 'portant what think 'bout . . . more 'portant observe p-person thinking . . . the mind."

"Person thinking?"

"Yah. Who thinking?"

Zack studied him curiously. "I'm the one thinking."

"No," Kai Li replied. "You observer . . . you w-watch p-person thinking."

Zack felt his mind strain.

Kai Li continued. "There t-two people . . . one thinking with m-mind racing . . . one observing. This is what Buddhist m-master teach."

Zack stared at him blankly then smiled.

Kai Li let out a big laugh. "Maybe get it?"

Zack laughed back. "Very strange, Kai Li!"

"But t-true. Observer be true s-self . . . other one be thinking s-self . . . call it m-mind, or 'ego' . . . like letter say."

"I don't know much about this, or about Buddhism. Maybe you're really a snake charmer?" He winked at him and switched the topic. "Do you go to school in China?"

"Was. No m-more. Work in f-factory."

"Is it hard?"

"Sometime . . . many hours."

"Doesn't your dad work?"

A brief sadness stole his face. "No dad."

Zack felt a pang of sympathy. "I see. Sorry."

———

Liyah followed Morningstar a couple of steps into the tunnel; there was enough light from the main cave for them to see about thirty feet in. Liyah tugged at the bottom of her tunic.

"That's it, Morningstar. Really." She tugged harder. "Let's get back. I can't come and find you if something happens. And I don't like tunnels at all. I mean it."

"Looks like it gets too narrow as it moves away from the cave," Morningstar replied. "I don't think it is a complete dead end, but there is no way of knowing."

"Nobody cares," Liyah said, irritated. "So, can we go now?" She let go of her, turned around, and began walking toward the entrance of the cave. Morningstar followed a few steps behind. The sun was sinking lower and as she looked out, she could see it resting above the trees; its rays shone directly in their faces, causing Morningstar to shift her gaze downward. When she did, her eyes caught the shallow footprint Liyah's sandal had left in the sand. Liyah was about to step to the left of it, closer to the middle of the circle.

Morningstar suddenly realized why there was something about the circle that troubled her, why the stones were neatly ordered, and why the dirt near the footprint was so much looser than the rest of the cave. A picture of the map flashed before her; the words near "The Caves" was marked "Sinking Sands." She yelled to Liyah. "No!"

As Liyah's head turned toward Morningstar, her foot landed— then kept going. The sand enveloped her sandal then swirled around her leg as it sank rapidly into the floor of the cave, pulling her down; as she shrieked, in a mere flash, the entire cave floor beneath her collapsed; sand, pebbles, and small rocks poured down below, like corn from the spout of some grain elevator, taking the stones and Liyah with them, a landslide of rock, dirt, and dust.

THIRTEEN

VOLCANIC DUST BLEW up from below, covering Morningstar as she stood, shocked, the toes of her blue-beaded moccasins jutting out over the rim of the hole. As the last of the dust settled, she peered over the edge, careful not to break off more and fall in as well. What remained was only debris and a deathly silence.

After a moment, the top of the pile began to move. Liyah rose slowly from under a blanket of the pebbles and dirt—stunned but alive. She brushed off her clothing and used her hijab to clear the dust from her eyes.

"You all right?" Morningstar cried down.

Regaining her composure, Liyah looked up, coughing lightly. "Yeah. I think so. But how am I going to get out of here?"

"Can you see how to get up closer to me, so I can pull you out?"

Liyah scanned the chamber she stood in. "There's no way. This must be just another cave."

"What can you see?" Morningstar's voice echoed into the chamber below.

"Well, it's pretty dim down here. The only real light is coming from where you are . . . from the hole. I can see a little ways but not far."

"Can you tell if it leads somewhere?"

Liyah's voice began to tremble. "No, not really. I just need to get out of here." Her voice rose a little in panic. "What are we going to do?"

"Well, walk in some direction keeping the light from the hole in view, then walk in a circle the same distance from the hole until you see something."

"I . . ."

"Just do it."

Liyah tried to settle herself. "Okay, okay. Don't worry. I'm just going to keep you in my sight."

She walked until the light dimmed then stopped. Keeping an eye on the light, she began walking in a circle.

"See anything?" Morningstar prodded.

"Nothing yet."

There was silence for a minute and then an echo of Liyah's voice a short distance away.

"What'd you say?" Morningstar shouted into the hole. "I can't hear you."

"A stream!" Liyah yelled back.

"A stream?"

"Yeah. It seems to be coming from the direction behind where you were standing."

"How far does it go?"

"I don't know. It gets too dark there."

"It's okay. We'll figure it out."

"How? I don't see how we can." Liyah replied, her voice breaking. She moved back under the opening and looked up at Morningstar.

"I could go get Zack and Kai Li," Morningstar suggested, "but I don't know what good that would do with you still down there. And you'd have to wait here by yourself."

"Oh, no! No. Don't leave me alone."

Morningstar took a gentle step back away from the lip of the hole.

"Where are you going?" called Liyah, terror in her tone.

"Nowhere. It's not safe here . . . I'm thinking."

"About what?"

"I'm thinking the stream must come out somewhere."

"So?"

"I mean it must join the stream we walked along . . . somewhere. It must come out of the hills, out of the cave."

There was a brief silence as Liyah absorbed the notion. She called up again. "But it might just go underground, not be a tunnel . . . or maybe come out on a cliff."

"Well, we don't know. But it's worth checking it out. It may be our only hope right now. Can you go farther down and see where it goes?"

"I can't go much farther than I was . . . there's not enough light. And I'm not going to get lost down here."

"Okay then, I'll go look for an entrance from the outside. I may be gone for a little while, but I'll be right back."

"No. NO! Don't leave me, Morningstar. Don't you leave me alone!"

"Don't worry. I won't be long."

"No, please, Morningstar," Liyah begged. "Please don't leave me. I don't like small places. And the dark makes it worse."

"We have no choice, Liyah. It's going to get dark soon. We have little time."

Morningstar left the cave to the pleas of Liyah. She made her way down the top part of the hill, then went around the side, looking for where the stream had disappeared. After a few minutes she heard the sound of the rush of water over rocks. She made her way up a short incline, reaching a small narrow rock plateau. On the other side was an opening in the hill, where the water flowed out. The opening was fairly wide and high enough for her to walk through without bending over.

She began making her way in, carefully. The stream took up the center of the cave, leaving a couple of feet on either side for her to navigate. *This must be the same stream that Liyah found inside the cave,* she thought. *If I follow this, maybe I'll find her.*

A short distance in, the darkness swallowed her up—she could now barely see three feet in front of her. Her pace slowed to a crawl. She waved her left hand back and forth in front of her, using her arm like a blind man's cane, checking for obstacles; with her right hand she traced the cave wall next to her, keeping it close.

The diameter of the tunnel started to narrow; her head bumped into the rocky ceiling. She bent down lower, moving on, sometimes walking like a chimpanzee, resting her weight alternately on her hands and feet. She called Liyah's name out into the black silence of the tunnel. *No reply.*

The stream now took up most of the floor of the tunnel. After sloshing through the water on her hands and knees a while, she noticed a very faint, dull light. She called out to Liyah again. *Still no reply.*

The source of the light grew brighter as the tunnel slowly widened. Finally reaching the point where she was able to stand up, she moved quickly along the side of the stream, calling out. "Liyah, Liyah! Can you hear me?"

Then, a muffled, echoed reply came. "Yes, yes . . . over here . . . over here." Morningstar sensed both panic and elation in it.

"I'm coming, I'm coming. Stay where you are."

Liyah's calls grew louder. "Hurry, hurry . . . Please hurry."

The tunnel took a sharp turn to the left, and out of the darkness appeared the shadowy gray form of a human. They saw one another at the same time and ran into each other's embrace.

"Allah! Praise Allah! Oh, Morningstar, I can't believe it," Liyah sobbed.

Holding onto Liyah's shoulders, Morningstar separated the two of them. "It's okay, Liyah. Everything will be good." She took Liyah by the hand. "C'mon. This way."

Liyah pulled her back. "It's too dark that way, Morningstar."

"It's the only way out. I know the way . . . It will be fine."

"I can't. It looks very dark . . . and closed in. It's really scary."

"It will be okay," Morningstar reassured her. "I will be right with you. Hand in hand, they disappeared into the blackness of the tunnel.

———

The sun was about to set, but its reddish-orange rays still penetrated through the trees. Zack was standing on the wall in front of the opening of the stone archway, looking off in the direction where the two girls had departed.

"Hey, man. Think I'll go get some more fuel for the fire."

"Not n-need bonfire," Kai Li replied. "You worry?"

"They should have been back by now. What could they be doin'? Don't they know it's gettin' dark?"

"Yeah, you w-worry."

"Well, no kiddin', Kai," he said, his voice exhibiting a sense of urgency and a hint of irritation.

"What we do?"

"We should look for them."

"What if come b-back and n-no one here?"

"They'll wait for us."

"No s-sure good idea. I always told s-stay one place."

Zack sat back down on the wall and returned to whittling. "Well, okay, we'll give them a little more time."

———

Liyah followed Morningstar back into the dark inner workings of the tunnel, trying not to ger her feet wet in the stream. A short way in, Morningstar paused and turned to her. "The tunnel gets a little narrow here but then widens back out at the other end. We'll have to get down on our hands and knees and sort of crawl a little."

"Oh, no, I can't. You didn't tell me that. I can't go any farther. Let's go back and find another way."

"There is no other way," insisted Morningstar, calmly.

"I just can't . . . You don't know."

"It's okay to be scared, Liyah. Everybody is frightened of something. It will be okay . . . Believe me."

Liyah went silent. The two were standing with their faces inches apart, yet they could barely make out each other's features.

"I can't . . . I just can't . . . I'm sorry!" Liyah begged.

"You can, and you must. There isn't any choice, Liyah. C'mon, follow me."

Liyah pulled back and started crying. "No. No. You just don't get it."

"Don't get what?"

Liyah's mind flashed back, back to her home in Beit Lahia. She was nine. There were explosions all around and gunfire in the street in front of their house. She, her brother, and her parents had gone to the basement to be safe.

Morningstar waited a few seconds for Liyah to reply, not hearing one, she repeated, "Get what, Liyah?"

Liyah brought her attention back to the tunnel and Morningstar's question. Her crying had subsided, but she found difficulty with her words, sputtering them out nervously. "In Palestine, when I was little, we had a lot of trouble."

"What kind of trouble?"

"There was always a lot of shooting, and it could be dangerous at times to go out in the streets. But it wasn't just the Israelis who we were afraid of; there are groups in our own city who fight each other. Most people are just trying to make a living and care for their families, but a couple of these groups are very extreme.

"My father runs a newspaper. He was educated in America. He's a well-known journalist in Palestine. He was always meeting with famous people and businessmen to get opinions from all sides. He tried to be fair and tell the truth. But no matter what he did, someone was always angry with him." Liyah paused to catch her breath.

Morningstar encouraged her. "Go ahead."

"Many times, they threw rocks through the windows at his building. One day a group attacked an Israeli business in the West Bank, in a town far from where we lived. The next day my dad wrote about it in the paper, saying the attack was unwarranted and that it would only hurt the peace efforts. But this group, the extreme religious people, they don't really want peace, and they saw my father as weak . . . and siding with the enemy. They arrived one morning and began throwing bottles and rocks at the house."

She paused briefly.

"My father called the police, who came quickly. There was yelling and scuffling between the group of extremists and the police. It got out of control, then fighting broke out. The police shot tear gas canisters at the crowd and started firing over their heads from behind their shields. Someone in the group yelled that they were being shot at; they started firing at the police. Bullets started hitting our house."

"My god, Liyah, that's awful. But why are you telling me this now?"

"Because you need to know why I can't go with you!" She took a breath. "My dad rushed us all to the basement. I followed behind my little brother, Khalib. My mother and father were then coming down the stairs after us when a big explosion went off. The blast blew them off the top of the stairs leading to the basement, not dead but unconscious . . . at least that is what I was told later. Someone had thrown a hand grenade into the house through the window.

"I was knocked against the far wall of the basement and fell down, and the ceiling caved in and landed on top of me, pinning me under big pieces of plaster. Khalib had made it into the next room—he wasn't harmed, but he saw our parents lying on the floor and thought they were dead. He stood there crying while the fighting outside continued. Sometime later, after the crowd had dispersed, the police came into the house to check the damage and found Khalib standing over them. They called the ambulance, and everyone was rushed to the hospital. They didn't think to look under the debris in the corner . . . for me."

Morningstar stared at Liyah, speechless.

"I was unconscious for a while, I guess. When I woke up, I couldn't move because of the weight on me. I got so frightened I thought I'd die just from that. I yelled for my father, but there was no answer.

"Darkness came and I still couldn't move; plaster from the ceiling was pushed against my face, and I only had a small pocket of space to breathe through. I was sure I would suffocate. I thought my family was dead and that no one would find me, so I screamed and screamed and screamed. I could feel my heart pounding in my ears.

"I remember finally giving up . . . maybe I passed out from fright or lack of oxygen, or maybe just fell asleep from exhaustion. I don't remember anything after that, except waking up in the hospital."

"How did they find you?"

"I was told later that Khalib had been in shock at the hospital, and my parents were still unconscious. The police had roped off the area around the house so no one could get in. A neighbor finally showed up at the hospital and after seeing they couldn't talk to my parents or Khalib, asked the nurse about me. No one knew I was missing. The firemen finally came and dug me out."

"I get it Liyah . . . I really do," Morningstar consoled. "And I'm sorry. I am," she said, gently. "But somehow you have to find the strength to get through this tunnel. It's not something I can do for you; it's something only *you* can do." She paused. "Do you remember the letter? About fearing?"

"Yeah."

"There is no death, Liyah. There is nothing to fear. I know the way out. And I'm here for you." She grabbed Liyah's reluctant hand and led her farther into the darkness. The tunnel soon narrowed, forcing them to bend lower and lower. Morningstar had to let go of Liyah.

Eventually they were reduced to crawling on their hands and knees in the middle of the stream.

Liyah stopped.

"What's the matter?" asked Morningstar.

"I can't do this. I'm telling you," Liyah protested.

"Yes, you can . . . c'mon . . . you can grab onto my ankle. Concentrate on holding on to *me* instead of where you are. We'll be out before you know it."

Liyah latched onto the heel of Morningstar's moccasin and followed her through the stream, but she soon felt her throat cramp up again, her breaths reduced to short, uneven bursts. She couldn't see; she felt the rock walls closing in on her. She cried out. "I'm suffocating, Morningstar. The walls. I can't move." She yanked her hand from Morningstar's ankle.

Gripped by fear, Liyah tried to stand but couldn't. She pushed out against the walls and started yelling in gasps. "Stop . . . STOP . . . we're going to die!"

Morningstar was caught by surprise; she turned suddenly to see why Liyah had let go, but they were in the narrowest part of the tunnel, and as she turned her head back around, it banged hard against a rock jutting out from the wall. She dropped, unconscious, face first, into the water.

The tunnel was so dark that Liyah couldn't see what had happened. She had heard a thud and could tell Morningstar's body had slumped, but that was all. She called out in a panic. "Morningstar? Morningstar?"

No answer.

"Oh, Allah."

Without hesitating, Liyah crawled up over Morningstar's limp body, grabbing hold of her shoulders she pulled up, bringing Morningstar's face out of the water. She pulled her to the side, laying her chest on a rock.

It was pitch dark. Images of being trapped in her basement coursed through Liyah's brain. The lump returned to her throat, but she didn't scream—there would be no one to hear her. There was no one there to do the saving, and no one would come. *It's just me. It has to be me. Stay calm . . . breathe. 'Breathe,' Mom would say. At least this time I'm not pinned down. This time I can move.*

It seemed the fear would consume her as she moved again above Morningstar, but her mind began to focus. *How am I ever going to get her out of here?* She thought of her dad—what would he do?

"Don't look down," he would say. "It's like being up high; concentrate. Don't look down. Just keep your eyes on the prize: look ahead. Always look ahead." She missed him so. She missed her mom. Their faces appeared before her then faded away. She lifted Morningstar from under her shoulders again; the fear eased a little more. *Breathe,* she thought. *BREATHE.*

Morningstar's head hung down but clear of the water, as Liyah dragged her a few feet at a time, yanking her toward her, resting, then repeating. Hunched over, struggling and exhausted, little by little she tugged and pulled Morningstar through the tunnel. The ceiling of the tunnel began rising, *just like Morningstar said,* and she was finally able to stand; she lifted Morningstar into her arms, carrying her the rest of the way.

Placing Morningstar against the rock wall at the opening where the stream exited, she sat down cross-legged beside her, Morningstar's head resting against her shoulder. She took in a deep breath and looked out over the far hills then down at the steep slope below her, wondering how she was going to get them back to camp.

Morningstar began to gradually blink her eyes open, at the same time trying to lift her head off Liyah.

"Careful," Liyah cautioned, steadying her. "Not so fast."

"What happened?" asked Morningstar, still groggy, rubbing the spot on her head that had smashed into the wall.

"You hit your head. It was my fault."

"Your fault?"

"Yes. I was afraid and panicking. I think you tried to turn around to see what was wrong and banged your head on a rock. I'm *so* sorry."

"I remember . . . vaguely. How did we get here?"

Liyah felt exhausted, but she had never felt more whole in her life. "I dragged you . . . You're heavy, you know."

Morningstar stared at Liyah in disbelief then smiled. "I'm very proud of you . . . That's just amazing."

Liyah smiled back. "Thanks, but now we have to figure out how to get down from here."

FOURTEEN

DARKNESS HAD FULLY set in by the time Morningstar and Liyah returned to camp to find Zack pacing along the top of the wall.

"Jeez, you guys sure took your time," Zack commented, appearing a bit miffed, as the girls approached.

"You find berries?" Kai Li asked.

Morningstar and Liyah stared at each other. "Oh, Allah!" exclaimed Liyah. "We forgot the bag in all the excitement."

"You forgot the bag?" Zack responded, incredulous. "How could you forget the bag?"

"Yes," said Morningstar. "We had an accident and lost it."

"Accident?"

"Yeah," Liyah responded. "We'll have to use the food in the packs for now. We can make it up tomorrow. Sorry. We'll tell you all about it later."

Zack helped Liyah set up the tents inside the cutout stone room where he and Kai Li had piled the branches. Zack placed large rocks on the ends of the ropes to tether them, since the spikes were useless against the rocky floor. Morningstar did her magic igniting the fire, assisted by Kai Li, as Liyah retrieved some of the precious food from the packs.

As the fire got stronger and the girls' clothes began to dry, Liyah and Morningstar answered more questions from the boys about their misadventure.

"'Mazin'!" Kai Li said, in a schoolboy way. "Very l-lucky. You b-brave, Liyah."

Liyah smiled affectionately at him.

"Sorry to bring it up, but we'll have another long day tomorrow," Morningstar counseled, "so we should probably get some sleep."

Zack stood up and started walking toward his tent then stopped abruptly. "Oh," he said, fumbling with the hip pocket of his pants. "I forgot something." He handed an envelope to Morningstar. On its front was the word *Having*.

"Where'd you get this?"

"Kai Li and I were scouting the ridge and walking through these rooms. I stuck it in my pocket and forgot all about it. Kai Li mentioned that the map showed the next one was somewhere near here. I just kept my eyes open . . . It was in a wooden box on the wall, a couple of rooms over."

Morningstar handed it back up to him. "Go ahead and read it. You found it."

Unsure, Zack initially resisted then gave in and sat back down. He opened the envelope and removed the letter, tilting it slightly toward the fire to get some light then began to read.

"Having, it says."

> *You have already come a long way, my friends. If you have found this letter, then you are almost halfway.*

Zack interrupted himself. "There it is again. Addressing us as if he or she . . . or it . . . knows who we are and that we are collecting these letters. And halfway to where?"

"I think m-mean m-mission." Kai Li replied. "Then home."

"Seriously?" Zack scoffed.

Morningstar turned to him. "Okay, Zack, we know. Go ahead."

Zack continued:

The third state of being, or truth, found within the Zah-re is called Having. Most cultures of the world live with an underlying assumption that it is the right of the individual to own things. This has come to be because humans, for different reasons, do not share the same sense of duty to care for the things in their possession, and those who care more do not feel the others will share equally in that responsibility, so they prefer to own things instead of sharing everything. However, this does not mean it is the natural order of things. It does not mean that 'having' is the same thing as 'possessing.'

There is another reason why people want to possess things. It has to do again with the ego. The ego latches onto things because it does not see our spiritual nature. It thinks that by having things in our possession—and owning these things—you become more important. Since the ego is the part of us that is insecure, it is always comparing itself to others. It assumes that the more things it has, the better off it will be, the safer it will be, and the greater it will be. Our ego acts insecure like this because it has lost its connection to our true self: the self that never dies.

"I dunno," Zack complained, looking around.

"Keep going," Liyah coaxed.

Zack returned to reading:

The things the ego chases to make itself feel 'important' usually have to do with money, food, houses, land, objects, fame, and power; and the more, of course, the better. But the ego is a creation of the brain and the imagination, and no number of things you own will ever be able to satisfy it. This is why, as we gain possessions, we feel we need more: more things, more recognition, more power. It is because we see ourselves as separate from all other things that we feel this need. We seek to remove the stress—the tension produced by feeling separate—by attaching ourselves to these things. But we are really not separate—we are one with everything.

On the other hand, the true self knows that it is real—the only real part of us. It knows it is infinite and timeless. It does not need to possess things because it sees abundance all around. It is willing to share things in its possession or give them away because it seeks the joy found in the giving. It understands that you can never really possess anything anyway. Like birds that must be set free, so too it is with the material things in life; we never really have them unless we are willing to give them away.

Zack kept the paper up but surveyed the others again, stopping at Kai Li.

"F-finish, Zack," Kai Li urged.

"Okay, okay, Kai-bo," Zack replied, holding the letter up to his face as if shielding himself from Kai Li's demands.

It is in this sense that we cannot really own anything, and those things which we seek to possess actually end up possessing us—because they keep us from being our true selves. When our physical bodies depart from the world, as they will, so will all those things we have attached ourselves to—all our 'possessions.'

When all people become their true selves there will be no need to have things in the way we have come to believe. At that time, we will all be free, connected with all things, having joy, having peace, and having meaning during the living years. This is what having means. It is what the ego suspects but can never admit.

Look within yourselves and to your lives. Seek to find the truth in these words, to understand what having means to you. Imagine yourself giving away many of the things which you do not actually need to live. Can you see that? How would that make you feel? Do you understand how these things have come to possess you?

You are the beauty and the light—each of you. And together, with others, you can become brighter than the sun. You do not need to own things to shine your light; possessions are outward things; the light comes from within.

"Pretty interesting," Liyah said, as Zack slipped the letter into its envelope. "Don't you think?"

"Yeah," Kai Li responded. "Very cool. M-master teach us 'bout 'tachments to things. Okay have p-possessions . . . but not m-make you better."

"Zack?" asked Liyah.

He remained silent.

"It's okay. You don't have to talk about it if you don't want to," Liyah assured him. "It doesn't really matter. But we're the only ones here, and these letters are starting to make me see that there are basic things that we share, in our cultures and in our potential, regardless of where we came from, what we look like, or what we were taught. I think talking about them can help us understand each other better . . . to ease this journey."

"That's nice, Liyah," Zack replied, "but I'm not a big talker . . . case you hadn't noticed."

"I know," Liyah, responded. "So maybe it's time?" She chuckled lightly. "My girlfriends and I talk about lot of things . . . like clothes and school and songs and boys." She turned to Morningstar and winked. "Much about boys."

Morningstar acknowledged her with a slight grin. "I have a few friends, guys and girls at home, too, Liyah, who do talk about lots of stuff. I'm more like Zack I think, though. When I talk about things like in the letters, it would probably be with my grandfather."

"I have a hard time speaking with my parents," Liyah replied. "Maybe because we end up getting into arguments, especially if they think I'm falling too far into 'Western ways.'"

"What does that mean?" asked Morningstar.

"It's just that they still live in an older world with many rigid customs, and I think this world is changing too fast for them. My name even reminds them of this."

"Why?" Kai Li asked.

"I'm actually named after the town Beit Lahia but spelled a little differently. The town is spelled L-a-h-i-y-a but pronounced the same as my formal name which is spelled L-a-h-i-a. My little cousin had trouble saying it, so shortened the sound to Liyah . . . it stuck. My dad insists that I use the correct name, but I disagreed . . . so you see."

"You do talk a lot," Zack snickered. "How'd we get on this topic?"

Liyah seemed lost for words for a moment then recovered. "Okay, so we were talking about having stuff. I asked what you thought about the letter."

"I'd have to think about it," he replied hesitantly. "Not sure what's wrong with having *some* stuff, like money or nice clothes. Where I live, money is power, especially to the gangs, and clothes show who you are."

"But maybe that's the point," Liyah replied. "Maybe that shouldn't be the case."

"Well, most people in my neighborhood, in Detroit, have little of it—money that is. So, when you have it, it means being on top—having power. How could 'having' this be bad?"

Liyah turned back to Morningstar, who was sitting calmly, gazing into the fire. Her faced was bathed in the orange-yellow glow from its flames. Liyah was struck by it. *She looks even more stately than she did that first day walking up the white stone path*, she thought. "Is that how you look at it, too?"

"For some people," answered Morningstar.

"Is it different for you? What's it like for you, living in America?"

Morningstar kept her eyes fixed on the fire. "I'm not sure what you mean?"

"I mean I've never been there. I hear a lot, but I really don't know what to believe."

"Well," Morningstar answered, "that's a big question. I haven't lived anywhere else, so I have nothing to compare it to. Palestine is as foreign to me and most Americans, I think, as it appears America is to you. And even my Lakota roots are foreign to most Americans and others."

"You're right, sorry. I guess I hear so many different things that I'm not sure what to believe."

"Like what?"

"Like, take money for instance . . . like in the letter. Many people say Americans are rich, yet I also hear that it is dangerous to live there because of murders and other crimes. How can people have money and be so angry at the same time?"

Morningstar paused a moment. "You might be asking the wrong person. I've never been rich. I live in a trailer in the middle of nowhere." She paused again, realizing that what she said was no longer true; she really didn't have a home anymore, did she? "And my whole family never had much money. What I know about other people and places I learned from the Internet or TV or at school. What I learned about life my grandfather taught me. I do know that some people in America are rich, like you say—if we are talking about money—but there are many who are poor. That's probably true of many places you go on Earth, although I don't know for sure."

"Do the poor people hate the rich people?" Liyah questioned.

"Sometimes that's how it might appear, but I think they're just angry. I don't believe they hate anyone . . . and the rich people are angry anyway, too."

Liyah stirred the coals with a stick; a flurry of sparks sparkled up into the night air. "Why is that?"

"Because it's not really about the money. Like I said, it seems to *come* with the money. It just appears to be the natural state of money, not people; at least that's what my lala would say."

"I don't know what you mean."

Morningstar looked over at the boys, who seemed were still listening intently; she returned to Liyah. "What I guess I mean is that money is just money, but it gets translated into things. If you are a seeker of *things,* then those who have more things than you seem to be better or have power . . . the letter says . . . because that is how you are measuring what you are worth. You give your power up to the money. My grandfather often said that real power comes from joy and happiness . . . from inside. That's what I think the letter is saying. The power from inside, everyone has, and no one can steal it. My lala said that real power does not grow from having, but rather from giving."

Liyah smiled, "It seems your grandfather teaches you good lessons."

Morningstar acknowledged by nodding her head, then continued.

"Once, when I was a little girl, I stole a doll from a friend. I was going to give it back eventually, but my grandfather found it in my toy basket. He knew it wasn't mine, so he asked how I got it. I lied; I told him I borrowed it from my friend Katiah. I think he knew I had taken it, but he never said anything about that, he just asked me what I thought it meant to *have something.* I said I didn't know, because I knew he was going to tell me something anyway, something that he thought would be important to me. It's the way he was."

Liyah interrupted her. "You said was . . . your grandfather *was.* You've spoken kindly of him so many times to us, but you never used that word. I know you love him. Did something happen?"

Morningstar suddenly found it hard to swallow, and her eyes began to well up; her voice became quieter, unsteady. "Yes. He died. When the tornado hit our trailer, he was inside. He was standing over me, protecting me. When the storm passed, he was nowhere to be found. After, when I was sitting on the stoop where the trailer used to be, wishing it didn't happen, there was a flash of light . . . and then all of a sudden I was here."

"I'm so sorry. I shouldn't have asked," Liyah replied.

"It's okay. I just miss him." She turned to face the fire again. "But with the doll, my grandfather sat across from me and held my hand. He told me that it was okay to feel good about something that you have, that things take on special meanings because over time we associate certain events and emotions with them—memories. In themselves, however, these *things* mean nothing. 'Take Katiah's doll for instance,' he said. 'I bet she has grown to really like it . . . almost love it you might say, because she has taken care of her, and talked to her, and the doll provided comfort back to Katiah. It would be natural for her to feel strongly about that doll and miss her if she were to become lost, wouldn't it?' I felt pretty guilty at this point, so I swore to myself as soon as he let me go I'd return the doll to Katiah . . . but that wasn't really the point to him."

"What was the point, then?" asked Liyah.

"He told me if something is more meaningful to someone else, then it is important that they have it, even if it is something you have or want. Everything is then put to its best use . . . and everyone benefits. In this way, both having and giving mean loving. 'This is our way, Sarah,' he told me; he would say that phrase when he was finished talking so that I would know it was important."

Morningstar turned to all three of them. "Then he told me that the best thing for Katiah is the best thing for me . . . that it was about her and not about me. And that it is *always* about the *other*, 'This is where we have become lost,' he told me. He explained that angry people are just people who had forsaken some of the things the ancients had taught and were now lost, and like little children who get lost, they are afraid. 'This happens when people put their faith in things instead of the Creator of All Things . . . the Great Spirit,' he said."

Kai Li stood up and approached Morningstar. He put his hand on her shoulder. "I see why m-miss him." Then he grinned from ear to ear. "He Buddhist, too."

"Thanks, Kai Li. I think he would like that," Morningstar replied. She then faced Liyah again. "I'm not sure that helps you, though," she apologized. "I guess I got carried away. It really doesn't seem to answer your question, I mean about living in America."

"Well, I guess I wouldn't be able to tell you what it's like living in Palestine, since I have nothing to compare it to either," Liyah shrugged. "But what you say makes me think that in their hearts people are just people everywhere. If your grandfather would have been able to sit down to dinner with my father, they would have agreed on that."

"I'm sorry too, Star," Zack said, lifting his head, gazing sadly at her.

Morningstar could feel moisture collecting in her eyes again. She turned away. "Okay, time to turn in."

————

Zack lingered by the fire after the others had retired, then wandered over by the stone archway. He stepped onto the wall and took in a few deep breaths, letting them out slowly, clearing his mind as Kai Li had taught him. He took a seat, dangling his legs, banging the heels of his sneakers against the front of the wall, then began scanning the night sky. Two moons beamed down, one directly above him, another rising above the trees. He turned toward the tents behind him, then back to the sky. His jaw dropped and his eyes grew wide.

"Jesus!" he whispered to the night sky.

FIFTEEN

A T DAWN, MORNINGSTAR rallied the others, then checked the map for their next destination: Signal Station. She and Liyah, refreshed from a good night's sleep and clean and dry clothes, set out up the path ahead of the boys. Kai Li waited for Zack, who appeared to Kai Li to be dragging his feet.

"You s-slow t'day," Kai Li kidded. "Girls way 'head."

"Yeah, well I didn't get much sleep," Zack replied, yawning. "We'll catch up."

"You okay?"

"Yup. Fine. Just tired. You might say I had a bit of a nightmare last night."

"What 'bout?"

Zack hadn't had a chance yet to say something to Morningstar about the moons, although it was on his mind. He knew she would be able to handle it, but probably not Kai Li . . . and certainly not Liyah. "Oh . . . nothin'. Nothin' worth talkin' about right now."

The four followed the path past the Sinking Hills, keeping a forest—marked on the map as the Land of Qom—to their left. The trees in this forest were spread further apart and had pale gray bark that formed loose layers around their trunks. The morning passed quickly, and they were able to maintain a steady pace into the early afternoon, only stopping a handful of times for water and to refuel. At the top of the rise, a solid gray object jutted up into the sky in the near distance. Losing site of it temporarily as they made their way through a small grove of trees, they followed the path as it leveled out of the trees, finally delivering them into an open field. Just on the other side of the field was a plain wooden building; behind the building a great stone obelisk rose into the sky.

As the others waited, Zack approached the building and peered into one of the windows. Observing no one, he pushed the front door open a crack and peered in; again no one. He motioned to the others.

Joining Zack, they entered the building together and walked around.

"This s-station on map," Kai Li declared.

"Almost the same set up as the cabin, including the fireplace," Liyah noted. "Except only one bedroom."

Zack and Morningstar removed their packs; Zack placed his to the side of the sofa, then sank down into a chair, not too dissimilar to the one he had claimed for himself at the cabin. "No one here," he proclaimed, his tone sluggish and disgruntled.

"Not a good sign," agreed Morningstar.

"But th-this is!" exclaimed Kai Li, crouched behind the sofa, out of view.

"What is?" asked Liyah.

"This." Kai Li stood up holding large packet. "F-food in here," he said, a big grin on his face. "I think maybe f-find 'nother p-pack. But find this."

Liyah took the packet to the table and displayed its contents: more bars, bags of raisins and dried berries, and another packet. Opening it she held up four large sandwiches, two in each hand. "Maybe someone is watching out for us after all?"

"Well," replied Zack. "I wouldn't go that far. But we sure could use those. I've been starving for days. Those bars and berries might help out, but I'm pretty tired of them. And pretty sure if I have to eat them much longer, I'll be as thin as him." He grinned over at Kai Li.

They took seats around the table. Liyah handed out the sandwiches. Kai Li opened his and pulled apart the halves before trying it. Zack wasted no time chomping into his.

"What is it?" asked Morningstar.

"Seems like peanut butter and jelly. But not exactly. Damn delicious, though!"

Morningstar tasted hers. "Yeah, a bit more bitter. But sticks to the roof of your mouth just like peanut butter."

Liyah laughed. "My dad is able to get peanut butter sometimes. It's like a treat at home. This jelly is pretty tasty too."

In minutes they had devoured the sandwiches. Kai Li removed the map from his pocket, stared at it for a few moments, then scanned the room; getting back up, he walked over to the door.

Zack called over to him. "Where you goin'?"

Kai Li fumbled around by the entrance, then returned, handing an envelope to Liyah.

Liyah looked up in surprise. "Another letter?"

Kai Li grinned. "M-map say zr4 here . . . in station. Easy to f-figure what m-mail box for."

Kai Li took a seat across from Zack. As they finished their snacks, Liyah opened the envelope and removed the letter. "Suffering," she said, looking around at the others.

"Pretty appropriate, I'd say, wouldn't you," Zack scoffed.

"So, should we read it or wait 'til tonight?"

"No point in waiting, Liyah," Morningstar replied. "Don't think we're going any further today. We might as well rest and freshen up here, then set out again in the morning."

"Yeah," Kai Li agreed. "Read now."

"Jeez," Zack responded, plopping his heels down on top of the table, shooting a disapproving look at Kai Li. "I was just beginning to enjoy myself."

Kai Li laughed. "M-maybe you secret B-buddhist, Zack? Just hide it, huh?" He laughed again.

Liyah nestled into her seat on the sofa next to Morningstar and began reading:

Why do you suffer? Is it the pain from anger? Hatred? Or maybe loss? Are you longing to be home? Do you feel troubled by your fears? Have you lost confidence in yourself? Wish you were taller, smarter, or prettier?

Do you feel you have failed someone—maybe yourself? Do you feel unwanted? Do you feel a desperate need to be appreciated? To be loved?

You are not alone. We all suffer, in greater or lesser amounts, in our lives. And too often. Why is this so? Why is life so hard?

The truth is that we have set ourselves up to suffer because we have attached ourselves to an outcome. We either believe that the past defines us and feel pain when that changes—or we expect that things will change in the future and they don't. Outcomes never exactly meet our expectations, and because that is true, we will almost always be disappointed by our expectations. Yet we do this all the time: We expect our parents to always be there for us—but they can't. We expect that people will behave a certain way—but they don't. We expect that life will be fair—but it isn't. We expect that someone will always be there to love us—and then they leave us.

Suffering appears to be the way of the world because most people view their relationship to the world through their ego—not their true self. As you have learned, the ego is the false self, and sees itself as separate; but the true self knows you are an important part of the whole, part of all things. The true self does not fear the loss of things or have expectations for others. Your true self loves because love is the only path to joy. It does not fear loss or death, because it knows neither is real.

When these things go away or end—and in time all material things do—or when someone fails to meet our expectations—as at some point they certainly will—the ego senses loss. If the ego cannot control these things, then it feels a sense of impending doom: a vision of its own death.

This is the suffering you feel: the false fear created in your mind by your ego.

We can find true peace, love, and joy only in the present moment, when our minds are calm—not looking back, nor into the future. It's only then that we become mindful of our connection to all things, of our place in the universe. We must shut out the jabbering noise of our ego, its incessant chattering and fear-driven, untruthful assumptions.

The true self (the observer self) knows that all things happen in the present—the now. It knows that the past is just a collection of those moments and the future is simply present moments that have not yet happened.

Suffering is therefore the domain of the ego, not the true self. When you dwell in the past or have expectations of the future, you will be having a conversation with your ego, and at some point, you will feel pain and suffering. When you live in the present moment and quiet your mind, you will not feel a sense of abandonment or suffocation, nor will you feel the pain of unmet expectations—because you will have none. You will only feel the joy that comes from your connection to all things.

Liyah lifted her eyes up from the letter, noting the others were still attentive. "Just a little bit more," she said, returning her eyes to the page.

When we love someone unconditionally, without any expectation of being loved in return, as a parent loves their child, we experience the giving of real love and the realization that that is enough—love is enough; but when we give with an expectation of getting something in return, we also suffer from that expectation. You are perfect as you are; believe this. Give your gift of love. You don't need to get anything back.

Our true self knows that we lose no one where love once existed, because love never dies.

It is just an illusion to think that the physical form defines anything permanent, or that material things have any real value. All things must pass, for by their very nature they are impermanent. If we attach a value to them and measure ourselves by that value, then that part of us will, at some point, die too. We will suffer pain from that addiction, and the inevitable loss.

Look deeply into yourselves. Study your suffering. It is through your knowledge of the roots of this suffering you will observe your true self. Cast off your ego. It does you no favors. It darkens your door. Lift up your heart and know that your light shines from within. It is this light that will show you the path out of suffering—the way to the present.

Liyah folded the letter, returned it to its envelope, and placed it on the table. "Any thoughts?"

"I told of . . . of s-suffering," Kai Li offered. "By teacher. S-seek why you s-suffer, then find truth . . . like Buddha . . . f-find s-self."

"I don't know Buddha's teachings, Kai Li," Liyah replied, "but my idea of suffering is that Allah did not make this a permanent world. I think this is like the letter when it says all things will eventually pass away. We learn that we must make the most of our time during our lives, because it will determine what happens after . . . after we die." She turned to Morningstar. "What about you?"

Morningstar had been caught up in her thoughts about the death of her grandfather and why she was so sad from missing him. Her eyes met Liyah's. "My tribe and many other First Peoples believe we are one with our mother, the earth, and that all things are connected. If we hurt the earth, then we hurt ourselves . . . and everyone suffers. Little Crow, a great Sioux chief and friend of my great-great-grandfather, taught that there are no superior beings or races. He said that everything is connected and therefore sacred. He said that no one thing is superior to another . . . that everything is part of the great creation . . . the Great Mystery."

Kai Li interrupted. "S-sound like Buddha, again," he said, glancing over at Zack, then chuckling.

Morningstar continued. "He also said no religion or belief is better than any other and that no one is more spiritual, more saved, or more perfect than anyone else. No one can claim God, or buy God, or be separate from what one may call God. He believed that together with what he called 'our relations' we become one with the Great Spirit. We have a saying in Lakota to describe this, '*mitakuye oyasin.*'

"My grandfather always told me these things when he spoke of Little Crow and his beliefs. He said that separation from what one believes to be God is the world's problem today. When we think of God as separate, outside of ourselves, we remove ourselves from the source of all things, then we are left struggling and blind—suffering. This is the teaching of Little Crow, and the Lakota who came before, and has been since."

Morningstar paused, sensing a heavy stillness around her. She looked around at her friends then continued. "I guess I don't feel that separateness the letter speaks of, but it's interesting to think about suffering from the attachments we make and the expectations we have.

Like what my lala said about the doll." She leaned forward to the table, resting her chin on her arms. "I'll have to think more on that."

Zack had become more attentive as Morningstar spoke. "I'm impressed, Star." he said, catching a notable look of surprise in Liyah and Kai Li. "Well . . . I'd say, for me, I was taught that suffering has two meanings. One is that Jesus suffered for us so that we might avoid suffering after this world ends, and the other is that we suffer because we have lost sight of God . . . as you said . . . and as the letter said. So, I guess this is also about being separate . . . I mean losing our way." He looked over at Kai Li. "But I do think this thing about living in the present is harder to get my head around." He paused, then turned to Morningstar, cupping his chin in his hand. "I'll have to think more on that," he added, winking at Morningstar.

Liyah and Kai Li burst out laughing.

"Okay, okay. I get it, you guys," she said, feigning irritation, "Liyah, let's start getting the fire ready for tonight."

"Sure," Liyah agreed, stuffing the envelope into the pack with the others.

"While you guys do that," said Zack, "Kai Li and I will go check out the lake. It should be a little past here, up the path. There's still plenty of sunlight."

———

The boys followed the path to the big stone structure just past the station. "Look," Zack joked. "The station is givin' the sky the finger. Must be a hundred feet high."

"Haha," Kai Li laughed. "'Bout s-seventy f-five. Like granite."

"Okay, Einstein. I stand corrected," Zack replied, his old sarcasm creeping in a bit. "Who cares if it's granite?"

"If granite, could be m-magnetic."

"So, what? Besides, I don't think stone is magnetic."

"Can have iron in it . . . m-magn-netic."

"So, what again?"

"Call s-signal station."

"And?"

"Maybe use to send s-s-signals."

"To who?"

"Not know."

"Well, Mr. Kai . . . I think you've got too much info stuffed between your ears, anyway. So, it's good to see there's somethin' you don't know."

Back along the path they arrived at a series of interconnected pools: sunken areas of smooth rock embedded in the earth; in them clear, mineral-green water bubbled gently, steam rising up off the surface.

Kai Li bent down and put his fingers in the water to test it, following with his entire hand. "Hot s-spring. Very warm," he said, glancing up at Zack.

"Hmm," Zack responded. "Let's check out the lake, then maybe on the return we soak in it?"

A short distance later, Crystal Lake jumped out at them as they followed the path to the right around a bend: a gigantic lake whose far end was not visible in the distance. Its water was crystal blue in color and so clear they could see the bottom quite a ways out from the shore.

Zack pried off his high-tops, peeled off his socks, and stepped gingerly into the lake. The cool water sent soothing waves of relief through his feet.

"Ahhh . . . Nice," he groaned. "Hey K.L., let's take a dip . . . clean off our clothes here. The girls already had their chance."

"Yeah, great," Kai Li replied, his voice filling with excitement. He hurriedly took off his shoes and socks as Zack returned to the bank. They stripped, instantly leaving all their clothes, Kai Li's glasses, and Zack's knife behind. High-stepping it, arms flailing, their two naked bodies ran across the small pebbly shore, then splashed their way into the lake. At waist high depth they both sank down, immersing their bodies and heads.

As the coldness of the deeper water hit him, Kai Li rocketed back up. "Jeez, jeez," he shouted. "C-cold."

Zack popped up a second later. "Holy shit, man! That's cold."

Acclimated, Zack swam out a short distance, treaded water, and called out to Kai Li, pointing with his head. "Hey, bud. Let's swim out to that rock out there."

"N-no swim," he called back, sheepishly.

"Okay, man," Zack replied. "No worries," Zack swam back toward him. "Well, Mr. Kai, we should probably step things up anyway. So, let's do the wash."

They gathered up their clothes from the shore and waded a few yards into the lake, along the embankment, so they could lay their clothes on the grass after washing. As they began dunking the clothes and wringing them out, Kai Li studied the tattoo on Zack's left shoulder: a lightning bolt piercing two purple clouds that poured down black rain. He had noticed it before, the day of the fire, but was too caught up in the situation to study it at the time.

"What mean?" Kai Li asked, pointing at the tattoo.

"The lightning bolt means power. It was a symbol of a gang I started when I was a kid, more like a club; but most of my friends moved away when their dad's left to find jobs someplace else . . . so it kinda broke up on its own." He rubbed his shoulder. "The clouds and rain? I guess I was feeling sorry for myself at the time," he added, his voice subdued.

Kai Li could sense a sadness in Zack's tone. "My dad, he gone t-too," he said. "No come back. He die when I l-little boy. M-mom later tell me he 'rested . . . then k-kill by Chinese p'lice after protest."

Zack wrung out his running pants, placed them on the bank, and grabbed his denim jacket, stepping back into the waist high water. He turned to Kai Li. "I don't think mine is coming back either."

Their eyes remained locked a brief moment.

Zack turned away and began wringing out the jacket. Kai Li finished washing the rest of his clothes, moving back and forth to the shore. Zack washed his red hoodie last, then joined Kai Li on the bank. They dressed quickly into the damp clothes then began walking up the path toward the hot spring.

Stopping at the spring, Kai Li observed Zack as he stared down at the steamy water, as if he was deciding what to do. "Still want t-to? Maybe put clothes on hot r-rocks . . . dry fast."

"Yeah, that might work," Zack nodded. "Good thinking, Kai-bo."

The two stripped naked again and laid the clothes along the flat rocks. Stepping into the middle of the largest pool, Zack found a spot about four feet deep to sit in, resting his head against the smooth ledge behind him. He looked up at Kai Li.

"Wow. This feels great! Jump in."

Following Zack's lead, Kai Li stepped into the pool, sliding down the smooth ledge into the swirling hot water.

"Oooh. Yeah . . . N-nice!"

"Indeed." Zack agreed, beaming a broad smile. "Yes, indeed."

"Close eyes. We meh-di-t-tate like be-f-fore."

The two closed their eyes and began breathing slowly, deeply, in and out, melting into their surroundings.

———

"Well, what do we have here?"

Both boys' eyes shot wide open, heads up with a jolt, witnessing Morningstar and Liyah approaching the pool.

"Where?" asked Liyah, her vision temporarily blocked by the back of Morningstar's head. As she stepped to the side, she saw the boys lounging in the stone pool. Turning away quickly, she took hold of her hijab and drew it across her face, even though the bubbly, steamy water partially obscured the scene.

Morningstar frowned down at them. "Were you two thinking of coming back at some point?"

Kai Li had covered himself with his hands, not certain what they could see. "Jeez, cut us a break, Mom," Zack protested. "We must have drifted off."

"Uh . . . huh," she drawled.

Kai Li slipped down a little farther into the pool, nervously avoiding her stare. Realizing that they couldn't see clearly into the water, Liyah turned back around.

"Oh, okay, we're so sorry," Zack replied, openly faking an apology. "Guess we'd better get going right away, then." He started to raise himself up on his elbows.

"No! Zack!" Liyah cried out, as both girls spun their backs to him.

Laughing hysterically, Zack eased down off his elbows. "I'll tell ya what. You let us get up and get our clothes, and we'll go start the fire while you two enjoy this nice hot bath."

"Deal," agreed Morningstar. The girls moved a short distance away, keeping their backs turned.

Slipping out of the pool, Zack and Kai Li began putting their somewhat drier clothes on. Before they finished, Morningstar turned around, stuck her fingers in her mouth and let out a piercing wolf whistle. Kai Li, pulling up his pants, tripped and fell forward. Zack shot his head around, but Morningstar was already facing away again.

"Very funny," Zack called out, acting irritated.

"Okay, we done," Kai Li exclaimed, after a few minutes.

The girls turned around. "All right, see you at the station," Morningstar said to both of them as they moved past. A moment later, she and Liyah could clearly hear Zack intentionally speaking too loud to Kai Li. "Now, when I give the signal, let's swing up behind that bush, and we'll be able to see without them knowing."

Liyah glanced over at Morningstar. "Boys," she complained, rolling her eyes. "I think maybe they are the same all over the world."

———

Back at the station, seeing the fireplace all set up and Morningstar's homemade fire-starting kit laying on the table, Zack and Kai Li attempted to start the fire. When Morningstar and Liyah returned, they found them still trying, unsuccessfully, to get it going.

Liyah went over to the packs and retrieved some snacks. "We're getting low on food again, you know," she observed.

"So what else is new?" Zack complained, his frustration with the fire showing.

Morningstar finished her snack then lent the boys a hand. In no time, a small flame rose between the gaps in the twigs. Once the fire was strong, they sat around the table, leaning comfortably back in their seats.

Liyah spoke up, breaking an extended silence. "Doesn't look like we're going to find anyone here," she said to Morningstar.

"Looks that way," Morningstar agreed, her tone subdued.

"We s-stay here," Kai Li replied, examining the map. "Someone come."

"Well, we can give it till morning, but we can't afford to wait here after that on the limited supplies. We'll have to move on."

"How long do you think it will take us?" Liyah asked.

"You have the map, Kai Li. What do you think?" Morningstar added.

"'M-maybe three, f-four day. We 'bout halfway. D-downhill though . . . be easier."

Zack looked across at him. "Wouldn't count on that, Mr. Kai."

"W-why?"

"Don't have a good feeling 'bout this freakin' place, that's all."

Calling it a day, the girls nestled into in their beds, Liyah on the top bunk and Morningstar below her. Lying on her back, Liyah spoke to the ceiling a few feet above her head. "I was thinking more about the letter—about love . . . and suffering. I think that if love never dies, then your grandfather is not really dead."

Morningstar remained silent for a moment, wrapped tightly in her blanket, eyes closed. "I guess maybe not," she replied, her voice barely audible. "Thanks. Night, Liyah."

―――――

Zack draped his heavy hoodie over the back of one of the chairs, moving it close to the fireplace to heat it up; his other clothes had already dried. He and Kai Li sat by the fire for a while, feeling its warmth before joining Liyah and Morningstar in the bedroom.

Finally retiring, and careful not to disturb the girls, they entered the room. Kai Li scrambled carefully up to the top bed, wrapping his blanket tight. Settled in the lower bunk, Zack drew his hands behind his head and gazed out the singular bedroom window. One of the moons could be seen peeking up above the tops of the distant trees. He closed his eyes, his mind drifting. *Soon I'm going to have to say something about this.*

SIXTEEN

———————

THE FOUR ROLLED out of bed, freshened up in the bathroom sink, filled the water packs, gathered their gear, and headed out. They followed the same narrow trail that had brought Zack and Kai Li to the lake the previous day, which ran along the entire lower bank of Crystal Lake. It meandered on past the southern tip of the lake, which fed the White River some distance farther south, and ended at a place on the map marked "Water's Edge." There they picked up the white stone path again, now labeled the "Long Trail" on the map.

With the sun directly above, they arrived at the mouth of the White River; there the headwaters formed, spilling out the clear, cold water of Crystal Lake into the river. Still fairly wide at this point, the river began its descent to the valley below, its pace speeding up as its breadth narrowed, cutting a wedge through the increasingly steep terrain.

By mid-afternoon they had reached a place where the path turned inland. In doing so, it passed through the lower corner of the Yellow Wood Forest, populated by incredibly tall trees with scaly black-gray trunks, and large twisted branches sporting huge yellow leaves. The trees provided them welcomed relief from the bright sun. Reaching the southern end of the forest, a grassy area opened ahead, sloping gently toward the valley; past that the White River again came into view.

Stopping before exiting the forest, they rested, taking a seat on the trunk of a large tree that has fallen across the trail. Liyah retrieved a small amount of remaining food from the backpack, along with some water to share. Kai Li took the map out of his pocket and began studying it.

"We should be good to go," said Zack. "We just have to keep following this path back to the river, right?" He glanced over at Kai Li for confirmation.

Kai Li handed the map to him. "M-must get to W-water Edge first. 'Nother m-marker there . . . no tell how f-far to valley."

Zack looked at the map briefly and then shuttled it to Morningstar, who had her arm out. As she checked it out, her eyes caught a few words in small, blurred letters farther along the path to the valley, past the area marked "Water's Edge."

"What do you think that says?" she asked Zack. "It's a bit smudged."

Zack looked at the map again. "There's an *x* with a circle around it . . . and *w, r,* something. I can't quite make it out . . . maybe 'sans' below that."

"Sans?" Liyah wondered out loud. "What could that mean?"

"Well maybe it's Sam or sands then?" Zack replied. "Can't tell."

Kai Li had been snacking on a piece of one of the energy bars, looking out across the land to the river. Zack tapped him on his thigh with the map. "Can you read that?"

Kai Li turned to Zack, appearing like he had just woken up from a dream. "Wha'?"

"Where'd you go, man? Can you read this here?" He pointed to the place on the map.

Kai Li held the map close to his face. "Not know. Can't r-read." He folded the map up, returning it to his pocket.

"I think we'll have pretty clear traveling the rest of the day," Morningstar noted. "The weather's nice, and we should be able to make good time along the path. The river is probably about several hours away. Maybe there'll be an area there where we make camp. We need to spend some time to find more food."

"I prefer to keep moving," Liyah responded. "I just want to get home. The sooner the better."

"We won't go too far without enough food," Morningstar replied. "And if we find enough, it might last us the rest of the way."

The four rested briefly before starting off again. It was Liyah's and Kai Li's turn to carry the packs, so they helped each other hoist them on their backs then set out after Morningstar and Zack, the four making their way down the last part of the inland trail . . . to Water's Edge. After a few hours, the path joined the banks of the river.

"Up ahead," Zack called back to the others. "Looks like a cleared flat area along the bank. Maybe that's what the map means by Water's Edge. We can fill the water pouches there."

The cleared area ended at a beach along the river, just off the path, the beach consisting of grainy sand and rocks; they made their way across the beach toward the water. Morningstar walked over in the direction of some larger rocks, seeking a place to set their gear. Nearing the rocks, she saw a wooden object sticking out from behind, right at the edge of the river.

Moving behind the rocks, a large wooden raft came into view, resting up against one of the rocks, half in the river.

Liyah had been watching her. "Find something?" she called out to Morningstar.

"Yes. A raft!" she yelled back.

"Raft?" repeated Zack.

The others met her by the rocks and checked it out; it was large, big enough for a number of people to sit on, and made up of sections of hand-hewn logs. They were fitted together with a kind of crude tongue and groove arrangement, bound tightly by strong fiber cords.

"How did that get here, do you think?" Liyah asked.

"I don't know," said Morningstar. "It *is* rather odd, isn't it?"

"No odder than anything else around here, girl," quipped Zack.

"What you m-mean?" asked Kai Li.

"I mean like this entire situation."

"Someone must have landed it here intentionally, since it doesn't appear there are many beach-like areas along this river," said Morningstar.

"*What* someone?" Zack questioned. "There's no life here, or anywhere for that matter. Haven't you noticed? Weird, man, no life at all . . . 'cept plants . . . .. and birds.

"S-someone live here . . . in cabin," offered Kai Li.

Zack looked over at him. "Did you actually *see* someone? Did you? No . . . well, there you have it."

"Okay, Zack," said Liyah. "Looks like everyone is tired and probably hungry. Let's get something from the packs and sit over there by the bank." She pointed to a small grassy area just past the rocks.

Once settled, Kai Li dragged out the map again. "I s-see wha' you mean."

"About what? "Liyah asked.

"'Bout letters. Look like *s* or *t* . . . or maybe *f*s . . . hard s-say. But if Water Edge, 'nother m-marker here."

"Where?" Zack questioned him.

"Here . . . Somewhere."

Morningstar surveyed the horizon. "The sun is getting low," she observed. "We should look for food and camp near here. If we keep our energy up, maybe we can make it back to the cabin in a few days."

After collecting their things, Morningstar and Liyah began looking for signs of berries and plants along the inland side of the path to add to the stash from the station. Zack walked a little farther down the path, finally returning with something in his hand.

"What got?" Kai Li asked, excited. "L-letter?"

"Yup," Zack replied, handing it to Morningstar.

"Where'd you find this?"

"You won't believe it. Just ahead, right off the side of the path there's a post with one of those wood boxes mounted on it . . . as if someone is expecting the mailman to come through here."

"No 'xpect mail-m-man. 'Xpect us," Kai Li replied.

Zack stared uncomfortably at him.

Morningstar turned the envelope over in her hands; it was made of the same strange fiber material as the others and blue in color. On the front of the envelope, in bold blue script, was the word *Forgiving*.

She opened it and took out the folded letter; its pages were also made of the same pressed fibers as the other envelopes and letters. She unfolded it, scanned it briefly, then refolded it and put it back in the envelope. She and Liyah then made their way over to a boggy area off the path, carrying one of the backpacks, and keeping the river in view behind them. There they found several varieties of berries growing along its edge, root vegetables as well. They gathered as much as they could stuff in the pack and hold in their hands, then returned to the boys, who were waiting by the beach.

The girls led them back to a clearing they had come upon while looking for food; they made camp there. The sun was setting, and there was a chill in the air. This time Morningstar and Zack scavenged for wood as Liyah and Kai Li set up the camp.

Later, sitting cross-legged by the warm glow of the fire, Liyah handed the envelope to Kai Li. "Why don't you read this one?"

"M-me?"

"Why not?"

"I t-too n-nervous."

"No reason to be," assured Liyah.

"I s-s-stutter m-more."

Liyah saw the terror in Kai Li's eyes; she gently took the letter from his hands. "Okay, another time."

"Morningstar?"

"No, go ahead, Liyah. You have a nice voice."

Liyah looked down at the envelope, removed the letter, unfolded it, then looked back up at everyone. "Forgiving," she said.

Tilting the letter toward the light, she began:

> During our lives we get injured and injure others—no one escapes. Mostly this happens unintentionally, but sometimes it is done out of spite or anger. It happens through both words and actions.
>
> Harsh words spoken in haste or anger can be as harmful as any action—words can cut like the blade of a knife, leaving scars—sometimes deep ones. Once said, the words cannot be taken back. Words and actions, both good and bad, echo for eternity throughout the universe. All that one can do is remove the sting from the wounds.
>
> Every action has an equal and opposite reaction in the science of physics, as you know, and so it is with hurt. Hurt leaves two scars: the first on the body or

in the mind of the receiver, the second, less obvious, on the side of the giver.

Insults, meanness, and even the absence of things like love or caring, are processed by our mind and ego and are often very damaging. We can find ourselves believing the messages that reside in the pain, over time incorporating these into our false image of who we are. And the giver of the blows does not escape either—an equal negative force imbeds itself into the mind and spirit of the person who has caused the harm, even into the very cells of their body. This wound is a form of guilt, whether recognized by the conscious mind or not, and it continues to harm the giver until it is released.

The ego feels guilt as a kind of death blow and does everything it can to rid itself of the pain; it tries to cover up our bad feelings about ourselves, this guilt, by blaming, and still hurting, the very people we have injured.

No one is perfect, not one of us. Not any of you—not your friends, your parents, or even your heroes. Not the members of any of your groups, your tribes—nor mine. We can only strive in that direction. Each time we hurt someone, we gain a scar ourselves. And we bring this forward in our lives, and to others.

If you close your eyes for a moment and think back in time, you will not have to go very far to remember an instance when you were less than loving to someone, perhaps even mean, or at least mean-spirited. Close your eyes and think of a time like that.

Liyah paused, Zack watched her as she set the letter in her lap. Then his gaze drifted over to Morningstar and Kai Li, their eyelids shut tight. Liyah took a deep breath and watched the flames as they danced along branches, then picked up the letter and continued reading. Zack closed his eyes.

> *Perhaps it was a time when you were little and disrespected your mother, or perhaps it was a time when you joined in with others in making fun of someone else, even though it was clear that they were feeling hurt. Although you didn't realize it, the energy released from that harm was reflected back to you, imbedding itself in your mind and the cells of your body, and in your spirit—planting the seeds of your own sorrow.*
>
> *Maybe it was the time you lied about something you did. Or a time when you felt injured by someone else and struck out in retaliation through your words or actions.*
>
> *Maybe you just felt betrayed by a loved one—perhaps your father—and you were angry and struck back. Now both of you are in pain.*

Zack thought back to when his dad had taken the job in Boston and returned home for the first time after months of being away, only to spend a few days, then leaving him and going back to Boston, for even longer . . . then not returning at all. It had been almost a year now. He remembered the last time, the fight they had—how he became so angry with his dad and he swore at him, told him never to come back. How could this anger he felt be his own fault? How could it harm him? Was this the pain he was feeling? *Is he in pain, too?* He was confused. A deep sadness fell in on him.

Liyah paused again; Zack opened his eyes and looked over at her. She turned, their eyes briefly locking. He sensed a strange connection with her. *She's so gentle,* he thought, *so caring. Could she have ever done anything mean to anyone? But maybe I've been a bit mean to her? And Kai Li? Maybe even to Morningstar?*

Liyah broke away, dropping her eyes back to the pages in her hand. She read on:

> Don't underestimate the pain that the other person may be in—from both the harm they may have caused you and the harm you may have caused them in your haste to get even.
>
> These pains create scars, scars which can only be released through the act of forgiving.
>
> You must forgive the one who hurt you, for this act of forgiveness is really for you, not them—it is to free you from the chains you create by carrying the burden of anger and guilt. By forgiving the other person, you give yourself permission to become whole again—to free your true self—to renew your spirit—to recover joy.
>
> Both forgiving the other and forgiving yourself are born of love. There is no other path out of pain. By releasing the other, we release ourselves. We let go of the need to be right. We let go of the anger and self-righteousness that reside in our ego—that weighs us down and robs us of the joy we were meant to have.
>
> Forgiveness is not about forgetting. It is about making yourself whole again. No one else can ever do this for us, and we can never do it for them. It is something we can only do for ourselves.

Liyah placed the letter back in the envelope and set it down beside her. She turned to Kai Li. "What did you think of that?"

"I like. Not 'zactly same as I t-taught."

"How do you mean?" Morningstar asked.

"F-forgiving like letter s-say, but compassion help forgive. If keep in heart . . . th-then forgive easy. I think it also 'bout s-suffering . . . like in other letter."

"Maybe compassion and love are really the same thing, Kai Li?" Morningstar suggested. "Or compassion requires love. What about you, Liyah? Is that what you're taught?"

"In Islam, forgiving is important too. It doesn't depend on getting an apology from the one who hurt you. You can forgive them without that. I never thought of it, but I guess this is a way of freeing yourself from being attached to the harm and not really to release the other person. So, in that way it seems much like the imam of my mosque teaches."

"Islam also s-say can't *get even.* P-people jus' get m-madder. Nothin can be even . . . is not p-possible . . . best forgive, else you offend Allah," Kai Li added.

Zack had been half listening, his thoughts still pulling toward his dad. Was his reaction to his dad fair? Was it equal to the hurt he had received? *How could anyone know this?* He turned to listen more to Kai Li and Liyah. *Maybe they're right,* he thought. *Maybe there's no point in trying to even the score. No such thing.*

"Yes, that's right," Liyah replied. "How do you know this, Kai Li?"

"I read lot. Remember it." His eyes met Zack's. "Forgiving 'portant for Jesus t-too. No, Zack?"

"Yeah," Zack replied, his voice soft, muted. "Yeah, very important," he added, more deliberately. "To forgive is to be like *him.*" His eyes met with Liyah's again. She nodded, smiling.

"And you, Morningstar?" Liyah said, turning to her. "You can't get away free here. What about you? Is there a thing about forgiving in your culture?"

Morningstar sat silently for a moment then began to speak in her quiet way. "My grandfather taught me that forgiving is important even to your body. He believed that sickness arises from not forgiving. He believed that all healing couldn't begin without it." She paused a moment, as if in deep thought, then looked around at the others.

"I think this could also be the message of the letter. That the 'pain' it mentions is *all pain* . . . that maybe the only way to get whole again is through forgiveness. Like my grandfather said, and Kai Li also mentioned before . . . we are all connected to each other . . . and to all things. I guess that means by injuring any of our *relations* we are just hurting ourselves."

"Much is s-same for Lakota and Buddhist, no?" Kai Li replied.

"Yes," said Morningstar. "It seems so, doesn't it?"

Zack studied Morningstar's calm, serious countenance. He was astounded by the wisdom of this young girl. He thought about his disregard for her when they first met, his competitiveness for her not to be the leader. His heart seemed to ache. He turned to face the fire; he had not felt this way in a long time, longer than he could remember.

SEVENTEEN

———

MORNINGSTAR AND KAI Li brought the backpacks to the lake, refilled the water pouches, then returned to camp. After breaking down the camp, before heading out, Kai Li studied the map, Liyah peering over his shoulder.

"A long walk today, but we can probably make it to the place where the sixth letter is . . . near Hooksett Bridge," Morningstar commented, picking up one of the packs. "Then we'd be back to the cabin the next day."

"Think so, t-too," agreed Kai Li.

"I've been thinking," said Liyah. "Why don't we save some time and use the raft? It would be a lot easier than walking. Hiking in these sandals is still hard on my feet, even though calluses are beginning to develop."

"We don't know the river," replied Morningstar.

It was already warming up quickly, and Liyah was not looking forward to another long day in the sun. She directed her attention to Zack and Kai Li. "What do you guys think?"

"Be fun," said Kai Li.

"Haha. A little adventurous for you, isn't it, Liyah?" Zack joked.

She smiled. "Maybe. Maybe not. *Perhaps* we could even make it all the way to the valley before nightfall."

"I don't know," insisted Morningstar. "It's pretty risky. We'd have to stop near the bridge anyway for the next letter . . . and we're supposed to stay on the path. Remember?"

"The river looks gentle here, Morningstar, even at its slow pace, wouldn't we make much better time than walking?" Liyah countered.

Kai Li took the map over to Morningstar. "Sh-show here path f-follow river close. Can go ashore any t-time."

"That's good enough for me," affirmed Zack.

"Zack an' me be like T-tom and Hu-kleby."

"Huckleberry," teased Zack.

"Who? Who is that?" Liyah asked.

"Two guys who went on an adventure together on a raft on the Mississippi," Zack replied.

Liyah shifted her eyes back and forth between them. Were they putting her on? "What is a Mississippi?" she asked.

"River . . . in 'Merica," Kai Li replied.

"And how would you know this, Kai Li?" Liyah asked. "It doesn't sound like a Chinese story to me."

"Cuz he's read every book ever printed," Zack replied, elbowing Kai Li "Haven't you noticed?"

Liyah looked at Kai Li as his face erupted in a big grin; she smiled too. *Things must be getting better between these two,* she thought. She turned to face Morningstar. "Do you have any idea what they're talking about?"

"I didn't read the book, but lots of people have."

"We on adventure!" Kai Li exclaimed.

"Not sure this is one I want to be on," replied Morningstar. Liyah noted the slight sarcasm in her voice.

"I'll find some branches we can use to steer, to stay close to the shore," offered Zack.

Liyah watched Morningstar's face tighten, her tone becoming more serious as she spoke. "There's no guarantee we'll find more beaches like this one to land the raft. And besides, there must be a reason why someone abandoned that raft here."

"M-maybe break loose. S-same logs as cabin," Kai Li said, defending their position.

Liyah had noticed that too. She wondered if the same person who left the backpacks and directions might have abandoned the raft. She knew they were all tired, too, even Morningstar, and maybe that was why they were able to wear her down until she eventually caved in. "I guess I'm overruled," Morningstar said finally, begrudging them a victory.

Zack and Kai Li retreated into the a nearby grove of trees. On returning, they placed the handmade poles on the beach. Zack removed his sneakers and waded into the water, making his way to the far side of the raft; lifting the underside of the submerged end, he rocked it until the other end, the one wedged against the rock, slipped down onto the sand. He then pulled hard on the front, as the others lifted and pushed the back. Struggling, they inched it from its sandy mooring and into the shallow water at the river's edge.

Kai Li, Liyah, and Morningstar placed all the shoes, including Zack's huge red sneakers, on top of the raft, then climbed aboard, hauling the packs up with them. Zack handed Kai Li the two poles. Taking hold of the rope that was attached to the front of the raft, he began wading into deeper water, towing the raft from the shallows.

Hauling himself on board with the others, Zack rolled up the bottoms of his wet, sagging jeans so he wouldn't trip. Kai Li followed suit, bringing his black pants up to his knees. They both then stood, unsteady, on opposite sides of the raft. Pushing their poles against the riverbed, they nudged the raft slowly forward, finally catching the easy drift of the river.

Liyah could feel the sun's warmth as it rose up through the powder-blue morning sky. Sitting next to Morningstar, both with legs straight out and heads supported by the backpacks, she loosened her hijab and let the rays strike her face as they cruised along, keeping a short distance from the shore; the light breeze over the cool water fluttered the edge of the hijab, refreshing her. She looked over at Kai Li and Zack, their eyes glued on the river, concentrating, lifting the poles at an easy pace, then pushing them down against the river's floor. She tapped Morningstar's leg. "We've come quite a way, haven't we? Hopefully we can make great time today without wearing ourselves out like before."

"I know," agreed Morningstar. "It is kind of nice here, though, floating along. I guess maybe I was wrong. It's good to not have to be hiking every minute of every day."

Liyah studied her. *Always looks so magnificent*, she thought. Yet hidden deep in Morningstar, she believed there were troubled waters. *She must be so lonely, losing her parents . . . and now her grandfather. I'm not sure I could have survived that. And here we all are, lost in nowhere?*

"You seem so serious most of the time. And sometimes even sad," Liyah said to her, mustering up some courage. "I can't tell whether you really have no fears or you're sad inside and don't care. Is there anything you are afraid of?"

Morningstar took in a breath and pushed it out with a sigh. "Well, I was really afraid during the fire. Seems like I've always been afraid of them. And afraid of the tornado too. I had a bad dream the other night, that it still sits there, waiting for me to return. Everyone has fears, Liyah. I think the letters are reminding me of things my grandfather used to say, helping me face those fears. But they also remind me of what I lost."

The raft brought them along at the same steady pace until early afternoon, covering a good distance. The sky above them remained clear; a distance ahead, a hazy fog hung over the water, and toward the horizon, on the left side of the river, a series of rounded hills glimmered in the sunlight.

"What do you think could be making those hills so shiny?" Zack called out.

"No idea," replied Morningstar.

Liyah retrieved the map from her pack, where Kai Li had stuffed it to protect it from the water. "The hills are here on the map, Zack," she said, then laughed. "They're called the 'Shining Hills,' of course. The only other markings on the map anywhere near where we seem to be are the smudged words." She handed the map to Morningstar.

"Bring here," Kai Li called to Morningstar.

In the two steps she had to take to reach him, Morningstar staggered like a drunken sailor, negotiating the gentle rocking of the raft as it carried them along with the flow of the river "Here," she said to him, "let me take over for you."

Kai Li exchanged the pole for the map. Morningstar began thrusting the pole against the riverbed; although not tall, she was strong. Zack noticed the difference and adjusted his strokes, maintaining a constant heading.

Kai Li studied the map for a minute. "*W . . . r . . .* mean s-something . . . not people's name."

"Well, what's that other word?" Zack questioned.

Kai Li took off his glasses and held them so that one of the lenses was at an angle to the page, focused on the smudge; he was used to doing this when reading small print books or mathematical symbols in some of his science texts. "Not say 'Sams,'" he said. "First letter fancy *f* . . . last letter is *s*."

"What is the *n* or *m* then?" asked Liyah.

"It more like *n* but fancy too, like *f*." Then he noticed that the color of the top of the *n* was a little different than the rest of the ink in the letters. He licked the end of his index finger and placed it on the smudge, rubbing gently; he looked again through the lens. The top of the *n* had been a residue of some kind and was removed with his rubbing. The letter was now clear; but it was actually *two* letters, not one . . . two *l*'s. Kai Li studied it for a moment, then looked up, his face going pale.

Zack looked over at him "Well, Kai-bo? Figure it out? Looks like you saw a ghost."

"'W. R.' mean White R-river, an' 'n' not *n* but two *l*'s." He paused. "So mean 'W-White River F-Falls,'" he said flatly.

Morningstar stopped poling and pointed downriver. "Zack. You see up there between the points where the two sides of the river jut inward?"

"Yup. See something?"

"There's like a line there. And the water beyond that line is a different color than the water just before it."

"So?"

Morningstar paused briefly then cried out, "C'mon, Zack! That could be a waterfall up ahead—what Kai Li is talking about."

"Jeez! And we're drifting toward the center," Zack replied. He started poling ferociously, slowly shifting the direction of the raft. Kai Li and Liyah glanced at each other, eyes wide, then watched Zack and Morningstar as they battled the current.

At first, they made some progress moving closer toward the bank, but the current was picking up speed as the falls neared—they were now being sucked back into the main flow of the river. As the raft eased into the deeper middle, Morningstar and Zack couldn't push against the riverbed with strong enough force to move the raft the other way, even though the river was only about five feet deep at that point. They began to float freely with the current, quietly but now swiftly, carried towards the falls . . . like a leaf in a brook.

The speed of water over the rocks below caused the water to rise and fall in a rolling motion, the waves rocking the raft up and down; Morningstar and Zack were forced to sit down with Kai Li and Liyah.

"Allah!" exclaimed Liyah. "What are we going to do?"

"Nothin'!" Zack uttered. "Absolutely nothin' . . . Nothin' we *can* do."

"But we'll go over the falls!" Liyah shouted. "Morningstar, can't we do *something?*"

Morningstar didn't answer. The falls were closing in, the current getting stronger by the second. She rose up on her knees, searching the river ahead. They couldn't be more than a few hundred yards away, and there was no telling how far down the falls fell before meeting the water below.

"We'll have to jump free of the raft when we go over," she said. "Otherwise, the raft may fall on top of us."

Kai Li's stomach rose to his throat. "I no s-s-swim," he said, his stuttering matching his anxiety.

"I don't either!" Liyah cried out, the pitch of her voice rising.

Zack joined Morningstar on all fours, gazing out over the river, searching for something—anything. As they raced ever closer to the edge of the falls, Morningstar noticed that the land and rocks to their left formed a sort of jetty, jutting out farther into the river than the land on the right. *The falls must begin there at the end of the jetty,* she thought. Following the line of the falls, a short distance toward the opposite bank from the jetty, were what appeared to be a handful of larger stones sticking up just above the surface, like a small island, their rounded tops peeking out above the water through patches of mist and fog.

"Zack!" shouted Morningstar. "Quick. Get the poles."

Zack picked up the poles, rocking with the sway of the raft and looking around. "What, what?"

"See those rocks up ahead just to the left? If we both push on the right side, we might be able to move the raft enough to the left to hang it up on those rocks. It's our only chance."

Zack handed a pole to Morningstar. "That's a real long shot," he said, as they both positioned themselves, drilling the poles into the river bottom, which was steadily rising as it neared the rim of the falls. They began pushing for all they were worth; the raft responded by moving slowly to the left. They poled with all their might, harder, faster. The raft began lining up more with the rocky island, but time was running out.

As Zack looked toward the falls, he suddenly realized that even if they were to make it to the rocks . . . and supposing the rocks kept them from going over the falls . . . they'd be stuck there. He knew there would be no way for them to make it from the rocks to the jetty—the force of the current would send them over the falls. One thing now seemed certain to him: *They had to get to the jetty.*

Zack stared ahead, trying to gauge the distance. He pressed Morningstar. "How far do you think it is from the rocks to the jetty?"

"Not sure. Maybe a hundred feet."

"Less," Kai Li said. "M-more like s-seventy."

Morningstar was great on expeditions, but when it came to estimating things like this, Zack figured Kai Li was probably better. He looked over at the rope lying on top of the raft, attached to the front. *If I could just get the rope to the jetty. But how? And how would I anchor it? . . . And it was too short, anyway.*

"Kai!" he shouted. "How long do you think that rope is?"

Kai Li spread it out a bit and sized it up. "'bout eight m-meters."

"Jesus! What the hell is that? . . . Feet! Feet!"

"Twenty f-f-five."

"What about those two hiking cords with the clamps in the backpacks?"

"N-nylon I th-think."

"Huh? . . . Wha? No, I mean how long? Christ, Kai Li!!"

"Each b-bout th-thirty."

Awfully close, he thought. "Get them! Now! And Liyah, untie the rope from the raft."

Kai Li removed the cords from the pockets in the side of the packs and handed them up to Zack while Liyah undid the knot in the rope, freeing it.

"Hook 'em together!" he said, looking down at Kai Li. Kai Li complied.

Handing his pole to Kai Li, he barked out an order. "Take over here for me and keep poling like crazy!" He grabbed the rope by the knotted end which Liyah had left tied and forced the hook on one end of the cords through the middle of the knot, clamping it on its own cord and thereby securing it to the rope. He then bent down to the metal ring where the rope had been attached; taking the clamped end of the first cord, he threaded it through the ring, clipping it back on the cable. He stood up, retrieving the pole from Kai Li.

Zack was working the pole again for all he was worth, with Morningstar doing the same. The riverbed kept rising as it approached the falls. He guessed the depth of the water to be less than four feet where they now were. *Wouldn't be much traction if I try to walk the rope across to the jetty*, he thought. *Maybe if I swim directly toward shore, perpendicular to the current? Could I make it to the jetty with the rope before the river swept me over the falls?*

He was running out of time. The raft was on a course for the rocks. Would it stop there and not go over? He set his pole on the raft, removed his sweatshirt to free his arms, stuffed it in one of the packs, then called to Morningstar. "Get it to the rocks, Star!"

Bare-chested, he then grabbed the rope end of the string of cables and shouted another order to Kai Li and Liyah. "You two. Put everything back in the packs and strap them on!" Stepping to the side of the raft, he tied the rope around his waist. Without missing a beat, he dove into the water.

"Zack!" Liyah screamed, too late. She watched in horror as he fought the chilly current, racing for his life, the river racing too, carrying him ever closer to the falls. She and Kai Li supported themselves on their knees while they helped each other with the packs, then sat back down, watching both Morningstar and Zack fight the river.

Zack was making gains toward the shore, but both he and the raft were nearing the falls. Thirty more yards until they would learn their fate. Zack picked his head up out of the water; the jetty was close. The riverbed had risen enough so that there was now only two or three feet of water below him. He let his legs sink until he felt one hit the rocks below; slipping and sliding along the riverbed, he half walked and half swam. *Any second now, almost there.* But every second was also bringing him dangerously closer to the falls.

Morningstar kept poling, steering, trying to hit the stones with the center of the raft. She looked at the rocks, then the falls; her heart sank. *We aren't going to make it,* she thought. *We're going to be a few feet off. We'll hit with the side of the raft, then slide over the falls.*

Overwhelmed, she looked over at Kai Li and Liyah. She could see the terror in their eyes. With only five yards to go she brought up the pole. *It was hopeless.* As she moved toward Kai Li and Liyah, the raft suddenly jerked, sending her to her knees. Looking up, toward the jetty she saw Zack; he was pulling on the rope, causing the raft to lurch toward the shore.

Zack was standing at the base of the jetty, yanking on the rope; walking backwards among the slippery rocks, he continued to tug with every fiber in his body. The front of the raft, where the cables were attached to the ring, began turning more toward him with each step. Morningstar got up and gave one last push with the pole as Zack fell backwards onto the rocks.

The raft crashed onto the small island of rocks jutting up above the water's surface; the force of the raft's momentum against rocks caused the entire front to rise up at a slight angle, almost spilling the passengers into the river. They began sliding down the raft toward the water. Kai Li quickly grabbed Liyah by her free hand to hold her steady. Slowly they moved up to the higher end, where Morningstar was catching her breath. The raft, balancing precariously, held their weight. The falls roared down over the edge of the river, crashing against the rocks below. A huge mist spewed back up, engulfing them. Holding on tight to each other, they turned their eyes to Zack, barely visible through the mist and fog.

The crash of the raft caused the cable line to go slack, freeing Zack to regain his footing. He moved a few steps toward them along the jetty. Finding a place where he could lean back against a rock while pressing his feet against two large stones in front of him, he once again tightened the rope by winding it several times around his waist. He leaned back; the rope snapped up, taut, about three feet above the water line.

The raft remained perched above the falls in the swirling mist, inches from an eternal drop.

EIGHTEEN

THE LIGHT FOG hanging over the cool water combined with the clouds of mist blowing up from the bottom of the falls to complicate things—they could barely see Zack. Morningstar signaled him. Zack saw her but didn't signal back for fear of losing his grip on the rope. He yelled to her, his voice barely audible over the roar of the falls. "Send Kai Li and Liyah over!"

Morningstar faced them. "We have to move out along the cable one by one over to the jetty. He's holding the line for us."

Liyah felt she was on the verge of losing control. Heights were one thing, the long distance to the bottom of the watery cliff from the precipice where they stood, but it was more the water. She imagined being sucked under by a whirlpool at the base of the falls, unable to swim. It wasn't the fall that captured her thoughts—it was the drowning. She grabbed onto Morningstar's forearm. "I don't know, Star."

"It's not a choice. We'll die if we stay *here*."

Liyah could sense her blood pounding in her ears and that same lump trying to rise in her throat. But it was different this time. This time she was able to relax her muscles, take more control of her thoughts.

"You come with m-me, Liyah," Kai Li said. "You be s-safe."

"I don't think that's a good idea," cautioned Morningstar, trying to outtalk the loudness of the falls. "If there's too much weight, we could pull the raft off the rocks."

"I'm okay, but I still don't think I'll make it alone."

"It's not that far," Morningstar assured her. "You'll be there in no time."

"Be fine. Water buoyant, w-weight be okay with cables," Kai Li said, his stutter fading as he focused his attention on their situation, and on Liyah. "I take her."

Morningstar's eyes bounced from one to the other. "Okay then . . . Liyah, hand me a backpack. Kai, you put on the other one."

Kai Li sat at the edge of the raft, holding onto the cable. His feet dangled into the water on the left side of their rocky island, facing Zack. "I hold cable with b-both hands. You climb on back . . . hold onto shoulders."

Liyah complied, easing herself onto Kai Li as he lowered himself into the water, snatching the cord with both hands, spreading his hands shoulder width apart, now facing downriver just feet from the rocky rim of the falls.

"Put your left hand on the rope between his hands," said Morningstar, "then place your right hand on the other side of his right hand." Liyah did as instructed. "Now rest your waist against his pack. This way you will have more weight on Kai Li most of the time. Are you okay with that, Kai Li? "

"I be okay."

Liyah let herself off the raft, clinging with all her might to the cord, resting herself against the pack on Kai Li's back.

Morningstar yelled, making sure they heard her above the roar of the falls. "Okay, now each of you has to move one hand at a time. Liyah, you have to pull down on the cable with both hands as Kai Li moves his hands, so that some of your weight is off of him temporarily. Kai Li will then start by moving his left hand froward along the cable toward Zack. Liyah, you then press your body against his again and slide your left toward his . . . then both do the same with your right hand . . . Got it?"

"Okay," Liyah said, her voice unsteady.

"'Kay," Kai Li yelled, his back to Morningstar.

"All right then. Start when you're ready."

Kai Li paused a moment then began pulling his body up using both hands. Liyah responded by pulling herself up with her hands as well. Kai Li then let his left hand go free and slid it about a foot to the left, grabbing back onto the cable. Liyah then pressed her legs against him on either side, lifting her chest a little, sliding her left hand the same distance close to his. Suspended by the cable and moving away from the tiny rocky island, the force of the current pushed the lower part of their bodies forward, placing additional strain on Kai Li. Morningstar noticed he was struggling. She called out to him. "You gonna be okay, Kai Li?"

"No easy . . . I hold on!"

The two began shimmying sideways along the rope, their legs and feet constantly being pushed out in front of them by the onrushing water; with their hands alternately sliding and grasping, they were paired now in what appeared like a high wire circus act.

Zack shouted encouragement from the jetty, stifled by the clamor of water smashing against the rocks below. Morningstar strapped the remaining backpack on and checked the stability of the raft. By moving carefully over the deck, she observed it would rock in different directions depending on where she stood. As the turbulent water rushed underneath, the raft rocked slightly, in fits and starts, atop the rocks.

She positioned herself on the right side of the raft so that her weight acted as a counterbalance to Zack's force on the rope. She sat there, watching Kai Li and Liyah sway along the cable, their lives dependent on the strength of Zack and their own will. At times like this, when she witnessed firsthand the power of nature's fury, her mind would get overwhelmed by tragic memories, and her own helplessness. She had to shut down her emotions—forget fear, forget pain, but in this moment she couldn't block out one notion that circled in her mind: *Will I lose these two as well?*

———

They were nearly halfway there, a little past the point where the two cables were joined together by their clamps. Kai Li's feet found a series of rocks along the bottom of the river, and he was able to use them to move a few steps along, resting his arms and shoulders briefly. They moved on.

Liyah squeezed her knees tighter against Kai Li. Even with the buoyancy of the water, Kai Li could feel the added weight pulling hard on his arms, and his stomach muscles ached from fighting the pull of the river. His left hand suddenly brushed against the knot where the rope from the raft joined the last section of the hiking cord. He knew he must be nearing the jetty. They could now hear Zack better, yelling as loud as he could, "Almost here . . . Just a little more . . . You got it, Mr. Kai! You got it, Liyah!"

But Kai Li's strength was fading. After cutting the remaining distance in half, he'd become so tired he was now only able to slide about six inches at a time. *I'm not going to make it, am I?* He took in a deep breath and pushed the thought out of his mind. His left foot then bumped into a large rock less than two feet under the surface; pressing hard against it with both feet, he was able to reduce the weight of the load. He paused, trying to regain his will to carry on, but felt himself frozen in place. He turned his head to the left and saw Zack, straining against the rocks.

Zack's shouts could be heard clearly now over the roar of the falls. "Hold on, Kai! Just a little more! HOLD ON!"

Unsure of the reason for the delay, Liyah squeezed harder against Kai Li's sides. "You okay?" she yelled.

Kai Li focused all his attention on Zack. He felt his spirit lift. "Okay. We go now, Liyah." He moved his left hand another six inches more toward Zack, toward safety; Liyah followed. They continued their dance, leaving the safety of the rock, slowly inching their way again along the rope.

A few agonizing minutes later, they were within reach of land. Kai Li's foot found the first big rock along the jetty. They moved closer.

Zack slowly brought his back and shoulders up, sliding the rope forward and easing Kai Li and Liyah down among the rocks. As Kai Li propped himself against a boulder, Liyah swung off his back, hugging him tightly, tears starting to fall. "That was amazing, Kai Li. You were great!" She then scrambled toward Zack, slipping and tripping over the rocks, her arms flailing. She wrapped her arms around him like a vice, tears now streaming down her face. "Oh, Zack! Thank you!"

Exhausted, Zack hugged her back, his own eyes beginning to well up. "We've got more work to do. Morningstar is still on the raft." He looked over at Kai Li. "Let's get him to a safer place, Liyah."

Zack jammed the limp rope under a huge rock, then he and Liyah helped Kai Li move a short distance up the jetty. "You two will be safe here. You can rest." He turned to face Kai Li directly. "Great job, man." he added. "Freakin' awesome!"

Zack crawled over the rocks back to his spot, then freed the rope. Still standing, he signaled to Morningstar through the mist, waving his hands wildly. Anchoring himself between the rocks, he wrapped the rope around a few turns, then leaned back. The rope pulled against the raft, snapping up above the waterline.

Kai Li and Liyah sent small rocks sliding down behind Zack as they caught back up to him. He turned to look. They were standing over him. "No time to r-rest," Kai Li asserted. "We help you."

Zack didn't argue.

———

Morningstar peered nervously down over the front of the raft to the rocks at the bottom of the falls. The view was surreal, she thought— even mystical; billows of mist parted the fog, and patchy rays of sunlight filtered through, enabling her to catch glimpses of the falls violently smashing against the giant boulders below. The sound of the relentless pounding of water against stone was all she could hear.

She gazed farther down the river, into the valley; she felt the pull of the falls urging her to the rocks below. *What would it be like— jumping into the void?* The mere thought grabbed her by her throat. She took a step back, coming back to her senses.

Staring back out again, her grandfather's face suddenly appeared, suspended in the mist, next to him a strange object: a vague form captured in a shimmering blue light. She heard a voice, not her grandfather's voice . . . a different voice, one that sounded familiar. It was low, and quiet, but she could make out what it was saying. "We are here . . . We are with you . . . Go to your friends." Then the face of her grandfather and the shimmering light vanished, replaced by the most beautiful rainbow she had ever seen. A great calmness swept over her. *It's time.*

Morningstar returned to the task at hand. She sat down on the edge of the raft, held onto the cord with both hands, then slid waist deep into the river. The cord pulled against Zack and slipped between his hands for an instant. Pulling back hard, he re-anchored himself between the rocks. Kai Li and Liyah responded as well, adding their effort to Zack's. The cord, which had sagged down to within one foot of the surface of the river, surged back to its original position, supporting the full weight of Morningstar and her pack. The flow of the water began immediately tugging at her, her legs drifting forward. She could feel the angry river trying to pry her fingers from the cord.

She moved out along the cable, sliding one hand then the other. The falls roared, and plumes of mist and fog engulfed her. She concentrated on moving quickly but cautiously. Shortly, her left hand slid over the hooks joining the two cords; minutes later she was halfway across.

The distance of the cord above the water was at its lowest point. Her feet touched the rocks below, but she was unable to rest on them. She kept moving, glancing to her left and squinting into the mist, searching for the others, her arms aching, her hands weakening. The current continually forced her legs up from behind. She fought a few more feet; her hand found the knot of the rope. *It couldn't be far now.*

She could now hear their muffled voices, especially Zack's with its deeper tone booming the same words of support he had called to Kai Li and Liyah. She turned her head again. Suddenly all three appeared out of the mist. Her spirit rose. Moving slowly but steadily, she inched along the rope, arms aching, but hands sure. Only three feet to go.

Kai Li moved toward her, hand over hand along the rope, getting ready to reach out to her. Morningstar tried to step up on the first big rock along the jetty, but slipped off, her weight pulling the cord down almost to the water level, submerging her. Zack's feet slipped slightly forward at the same time. Regaining his footing, he and Liyah yanked the rope taut, causing Morningstar to bob up and down like a buoy in the harbor. With each bob, the now lighter raft rocked on top of the boulders, loosing itself from its mooring.

Kai Li was still a few feet shy of her. With only two feet of rope left between the two, the raft broke free. In seconds it was drawn over the falls. As it rode the falling waters down, the rope that Morningstar was holding onto was pulled into the water. The momentum of the falling raft could not be overcome by the combined strength of Zack and Liyah. Liyah was thrown down onto the rocks, and Kai Li was yanked forward and forced to let go of the rope.

The raft splashed into the water below, pulling hard on the cords and pinning Zack against the rocks. Kai Li heard Zack scream out something, but he was focused on Morningstar, now dangling from the rope over the edge of the falls, only her arms and head visible above the falls.

"Pull it sideways toward the shore!" Morningstar shouted up to Kai Li.

He tried but there was too much force on the cord against the rock on the jetty. He called out to Liyah, "Liyah! Help! NOW!"

Liyah had moved over to Zack, trying to free him. She glanced at Morningstar, then Zack. "Sorry Zack, I . . ."

"Never mind," Zack groaned. "Go . . . GO!!"

Liyah stumbled across the rocks to Kai Li. "Help pull her that way!" he said, pointing to the bank.

Together, standing on the same side of the rope, they yanked and yanked, getting whatever leverage they could from their feet against the rocks in the shallow water at the end of the jetty. Slowly the rope followed them, drawing Morningstar's body along the falls toward the rocks, where the jetty met the falls.

"More. More!" shouted Morningstar.

The two wrestled the rope closer. Morningstar stuck out her right leg, searching for a rock. After a few tries, her toe caught one. "More!" she yelled to Kai Li and Liyah.

They pulled with every ounce of strength they had. As the rope inched a little closer, Morningstar found the footing she needed. She scrambled up the last remaining rocks to Kai Li and Liyah—and safety.

Kai Li headed urgently up the rocks, calling back. "Zack in trouble."

The three gathered around Zack, pinned against the rocks, unable to move. He looked up at them, moaning. "My knife."

Morningstar pulled up his pant leg, drawing the blade from the sheath. She began to cut at the rope, but no strength remained in her arm or hand. She stared at the rope in dismay. Kai Li stooped down and placed his hand over hers, gently taking the knife from her. She turned to face him.

"It okay," said Kai Li. "I do." Morningstar relinquished the knife.

Kai Li hacked at the rope, stabbing and sawing. In less than a minute, he was most of the way through it. He told the others to stand clear. Backing up a step, he leaned over, then cut the rest of the way through.

Snap!

The rope whipped wildly, then disappeared over the falls.

Liyah unraveled the remaining portion of the rope from around Zack's waist and cast it aside. Zack, still in pain, was able to sit up; burn marks lashed his stomach where the rope had pressed and scraped against his skin, and large bruises were already showing on his back. Liyah took his sweatshirt from the backpack, wet it, and dabbed it softly on the wounds.

They sat together at the top of the jetty, Zack recovering, the others resting. Kai Li was looking down, clearing the water and dirt from his glasses with the sleeve of his jersey. He slipped the glasses back on, securing them above the bridge of his nose. As he looked back up, his eyes caught Zack's. He could sense the honor in Zack's stare. He winked. Zack smiled back.

NINETEEN

THE LIGHT COOL breeze near the falls chilled their wet bodies. Each grabbed their shoes and anything dry they could find to wrap around them from the waterproof packs. Zack slipped into his denim jacket, the soft lining protecting his wounds. Grabbing his sweatshirt from Liyah, he tied it around his waist, hoping it would dry during their afternoon travels.

The four moved carefully along the jetty and ascended a small steep hill. On the other side they found a narrow dirt path that followed the bank of the river. Once a short distance past the falls, they emerged from the mist and fog. Morningstar retrieved the map and studied it. "Seems like the only way to get back on the white stone path is to cross back over the river at this place called Hooksett Bridge," she said, pointing to a spot on the map. "It should be close to the end of these white cliffs," she added, looking at the rock ledge jutting up, just ahead.

The sun was now high, and its warmth helped dry their clothes as they made their way along the path. The cliffs shot several hundred feet straight up above them on their left, the river could be seen at the bottom of the steep embankment to their right. The height of the cliff and the narrowness of the path created a dizzying effect. Liyah and Zack hugged the cliff-side, dragging her left hand along its face to stay close.

They continued on downhill. Whitecaps were soon visible on the river below. The path's descent became steeper, and at this closer vantage point they could see the undulating, rapid flow of the water sweeping over the rocks, hidden beneath the riverbed. The closer they got to the level of the river, the angrier the river appeared.

The path edged inland for a short distance, the river disappearing from sight briefly. The trail then swept around a turn, dumping them back out.

"Look," Liyah called out, pointing her arm straight ahead. "The bridge!"

They slowly approached the base of the bridge, then stopped to survey the situation. To their left, an indentation had been cut into the ledge, allowing for more room to access the bridge from the path and a place to secure the cables. Morningstar stepped up to the part of the path that served as a sort of platform for the entrance onto the bridge itself. She searched for the continuation of the path on the other side of the platform but found none—it simply ended at the bridge.

Morningstar turned back around, facing where the bridge cables were anchored. Three sets of four giant metal eye hooks were embedded into the stone, holding all the cable ends. The first set supported the walkway of the bridge. A second set was parallel to the walkway hooks—four feet above—and the third set of hooks a few feet above those. The cables spanning the length of the bridge were made of some kind of heavy, twisted wire, something like cables for a ski lift, but thinner.

The walkway of the bridge consisted of narrow wooden slats held in place by the four cables running from the base of the cliff to the other side. Each slat step was less than a foot deep and designed to span the width of the bridge. Moving forward along the bridge, each was separated from the other by a small gap, through which it was easy see the churning river far below.

"Looks like the bridge slants downward somewhat before reaching the other side," Morningstar said to Kai Li, as he stepped up onto the platform.

"It also dip in m-middle," Kai Li observed. "M-make me l-little nervous."

Kai Li also noticed the slats were not physically attached to the cables but rather wedged between them in a woven fashion—the tension from the taut cables holding them in place. The slats resembled unfinished wooden planks from a lumberyard; all were severely weathered and many of the damaged slats had only part of the slat remaining. In some places there were big gaps where the slats were missing altogether. He turned to Morningstar.

"L-look bad."

"Like something right out of a horror movie, I'd say," she replied.

Even its shadow on the river below reflected this view, appearing like an abandoned, broken railway track to Kai Li. "Yup."

Morningstar called down to Zack and Liyah. "This has to be it. The path doesn't continue past this point. We have to cross here."

"Really?" questioned Zack, in a halting voice.

"Yes," Morningstar replied, matter of factly. "Really."

Liyah and Zack stepped up onto the platform.?

"What do you think, Kai Li?" Morningstar asked. "I mean about getting across?"

"It in bad s-shape. Cables look okay though, and it n-narrow 'nough so arms can r-reach 'cross."

"We can go as teams," Morningstar offered. "Liyah, you and I can go together. Zack, you can help Kai Li. Okay with you?"

"This seems way too dangerous to me," Zack replied. "Maybe we should find another place to cross."

"We can't do that, Zack," Morningstar insisted. "The path ends here. And there's no other bridge. This is the only one on the map."

Zack fell silent.

"As much as I don't like this either, Zack, I have to agree with her," Liyah added. "It's the only way."

"I don't know. I don't like it," Zack complained.

Morningstar turned and moved forward, stepping onto the first slat suspended in between the cables; her right hand grasped the cable about eye level next to her; she did the same with her left, arms now completely stretched out. If the bridge was another foot wider, her reach wouldn't have covered the span.

Stepping forward onto the second slat with her right foot, she slid her right hand forward so that it remained directly above that foot; she did the same on the left side. As she took a few more steps along the slats, she felt the bridge sway ever so slightly. She looked down at her feet, but her eyes continued on . . . to the whitecaps far below. She lifted her head back up. "My grandfather told me if you focus your eyes straight ahead on something, you won't get dizzy."

"You're crazy, Morningstar!" Zack protested.

"C'mon, Liyah," Morningstar encouraged. "It'll be fine. I'll help you get across."

Liyah approached the end of the bridge, grabbed onto the cables on either side, and placed her foot on the first board. Morningstar moved forward one more step, allowing a little more space for Liyah; as she did, Liyah sensed a tiny vibration in the cables. She gripped tightly on the cables, took in a deep breath, and held it.

"Breathe, Liyah, breathe!" instructed Morningstar. "It'll be fine," Morningstar repeated. "Everything is going to be okay."

Liyah slid her hand forward and stepped fully onto the first slat. She stood there for a moment, then took another step. Then another. Right behind Morningstar.

Morningstar glanced over her shoulder at her. "Stay close; we'll be across before you know it."

Liyah, eyes locked to Morningstar's back, managed a strained, "Okay, I think I can do it . . . please just go really slow and don't make this thing sway."

The two girls set off deliberately, cautiously, along the bridge.

———

Kai Li and Zack were now next to each other on the platform of the bridge. They had watched intently at the first few steps that Liyah and Morningstar had negotiated. "I n-not know 'bout th-this," said Kai Li. "S-stomach queasy."

Zack remained silent. Kai Li turned to face him, to get some reassurance, but it was Zack who seemed to need it.

"You okay? L-look like see ghost."

"Fine," Zack mumbled.

Kai Li turned back around and inched closer to the end of the platform; he slid his right hand carefully onto the cable, then reached his left arm out to the other cable, having to stretch to grasp it. Repeating the actions of Morningstar and Liyah, sliding each hand

and corresponding foot alternately forward, he began moving down the bridge. He could feel the vibrations from the girls as they, too, moved on their way, only a short distance in front of him.

In this manner, Kai Li made his way to the fifth board and then stopped, wondering why he hadn't felt the bridge sway when Zack got on; he turned to look back. "Z-zack?"

No response.

"Zack!"

"Yeah, I'm comin'," Zack mumbled. He grabbed the cables and nudged his right foot onto the first slat, but the cables, while okay for the others, were below the level of his shoulders. He backed off the step then latched onto the upper cables, repeating the process. The bridge swayed ever so gently; Zack gripped the cables tightly and stopped.

Kai Li noticed Morningstar and Liyah had extended their distance from them. After moving down the bridge a little farther, he paused to rest and wait for Zack. He heard Morningstar call out. "Everything all right back there?"

"Okay here," Kai Li called back.

———

Morningstar and Liyah returned to their navigation of the bridge. They moved ahead slowly but steadily. "Doing great, Liyah," Morningstar said, as she glanced past her to see the boys were falling farther behind. Even at a fair distance away now, though, she could tell Zack was struggling—there was no grace in his motion, just the halting, stiff movements of his arms and legs.

Liyah stopped on the slat that was two behind Morningstar. "Something wrong?" she asked.

"I think Zack's having difficulty."

"In what way?"

"In general."

"Maybe he's not good at balancing?" Liyah suggested.

"No. I don't think so. He's pretty athletic . . . I don't think it's that."

"Then what?"

"I think he's afraid," Morningstar said, her voice calm, serious.

Liyah laughed. "Zack? Don't be silly. He's not afraid of anything . . . he grew up in the city streets, with gangs—like we see in American movies at home."

"It's not that kind of fear, Liyah. His fear is of high places. And that can be even more crippling than the threat of violence."

"How can you be sure?"

"I'm sure. And I'm afraid for him. And I'm afraid for Kai Li, too. If Zack gets in trouble, Kai Li may not be able to help him."

"I'm sure they'll be alright, Morningstar. If I can do this, so can they."

"I hope so."

Liyah continued to shadow Morningstar, only a few slats behind, as they approached the halfway mark, where the bridge halted its downward slope and began to rise toward the other side. Morningstar stopped and turned around again to check on her. She motioned her with one hand, "Hold up. There are a few places ahead here with a lot of broken and missing steps."

"Okay," Liyah replied, nervously. "What should we do?"

"Wait here, I'll check it out . . . Be right back."

A few minutes later she returned.

"Two boards are completely missing, and there are two badly broken ones right after those. The first one is cracked with a gap open on the right side and the next one similar but missing a big piece on the left. After that it looks pretty much like what we've been seeing all along."

"It will be a little tricky for sure," said Morningstar, "but nothing we can't handle. I think if we place our feet directly on the cables, like walking a tightrope, we'll be fine. Just step where I step . . . and stay close."

Liyah stared down through the big gap between the missing boards, then took a step back. "I don't know, Star. I'm not sure I can."

"Sure you can. We just need to slide one foot along each of the two middle cables while we hold on tight to the cables above. Put your feet right behind mine."

Morningstar led Liyah to the last good slat before the gap. "Okay, are you ready?"

"I guess."

"Do *exactly* as I do . . . and stick to me like glue. That way if anything happens you can grab onto me."

"Happens?" she whispered.

Morningstar positioned herself on the slat; her hands reaching forward, she grabbed onto the wires at shoulder height on either side of her, then slid her right foot along the second base cable in from the right, her foot at a slight angle—the arch within her moccasin resting on the cable. "Imagine yourself as a tightrope walker, Liyah."

Liyah mimicked her movements: first the right foot, then the left, sliding her hands along the twisted steel cable. Carefully but steadily, they slid their way across the gap, approaching the broken boards.

"They may not be safe even though they are secured on one side," Morningstar told Liyah. "Stay on the cables."

Once across the last ones, they continued on over a handful of solid slats, then paused to regroup. Morningstar turned to Liyah, placing her hands on Liyah's shoulders. "You're very brave. I think maybe I was more frightened than you."

Liyah gave her a half smile. "I'll never believe that one."

———

The girls were a good distance ahead by the time the boys finally made it to the gap. Kai Li, a handful of steps ahead of Zack, had been thinking about the letters and his fear, breathing and trying to gain every edge he could over the situation. He was wondering again about Zack. *Could he really be afraid?* He turned his head over his shoulder. "Hey. You okay?"

No response.

"Zack," he repeated, louder. "Okay?"

Kai Li made his way back. "What wrong?"

"Can't do it," Zack stammered, his words scarcely audible. "Thought I could, but I can't."

"Why n-not?"

Zack simply stared at him.

Kai Li appeared stunned. "You 'fraid h-heights?"

Zack looked at him sheepishly. "Y-Yeah."

"Who would th-think?"

"Don't say anything to the others, okay?" he beseeched Kai Li, his voice almost commanding at the same time.

The total reality of Zack's fear hit Kai Li. "Sure. N-no worry. I get you 'cross."

Zack, white-knuckling the cable, thrust his head back and to the side several times, as if pointing. "The pack. You have to take it." Zack demanded, voice cracking. "When it shifts it freaks me out."

"S-sure"

"Just undo the straps and take the pack," he repeated.

"But I h-have to l-let go," Kai Li returned.

"You can hold onto me as you take it off," he insisted, his voice shaky, tone edgy "I'm *not* letting go of these wires."

Kai Li moved closer. Zack's face looked like all the blood had drained out. Kai Li let go of the wire in his right hand as he circled around behind him, holding onto his body for safety. As he removed the strap on the right side, the pack tilted at an angle on Zack's back. Zack shifted quickly to adjust his balance.

"Careful. Careful," Zack cautioned.

Kai Li re-hooked the strap so he could loop it over his shoulder, then tended to the left one. When it was free, Kai Li re-hooked the left strap and removed the pack from Zack's back. He then slipped the pack on himself as he pressed against Zack for support.

"Shit, man! What are you doin'?" Zack blurted out, pushing back against Kai Li.

Zack's sudden movement caused Kai Li to lose his balance; he lunged for the cable on his left, holding on with both hands as he fell to his knees; he was now in an awkward position, looking straight down at the river, feeling like he might slide off the slat any moment.

"Jesus! Jesus!" Zack shouted.

"No worry, no worry!" he assured Zack, the sense of urgency disabling his stutter. He stood back up slowly, then leaned against the outer cable as he tightened the straps of the pack.

Zack felt the movement of the cables. "God, Kai Li! What's goin' on?"

"Minute."

"What?"

"No worry. All good. I come front now. No move."

Once again in front of Zack, he eased up to the next slat. "Just follow now. Hold onto p-pack if need."

Zack stared at the series of broken and missing slats. "We have to go back."

"No can do," Kai Li replied.

"Yeah, well, we can't get over without something to stand on."

"You hold on pack . . . put f-feet on cables behind mine."

"It won't work," Zack protested. "I can't do it."

Kai Li started moving forward anyway.

Zack panicked. "Shit!" he shouted, lurching ahead and grasping at the pack.

As Kai Li tightrope walked the two cables, Zack inched each sneaker along the cables with each of Kai Li's steps, 'til they met the heels of Kai Li's.

Very slowly but with even, steady movements, Kai Li led them along the middle cable wires underneath their feet. They passed the spot where the first missing board would have been, and then the second. As they approached the end of the gap, Kai Li looked ahead at the two broken slats to assess his next move. He had been so caught up in his plan to get across the gap he hadn't considered the next two boards were going to pose a different problem. They would have to either move first to one side and then to the next to step on each of the boards, or they would have to continue what they were doing and step over them. *The boards look like they'll hold*, he thought, but then decided not to take a chance.

"Two broken. We go over."

Kai Li tapped the side of Zack's leg as he stepped forward. "M-move now."

The first board remained wedged to the left between the wires with the missing end on the right. Kai Li raised his right leg and stepped along the cable over the slat, setting it down on the cable on the other side, leaving enough space for Zack to place his right foot.

Zack stepped over the board and set his foot down behind Kai Li's, but the added pressure of their combined weight on the cable caused the board to dislodge from the grip of the other cables. The right end of the board then snapped up between the two inner cables. Gravity did the rest, snatching the entire board from under them, sending it spinning like a helicopter blade to the rapids below.

The flying slat entered Zack's peripheral vision. He jerked his body in its direction. The motion was just enough to cause his left foot to miss the cable as it came down. Falling to his left, his knee came down hard on the cable, pushing it out from underneath Kai Li. He lunged to try to make it to the first good slat ahead of him, landing on his stomach across it, his head in between the cables in front. He stared down wide-eyed at the violent river.

Kai Li's fall shook the cables again, causing Zack to lose his balance and slip sideways between the two side cables in the middle of the gap; his butt hit the cable behind him, breaking his fall temporarily, allowing him to latch onto the side cable in front of him. He then managed to get his arms on the other side of it, his armpits now locked around the cable, saving him from tumbling to the river below.

Kai Li was thrown into pure reaction mode. He stuck his head between the cables and looked back underneath the walkway for Zack; there he was, body dangling on the side of the bridge, suspended by only the outer cable, facing downstream. "You okay? he yelled out.

No reply.

Kai Li instantly refocused. "I come! Hold on! I come!" He pushed his hands against the cables and raised his chest, at the same time bringing his knees up to the board to support his weight, then turning, sat down on the slat, legs dangling, facing Zack's side—only an arm's length away.

Zack, eyes clamped shut, let out a feeble, high pitched, "*Heeelllppp!*"

"Right here . . . no let go . . . I get you!"

Zack groaned.

Kai Li could tell Zack had no leverage, he couldn't pull himself up—and there was no slat for him to grab hold of. Kai Li was also certain he was not strong enough to lift Zack out by himself and felt Zack might pull him down if he tried, anyway. But, with the cable lodged in his armpits, Zack could probably hold on longer than if he were hanging by his hands; it could give him a little time to try to get him to safety—he knew too, though, that Zack would weaken—eventually.

Kai Li stood up on the slat. Edging to the side of the bridge, he reached for the cable above his head. Soon he stood on the outer base cable facing Zack, who hung suspended on the single cable, eyes glazed, staring out over the river. Taking another step, he positioned himself close to Zack.

The cable swayed. Zack gripped it like a vise with his armpits.

"Jeez! Jeez!" Zack then slowly opened his eyes, keeping his head rigid as he looked out over the side of the bridge. Finally able to speak, he pleaded, "Help me, Kai Li. Help me!"

"No worry, Zack. I get down, pull you up."

Kai Li squatted, still holding onto the cable with both arms extended, then he realized he couldn't get low enough without having to let go of the cable. He stood back up. "Try somethin' else."

Zack groaned again.

Kai Li maneuvered back to the slat where he had been sitting before. He could see Morningstar and Liyah down the bridge, making their way toward him, but he couldn't wait.

He eased himself down, sitting on the slat facing Zack with his legs dangling down. Bending backwards he eased his body down until his upper body was completely below the slat, the back of his head toward Zack; he could see the white caps rippling below. He closed his eyes for a moment and took a deep breath. With the narrow slat caught under his knees, he was now suspended below the cables, his back and the pack facing Zack—less than a yard away.

He called out, "Zack, look to right . . . You see me?"

Zack slowly rotated his head to the right, eyes pinned to the side of his head, searching . . . then down. "Jesus! Oh my God! What are you doing?"

"You reach me? With legs?"

Zack appeared frozen. Kai Li prodded again.

"Zack?"

No response.

"Think of letter," Kai Li said calmly to him. "No fear. I h-here. Breathe . . . 'member? Breathe."

Zack took a deep breath and closed his eyes. He paused a moment, then opened his eyes; there was Kai Li, upside down, the backpack facing him. He stretched out his right leg. The toe of his sneaker hit the pack.

"That it . . . put foot on pack."

"I c-can't."

"Yes . . . Yes can. Push 'gainst me . . . take weight off cable."

Zack stretched his leg out further, resting his foot on the top of the pack; he pressed down, then pressed down harder. His body rose, removing some of the pressure of the cable against his armpits; he was then able to slide a little to his right, inching closer to Kai Li; he pushed again against the pack—this time with more force. He moved a foot nearer.

Kai Li sensed a tremendous strain on his knees. He forced his heels down toward the water so he wouldn't slip off the slat. He strained as Zack pressed against the pack again, literally walking up the backpack.

Zack reached up to the next highest cable and hoisted up his body. Now standing, he stared down at Kai Li.

Kai Li tightened his stomach muscles—like he had done so many times during his nighttime martial arts classes he was taking—and sat back up on the slat to the left of Zack, facing away. He held up his arms to Zack, who grabbed hold of his wrists and raised him to a standing position. Kai Li pivoted on the board, his eyes meeting Zack's. "Told you," he said.

TWENTY

———

NAVIGATING THE REMAINDER of the bridge without further incidents, they arrived safely on the platform at the far end. The sun was sinking in the sky, and a sense of urgency to get back on the white stone path set in. To the rear of the platform, they spotted a narrow path and followed it beyond a small stone wall, making their way to the top of a hill. From there they could see the edge of a dense forest not far away.

"From the map, that must be the Black Forest," Morningstar observed. "The path we're on should lead us back to the white stones, and we can camp near the entrance to the forest. We could be back to the cabin before nightfall tomorrow."

She handed the map to Kai Li. He folded it and stuck it in his shirt pocket, adjusted his pack, then took the lead down the path followed closely by Morningstar and Liyah.

There were still a few hours of daylight left when the trail they were on abruptly ended, meeting with the white stone path. Behind them they could see blue cliffs rising above the river, and the Black Forest just a short distance ahead. They continued on the trail, crossing a gentle sloping field, and finally landing at the edge of the forest where they rested. Sitting by the side of the path, they shared a portion of the meager food supply that remained.

"M-marker near here," Kai Li said, remembering the map. "Keep eyes open."

Liyah turned to Zack. "What are you thinking about? You've been pretty quiet."

"Just some stuff," he replied, drawing circles in the dirt with small stick.

"Like what?"

"Oh . . . I don't know. I guess I'm still amazed at what Kai Li was able to do back there . . . on the bridge. It all kinda reminded me of a nightmare I had but helped get over something, too."

Liyah caught his eye. "Yeah, well, we were worried about you guys, you know."

Zack grinned. "Yup. Thanks, Liyah. I was worried about me, too."

They all laughed together, for the first time.

"Time to get going," Morningstar said as she stood up and scanned the path ahead. She then turned to Kai Li. "Do you see that thing sticking up over there by the entrance into the woods.?"

"Big t-trees," Kai Li replied.

"No, I mean, before the big trees."

"N-no. Where?"

"Follow the path . . . before you get to the forest . . . sticking up on the right."

"See s-somethin' . . . yeah."

"It looks like a post to me." Morningstar added. "Maybe like the ones that we found some of the letters in?"

"You eagle eye, okay," Kai Li said, excited. "Like grandpa s-say."

They headed back down the path, making their way to the post. Kai Li opened the top of the box, retrieving an envelope; he handed it to Morningstar. She glanced at the word written on the front, *Leading*.

"Why don't we wait to read this by the fire later?" she said, stuffing it into the pocket of the pack that held the other letters.

Moving on past the first trees, they crossed over a shallow stream, and stepped along a series of high, flat rocks that bridged a stream; the stream flowed from the north, out of the forest, and down to their left, toward the river. Just beyond the stream, off the side of the path, was a small field.

"This will do," said Morningstar.

"Shouldn't we look for some food?" Liyah asked.

"I don't think we'll find any around here," Morningstar replied. "You can look if you like, but don't stray too far . . . stay within eyesight."

"I go w-with Liyah," said Kai Li. "We get wood, t-too."

Just as the sun sank below behind trees, Liyah and Kai Li returned to camp, dragging a few dried branches. "We couldn't find any berries," Liyah complained. "And there wasn't much wood either. We'll have to make do with this." They dropped the branches next to the spot Morningstar had picked for the fire.

"Not much we can do about it," Morningstar replied. "We're going to have to go without dinner. We can find something near the cabin."

"That's a day away," Zack replied, disgruntled.

"Yeah," agreed Morningstar, "but we had a snack only a few hours ago, and we need to keep what's left in the packs to provide energy tomorrow . . . and just in case."

"Just in case what?" asked Zack.

"Just in case," Morningstar repeated, as she began removing the water sacks from the packs. "We need to think about washing up. Liyah and I will start the fire. Why don't you two go first. Take these." She handed them the sacks. "I'll need your knife, Zack," she added.

"Aye, aye, Captain," he joked, taking the sacks from her in exchange for the knife, then heading off to the stream with Kai Li.

Liyah turned to Morningstar. "I think he's back."

"I heard that," Zack responded, not bothering to turn around.

———

Shortly the boys returned with the water, then the girls then took their turn by the stream. They returned to camp as the sun tripped below the horizon. Twilight was upon them.

There was a chill in the air as Kai Li and Liyah sat down together next to the fire. Zack went into his tent and brought back his denim jacket, tossing it to Kai Li as he took a seat on the other side of Liyah. "Here ya go, sir. That shirt can't be too warm."

Kai Li gave Zack the thumbs-up and waited for Morningstar as she fetched the envelope. When everyone had settled down, she opened it, removed the letter, and handed it to Zack.

"This is number six?" he asked, opening it.

"Yup," replied Kai Li. "Not s-see seven on map."

"I don't think it matters," Liyah responded. "I'm afraid we've failed our mission. We never found the book."

"We might as well read it anyway," Morningstar replied.

"Yeah, s'posed read all," Kai Li said confidently. "L-look for clue."

Liyah encouraged Zack with a nod. "Go ahead."

The fire crackled, spitting tiny embers into the early night sky. Zack began to read.

"Leading," he said, reading the title then pausing:

There comes a time when we all must lead. Not in the same sense of a military leader or captain of a team, but to help others in a different way, and to help ourselves. In this sense, leading does not have to mean raising a sword high and charging into battle. There is a more important fight that requires all of us to be leaders. This fight lies within us. It is the fight to free the true self.

Our first challenge is to lead for ourselves—not to dominate, but to surrender. As you have learned, we become who we were intended to be only by quieting our egos and allowing space for the true self. In this sense we give ourselves grace—freedom from the ties that bind us. By rising up to this challenge, we lead ourselves out of the maze of intertwined false messages and habits that have taken control of our lives. The sooner we do this, the more joy we will have in our lives and the more ready we will be to be true leaders, not leading by the voice of commands but by the unspoken voice of our hearts.

Once we have become whole, our second challenge is to set the stage for others—to help them find their way, too. Although we cannot do the final lifting for them, we can lead by example. We can become a signpost for them, showing them the way.

It does no good for us to just find our own path. In order to alter the course of the world, which has been sinking into pain and chaos, we must help others . . . who in turn will help others . . . until we reach a critical point when this process will be self-sustaining and unstoppable. The world will finally be able to achieve peace and harmony. No government, religion, or single leader can lead us there. It is up to each of you. And it relies on your commitment to yourself and to the others you will touch. It must be a groundswell—it cannot happen by edict.

There is no one other than yourself who can break the bonds of the ego and establish a path of joy for your life. It is a singular battle where you serve both as soldier and leader. Others may provide guidance and be good examples for you by having overcome their own personal battles, but they cannot conquer your fears, or know intimately the chains that you struggle to break. You must lead yourself out of your bonds—there is no other way. Once we are finally free and live in our true selves, then, and only then, are we ready to help lead others, to the point where they can then do the same.

In order to learn how to lead, we can get direction and encouragement from others who have found the path. These people become our mentors. In other personal struggles during our lives, we often refer to these people as our heroes, but even they will tell you that they are just behaving as their inner messenger guides them. It is a lesson for all to learn: without developing the inner strength to get us through our trials, we will not become all that we can be. Our heroes and mentors become our guides. They inspire us and help jump-start our own awareness and healing. We, in turn, help lead others in the same way.

Time is running out. You have been brought here to learn who you truly are, and to then become the seeds of change and healing for an overwhelmed and broken world. To become leaders, therefore, requires you to become your own heroes.

This is your challenge.

Zack folded the letter, placed it in the envelope, and handed it back to Morningstar, who glanced around at the others. "What do you think?" she asked quietly.

"I don't see how this is going to help us find the book," said Liyah.

"Me either," Zack agreed.

"I guess maybe it's not intended to," Morningstar replied. "But I think we can't worry about it. We've done the best we could, even if we don't find it. We just need to get back to the cabin and see what lies in store for us."

"I wouldn't get my hopes up," Zack cautioned. "I'd say nothin' is in store. We're gonna run out of food . . . then what?"

Morningstar let his comments pass. "What about you, Kai Li?"

"Buddha s-say n-no attach to outcome."

"What does that mean?" Liyah asked.

"Like letter . . . m-mean is what is. No worry 'bout th-things can't change."

Morningstar studied him. "You like these letters, don't you?"

"Yeah . . . Make sense."

"Well, tomorrow maybe we'll know about the ending."

———

It was a restful night for everyone. They took their time packing up, sharing the smallest portion of the food left to get them going, finally heading along the white stone path and into the Black Forest. A short distance in they came upon a large wooden sign with burnt lettering:

This Way Not for the Living
Do Not Tread Here!

"Good 'nuff f-for me," Kai Li said, emphatically.

"We can't go back," Morningstar insisted, unflinching, "We have no choice."

"She's right," Zack agreed. "It's just some kind of stupid scare tactic."

Kai Li looked at the sign. "It w-work."

"Besides," added Liyah, "this is the path. Nothing can harm us if we stay on it. Right?"

"No s-so sure, Liyah."

"Well, let's get on with it," Zack announced, turning up the trail and leading the others further into the woods.

They walked easily until about noon, when the path started to rise, speckled with outcroppings of large rocks. By early afternoon, the trees around them had become more densely packed, their tops shooting far up into the sky directly over them, the dense spruce-like needles latched together, blocking out the sun. Morningstar thought she had never been in a forest this dark—almost nighttime in the middle of the day. As the path began to meander through them and around the rocks, she sensed they were losing valuable time; she was no longer certain they'd make it to the cabin before dark.

Stopping for a rest, Morningstar and Kai Li studied the map.

"What think?" asked Kai Li.

"I think we can't chance getting all the way to the cabin. Probably best to make camp early, eat the rest of the food, then get to the cabin in the morning."

"Where we gonna find a space for the camp around here?" Zack questioned. "And without burning the place down . . . us with it?"

"We have to keep going until we find something, anything," Morningstar replied.

Back on the path they moved along steadily, eventually coming upon a brook. The brook flowed down to them, parallel to the path; before reaching them, it veered to their right beyond a small clearing.

"Might be our only hope," Morningstar said. "We can use the needles to start the fire, but we have to keep it small, given the closeness of the trees."

"Yeah," agreed Zack, winking at her. "We don't want to go through that again, do we?"

They set down the packs and began their tasks to make camp: branches, water from the stream, tents, and fire pit. Kai Li and Zack completed their rounds and fashioned a place for the fire, carving out a shallow hole to hold the kindling and placing the stones around it to protect the fire from the wind and the forest from the fire. They sat down next to each other with their backs against a large rock, waiting for the others to return from the stream.

The girls returned with the water. "No berries," said Liyah. "We'll have to finish off what's left in the packs. It's not much but should keep us 'til tomorrow morning."

Morningstar and Kai Li got the fire going, and they sat around it, eating what they hoped would be their last meal of the journey. It was nearly black in the woods already; the piece of sky they could see above them was also now dark. Morningstar hoped the sky would stay clear so the moons could provide them some light.

The four stared silently into the fire as an undercurrent of anxiety hung in the air. A light wind blew through the treetops, and the sweet, dank smell of the forest filled their senses.

Liyah watched as a small flame encircled the tip of a stick she was using to poke the fire. "We are very near the end of our journey," she said.

"I'll believe that when I'm back in Michigan," replied Zack. "Even if we get to that cabin, it doesn't mean we'll get back home."

"What do you mean?" Liyah asked.

"I mean we may get back to the cabin okay, but we didn't do what we were supposed to. We never found the *Book of Universal Truths.*"

"Yes we did. We have the pieces," Liyah replied, trying to reassure herself as much as Zack.

"We have *some* pieces . . . maybe," Zack responded. "And we sure haven't found any actual *book.*"

Liyah frowned, then shot a worried glance in Morningstar's direction.

"We still have time left before we get there," Morningstar replied, interceding on Liyah's behalf. "Besides, we've done all we can. We have to trust it will be enough."

Zack glanced over at Kai Li, who had remained silent, looking intently up into the trees; Zack followed his gaze, but only found the treetops, waving gently in the wind. "I don't see anythin' there," he said, chuckling. "What's up with you? Where'd you go?"

Realizing someone was speaking to him, Kai Li brought his attention back to the group.

"I don't see anything," Zack repeated, then smiled. "Somethin' in the trees?"

"No," Kai Li said softly. "Guess n-not."

Liyah sensed he was holding back. "Something the matter?"

Kai Li looked over at her. "No. It okay," he insisted halfheartedly.

"Well, that's hard to believe, Kai-bo," Zack kidded, "You look like you've seen a ghost."

"You *are* a bit pale," Morningstar agreed. "Even in this light."

Kai Li felt the pressure of everyone staring at him. "Wind 'mind me of s- somethin'," he begrudgingly admitted.

Liyah could tell he was troubled. "What is that?" Liyah asked, gently.

"Ghouls," Kai Li said without a stutter.

"Ghouls?" Liyah repeated.

"S-spirits . . . ghosts."

"What kind of spirits?"

"Bad."

"Why are you reminded of them?" asked Morningstar.

"Wind in t-trees . . . warning."

"Of what? You kiddin' us, man?" Zack asked as if hoping for an acknowledgement that he was playing with them.

Liyah gave Zack the eye, then turned back to Kai Li. "I'm not sure what you mean. Can you tell us about it?"

Kai Li hesitated to talk about it. He didn't want to conjure up his childhood demons; he hadn't thought about them in a long time.

"Go ahead, Kai Li," Morningstar reassured him.

"It n-nothin' r-really," he said, studying each of them before continuing. "Just my f-father use tell me 'bout Chinese g-host. One he say p-part ghost and also ghoul . . . call him *Gui Shu*."

"I'm havin' a hard time with this," Zack interjected. "There are no such things as ghosts. Everybody knows that."

"Stop it, Zack," Liyah said, shooting him another hard look.

"Just sayin'," he said, backing down, but trying to defend against her stare.

"It actually depends on what Kai Li means, Zack," replied Morningstar. "There are spirits, what my people refer to as the souls of our ancestors . . . and of course the Great Spirit."

"You said ghouls," Liyah added. "We have Arab spirits called exactly that. It's a word which means demons."

Zack rolled his eyes.

Liyah ignored him and continued. "But ghouls live in empty places, like the desert. They appear as animals but can change into any shape. The stories say they lure people away, slay them, then drink their blood . . . maybe even eat them!"

"Seriously, girl," Zack said, shaking his head. "You think I'm the problem, but I wouldn't say you're 'zactly helpin' out here."

"No, no, no. I mean that they are just stories. It isn't real!"

"Maybe w-why Gui Shu p-part ghoul," replied Kai Li. Was m-man, then change f-form, and live in f-forest . . . in t-tree. S-some lure you away . . . down endless r-road."

"Maybe as far as the story goes, Kai Li, but goblins, ghosts, and ghouls are not real," Liyah assured him.

Morningstar watched him for a moment. "Fire is magical, isn't it?" she said. "It seduces your senses, then draws your mind to its musings. My lala would say that it 'brings out the souls of our relations.'"

Kai Li turned to her. "Past s-souls?"

"Yeah . . . usually. But we believe that souls exist in all things, in the past and now, and that all things are related."

"My t-teacher say same."

"Well, I don't know much about Buddhism," Morningstar continued, "but actions give most people away—about what they really believe."

"In Islam," Liyah added, "fire is often a symbol of hell, a punishment for those who did not do good deeds when they were alive. I think this is also what Christians believe. Is that right?" She turned to Zack who was poking at the fire but still listening.

"I s'pose, although I'm not sure many people still believe in the fire part exactly . . . more like a symbol."

"Islam teaches that each person possesses a pure soul when they are born, and if they do good deeds in their life, the soul is nourished and grows. When the person dies, the spirit remains. This is what is meant by life after death."

"I don't really know a lot about the Christian religion, actually," Zack said. "Some of the things you are saying seem similar, but I was unhappy at home and didn't like the rules and stiffness of the church, so I didn't really pay much attention. I had friends who felt the same . . . there was something about the behavior of many people there that seemed pretty hypocritical."

"What 'bout Jesus, though?" Kai Li asked. "Y-you talk lot 'bout him."

"Well, that's sort of what I mean," Zack replied, his tone more serious than the others could remember, his voice low and steady. "Lots of people sayin' his name . . . but not followin' what he said. I guess I just feel close to him . . . like he's part of me or something. I see him as a true spirit, who believes in me . . . and the world—that you can achieve goodness in this life, that you don't have to wait for the next. And yes, that your soul will live on. So, I guess this is much like what you're all saying." He smiled. "But I still don't believe in ghosts."

"What 'bout angels? They n-not ghosts?"

"Don't know how I feel 'bout angels," Zack laughed. "Sometimes I wonder if they don't actually exist, but if they do, they're not the souls of people. I think they're probably separate, but still not like ghosts. There are no such things as the spirits you guys are talking about, anyway. You even said so yourself, Liyah."

"I think souls are special spirits," Liyah countered. "Many Arab people still believe that genies are real spirits. I guess maybe that's kind of like the angels, not like souls of people. They live in a kind of parallel world and only show themselves from time to time."

"J–just l–like ghouls!"

"Perhaps, Kai Li. But like Zack, I don't believe in genies or ghouls," Liyah emphasized.

Kai Li stared back into the flames. "Buddhists say fire b–base element."

"My people believe this too," Morningstar added. "Earth, water, wind, and fire. Everything is made from these elements. Maybe that's why so much can be seen when you look at fire, why it attracts the eyes of everyone—where some spirits may live."

"Why do you believe so much in spirits anyway? Is this Buddhism?" asked Liyah.

"No. Buddhists say s–spirit work in p–progress. It karma . . . 'bout the m–mind. You plant good s–seed, you get good f–fruit . . . now and future . . . l–like what you s–say Liyah: good thoughts an' action m–make good s–soul. I taught this carry on t–to future."

"So then why are you so afraid of spirits?" Zack asked, stirring the coals of the fire to generate more heat.

"Chinese believe in many s–spirit. I l–learn from o'zer k–kids an' my f–father."

"What other spirits?" Morningstar prodded. "You mean other than the Gui Shu you mentioned?"

"Maybe we should get off this topic?" Zack complained.

"Don't listen to him, Kai Li," Liyah advised.

"Well, one call *R–Ri Ben Gui Bing*. It bad s–spirit. . . Jap'nese soldiers who d–die in W–world War II. Ghosts wear uniform of s–soldier with l–long knives 'n' rifles. Very scary."

"Doesn't sound very scary to me," Zack teased.

"I thought you weren't interested, Zack. Go back to our fire," Liyah admonished.

"Just sayin'."

Liyah signaled Kai Li to continue.

"Scary not cuz s–soldiers but cuz uniform r–remind Chinese of bad t–time when many Jap'nese soldier occupy Chinese l–land. Kill m–many people with knife and g–gun—helpless p–people . . . women 'n' children. S-steal 'n' rape, t-torture. Chinese no f-forget. When s-see ghosts, f-feel death near."

"Why are you afraid of these ghosts?" asked Morningstar.

"Cuz I p-part Jap'nese, part Chinese. Dad part Jap'nese an' his d-dad, my gran'father, he Jap'nese s-soldier . . . m-marry Chinese girl. M-my dad born in China. My m-mom Chinese. Some p-people no like my d-dad jus' cuz he part Jap'nese. They make f-fun of me in school 'n' frighten me when I l-little with stories. I very s-scared. Wind in t-trees remind me of s-spirits."

"Are there other spirits you see?" Liyah asked.

"M-mostly only Gui Shu and Ri B-ben Gui Bing cuz learn f-from kids and my d-dad. But also s-stories of others like *Wu T-Tou Gui*; he headless g-ghost.

Liyah smiled. "Well, you are safe with us. No ghosts here."

"That's right, Kai Li. No ghosts here," said Morningstar.

"No ghosts anywhere," Zack added.

Several hours passed, and the breeze picked up again, stirring the trees. Kai Li shifted uneasily in his sleep. The moons had risen, sliding in and out between the clouds. Their beams broke in between the clouds and flashed shadows of the thrashing tress against the roofs of the tents. Kai Li opened his eyes and followed the images. He again sensed the presence of bad energy, tuning his ears to the wind as it whistled in low tones through the trees.

A sudden gust of wind blew through the camp and extinguished what was remaining of the fire; Kai Li sat up, pushed aside the tent flap, and peered out. A stream of smoke rose from the coals of the fire. The smoke seemed to take the shape of a panther, then blew past the tent in a rush, the shape dispersing. Was he just imagining it? The fine hairs on his arms stood on end, and his heart thumped against his ribs.

He wanted to wake the others, but he also wanted to be brave. His mind raced. He tried to concentrate on his breath and relax, but nothing was working. Then his eyes caught a glimpse of a specter rising from behind one of the big boulders a short way from his tent;

it was the florescent light-blue form of a female, shifting and twisting gracefully as she rose, her long yellow hair flowing, blown by the gusty wind. He was mesmerized.

The apparition smiled at him, her motions gentle, eyes kind; his tense muscles relaxed. The form signaled him, moving her hand in a slow, wavy motion to approach her. He thought he must be asleep, and this a wonderful dream. Leaving the tent, he moved toward her, advancing like a sleepwalker, staring blankly forward—as if on some vague undefined mission.

He passed the end of the boulder and moved around behind it. The beautiful lady smiled down at him; he smiled back. Her face then turned from blue to orange, then red; he blinked hard several times trying to make out what was happening.

The soft form suddenly became more angular, taking the shape of flames, shooting pointed fingers of yellow light upward. Was it a fire? But the fiery digits turned into the fangs in the gaping mouth of a triangular-headed snake.

As the snake bore down on him, Kai Li's eyes bugged out of their sockets. He ducked, letting out a bloodcurdling scream. He tried to run but tripped over a root and fell to the ground; he screamed again, covering his head with his arms. Liyah and Morningstar sprung out of bed, staring at each other as their brains tried to catch up with their bodies.

Zack grabbed the knife he kept close to him at night; he bolted out of the tent into the night air. Morningstar and Liyah were quick to join him.

"What's going on Zack?" exclaimed Morningstar.

"Where's Kai Li?" Liyah asked.

"I think that was him screaming. Over th—"

"Help! Help me!" Kai Li yelled.

Zack rushed in the direction of the screams, circling around the side of the rock. Sprinting behind it, he found Kai Li, squirming on the ground. No one else was there.

"What the hell is going on, Kai?" Zack shouted, grabbing hold of Kai Li.

Kai Li heard the familiar voice but was afraid to look up for a moment, thinking the monster snake might still be there.

"Kai Li!"

He twisted his head and peered up at Zack from between his forearms. Slowly he uncovered his head and looked around. It had gone.

"What are you doing?" demanded Zack. "You scared the crap out of us!"

Kai Li was still wide-eyed, breathing in short gasps. He collected himself, stood up, and looked at Zack. "B-big s-snake!" he panted.

"What?"

"S-snake!"

"Where?"

"'Bove m-me."

"Above you? How can that be?"

"W-well . . ." Kai Li now struggling with how to explain what he saw—if indeed he saw it. Maybe he was just having a nightmare. *But it was so real!* he thought. *It had to be.* "I s-see a ghoul . . . s-snake . . . attack m-me."

The girls joined them. Morningstar turned toward Zack. "What's the matter?" she asked, anxiously.

"He was having a nightmare," Zack replied, seeming a bit nervous. "Kinda freaked me out."

"No. Goblin . . . s-snake . . . uh . . ."

Liyah reached out to Kai Li, gently grabbing onto his arm. "You really scared us!"

They had only taken a few steps toward the camp when Morningstar stopped suddenly. Zack stumbled into her. "Hey! What are you doing?"

"Ssssh!" she whispered. "I hear something."

"What?" Liyah whispered back.

"Voices."

"W-where?" asked Kai Li.

She pointed past the camp. "Over there."

Muffled voices filtered through the woods, not far away, then began getting louder.

"Quick!" Morningstar urged. "Back behind the rock!"

Twenty-One

Tᴀᴇ ꜰᴏᴜʀ ꜱᴄʀᴀᴍʙʟᴇᴅ behind the boulder, hearts pounding. The voices stopped. Zack waited, then tentatively poked his head around the corner; he heard the voices again, but he couldn't tell what they were saying. A foreign language? Men for sure, some laughing.

The voices got louder. Someone appeared in the open, beyond the camp. Zack yanked his head back.

"What do you see?" gasped Liyah.

"I saw someone come around from behind some rocks. He's wearing a kind of outfit or something. Didn't get a good look."

Zack hugged the surface of the rock and inched his head forward once more. A group of three moved toward him, then stopped. The others stayed by the rocks, watching. It was dark, but the moons cast enough light for him to make out their images. They all had on some kind of military uniform, which glowed in an eerie way. He couldn't see their faces clearly under their helmets, but he could hear them speaking. It sounded like gibberish to him.

One of the three appeared to be the leader. He was wearing a different uniform and had a large piece of paper in his hands that he was showing to the other two; he had a mean tone to his voice as he shouted, pointing at the paper. His uniform was colorful and iridescent; the others wore dull brown ones.

Between the moons and the glow from the outfits, Zack could easily make out details of the leader's uniform: two rows of brass buttons down the front and matching gold-colored embroidery on the sleeves, shoulders, and around the collar; his helmet also appeared different, with a funny brim and some gold-colored stripes around it; spots of bright red on his wrists, and streaks of yellow near his neck, chest, and belt—red as well above his helmet in the front. His hands were covered by white gloves that fluoresced brightly, appearing blue—like white clothing under a blacklight—as did the white object attached to the top of his helmet. He had a sword of some type at his side that had a pulsating red handle, with gold trimming along the sheath.

He glanced at the group of other soldiers waiting by the rocks. They had some spots of red and gold in various places but had simpler uniforms, wore plain helmets, and carried small backpacks. The soldiers all had rifles and were wearing some kind of army boots, with the exception of the leader who was looking at the map; he wore knee-high black boots and carried a riding crop in his hand.

The leader stopped shouting, took his eyes from the map, and began looking around. As he turned to where the four were hiding, Zack pulled his head back sharply, holding his breath. He turned to the others, signaling them to be quiet.

Peering around again, he could see the soldiers were talking among themselves; he still couldn't make out their faces—only a fuzzy light-blue cloud instead. He turned back to the others, whispering.

"A bunch of soldiers not too far away. Over near the rocks, just past the camp. Looks like seven or eight of them in all, but maybe more behind the rock. I can't tell."

"What are they doing?" asked Morningstar, her voice hushed.

"The leader and a few others were looking at a piece of paper at first, maybe a map or something, but right now they're just standing around. There's something very strange about them."

"L-like w-what?" asked Kai Li.

"There's something weird about their uniforms . . . they glow. And I should be able to make out some faces, but I can't. It's kinda like they don't have any."

"Don't have any faces?" Liyah questioned.

"Yeah, there's just a blue foggy light."

While the others continued to whisper, Kai Li crept on the ground to the other side of Zack and inched around the rock. His eyes almost exploded out of his head. He tried to stand up and jump back at the same time. Losing his balance, he tripped into Zack.

Zack fell down on one knee, turned, and whispered harshly. "Jeez! What are you doin'?"

Kai Li looked back at him, wide-eyed, but couldn't get any words out of his mouth.

Zack witnessed the terror in Kai Li's eyes. "What? What? What is it?"

"S-s-s so . . . s-sol d-d-d . . ."

"Soldiers . . . yes, I said that," Zack responded.

"N-no . . . n-no . . . n-no s-s-soldiers. No r-real."

"Not real soldiers?" Liyah whispered.

"R-r-r-i B-b-b-b . . ."

"Jeez . . . spit it out will ya!" Zack pressed impatiently.

"R-r-ri B-ben."

"What?"

Frustrated and frightened, Kai Li paused for a second then loudly blurted out the words. "R-ri . . . B-ben . . . Gui . . . B-bing!"

"Huh?" Zack replied, taking a step back, stunned.

Kai Li took a short breath. "Soldiers. Ghosts."

The girls looked at each other, to Zack, and back to Kai Li.

Morningstar crawled to the end of the rock. There were the soldiers and their glowing uniforms. They appeared agitated. The soldier with the gold buttons on his uniform was saying something to a few of the others and pointing toward them.

Morningstar withdrew and returned quickly to the others. "I think they heard Kai Li. The soldiers are headed this way."

"Oh no!" exclaimed Liyah.

"We need to get our stuff from the camp and get back on the path," Morningstar suggested. "But they'll see us."

"They're gonna run into the camp any minute," Zack replied. "They can't miss it. I'm surprised they haven't noticed the hot coals yet."

"I'll distract them," Morningstar offered. "Even if they suspect something, they couldn't know how many of us there are. If I run before they get to the camp, they may think it is only me."

"But what if they catch you!" Liyah protested.

"I'm better at finding my way through the woods and back again than any of you. They won't catch me."

"I dunno," Zack countered. "We should stick together."

"If we stick together, we will all be caught. When they begin following me, Zack, you take the others back around to the camp. Pick up our packs and head up the path toward the cabin. I'll lead them downstream then circle back. Meet you a ways up the path."

Zack complained. "But—"

"No buts. Move as soon as they begin following me," she commanded. She sprang out from behind the rock, running across their field of vision, then making a right—toward the stream.

One of the soldiers yelled something out. He began chasing Morningstar, shouting back to the others; they began jogging slowly behind, their rifles in hand.

Zack waited until they all had disappeared from view, then hustled Liyah and Kai Li back to camp.

Morningstar ran as fast as she could, unburdened by the backpacks, rifles, and stiff boots the soldiers had to deal with. She flew like the wind, her dark braids bouncing behind in the moonlight, her moccasins sweeping silently across the pine floor of the woods. Faster and faster she went, sailing between trees and around rocks, weaving her way a short distance from the stream and farther into the woods, never looking back.

The two closest soldiers ran as fast as they could but were losing ground. They could see her disappearing as she ran on, outdistancing them. They slowed their pace.

———

Zack, Kai Li, and Liyah began hurriedly breaking down the camp and gathering up their belongings. Zack helped Liyah with one of the packs and put the other on himself; he then scattered the coals from the fire, covered them with dirt, and led the way to the path—away from the soldiers and toward their final destination.

They moved along briskly, finally resting after a short time.

"What if s-she n-no come?" Kai Li asked Zack.

Zack paused, studying both of them. "We'll have to go on without her."

"We can't leave her behind," Liyah insisted.

"We have no choice."

"But Zack," Liyah implored.

"No point in worryin' now," Zack replied. "Let's wait here for a while, under cover of those rocks over there."

———

Thinking she had finally lost the soldiers, Morningstar slowed her pace and veered slightly to her right, circling back to locate the stream. From there she would be able to follow it back upstream, eventually meeting the path just beyond the camp.

The soldiers had already given up. They regrouped and headed back until they found themselves stumbling across the rocks lining the fire pit. They fanned out in a close circle to search the area, then returned after finding nothing.

Morningstar continued working her way through the woods, looping back toward the camp and hoping to find the stream. It was eerily dark in the woods, even with both moons above. Soon, her eyes caught the gleam of reflected light in the near distance. She moved toward it, and as she got closer, she could see it was the reflection of light upon water. She had found the stream.

She squatted down and brought some cool water to her lips. Wasting no time, she headed back up along upstream, then moved away from it toward the far side of the camp, closer to where she could rejoin the white stone path.

Passing a short distance from the camp, she didn't see any soldiers, nor could she see anyone along the path, a short distance away; she made her way to it, then set off at a quick pace to catch up with her friends.

After a few minutes of walking briskly along, she noticed forms up ahead, off to the side of the path, close to the stream; she counted seven in total, just standing there; she saw the glow of their uniforms. Slowing her pace, she moved off to the left of the path, keeping low and concentrating on not making a sound. At this distance they would likely hear the snapping of a twig, she thought.

She could now hear them talking in that foreign tongue, the one Kai Li had said would be Japanese, and she could see the uniforms more clearly, radiating red and gold in places, a strange blue light emanating from their hands and faces. In order to be certain that they wouldn't detect her, she moved farther away from the path, into the brush and trees, moving slowly, staying low, stepping carefully.

Assured she was a distance beyond them, she turned slightly to her right, seeking the path again. The woods were deathly quiet. She could hear only her breathing and the wind as it passed through the trees. She moved on. The gurgling of a brook again reached Morningstar's ears. She followed the sound to the stream, then stepped onto the path, breathing a sigh of relief.

Passing a large group of large rocks, she heard a soft. "Psst."

Morningstar turned her head to see Liyah, running onto the path, all smiles, her eyes beaming with happiness. Zack and Kai Li joined them as they embraced.

"Thanks for helping us get away," said Zack.

"Thanks for watching out for these two," Morningstar replied. "And for waiting."

They started up the path but hadn't gotten far when they saw dim greenish-yellow lights coming from the woods; they stopped. "It can't be them," Morningstar said. "They're behind us."

In an instant, a dozen or so ghoul-like figures emerged from the woods, walking slowly toward them, chatting away in Chinese and laughing loudly; a few of them bumped into and pushed each other like drunken pirates. They appeared to be fighting over a basketball, like boys at a playground—except it wasn't a basketball. It was a head.

The four watched in horror as the headless one tried to get his head back from three others, playing a kind of keep-away with it. The light from the moons pierced through them, pausing only briefly to provide some substance to their bodies and clothing, like the way the features of jellyfish are lit up by the sun's rays, giving form to their tentacles and filling their bodies with a semitranslucent gelatin, except this gelatin was multicolored.

The ghosts all wore different clothing: a few in prison uniforms—gray-green pants with orange shirts; a few in ancient military outfits, like the Mongols of old China; some were in ordinary peasants' clothes with the traditional cone-style broad-brimmed hats of the rice workers or junk sailors; a few looked like spiffy politicians, one wearing an armband with the modern Chinese flag as a symbol and one wearing an old army hat exhibiting the Chinese Red Army logo of the 1960s: a hammer and sickle.

There didn't seem to be a leader—more of a motley gang of thugs and trouble-minded bullies. They suddenly stopped and stared at the young visitors, still laughing and talking loudly, their yellowed teeth long and protruding like those of a skeleton, sunken purplish eyes bugging out of their gaping sockets. The one who was trying to get his head back finally retrieved it and was placing it back on his shoulders. Two others had removed their heads and were carrying them in the crook of their elbows, while one other had his head on backwards and was standing there with his eyes, and the back of his sandaled feet, facing the four fearful teens.

"Wu Tou Gui!" Kai Li shouted.

"Wu-what?" Zack demanded in a confused but commanding tone. The ghouls heard Kai Li and looked at him. Zack and the girls were all still walking backward very slowly as Kai Li stopped but kept talking.

"W-wu Tou! Wu T-tou Guuiii!" he said again. "They g-ghosts d-d-do bad things in l-life . . . many be-h-headed . . . m-must w-w-wander f- forever in n-night."

The ghouls looked around at each other; roaring laughter came from their ranks. One of the headless ones came forward and stood next to the one with his head on backwards. The backwards-headed ghoul pointed to the headless one and started talking in English to Kai Li. "Chen here lose his head. You have it?"

The ranks broke out in laughter again, slapping each other on the back and jabbering. Kai Li stood speechless, his mouth unhinged.

"What matter boy?" he continued. "Ghoul got your tongue?"

More hysterical laughter.

"You think we not speak English? We speak all languages. We kill all type people— not play favorites." He smiled a great ghoulish smile with his big rotten teeth.

There was more laughter, and nervous moving about by the other ghouls.

"You right, boy!" he added. "We Wu Tou Gui—the condemned. Some kill in olden days, like those—" he pointed back to the ones dressed like Mongols. "They ride with Genghis Khan . . . kill hundreds of thousands . . . women . . . children . . . all. When empire fall, they executed. And those—" he acknowledged the two carrying their heads and dressed in modern clothing. "They kill for money . . . or maybe just because. And the one with the armband with stars, he kill demonstrators in square and other people who make trouble for state. He and me die normal death, not beheaded. I surprised to be Wu Tu Gui. But someone who punish us all think different, maybe, heh?"

Kai Li said nothing. He just stared at the ghoul.

"Maybe you not know me?" the backwards ghoul asked. "I think maybe you too young . . . But I know *you*." He laughed an evil laugh.

The other ghouls began laughing again too, but the backwards ghoul rotated his head on his shoulders and glared at them, saying something in Chinese. He rotated his head back to Kai Li.

"You see," he continued, "someone I sentence to death. Not kill him myself. He professor at college . . . make trouble for government. That—"

He stopped suddenly, looking past Kai Li and the others. Soldiers began appearing on the side of the path, past some bushes; they caught the attention of the backward-facing ghoul. The soldiers noticed the ghouls a split second later. When they were within thirty yards, they stopped. The leader of the soldiers shouted something in Japanese. The ghouls got very agitated and started grumbling, talking to each other and pointing at the soldiers. The four turned around. There they were again: the Ri Ben Gui Bing. Now in clear view, the light from the moons illuminated their uniforms, ghostly with their incandescent glow—more uniform than man.

The leader stood there straight backed in his black military pants and jacket, a samurai katana at the ready across his hip, its pearl- and ruby-studded handle shooting rays of light into the dark night. His jacket radiated gold beacons through the wavy stripes on its cuffs and collar and the polished buttons down its front; on his head sat a ceremonial military hat, with shiny black visor and short tubular crown, complete with chinstrap—at its front a large plume, red and bushy at the base, airy white at the top.

Withdrawing the honed, polished, curved steel blade from its sheath, the leader waved it in the air above his head; bringing it forward, he then shouted something to the others. They all began marching up alongside the path, moving closer.

"Remember what we were told," Morningstar cautioned. "Stay on the path. Always on the path." She started stepping back, slowly.

Liyah whispered to Zack. "You remember when Kai Li told us about the dead soldiers?"

Zack kept staring straight ahead. He whispered back. "Yeah, a little. What about it? Now's not really the time, is it?"

"Well, I think he was talking about these soldiers."

"It was just some kind of ghost story." Zack replied, holding his finger to his lips.

"That's what I mean. He said they were soldiers from Japan who had invaded eastern China prior to World War II, killing many thousands of people—gruesome stories of death, rape, plunder, and suffering. He said that when the war ended, when the Japanese were defeated by the Americans, they went back to Japan, but the Chinese never forgot. They believe their bad spirits still roam the countryside at night looking for more victims. Kai Li also said his grandfather had a connection to those soldiers somehow."

"I still don't see how that is going to help us," Zack replied under his breath.

"They're just apparitions," Liyah insisted. "They aren't real."

"They look pretty real to me," Zack replied.

Kai Li was in the immediate path of the ghouls, and they were getting wild and more menacing. Liyah glanced at the soldiers and then the ghouls. She then called out to him.

"Kai Li," she said clearly, firmly, "there are no such things as ghouls and goblins. These soldiers are still dead and cannot harm you. And the ghouls are receiving their punishment; they have power over you only if you believe in them. The power to turn them away is yours. It's in your mind, Kai Li."

The backward-looking ghoul was still staring at Kai Li. He finally completed his sentence: "That professor was your father." Then he grinned a very foul grin.

Kai Li looked right into the hollow sockets of his eerie eyes. He blinked slowly, as if his brain was processing what he heard but was overloaded with the information. As his eyes opened again, his entire demeanor changed.

"This is not real, Kai Li," Liyah implored. "Don't believe in what you see . . . believe in me . . . believe in us . . . believe in your dad. Remember *him* and that we believe in you."

The ghoul with his head in his hand moved forward toward Zack who raised his hand with the knife in an attempt to scare him away. The ghoul kept coming. Zack lunged and slashed at the ghoul, but the knife, his hand, and his arm travelled right through it as if he were trying to cut through smoke. Zack took several steps back, dropping the knife. The ghouls stopped and laughed a threatening laugh.

Kai Li watched this happen out of the corner of his eye, not willing to look away completely from the backward-looking ghoul. It moved toward him. Liyah pleaded one last time. "It is your dad who is real."

Kai Li closed his eyes but held his ground. His thoughts travelled back in time to when he was little and walked along another path, holding his father's hand. And then in a stream of consciousness, like a blinking old-time movie, memories flashed before his eyes: moments of happiness when he rode atop his dad's broad shoulders and held onto his head, dinners with him and his mom, walks in the park. So many memories he had tucked far away into the recesses of his mind. Then his dad's face began to fade; the last image was of himself, tears rolling down his face by the side of a grave, his mother calling for him, "Come away, Kai Li. Time to go . . . Come be with me."

The ghoul's wavy form fully enveloped Kai Li. Zack and Liyah looked on in horror. Morningstar's attention had shifted to the soldiers behind them, fast approaching. She turned back, hearing Kai Li cry out, "D-daddy! D-daddy . . . Dad!" They saw him reaching out his arms, unafraid, joy his voice.

The soldiers had moved onto the path, now only a few steps away from the ghouls and the four comrades, when a thundering *whooosh!* sound swept above them; a great shadow blocked the moonlight, blackening the night sky. A gigantic object passed not ten feet above their heads—a massive serpentine body. It dipped lower, bearing down on the backwards-facing ghoul and the headless one who had attacked Zack, forcing them off the path. As this monstrous flying beast passed by, it flapped its gargantuan wings, casting the remaining ghouls high into the air, far above the trees, and into the forest.

The soldiers stopped dead in their tracks, their heads tilted up, following the serpent. As the beast passed by, it rose up in the air, tilting its giant wings, carving out a return path, as if it were a great phantom jet. The scales on the wings flashed deep purple in the moonlight; a long green tail, double forked at its end with yellow spears, swung behind, dangling between two huge stocky legs.

The beast completed a half circle and began its return dive, heading for the soldiers. The moons' glow now shone down on its front, illuminating an enormous orange head with short triangular ears, and a white patch between two large red eyes; its huge nostrils flared. It opened its mouth wide as it swooped down, exposing its bright white dinosaur teeth—a fiery red, double-forked tongue fell out over the teeth, like a panting wild dog.

The soldiers raised their rifles on command and fired at the flying serpent; they reloaded and fired again. The beast closed in, gliding, descending. Its elephant-like rear legs crushed two of the soldiers as its huge tail swept the others away—only the leader was left standing. The two ghouls who had been forced off the path turned their iridescent eyes toward it as it banked and readied another assault. Down it came again.

The leader took a pistol from its case at his side and started firing, waving his sword at the same time, yelling in Japanese. The great beast bore down on him and the two ghouls, its mouth open wide, its sharp white teeth gleaming. A short distance from its targets it rolled its red eyes and released a torrent of fire from its nostrils; the flames reached out like giant gas torches into the night air, melting the steel katana instantly, disintegrating the leader's hand and forearm. He let out a bloodcurdling scream. Turning its head to the side, the serpent let out another blast of fire and heat, vaporizing the two ghouls, leaving only a wispy gray column of smoke rising up from the ground.

The leader was still screaming at the loss of his arm as the beast passed overhead; it reached down with the claws of its short forelegs, snatching him up between the brass buttons on the front of his uniform and sweeping him into the air. Up, up rose the great serpent, like an eagle with its prey, beating and flapping up and over the treetops, until it was but a black silhouette against the high moons.

Morningstar, Liyah, and Zack had all fallen down to the ground to avoid all the swooping, flapping, fire, and wind. Kai Li had remained standing.

As Zack and Morningstar slowly stood up, Kai Li walked over to a shaken Liyah and helped her to her feet, then hugged her.

Zack and Morningstar heard Kai Li thanking Liyah for her belief in him. He was smiling and speaking with barely a hint of a stutter, and once again pushing his glasses back upon the bridge of his nose. They walked over and joined him and Liyah.

"Very wild . . . No?" Kai Li said.

Zack stared at him in disbelief. "Wild? That's all you have to say? You act as if nothin' happened here. A minute ago, you were a scared rabbit who thought he was about to be lunch for a pack of coyotes."

"Yeah, well . . . I figure out."

"Figured what out?" Morningstar asked.

"Liyah r-right," he grinned. "No such things as ghosts."

"Huh?" Zack replied, incredulous. "How can you say that? We *all* saw what just happened."

"Yah, but no real."

Zack shook his head. "You've really lost it." He turned to Morningstar and Liyah. "I think he's in shock."

"No s-shock. I hear things and see things when ghoul try to kill m-me."

"Like what?"

"Liyah right. I bring ghosts to us . . . you s-see them cuz you believe m-me, but these ghosts only my ghosts. Liyah t-tell me she believe in me. I call to my d-dad to help. He come."

Liyah remained silent, trying desperately to hold back her tears.

"Your dad?" Zack asked, confused. He looked around as if Kai Li's dad still might be there. The only thing he noticed was that all the soldiers and ghouls had disappeared, not even a trace left behind.

"And what about that monster?" Zack added. "Not real either?"

"No m-monster . . . dragon."

"Dragon?" Morningstar questioned.

Kai Li's eyes locked with Zack's. "No real like us. R-real in spirit."

Zack smiled. "It certainly looked real to me, man."

"Did you call it here?" asked Morningstar.

"Dragons great Chinese s-symbol. They good omen . . . m-mean hope . . . bring power and luck. They come when they n-needed. If believe . . . they know. I tell my dad I believe in him and good spirits, and in you three. I ask him to save you . . . s-send dragon for you."

Kai Li could see tears in Zack's eyes. "Besides," he added, "we safe on path anyway, r-right Zack?"

Morningstar bent down, picked up Zack's knife, then handed it to him. "C'mon," she said. "Let's get out of this forest."

Twenty-Two

———

WEARY AND HUNGRY, the four made their way in the moonlight along the white stone path, through the cool night air. Zack led the way, the hood of his sweatshirt pulled tight over his head, followed by Liyah, a blanket draped across her shoulders over her blue dress blazer; Morningstar, warmed by her long-sleeved tunic, checked behind her to make sure Kai Li, consumed by Zack's oversized denim jacket, was following closely.

The last of the moons began to sink below the treetops, and the faint beginning of twilight was upon them when they reached a fork in the trail; the path split in two opposite directions. Without the moonlight, and twilight still dim, they found the map difficult to read.

"What we do?" Kai Li asked Morningstar.

"Not sure," she replied. "Let me think."

"Isn't this the place where we started the loop?" Liyah asked.

Morningstar walked a short distance up the path to the right and turned around. "I believe you're right, Liyah. Good work. We go left here."

"Another Lakota," Zack commented, tapping Liyah on her shoulder and laughing. He passed by and headed up the path.

"We close now," Kai Li added.

———

Liyah looked down at her sandals, remembering the pain of the first days, the blisters and cuts, the fear, the tears. She looked around at the others, everyone seeming to be caught in their own thoughts. No one had spoken a word since they left the fork. Then suddenly the path opened into the small field behind the cabin, and the white stones ended. Kai Li rushed to the cabin, looked in the windows, then motioned wildly to the others. "No one here . . . C'mon!"

The door was open. Once inside they quickly removed the packs and set them in the same place they had found them so many days before. Nothing in the cabin had changed, with the exception of a new fire in the fireplace and food on the table. They sat down on the sofa and chairs, helping themselves: more energy bars, fruit, and some vegetables. Not fancy, but what they had become accustomed to over the last several days.

Liyah filled the cups from the packs with water from the pump in the bathroom. The only sound that filled the cabin was their chewing and the crackling of the fire. Kai Li finished eating first. He gathered all the envelopes from the backpack and brought them over to the wooden mailbox by the door.

Zack glanced over at him. "Hey, man. What's up? What are you doin'?"

"I put letters in box."

"Why?"

"We s-s'posed to, no?"

"What makes you think that?"

"Not f-find book. These all we have to give."

"Well go ahead, but I don't think anyone's coming to pick them up anyway," Zack answered, turning back, his voice trailing off in a disappointed tone.

A few seconds later, Kai Li let out a yell, startling the others. "It here!"

"What?" Liyah called back.

"O'zer letter!"

"What other letter?" Liyah asked him.

"Seven letter."

"Seven?" questioned Morningstar.

"Yah," Kai Li replied as he brought all the letters back to the table. "Must miss on m-map . . . in s-same box as first."

"Wonderful," Liyah exclaimed. "The letter, the fire, and the food must mean someone has come here for us, as promised."

"We still failed to bring back the book," Zack reminded her, pouring water on her enthusiasm.

"Well, sit back down, Kai Li, and let's read it," Morningstar said. "Liyah, why don't you do the honors?"

Kai Li handed the envelope to her, sliding it gently onto her palm. She ran her fingers gently over the papyrus-like paper, pausing briefly before opening it; she wanted to read the final words but felt the news might not be good. After a moment's hesitation, she removed the letter and took a deep breath. "Loving," she said. "That's the title of this letter." And then she continued without looking up at the others, reading the entire letter without interruption:

My Fellow Travelers:

Look upon these past days. Could you have completed your journey without the others? What have you seen? What have you learned?

Did you not expose your own weaknesses? Did you not face your fears and find them to be without substance? Did not your anger or judgments get in your way? Do you see that the path you were headed down before you came here would not get you where you needed to go?

Did you not witness the strength in the others as you traveled a new path? Did they not honor you with this? Do you see their light—and your own? Did you find love—for them, for yourself?

You have come a long way. You are almost home.

*The final state of being is **loving**. The Zah-re teaches that loving is the beginning and the end. We are born* as love but become lost, so the journey of our lives is one of finding ourselves again—of returning home, to love.

Without love, joy is not possible. With love, joy is automatic. The act of loving breaks the chains that bind the true self and frees the light of the universe. Because we were born as love, its spark still lies within us. Rekindling your light is the only way out of the **ego**, the **fearing**, the **suffering**—the darkness. Shining your light for others then becomes your natural mission in life. In this way, and only this way, we will all become what we were intended to be as individuals: whole.

The young child is born of innocence, absent of the false self's fears. She is born naked, and she has no expectations. She lives in the moment, with nothing, so **surrendering** has no meaning. Possessing nothing, she suffers no losses. She has not injured others, nor has she been injured, so there is no need of **forgiving**. She has only one identity—she is love.

How does this child of the universe become lost?

As we move down the road in the journey of our physical lives, we become entangled in a web of unknowing. We believe what we hear and what we see. We are unaware that this world we have entered, and the people upon whom we rely, have lost their way—lost the light.

Shadows begin to diminish our own glow, and the darkness moves in.

The further we go the more we get lost. We attach ourselves to possessions because we have not learned the lesson of what **having** means. We find ourselves unable to forgive. We lose the magic behind the gift of our birth—**our true selves.**

After a time, our ego—that false self—begins to rule our actions. It seems only when we are broken and desperate do we begin to question how we arrived to this point. Only then do we turn our eyes inward—toward the heart, seeking answers, looking for a way out of the darkness.

We learn that in order to keep our light, we must give up old notions. We must overcome the ego, and then we must begin **leading** others in their struggle to do the same.

Love fears not, has not, suffers not, and forgives all. It is the surrendering of all false beliefs. It is the state of oneness with everything—the natural way of the true self. As we reconnect, we once again find love, and light. Compassion springs automatically from this love—it conquers hate. Hate is born of fear and judgment, but compassion is the absence of both.

Love is the path of the white stones—the safe path. The only path. Love is truth and can speak no lies. Love is the light that defeats the darkness.

We must all learn how to love, because only in the presence of love do we survive. Love is central to all religions and spiritualities, as are compassion, caring, and connectedness—all of which come from love.

We are all of the same energy, the same beginning. This is the mystical truth that binds all beliefs and all spirits, living and past.

The little boy who loses his light in his journey to become a man must make the return journey. He must find again that which he has temporarily lost—he must become the child once more. It is there where his light resides. Until he does this, he will remain at sea . . . alone . . . with no safe harbor.

You, my children, my friends, my fellow travelers, have not yet been so far along your road that your journey back need be a difficult one. You have a chance to save your light, your life. You have a chance to lead the best life you can—a meaningful life, a joyful life—and let your light shine the way for others.

You have been chosen.

The tribes of the earth have forgotten that they are one. They have become separate. They, too, have become lost. They have not listened to the wise among them, those who have tried to guide them to the light. They have not listened to their hearts. They have renounced the mystical in favor of the ritual, replaced the divine with doctrine—turned their eyes from the sacred to a sacrament. Yet all is not lost. A great awakening stirs.

The kindling awaits the flame, and you are the spark.

You have a choice now. You can return home and live in a world you once knew. Or you can return home and free that world—the one that has been waiting so long, so long for someone to return with the light.

This is the challenge of your life. It is the challenge of every life. The people of Earth are so close, but they could still lose it all. The air is thick with energy and anticipation.

Blindness begs for the light. All that is needed is the light of a few to be passed on to others who in turn pass the light to even more. This will ignite the fire that will burn with the flame of love, and make the world bright, whole again.

You each have the same light, but different skills. If you choose to follow this path, it will take the strength of each of you, and all of you together, to reignite the flame. You will have to strive at this until the critical point is reached, and love is found.

This is the challenge to which you must rise.

You must not fail yourself. You must not fail each other. You must not fail.

Liyah placed the letter on the table. They sat there, quietly, watching the fire dance, listening to it snap, breathing in its smoky essence.

Zack broke the silence. "I think I finally see what he is trying to tell us," he said quietly, reflecting on all he had been through with his new friends. "I'm sorry for so many things. I don't know how I can help, but I'm willing to try."

Liyah put her hand on top of his. "I think we all have regrets, Zack. We've all been blind in our own way."

"Not know what letter m-mean by 'choice.' What we s'posed to do?"

"I don't know, Kai Li," Morningstar replied, "I don't know what we can do by ourselves, or how we are expected to act together. Maybe there is more to find out."

"There must be," added Liyah, taking her hand from Zack, then picking up the letter and searching through it, turning over the pages, as if she could find some missing clue.

Zack stood up and wandered over to the window. "How are we supposed to get out of here?" he said, staring out at the stream of smoke rising above the trees. "How will we ever get home?"

As Zach returned to his spot at the table, Kai Li went over to the mailbox. He had been thinking: Maybe if there was a pen, he could write a note, explain that they really tried—that they were sorry? An apology. Yes, maybe that could do it?

His fingers moved hastily, awkwardly, as he searched underneath the letters, fumbling around the bottom of the box. He tried again; no pen. He removed all the envelopes and began sorting through them, finally picking out one; not one of the seven, but the one that they found when they first arrived at the cabin. He opened the envelope, unfolded the pages, then scanned the writing, looking for something. Maybe a clue?

Liyah called over. "What are you looking for, Kai Li?"

"Jus' checkin'."

"For what?" asked Morningstar.

He kept reading, answering slowly. "Jus' somethin'."

There was a longer pause.

"That it!" he shouted.

"It?" Zack questioned.

"Kn-knowledge."

"Knowledge is what? What are you talking about?"

"Mean not b-book."

Morningstar was walking toward him with a quizzical look on her face. "Not the book?" she asked.

Zack looked over at the two of them. "Are you okay, Mr. Kai? I think maybe you're losing it again."

"No . . . Mean, *yes*."

Liyah let out a laugh. "Maybe you're right, Zack."

"It here, in letter," Kai Li replied. Morningstar looked over his shoulder at the letter as he continued. "Must read from *Zah-re*. Must all r-return together, o'zerwise no l-leave this place."

"No kidding," Zack replied. "Thanks for reminding us of the trouble we're in."

"No . . . w-wait . . . I finish. S-say something jus' 'fore that." The pages shook in Kai Li's trembling hands as he glanced back down at the words on the page. "It say in order to f-find way home m-mus' bring knowledge b-back. If return without, all p-perish."

"I don't follow you. How is that any different?" asked Liyah.

"Don't see?" Kai Li insisted. "It knowledge."

Zack kicked his heels up on the table and laid back in the chair. "Knowledge? I still don't get it."

"M-mean it not book . . . It knowledge!" Kai Li emphasized.

There was silence for a moment. "Yes, yes, I see," Liyah said, beaming. "All along we didn't have to bring back the actual *Book of Universal Truths*—just the knowledge."

"And the knowledge is with *us?*" asked Morningstar.

"Yes," Liyah added. "We have done all that was required. We made it through the Valley of Fear and all the trials, and we found the letters. They represent the knowledge from the *Zah-re*. And we returned together, carrying its meaning."

Zack sat back up. "That could be," he said, more energized. Then he sank back in the chair, sounding more depressed again. "If we did everything right, why aren't we home then?"

"Well, there is one positive thing though, isn't there?"

"What's that?" he asked.

"We have new friends!" Liyah replied, laughing.

"Yeah, well, I guess you're right about that," Zack agreed, smiling at her.

"And another thing," said Morningstar.

"And what is that, oh Wise One. . .?" teased Zack.

"We overcame many obstacles, and in the process, many fears. Don't you think?"

"Yup," agreed Kai Li. "She right. Not just dangers, but things we think we 'fraid of, no? Like the fire Morningstar took us through, right? And making it across that bridge . . . pretty scary, Zack. You made it through though, and actually help me be less afraid, too."

"And Liyah freaking out in The Caves then saving me," said Morningstar, chuckling.

Liyah jumped in. "Well, let's not forget about those creepy ghouls and soldiers, huh? I mean Kai Li conjured up his worst nightmares somehow, didn't he? Then ended up saving all of us . . . I think . . . like some sort of magician."

Zack let out a belly laugh. "And then there was the falls, too," Zack added. "Holy crap! I think we were all heroes then." He started laughing and laughing again and again, until he couldn't stop.

The laughter became contagious; they could hardly catch their breath.

After finally settling down, Morningstar joined Liyah and Zack at the table as Kai Li paced back and forth between the table and the fireplace, staring down at the floor. He finally settled back down in his chair and picked up the small wooden box that still sat on the middle of the table from when they had first gotten there. He took the letter from his pocket, unfolded it.

"No more clue," he said to the others. He tried to put it back in the box, but the box was locked. He tipped the box on its side; there was the key, once again taped to the bottom. He removed it and started to insert it into the keyhole.

Morningstar had been watching him. "That means someone may have put something else in the box," she said, matter of fact.

"What does?" Liyah questioned.

"We didn't put the key back on the bottom of the box," replied Morningstar. "We left it on the table."

"That's right," Zack agreed.

Liyah clasped her hands together as if in prayer. "Praise Allah. Maybe there is hope. Maybe someone's still here . . . the person who brought the food and started the fire."

"Well, that may be," replied Zack, "but I'd hold off on any praises right now."

Kai Li was so absorbed with the box that he had not taken in a word of their conversation. He turned around, holding the box in his hand. He stared at the others, eyes wide open.

"Oh, no," said Liyah. "What is it now?"

"M-more in box."

"You're kidding? What?" Zack asked.

"M-more env'lopes . . . an' a few s-small box."

Liyah's jaw dropped. "Please no more tasks. I couldn't . . ."

"Take them out, Kai Li," Morningstar interrupted. "Let's get it over with."

Kai Li removed the envelopes from the box and returned the map and *Loving* letter in their place. He counted five envelopes and five small boxes. Four of the envelopes and boxes each had a number from one to four marked on them. The fifth box had an *X* marked on it; on the other envelope was written, *Open First*.

216

Kai Li picked out the envelope marked *Open First*, leaving everything else on the table next to the box. He slid his finger inside the envelope, lifting out the flap, reached in, and removed the letter. He handed it to Morningstar.

Morningstar glanced quickly at the others, then began to read:

> *Congratulations to all of you. You have come a long way, and you have done well. You will be returning home soon, but there are a few things you need to know.*
>
> *What you have been through was designed to enlighten you—to make you wiser, and to heal you. You have found great strength in yourself and your fellow travelers. You have found the Seven States of Being within the words of the Zah-re. And you have returned with that knowledge.*
>
> *These are also the messages of your great prophets. The words represent the path into the light. Cherish them and share them—always.*
>
> *Before we prepare for your return home, I would like to present you with a few gifts to take with you in remembrance of your journey but also to help you along your way in an even greater journey. It is your choice whether to accept the challenge that comes with them.*

Morningstar placed the letter on the table, but before any of them could speak, a low vibrating sound filled the room. It grew quickly louder, its pitch higher and higher—like an airplane engine revving up. They looked around at each other, simultaneously covering their ears. The noise stopped. Morningstar, Liyah, and Kai Li looked over at Zack, who was staring toward the hallway, his face pale, eyes wide. They turned toward the hall.

There, not more than ten feet away, a shimmering, multicolored light emanated from a translucent egg-shaped orb about eight feet high and four feet wide. Its surface was aglow in a purple-blue haze, then the color then changed to a beautiful green and then to yellow as it moved inward. Around the center the most brilliant of reds sparkled, and at the very center itself, was the purest white light. The object now emitted a steady buzzing sound, barely audible.

"Jeez!" breathed Kai Li.

Twenty-Three

A VOICE EMANATED from within the orb as it moved closer to the fireplace. "Welcome," it said, in a scratchy, high-pitched tone. "I do not mean to frighten you. I am Ooray. I have come to guide you safely home." As it spoke, its form changed in resonance with the pitch of the voice, like an amoeba, but glowing with radiant light, its colors constantly mixing and pulsating.

Kai Li, Morningstar, Zack, and Liyah all remained silent, awestruck, staring blankly.

"I see you are overwhelmed," it continued, the voice now more steady, more decipherable, more feminine. "This is understandable. You have come a long way . . . not only in distance, but also as friends. You have been through much together. Yet the journey is not over. The time is short, and for the people of Earth there is much to be done."

It paused.

"I come here from a far place, sent to prepare you for the greatest journey of your lives: the mission to rescue your fellow humans from a living death and from ultimate destruction. The four of you have been chosen to open a door for them to a better way, a way of peace and joy . . . in harmony with the intentions of the universe."

The four glanced sideways at each other, afraid to look fully away.

The orb continued. "The first gift is for you, Zack. Liyah, please open the box and the letter marked with the number one and present the gift inside the box to him, then read the letter out loud to the group."

Liyah stood up, her hands shaking, and approached the table. She gingerly picked up the box along with the associated letter, lifted the lid gently, then removed the protective material surrounding the object within; she withdrew a pendant, attached to a silver necklace. The incredible beauty of it stunned her: a deep blue sapphire gem the size of a quarter, in the shape of a heart, countless facets on its face reflecting the light from the fire, causing it to shimmer like a blue diamond.

Turning to Zack, Liyah slowly lowered the pendant until it dangled from the chain, visible to all. Kai Li gasped. He placed his fingers below the stone; supporting it ever so gently then raised it to his eyes for better inspection. "Word, ins-side," he said, looking at Zack.

Zack bent down, studying it; inside the sapphire pendant, were two words, silvery in color, attached together: "TrueHeart." The words floated, as if suspended in water.

"Wow," Zack said, taking it from Liyah and holding it for her and Morningstar to see. As he rotated it for them, to their amazement, the words appeared the same, not sideways or backwards . . . no matter what the angle or who was looking at it.

"It reminds me of the magic kit I got when I was seven," said Morningstar. "But I think this one is real."

Liyah took the necklace back from Zack and slipped the chain over his head. The jewel rested against Zack's chest; its deep blue light reflected in the golden cross in Zack's ear. While Kai Li and Morningstar sat silent, mesmerized by the stone, Liyah took up the envelope with the *1* marked on it, slid her fingers inside and retrieved the letter, and placed the envelope back on the table; then, diverting her eyes from it, she scanned the faces of her friends waiting in breathless anticipation, their eyes bouncing back and forth between the stone and the orb.

Before Liyah could start reading, the orb spoke again.

"You have come far, Zack. You have been lost in the streets of a great city, yet you never lost yourself. You reflect the terrible pain that city has experienced, but you now have a chance to save it. It is burdened by a great darkness and the people are suffering. For so many there, their world is broken, and they cannot fix it by themselves. Hope has dimmed in their lives. You can bring back the light that will overcome the darkness . . . there and in other cities.

"All this time, in your heart, you have protected the message of Jesus: of peace, love, and compassion. You hid it so well that you had forgotten it at times yourself . . . to fight your battles in the streets, at school, and in your home. You were tough, but only because you had to be. Your gentle heart remained safe . . . behind a false facade.

"You hid your true self. But you survived where many others fail. Through your new friends here, and the challenges you overcame with them, and by yourself, you found what it really means to be strong. And you have added their strength to yours.

"You have shown great courage, Zack. You dared to look within and rescue the child. And you have proven your ability to lead others, to have them follow you along the right path. Above all, you have opened your heart and found it to be the heart of Jesus . . . as it always was . . . as it always will be."

There was a pause. Kai Li and Morningstar looked at Zack and Liyah, mouths agape.

Ooray spoke again. "Listen now to the words of Liyah. Go ahead, Liyah."

A mist surrounded Liyah's eyes. She brought the letter up and began to read, slowly, clearly. "'Behold the TrueHeart, protector of self and beacon of love. You have earned the right to wear this, if you so choose. You will forever be in its care, and it in yours. From this day forth you will be both its guardian and its disciple. You will be charged with delivering its message to the world and protecting its radiance for future generations. It comes to you with a price, paid dearly by all those who came before, upon whose shoulders you now stand. If you accept this TrueHeart and the responsibility associated with it, look into the eyes of the one who reads this to you and repeat the following.'"

Zack was ready. For the first time in his life, he felt truly certain; there was no hesitation. He looked into Liyah's eyes and nodded his head; she returned a smile, eyes tearing up. She glanced down again at the letter and read, "'I, Zack.'" She waited.

"I, Zack."

"'Following in the greatness of those before me, accept this TrueHeart,'" Liyah continued, looking again at the paper and then back at Zack.

"Following in the greatness of those before me, accept this TrueHeart." Zack repeated.

"'I accept it as a symbol of the power of love over fear, and the strength of compassion,'" Liyah said, their eyes lingering for a moment.

Zack now stood before her like a sentinel, shoulders squared and pressed back, legs locked together, arms down by his side, head rigid like a statue, and his eyes fixed on hers. "I accept it as a symbol of the power of love over fear, and the strength of compassion."

Liyah paused for an instant, overwhelmed by the transformation happening before her very eyes; she was drawn fully into the ceremony. Her eyes softer, her voice quietly confident, she continued, "'I shall protect it always, holding its message forever in my heart.'"

"I shall protect it always, holding its message forever in my heart," Zack replied, without hesitation.

Their eyes locked once again. Liyah looked away, overwhelmed by the power of the connection. Could this be the same Zack she met less than a week ago? She looked back at him, her face aglow with the pride she felt toward him. Her eyes welled with tears. "'And share its power,'" she said.

Zack looked into her eyes and found the same connection. He was caught off guard. He paused, then repeated the words confidently, slowly, losing himself in the moment, "And share its power."

Lost in his gaze, tears began to roll down Liyah's cheeks. She thought she could see his soul shining brightly through the windows of his eyes: the proud soldier, the conqueror of fear, the holder and protector of the TrueHeart. He had accepted love and compassion as his guiding star—the transformation was complete.

Zack strained to collect himself, thinking his insides were falling apart. His hands began to tremble, his knees weakened. He could no longer avoid the message in Liyah's eyes: their souls were now connected. His body remained poised, but his soldier's heart was melting. He reached his hands out gently to meet hers. Tears suddenly poured down his face.

Liyah flung her arms around his neck. She hugged him as if she were seeing a lost loved one after too many years apart.

Once settled, they sat back down and faced Ooray.

"The second box and letter are for Morningstar," Ooray said to them. "Kai Li, present the gift to her. Morningstar, please stand for Kai Li."

The envelope with *2* marked on it was in Kai Li's excited hands in seconds; he removed its contents, glanced it over briefly, set it on the table, then picked up the box and opened it. He lifted up a silver necklace. *Very plain, simple,* he thought at first, but nonetheless beautiful. As he looked at it more closely, however, he noticed it consisted of thousands of little pieces.

Kai Li removed his glasses and held them up to it, just as he had done with the map, days before. While appearing as a solid chain to the naked eye, it was actually a network of little stars, all of the same size, each one connected to the six neighboring stars in a kind of three-dimensional grid. Then he noticed something even more amazing: Each star moved freely in the space surrounding it—they seemed attached somehow, but without any direct connection, and no seams. *How is that possible?*

Stunned, Kai Li looked at Morningstar. "'Mazing!" he blurted out, handing it to her, along with his glasses. "Made of s-stars. Check out . . . float f-free."

Morningstar inspected it, using his glasses as magnifiers, then passed the set over to Zack and Liyah.

Before anyone else reacted further, Ooray began to speak. "As living beings across this universe gain the capacity to wonder, they inevitably search for the meaning of life. They look to the stars, and for answers from their gods. They develop sciences to understand how changes in chemistry and physical properties created life. And they send probes into the darkness of space to seek other life forms, hoping the answer may be there.

"I am part of that search, begun from another place in another galaxy. We continue to search to understand the meaning of life and the origin of universes. In the course of our search, we have gained much knowledge, but found no answers.

"This journey has brought me to many places, such as your Earth. I would like to tell you that I have the answers to save you the time—

to let your minds rest in peace. But I do not have those answers. I can only tell you what I have found, and that is simply this:

"The capacity for intelligence inevitably creates an explosion in knowledge, which leads to longer life spans, faster transportation, as well as a great assortment of *things* . . . things to own . . . things to distract the mind. But the source of knowledge seems to be a bottomless well. The more we know, the more there is to know, and the more we feel we *need* to know. The tendency for intelligent beings is to move away from their fear by occupying their time with the search for knowledge, and the pursuit of things—the hope being that ultimately knowledge, and understanding the meaning of life, will bring joy. While this is a truly noble and worthy effort, it can also be a deception.

"Your ancestors, Morningstar, brought you a great gift. Like all humans, they were filled with wonder about their universe. They gazed up in amazement at your moon and stars. And they thought about how they arrived there . . . and where their spirit would go when it was time to give up their bodies. But they were not confused by many possessions, of distant travel, or of the increasing complexity of the world.

"Their lives, while considered less civilized by those who took their lands, were just simpler. Your grandfather was right. Their advantage was they were not distracted by *fear* or *having*, so they had more time for *being* and understanding what that meant. They spent their time living, connected to all their *relations*. They were not savages, not ignorant, not uncivilized. They were observers. They were closer to their true selves than most other humans are today.

"Your ancestors knew that each individual is unique, a special envoy of the Great Spirit. But they also understood that all things are connected, that the mountains, the trees, the animals, and the people all existed in a special harmony—that all nature is one, and that it has always been this way, and will forever be this way. By communing with nature, and respecting all their relations, they came to know this in their hearts. They found awe in the rising sun, peace in the starlit sky, and love in every moment. This *oneness* is the gift they brought to you, and to everyone.

"The spirits of the dead are indeed to be revered, as your ancestors believed. By honoring them we honor ourselves, and we accept our special place in the fabric of life. The spirits of those who came before and those who come after are eternally connected. There is no beginning, and there is no end. In this sense your grandfather and your parents are also time travelers, like me. They are here with you . . . and you with them.

"So, Morningstar, it is this same gift I ask that you give to others. You are connected to your ancestors and to all your relations—to all that came before. And you must be the bridge to all that will follow."

Morningstar's eyes welled up; she was on the brink of tears but held them back. The only tears she had cried since her father and mother died were the few that left their tracks in the dirt on her face, when the tornado destroyed all that was left in her life.

"Kai Li," Ooray added, "please present the gift to Morningstar, and read the letter."

Kai Li took the necklace from Liyah and placed it around Morningstar's neck, then took a step back and looked at her in admiration. His hands trembled as he picked up the letter and nervously began to read. "'Morning-s-star, b-behold the Web of L-life, messenger of con-connectn-ness, and s-symbol of circle of l-life . . . life with n-no begin or end.'"

He looked up at Morningstar for an instant, embarrassed, and then down again to the paper. "It very l-long," he said.

Liyah got up and came over to him. She took the letter from him and began to read. "'Morningstar, you have earned the right to wear this Web of Life and, if you so choose, you will forever be in its care, and it in yours. From this day forth you will be both its guardian and its disciple. You will be charged with delivering its message to your world and protecting it for future generations. It comes to you with a price, paid dearly by all those who came before, upon whose shoulders you now stand. If you accept the Web of Life, and the responsibility associated with it, look into the eyes of the one who reads this to you and repeat the following.'"

Taking her seat, Liyah turned the letter over to Kai Li.

"Go on, Kai Li," Morningstar said softly. "I'm ready. You'll be fine."

Kai Li continued, self-conscious of his stuttering. "'I. . .M-m S-star 'cept this Web of L-life.'" He lifted his eyes to her.

"I, Morningstar accept this Web of Life" she repeated, eyes forward, posture straight but relaxed.

Kai Li focused his attention again on the letter, his eyes darting back and forth trying to recapture where he had left off, the delay making him more nervous, his stutter worse. "'I 'nowledge it as s-symbol of c-connect n-ness of all th-things.'"

Morningstar paused, waiting for Kai to return eye contact. He continued to stare at the piece of paper in his hands until the silence became deafening. He tilted his head up to see if there was a problem; their eyes met again. Morningstar smiled. "I acknowledge it as a symbol of the connectedness of all things," she repeated, more slowly this time, taking in the meaning of the words.

Kai Li continued reading, "'And of l-life ev-l-lasting, without b-begin or-or end.'" *Why can't I even seem to read a short sentence out loud without stuttering and stammering badly?* He glanced up at Morningstar, apologetic.

Morningstar's eyes met his. She took his hand. "And life everlasting, without beginning or end," she repeated. He could feel the power of their connection. After his run-in with the ghouls, his stutter seemed to disappear, he seemed strong like that, but now, with this nervousness, it was back. He felt himself melting.

"I so s-sorry," he said, tears forming in the corners of his eyes.

"Shh," she whispered. "It's all right. It doesn't matter."

He brought the letter up, took several slow deep breaths, and continued. "'I p-protect it always.'"

"I will protect it always," she stated, her heart full of the pride of a warrior.

"'Keepin' it m-message ever in h-heart.'"

"Keeping its message forever in my heart," followed Morningstar.

"An' share it power.'"

Morningstar stood tall, eyes flashing. "And share its power."

With her thumbs she wiped the moisture from under Kai Li's glasses, put her arms around him, and hugged him. "Thank you, Kai, you were wonderful. Thank you for being you."

"S-star. You my true f-friend. I love you."

They turned to see the smiling faces of Liyah and Zack.

Ooray spoke again. "The next one is for you, Liyah. Morningstar, please present the gift."

Kai Li took his seat. Morningstar picked up the envelope with the number *3* marked on it, opening the box, as Liyah joined her; she removed another necklace, holding it by its silver chain.

Dangling and twisting at the end of the chain was a crystalline jewel about the size of an olive, shaped like a water droplet. It was deep blood-red in color; its many facets sparkled.

Liyah couldn't believe how truly breathtaking it was. She bent down slightly to accommodate Morningstar as she slipped the necklace over her head.

Ooray addressed Morningstar. "Before you read, I would like to say something about this gift. Resting against your chest, Liyah, is the Timeless Teardrop. It has been forged by the anguish and pain of all those who have come before. Each facet of its surface reflects the suffering that is the history of humankind. The source of its light can be found in every sickness, every heartbreak, every pain, and every sadness that has ever existed, recounting for all humanity its tortuous journey.

"It is a reflection of that pain but also a symbol of hope. It reminds us that we all share this history of suffering. No race, nor any society, is free from the shadow of suffering, yet all have been responsible for its cause. Wars, the mean-spirited abuse of power, religious fervor and persecution, greed, fear, retribution, and blindness to our oneness has been universal. From the first human tribes to the most sophisticated of modern societies, humans continue to inflict needless suffering upon their fellow relations.

"Your people, Liyah, know this as well as any. They have had grievous pain inflicted on them throughout their history, and many now seek to revenge this pain on others. But they are not alone.

"The facets of the Timeless Teardrop reflect the power struggle of dominant males during early human evolution, the clash between hunter-gatherers and the move toward civilization, the religious intolerance between all faiths, and the wars over political boundaries.

"Blood, torture, death, meanness, iniquity, and inequity flow from the pores of all mankind, from feudal manors, from Chinese empires, from Greek city-states, from the Roman Colosseum, from British colonialism, from the Spanish conquistadors, from Irish terrorists, from Japanese aggression, from the Soviet prisons, from Germany's death camps, from American slavery and the treatment of their Indigenous brothers and sisters . . . and on and on. The Timeless Teardrop signifies all this.

"No one is innocent, and no one left untouched. When we behave like this, we hurt only ourselves, and most importantly, our collective, most precious children—teaching them fear and hate. And so, the cycle goes on. Liyah, this is your history, and the history of your friends who stand here by your side. If you choose, you can help lead them, and those whose lives you will touch, away from this dark path and into the light, through compassion.

"I have chosen you, Liyah, for this gift because you have shown compassion toward your brother in his growing years, and now his troubled years. You saw in Zack his potential for goodness even when you couldn't understand his roughness. You believed in Morningstar from the moment you met her. And you helped Kai Li believe in himself in his hour of need. You show it each day by honoring people in every way. You are a symbol of hope."

Ooray paused. "Go ahead, Morningstar."

Morningstar smiled at Liyah and began reading. "'Liyah, behold the Timeless Teardrop, formed from the tears of the multitude— every tear ever cried over the course of human history. It is now time in the journey of mankind to come into the light. Suffering has reached a flashpoint. The guilt and burden of the pain belongs to all, but the weight is too heavy to bear any longer. You can help others see this, and lead them on the path out of suffering, through awareness, understanding, compassion, and forgiveness.

"'I ask you, Liyah, to accept this Timeless Teardrop, the symbol of human suffering, and the ending of that suffering. If you so choose, you will be forever in its care, and it in yours. From this day forth, you will be both its guardian and its disciple. You will be charged with delivering its message to your world and protecting its radiance for future generations. It comes to you with a price, paid dearly by all those who came before, upon whose shoulders you now stand.

"'If you accept the Timeless Teardrop and the responsibility associated with it, look into the eyes of the one who reads this to you, and repeat the following.'"

Liyah shifted her eyes over at Zack, who winked at her; then Kai Li, who gave her a thumbs-up; and back to Morningstar. She took in a deep breath, then nodded.

Morningstar continued. "'I, Liyah, accept this Timeless Teardrop, symbol of suffering and hope.'"

"I, Liyah, accept this Timeless Teardrop, symbol of suffering and hope," she repeated nervously.

Morningstar studied the next words, then looked up, her eyes locking with Liyah's. "'Its reflections will be a reminder of that senseless suffering.'"

"Its reflections will be a reminder of that senseless suffering," Liyah said, her voice more sure.

"'Of all people from all nations,'" Morningstar continued.

While Liyah's nervousness had faded, her emotions were beginning to rise. She thought about those words, of how people from every country throughout history had experienced not only sadness from hellish wars, but also sickness, poverty, and pestilence; as she looked into Morningstar's eyes, she saw this reflected in the stories of the Lakota and all First Nations people.

"Of all people from all nations," she repeated.

As Morningstar looked at the next words, she, too, thought of all the Indigenous nations, often in combat with each other over the many years, even before the white settlers arrived, and of the great nations of the world still living with the remnants of hate and retribution. Then memories of her parents and her grandfather infiltrated her mind. She fell silent.

Morningstar collected her thoughts and gazed into Liyah's eyes. "'And the believers of all faiths,'" she said, quietly, softly, her voice trailing off as her own emotions, long buried, began to emerge; she had tried for so hard to deny her feelings—feelings resulting from deep wounds, bearing great pain, and suffocating her happiness.

Liyah was now truly beginning to fall apart. Her mind wandered home to her family and friends, to all the people of Palestine, to Islam—her own faith . . . then to the sworn enemies of her people, the Jews. She thought about how strongly they believed in their faith too, and how much pain had been inflicted by both Palestine and Israel on each other. And then suddenly visions of the Holocaust filled her head:

the mass starvation, torture, and death of harmless people, people no different than her, or Morningstar. *After all, we are all connected, aren't we? The believers of spirits, the wanderers without a home, the First Peoples, the Palestinians, the Jews . . . her and Morningstar. All that suffering . . . and it continues still.* Liyah's eyes welled up with tears.

Morningstar saw the reflection of this in Liyah's eyes. She tried to look away but was unable. A strong, unbreakable magnetic force drew them together.

"And the believers of all faiths," Liyah managed to repeat.

Morningstar had memorized the next words but couldn't get them out. They were blocked. She didn't understand the emotions that were overwhelming her. She tried to remember when she had felt like this before but couldn't. Her whole body began to tremble from within. She was letting go. So much had been kept inside for too long. She forced herself to continue, and as she did, Liyah could sense her pain.

"'And all the innocent children, throughout the world, over all t-time,'" she finally said, haltingly, stammering.

"And all the innocent children, throughout the world, over all time," Liyah repeated.

Morningstar's thoughts shifted again to her grandfather, and suddenly she could no longer hold back. Tear drops began to trickle from her eyes, then forming a stream over her cheeks. No longer able to maintain eye contact with Liyah, she bowed her head in great sadness.

Seeing her friend in such pain, Liyah forgot her own sadness; gaining great strength from her desire to be there for Morningstar, she put her own emotions on hold. Reaching out her hand, she gently lifted up Morningstar's chin until their gaze fixed once more on each other.

Morningstar looked into the mirror of her friend's eyes and saw her own face, tears streaming. She could feel the kindness beaming from Liyah like a beacon. She finally knew it was okay—okay to grieve for her parents, for her grandfather; okay to be sad for the children; okay to be weak at this moment, to need her friends.

Smiling through the tears, Morningstar pressed her hands against Liyah's face. Kai Li and Zack, concerned about the long silence, and unable to see Morningstar's face, stood up and moved toward them. "You okay, Star?" asked Zack as they neared. Morningstar turned and flung her arms around him, then Kai Li. Seeing her tears for the first time, the boys were speechless; they remained at her side for a few moments, until Liyah signaled to them that everything was okay.

As Morningstar's tears subsided, she picked up the letter she had dropped on the floor in the middle of everything. "'I will keep its message forever in my heart,'" she said, then looked up at Liyah. Liyah's eyes were clear. *She looks radiant*, Morningstar thought. *She has been reborn.*

"I will keep its message forever in my heart," Liyah replied, carrying herself with pride, with the voice of a leader.

"'And share its power,'" Morningstar added, finishing.

"And share its power."

Morningstar hugged her. The boys came up and did the same. Liyah then tapped Kai Li and pointed. Without a word, Kai Li knew exactly what to do; he retrieved the letter and box marked *4*. He then turned around to face the others. As he did so, Zack held out his hand. "You might as well give it to me to read, obviously. And the gift must be for you." Kai Li knew Zack was right. *How am I going to get through this?* But after watching the others, he had gained some renewed confidence. He started concentrating on his breathing.

The girls moved over to the sofa to sit down while Zack read to Kai Li. Zack tore open the end of the envelope, slid the letter out the side, and unfolded it. He set the letter on the table, then opened the box.

"Another jeweled necklace," he said as he lifted it by its chain up to the level of his eyes. "And, of course a magnificent one at that." He showed to the others.

The jewel was about the same size as the TrueHeart and Timeless Teardrop but was colorless—a crystal in the shape of a torch. The setting for the crystal began as a pointed handle, then widened as it flared up over the base of the crystal, creating silver flames; the crystal itself was also in the shape of a flame.

Zack held the crystal high, studying it as it caught the light, sparkling in brilliant reflections of all the colors of the rainbow—millions of specks of light bursting from all sides in a dazzling array. Together the silver base and diamond-like flame created a torch of absolute beauty. The chain was secured to opposite sides of the base at the very top of the silvery setting, so that as it was draped around the neck, the torch would always be upright.

Zack placed it over Kai Li's neck, then picked the letter up off the table.

Ooray, who they seemed to have totally forgotten for an instant, began speaking again. "Kai Li, behold the Torch of Truth. Its flame shines pure light from all the universes since the beginning of time. It is a symbol of enlightenment. In its presence, only truth can be seen or told.

"All knowing beings in all the galaxies are on a great search. They seek to understand who they are . . . why they are . . . what *everything* is . . . and why *anything* is. In a seemingly impossible quest for this elusive knowledge, they elevate the entire human species, helping it rise from the muck of its ancient beginning. The great individuals who risked their livelihoods and lives in this pursuit are the torchbearers of wisdom. They are the teachers and the preachers. They bring us the message of truth, and in the process, they help reconnect us to our spirit.

"Knowledge is a wonderful gift, because once truth is discovered, it is no longer lost. Each piece of new knowledge creates a stair upon which we all can stand, and from there we are able to reach the next step. It is a wondrous progression that leads us all to better understanding of our important position in the cosmos, and our importance to each other. Knowledge is also collective. What is learned over time is like a rising body of water, lifting everything along with it.

"There are many men and women throughout human history that have brought enlightenment to the world. Oftentimes they are unappreciated, or even persecuted. Through great personal sacrifice they have taken others to that next stairstep. Their message may be centered in medicine, physics, art, philosophy, or any other discipline. It can be either scientific or spiritual. The enlighteners shine the light of truth in the darkness. They show us the way.

"A great share of many of these enlightened ones come from your close ancestors, Kai Li. There is much wisdom in the ways of the East. I have chosen you to carry the Torch of Truth forward, to take it from those who carried it before you . . . to raise it high . . . to shine its light for all to see. Each time you light the way for another they are then able to do the same for someone else. In this way the light of truth will bring the world out of the terrible darkness of ignorance and fear. It will take the collective knowledge of all to unleash the full power of the light.

"This light can be given to everyone, and anyone can be the passer of the light. This is the message you must carry. This day I give the torch to you."

Zack began to read from the letter.

"'Kai Li, your passionate pursuit of knowledge and your unfailing belief in the path of truth has not gone unnoticed—the light is already within you. I ask you to accept the Torch of Truth, the symbol of knowledge and enlightenment, shining forth the light of the universe. If you so choose, you will be forever in its care, and it in yours. From this day forth, you will be both its guardian and its disciple. You will be charged with delivering its message to your world and protecting its flame for future generations. It comes to you with a price, paid dearly by all those who came before, upon whose shoulders you now stand. If you accept this Torch of Truth and the responsibility associated with it, look into the eyes of the one who reads this to you and repeat the following.'"

Zack took his cue, lifting his eyes from the page to meet with Kai Li's. Kai Li was fidgeting, his eyes darted to the side when they first made contact with Zack's but returned. Kai Li took his finger and pushed his glasses back firmly onto the bridge of his nose; a few beads of sweat appeared on his forehead. He knew *this* was not going to be easy.

Zack looked at the letter, slowly reading the first line. "'I, Kai Li, accept this Torch of Truth, symbol of knowledge and beacon of truth.'"

Kai Li drew the fabric from his pant legs between his thumbs and forefingers and began playing with it. "I, K-K," he began, then stopped. He concentrated again on his breathing, turning to see the girls; both were smiling broadly, nodding. He faced Zack.

"Hey, Kai-bo," Zack said under his breath, then winked. "Where'd you go?"

It caught Kai Li by surprise. He paused a moment, then smiled, and winked back. Without hesitation he replied, focusing like a laser on each word. "I Kai Li, accept . . . this . . . T-torch . . . of . . . Truth . . . symbol . . . of . . . knowledge . . . b-beacon of truth."

Zack smiled again. Kai Li grinned.

Zack continued. "'By its light, the path will be illuminated.'"

"By light, path w-will be luminated." A warm feeling radiated through his bones . . . his stuttering fading.

"'And universal truths unveiled.'"

"An' universal t-truths unveiled."

"'I will keep its message forever in my heart,'" Zack read, then looked up to see Kai Li, eyes bright, demeanor calm yet confident.

With a clear voice he repeated, "Will keep message forever in heart."

Zack took a step back, stunned, his face at first serious, then softening. They stood in silence. Zack could sense the strength within Kai Li; it radiated outward, filling the room. There was a subtle exchange between the two of them—a slight movement of the eyes, the softening of their faces, a hint of a smile. It was a silent conversation, held between two males throughout the ages, an implicit understanding. They were bound together—brothers.

Zack nodded, then spoke the last line. "'And share its power.'"

"And share its power."

The two embraced.

Liyah and Morningstar, who had sat quietly through the whole exchange, rushed up to join the boys, in tears. They hugged then broke out into great excitement, laughing and all talking at the same time.

In the middle of all the commotion, Kai Li suddenly remembered that there was still one more box to be opened. He went over to the table, picked up the remaining box, marked with the number 5, and turned to face the others. "Almos' forget . . . one more."

"You have come to the end of your journey here," Ooray said to them. "It is time for you to go home. During your short time here, you have all become what you were always capable of being. The light within each of you beams outward. Through each other you have learned that the same light resides in everyone, no matter how hidden or dim it may be. It is the light of the universe. It represents the essence of all life. It is a message of hope and joy . . . and it belongs to all.

"You have accepted a great challenge. Your mission is to bring forth the inner light that every person possesses, so that your world, and the whole universe, can share in its glow. The message you will bring is that of the salvation of *joy*. While this may seem impossible to you, I have provided each of you with the tools to accomplish this task.

"By now, you should realize that within you, you have the power to affect great healing. You have already healed yourselves and each other. You are stronger, and more whole, than you have ever been, and together you are even stronger. I have provided you with something else to protect and guide you on your next journey. You will find these in that box marked 5 in Kai Li's hands."

Kai Li didn't waste a second. He opened the box and lifted out its contents: four identical bracelets. He laid them on the table.

"There is one bracelet for each of you," continued Ooray. "Please put them on."

Each took one of the bracelets and placed them around their wrists.

"If you look closely at these, you will notice that the band is the Web of Life, cast of the same material as Morningstar's necklace, but wider, and thicker. Attached to each bracelet are smaller versions of all three jewels: the TrueHeart, Timeless Teardrop, and Torch of Truth. The original Web of Life that you wear, Morningstar, along with the necklaces, have special powers. By holding them before the eyes of others, its meaning will be realized by the one who looks at its light; they will then be able to help carry the message of the light to others. In addition, the light from the four gifts has powerful protective qualities. The reflected light can be transformed into other forms of energy, of heat, cold, wind, magnetic force, and gravity. By experimenting with your own gifts, you will discover these great powers. However, the forces can only be used for defensive purposes, to protect you, and are powerless to cause permanent harm to others.

"These bracelets are a reminder of the important things you must carry in your heart at all times, the tools you need to do your work. But these bracelets have some special powers, too. While they are not as powerful, individually, as the jewels or Web of Life, they can be used to summon the others. If you hold the bracelet up to the light, any light, so that a particular jewel, or the bracelet itself reflects the light, and you center your thoughts on the one who carried the original gift, they will be summoned to assist you; their gift and their bracelet will shine with unusual brightness. All they have to do is clasp this gift over their heart and they will be transported to where you are. All time will stop for them until they hold their gift to their heart once more and are returned home. The bracelet also holds other powers that you will discover over time.

"Your mission is to reach out to others, especially those who have lost their way: the angry ones, the ones who live in sadness, those without hope, those that live only for themselves, and those without joy. You are to bring them the messages of these gifts. Once given, the messages will pass from one to one, and many to many, until the goodness within everyone lights up the universe . . . and fear is conquered.

"I now free you to return home, to begin your work. Rest here tonight and gather your strength. In the morning make your way to the place where you found each other, to the field of the circle of stones. Gather together in the middle, holding each other by the hand. With the other hand, clasp your gift over your heart. Trust in its power and believe in its message. Go in peace. Let love and compassion be your guides."

They all watched as Ooray disappeared in a split second, like the turning off of a light switch. Kai looked over at the others. The faces of his friends reflected the bewilderment of what had just happened, but also the seriousness of the mission before them.

"It's still not clear to me where we're supposed to start," Liyah said. "Or how we are to go about it."

"The way will become clear, I'm sure," responded Morningstar in her calm, reassuring way.

"Maybe," replied Zack. "But I still wonder if I'm dreaming, or if someone isn't really playing a prank on us."

Kai Li winked at him. "We 'bout to find out, no?"

Twenty-Four

———————

THE EARLY MORNING air carried a slight chill. Zack handed his denim jacket to Liyah to provide some added warmth over her thin jacket. Morningstar led the way across the yard to the edge of the trees, then into the woods along the narrow path. Arriving at the fork in the path, she found the upside down "V" cut into the side of one of the trees—her mark. *It would not be far now.*

Zack pulled up alongside her and glanced over. "I wanted you to know that no matter what I said before, I appreciate your patience, and your skills, of course. He smiled. "You kept us on the right track. You're a true leader. Sorry about before."

Morningstar stopped, turned, and returned his smile. "I know, Zack. I have always known. As for leadership, I think we all have to take up that role now, especially you."

Zack laughed. "You are right as usual. You can count on me to be there if you need me. You rock, Star!" He grinned. "After all, the expression was made for you, wasn't it?"

"Very funny, Zack. You can count on me too. We all just have each other . . . for now."

Kai Li and Liyah caught up to them. Kai Li reached in his pants pockets and pulled out two cell phones. "This one for you, Zack. An'

this one yours, Liyah. I almos' forget. I put them in sealed pocket
of pack when we first leave cabin. Forget 'bout them till we take
everythin' out of pack this mornin'."

Zack laughed, "Always full of surprises aren't you, Mr. Kai?"

The mid-morning sun was bright, the sky a cloudless powder blue,
as they entered the clearing. Morningstar pointed to the stone at the
edge of the circle where they had met Liyah that first day. "Here we
are. Almost home."

The four approached the stones and formed a circle as they had
been directed. Liyah and Morningstar stood across from each other,
Kai Li and Zack in between them. They held hands, silent with
anticipation.

"How are we going to know what to do when we get back?"
asked Liyah.

"I think it'll become clear, Liyah," Morningstar replied. "The
first thing to do is get back safely. The rest will follow. I guess."

"Well, 'fore we try," said Kai Li, "I want to thank you all. I learn
a lot . . . more with you than ever could learn on own, at home in
Hong Kong."

Zack gave him a thumbs-up. "No one learned more than me. I
had a lot of growing up to do. Probably more still, huh?" He winked.
"But without the three of you I may never have found this path . . .
the right path."

"We all learned a lot, Zack," added Liyah. "And I, too, am very
grateful. I will miss you all."

"Maybe no," replied Kai. "Have feeling we see more before . . ."
His voice trailed off as his eyes widened, staring in Zack's direction.

"What are you lookin' at Kai-bo?" Zack joked.

The girls pointed toward him. Zack quickly scanned his body.
Nothing there. He looked at them again, still pointing at him. He
turned around.

A wavy spectral vision was moving slowly toward them, hovering
inches above the ground, its vague image bathed in multicolored light.
It stopped just before reaching them. It was Ooray. The soft, quasi-
female, sometimes almost male, voice addressed them as before, the
image pulsating in tempo and color with the vibrations of speech
emanating from within.

"There are a few final details you will need to know to carry out your tasks. And one last stop you must make together before you finally get home." As Ooray moved past Zack to the center of their circle, a gentle, warm breeze tussled their clothing and hair.

Now settled in the middle, Ooray continued. "As you know, you will need to use your powers to be successful in your mission, and so they don't fade over time. You must practice as the opportunities arise. There is no time to waste. Together you will always be more powerful than each separately, but you also have the capability to learn and apply some of the others' powers as well.

"Morningstar, I'll use you as an example since you hold the Web of Life—the symbol of the connectedness of all things. The others do not yet know the full power of your understanding of what that means, like you do. But they can learn from you. Just as you can learn the depth and power of compassion from Liyah, knowledge and truth from Kai Li, and of love over fear through Zack's TrueHeart. You each have special powers, but you are not truly whole without having some of all the powers, together. The bands provide the ability to channel the combined powers. Your gifts are your special power. Listen to each other. Practice. Then lead.

"By leading I mean living through your actions and passing the powers on to others. For the four of you cannot heal the world. Not in a million lifetimes. Only by passing the power on to others, who then pass it on to others, and so on, multiplying the reach of the powers geometrically, will everyone be reached. In order to do this, you can pass on the powers by infusing an object you hold dear with the power—through your energy and thoughts, then give that object away to the person who will have seen the light and can now lead others. In this way, over time, all humanity will be blanketed, and the great darkness lifted."

"But how can we do that?" asked Morningstar.

"All things are made from energy: all matter, the sun, the stars, your thoughts, light itself, and yes . . . even love. By looking at an object you now have the power to transfer some of the energy into it, as I have for the gifts I gave each of you. You are just apprentices, but you will learn to control your thoughts, to focus on each of the powers when needed, and even to manipulate time itself. Through practice and good actions that power can grow, and then be shared with others. But much of that power is now already part of you. I will show you."

Ooray left the circle and moved closer to the nearest granite slab. Rays of colored light shot out and enveloped the stone. Seconds later, Ooray removed the light source from the stone, but the stone continued to glow with a bright-orange hue.

"Now," Ooray said, "each of you hold out your hands toward the light."

They did as they were instructed.

"Concentrate on receiving the warm glow of the stone into your body through your hands."

Nothing seemed to happen.

"Concentrate more."

Still noting at first, but then narrow mists of orange light suddenly began radiating toward Kai Li, who was in his meditation mode, finally reaching the tips of his fingers.

"Close your eyes like Kai Li and keep trying. Feel for it. Become one with the stone. Absorb its light."

They tried again. Slowly, sporadically, waves of light left the stone and travelled to the hands of each of them. After a moment, the orange glow of the stone was no more."

Ooray pulsated again in alternating spectral colors. "Open your eyes now."

They looked at the stone then around at each other.

"Jeez," said Zack in astonishment. "I could actually feel the light . . . but it's too hard to describe it."

"Well done," said Ooray. "It is the beginning. But, now there is the one last thing I spoke of. You must go together to where Zack lives, and then Kai Li, Liyah, and Morningstar will return home as well. But don't worry. I will accompany you this time to guide you. Get prepared again to go."

Instinctively Liyah, Zack, and Kai Li looked over to Morningstar. She glanced down at the ground for a moment then back at her friends. "How about a hug for good luck?"

"Getting soft are we?" Zack teased.

They laughed and then came together for a final embrace. Spreading apart again, they took their positions. Reaching out with their right hands, bracelets on their wrists and necklaces dangling down, they formed a wheel by grasping each other's hands, one on top of the other. With their left hands they held each other by the waist.

"Okay," said Morningstar, "Zack, close your eyes now and imagine being back where you were before you came to us. Bring us there."

As the others closed their eyes Morningstar cast a last glance up at the sun. She could feel its warmth on her face and felt the electricity in the air; it reminded her of the feeling she had as she sat upon the stoop by her home, what seemed so long ago now. Closing her eyes, she let herself go with the feeling. Sensing that something was about to happen, they all closed their eyes even tighter. The air grew heavy. The hair on their arms stood straight up. A high-pitched whining sound vibrated faintly in their ears, then grew louder. The wind picked up, wildly tossing their hair. There was a sudden flash of light and then . . .

POP!

The grass where they had been standing twisted about in wavy swirls . . . but they had vanished.

———

The thunder cracked and the sky lit up with lightning. Zack's eyes flew open. Over him stood a boy in dark clothing holding a gun; next to him were two others, one holding a chain, the other a knife.

Where am I? What's going on?

Trying to overcome his confusion, he looked up. The gang leader was staring at the others, taken aback for an instant by the bright flash of light that had arrived as he was about to tend to Zack. He looked back down.

"Yo! Time to pay, dude! Stand up!"

Once Zack was to his feet, the boy aimed the gun at him. He noticed the necklace. "What you wearin' there, man?"

"What?" Zack managed to ask, still trying to put all the pieces together.

"Don't give me that crap, man! There . . ." he pressed the muzzle into Zack's chest just below the sapphire pendant.

Zack looked down. The pendant flashed its deep-blue color in the moonlight, which seemed to speed between the layers of storm clouds. His memory was jolted into hyperdrive. "Jesus!"

"Jesus is right, boy. But even he ain't saving *you*."

Zack's eyes bounced between the leader and the two other gang members like a pinball.

"What's wrong w'ich you? Gimme that." He reached for the pendant; Zack stepped back. The boy reached for it again.

"No!" Zack refused, emphatically, holding his ground.

"You goin' down, fool! But why don't you dance for us first?" He aimed the gun at Zack's feet and pulled off two shots. Zack jumped back. They laughed.

The moon snuck into full view for a moment, illuminating the boys. This time Zack got a good look at the leader: a few years older, and much bigger than he had appeared in the dark school. Fierce anger spewed from his eyes.

The boy aimed the gun again, this time right at Zack. Zack froze like a deer, expecting the worst at any moment. But suddenly there was another flash of light, then another, and a third. The gang members turned away to shelter their eyes. When they turned back around, they stared in disbelief.

Zack, still facing the gang, saw the flashes, but with his back to the light wasn't forced to shelter his eyes. He noticed they were looking at something over his shoulder but was afraid to peel his eyes off them. When he finally turned around, a stunned look came across his face. He found himself looking at Morningstar, then Kai Li, and Liyah. They were gathering themselves together, a short distance from him, looking a bit stunned as well.

Kai Li looked over at the gang members and was the first to speak. "Look like you see ghost. Ooray said we to come here, 'member?"

The gang leader was bewildered. "What the f—! Where'd you all come from?"

"Doesn't matter," Liyah responded. "What's going on here? Looks like you got yourself in trouble, Zack."

The leader regained his composure and took a step toward them. "What's it to you, bitch? Looks like you just joined the party. You can watch your friend here bite it if you like. Then I'll get to you three."

The other gang members came up alongside the leader, and they began to push Zack around. Kai Li, Liyah, and Morningstar looked at each other, confused. Suddenly, Ooray appeared in a flash of blue light next to Zack.

The gang members stopped in their tracks, staring wide-eyed at the vibrating orb. A red laser-like beam suddenly shot from Ooray and hit the chain dangling in the hand of one of them. In an instant the chain became white-hot; the gang member dropped it like a hot poker. Another beam struck the knife in the hand of the other; the knife flew away as he gripped his hand, screaming in pain.

The leader raised the gun and pointed it to Zack's head. "Do anything else," he yelled, "or I blow his head off."

Ooray's spectral, swirling light expanded, engulfing all three gang members. As the light receded, they were left frozen in time; the gun fell to the ground. Zack, unaffected by the light, backed away and gazed over at Ooray. "Jeez, Ooray. Thanks. I forgot about this," he managed, his voice quivering slightly. He stared at the gang members who remained standing in place. Finally composing himself, he added, "Not a good situation, huh?"

"I say you get that right," kidded Kai Li. "But 'mazing!"

Ooray's form blinked and vibrated as its voice came to them again. "As I said, you will learn how to do things like this, but your powers cannot severely harm anyone. You must find ways to avoid these situations whenever you can, because if you are off guard, you may not survive."

"Are we to go home now, Ooray?" asked Liyah. "I thought maybe there was something else. We didn't really help at all."

Ooray's colors swirled. "There is one more thing. I have put these young men in a force field so that you can use your powers to teach the leader. I will show you. Morningstar, step forward please."

As Morningstar stepped closer to the leader, the jewels in her bracelet caught the moonlight. They sparkled brilliantly.

"Now, we will take him back in time . . . far back. Hold onto your necklace with your left hand and remember what it symbolizes: the connectedness of all things throughout all time, past and future. Point the fingers of your right hand, the one with the band of jewels, toward his head. Concentrate, and I will guide time and its memories."

Ooray then directed its voice to the others. "Zack, Liyah, Kai Li, join her and do the same, pointing the hand with the bracelet and holding onto your gift with the other. Although much can be accomplished with the bracelets, your special gifts add power, until you learn and become like me. Now, keep concentrating."

They obeyed. The bracelets sparkled like crystalline candies in the moonlight. Soon, Zack's TrueHeart, Liyah's Timeless Teardrop, and Kai Li's Torch of Truth sent wide beams of red, blue, and white light onto the leader's face.

"He will feel the power of the jewels," Ooray assured. "He will see truth. He will see the collective pain of his ancestors, as will you. He will feel compassion. You will see what he sees, hear what he hears, feel what he feels. But his comrades will see nothing, hear nothing, and feel nothing. I will begin."

Their silver bands hummed. The beams held steady. The moon danced above.

Ooray used the force provided by his students to send the leader's mind back to a time long before he was born . . . back . . . back to past relatives and their times; back to the days of the sailing ships raiding villages on the African coast, taking natives from across the sea to America, and into slavery.

The leader was there. He was one of them. He was placed in shackles and forced to endure an arduous ocean journey during which many became ill and died . . . all this in an instant of time. He saw the fields of a plantation before his eyes and felt the hot sun beating down upon him; he was thirsty but received no water; he winced in pain as his back split open from the whip of his master. He felt wild anger but could do nothing to retaliate. He felt his wounds gush warm blood. He cried out for his homeland and his family.

In an instant the leader became someone else: a Black soldier in a blue coat, fighting. Many dead lay near him; the air was thick with smoke and the hum of lead bullets whizzing past. He held a rifle in his hands, felt the itch from the wool uniform under the hot sun. There was a surging of his fellow blue coats then a counter surge by the army in gray. Death was all around. A bayonet pierced his left shoulder, and he was pushed to his knees.

Suddenly it was 1925; he found himself standing on the streets of New York City, holding a rag in his hands, buffing the shoes of a White man in a tan suit. The man got up, stepped out of the chair, tipped his hat, and handed him a coin. He looked back up at the man, pushed up the visor of his newsboy-style hat with his thumb and forefinger, and found himself saying, "G'day, sir! Thank you, sir!"

The sun caught his eye as he watched the man move away. When he looked back at the chair, it was no longer there; in its place was the body of a man wearing a U.S. Army jacket, pants, and boots. His helmet was lying next to him on the ground, along with his machine gun. He was dead. It was 1944.

"What are you waitin' for?" a voice behind him boomed. "Grab the gun . . . and belt too. We need all the bullets we can get. Let's go, boy! Hop to it! And get back in the foxhole. Those Nazi sons 'a bitches will be shellin' the beach again any moment."

He found himself rolling the soldier over, removing the strap holding the bullets, putting it over his other shoulder; he then grabbed the last hand grenade from the dead soldier's belt along with the machine gun. Holding his rifle in one hand and the gun in the other, he ran through the sand toward the foxhole, leaping into the trench as a shell from artillery struck nearby, blowing him through the air until he finally landed on his back on the beach. He looked up and saw the sun's light again, filtering through the smokey haze.

There was a flash; he was in Detroit; he was seven; his mother had just been beaten in her bedroom, again, by his drunk stepfather. He felt the same feeling all over, as real as it was then, too frightened to help his mom, because he knew he would be next . . . and then the guilt for not doing so.

Flash forward five years: His stepfather is at it again; he has the look of the devil in his eyes. He thought his stepfather was going to kill his mother for sure this time—he was beating her senseless. He intercedes. His stepfather punches him in the face and knocks him down . . . he's helpless again. But this time, he is filled with rage. He disappears and returns moments later, with a gun.

It is now the very next day; he is standing in his grandmother's living room in the tenement she lived in—small and cluttered. There were people crying in the other room; there were police; they tried to speak low, but he could hear their voices.

"She's dead, ma'am . . . beaten to death . . . and it looks like someone shot her husband in the head," one of the policemen was saying. He hears his grandmother as she begins to wail, "Not my daughter. Oh, God! Not my baby!"

He turns and runs out of the apartment; makes it down the hall, down the stairs, and into the trash strewn front yard; he is free. He looks up at the sky; the sun is a big ball of yellow. He runs and runs, tears streaming down his face. He hides . . . and waits. The sun sets, and the night passes. It takes only a few seconds in his mind as he replays the event, but to him he feels those hours in full—those long, endless hours.

It's two days later; he is starving and fishing through trash cans. Several boys surround him; they offer food; they take him in. He sees the insignia on their jackets—the one he now wears on his skin.

Another flash. He sees Zack; he blinks . . . and blinks again. He looks at Liyah, holding tight to her necklace; the bright ruby beam steals his attention. Compassion pours forth into his mind like a river. He is taken on another journey, wearing the shoes of others, not those of his relatives of the past.

It is 1831; he is fourteen; he is a Choctaw. He and members of his tribe have been forced from their homes in Mississippi and are on a long march west to a reservation in Oklahoma, set aside by the United States government for "Indians," no longer indigenous, but aliens—refugees. Their travel has been so long and arduous that many have died, especially the very old and the very young; it is the saddest of times for his nation. A sickness has set in among them, and it is difficult to go on. He weeps inside for his people. But he is a strong boy and finds the courage to go on and to help others. He brings water to the old; he brings food to the very young, and he holds their hands; he tells funny stories at night to lift their spirits; he speaks of the bravery of all warriors from all tribes. A young girl of eight who lost her parents begins to follow him around . . . she will never be far away. He knew her parents; he watches out for her until she is safe at the reservation. All of this he, the leader, sees . . . in the blink of an eye.

He turns to Kai Li. It is now 1937 in Nanking, China. Japanese troops are brutalizing the town, raping women and killing everyone, the old as well as the young. He has become a young girl of nine wearing her favorite party dress; she is in the back room looking into a mirror and smiling.

Army soldiers break into her home and begin pumping bullets into her family; she is scared, and she hides under the bed. After the shooting stops . . . hours later . . . she crawls out but will not go into the other room—she knows what she will see. She is found the next day, sitting in the corner of the room, still in her favorite dress, with a blank look on her face.

Suddenly it is 1963; he is in a suburb outside of Hartford, Connecticut; he is ten; he is White. It is a cold winter morning, and he is sitting by himself in the back of a yellow bus; he is on his way to school. He is wearing a heavy, checkered coat and a colorful wool snow hat, its flaps pulled down over his ears . . . tie strings dangle down from each side. He is nervous; he is hoping that the older boys in the back will not pick on him again; but he is unlucky. Several of the boys move up behind him and start taunting him. They make fun of the acne that has taken over his young face; they mock his hat; they pull it off his head and toss it around. They begin pushing him back in his seat; they rub his head with their knuckles and spill the contents of his book bag in the aisle of the bus. Finally, one of the boys spits on him, and another throws his hat out the window. The bus driver, studying his mirror, tells them to sit back down. But the damage is already done. He doesn't even feel anger; he just feels fear and shame. He is terrified but feels somehow, wrongly, that he deserves it. He will carry this feeling with him, just below the surface . . . his entire life.

He looks around; the boys are gone. He is now a young girl at the edge of a waterfall; she is hanging on a rope; she is yelling to the shore to another boy who is her lifeline; if the boy cannot hold on, she will die . . . she knows it. He looks over again to the shore and can see the boy's face now. Suddenly, Zack's face appears.

Ooray's voice overrides all their thoughts "You may release him now." They do so, resting their hands at their sides. Ooray continues. "Morningstar, you have all seen this together. Take the boy's hand so he is connected to you, and I will tell him what has happened."

Morningstar sees that the leader has rejoined them, but that he is stunned and unable to move or speak. She approaches him. She glances briefly at the other gang members to make sure they are still blocked from harming anyone. Holding out her arm, she then takes the boy's hand in hers. He feels her energy flow into his veins. The moon's fullness reflects off her face. He looks into her eyes.

Ooray speaks to him. "The three others have come here to save a friend, the boy you wished to harm. His name is Zack." A light appears above Zack. "But it is you who they are really saving. You have this one chance to reclaim your life . . . to change its course . . . to live a life with meaning. We have all seen what you have seen. There is great pain in the world; there always has been. But the world is at a point now when it will finally tip one way or the other. Humans will either slip into oblivion or help one another honor their inner nature and become the light that they were intended to be.

"All things in this world, past, present, and future are all connected. We are a product of the stars. We are one with all that has been or will be. As the actions of others have affected our lives, so our own actions reverberate through time and affect all things—for good or for bad. Because we are all part of the same web of life, all things will feel our pull as we tug on the connecting strands, like a bug in a spiderweb, no matter how slight our tug or how far away we may be, in distance or time.

"The slave on the plantation, the young man in the blue Union coat, the shoeshine boy, the soldier in the foxhole in World War II, these are all your relatives. They have struggled in their own way, in a world of trials. Their paths have led to you. Do you want to let them down and give up on your own life, no matter how difficult it has been?"

The light above Zack moves over Liyah. "This is Liyah. She too comes to help you see the path. Her relatives have had difficulties throughout history, not unlike your own. She was chosen to be the one to give you the compassion she has fought hard to hold onto. She showed you the pain of other cultures and peoples, did you not feel for them? They are one with you. They inherited their history, too; and like you, they are just trying to live their lives. They are connected as well, because they are part of this great web of which I speak.

"But you are connected to them in another special way. The Choctaw girl who was shown grace by a young boy will raise a family; she will pass this kindness onto them. From her daughter's granddaughter a child will be born to a Lakota Sioux, and they will have, as their daughter, someone who will extend a kindness to you . . . that girl is Morningstar, the girl who holds your hand to heal you.

"The boy who was bullied on the bus will grow up and move to Detroit; he will open a convenience store; he will carry a gun to protect himself from other bullies. There will be a misunderstanding late one night, and he will fire the gun, mistakenly thinking he is threatened; he will miss the person he is aiming at and shoot Zack's grandfather, who was stopping by to get some cigarettes on his way home from the night shift at the assembly plant. He will not return home. His son, Zack's father, was nine at the time. He has not gotten over it.

"The Chinese girl will recover from the Rape of Nanking; she will grow up and become a Buddhist; she will learn to forgive those who took her family from her; she will teach her children the power that is in forgiveness . . . and they will teach theirs in turn. Her granddaughter will marry a Japanese man, and they will give birth to a boy. That boy is Kai Li." The light shifts to Kai Li. "He has come here to help you learn to find the truth, to forgive others as well . . . to forgive yourself. He has come here to free you."

Ooray paused, then went on. "Gangs, like yours, come in many flavors: Black, White, Asian, Latino, and many others. The members have arrived from many directions, traveling many paths, through no fault of their own. And, like them, your journey was not your fault, either. We are all a product of what has come before: our individual past, our family past, and the collective past of all humanity. But it does not mean we are bound to it.

"Your path has been more difficult than most; of this there is no doubt. Your relations who were forced to come to America bore the physical chains of slavery — yet many were thinkers, leaders, and even royalty in their homeland…and all were fathers, mothers, and children of equal humanity to all others on this Earth. Your parents and their parents, though free, bore shackles as well. They were chained out of equal opportunities, much like others who are poor, unlucky, homeless, or whose skin color did not match the one needed for entry.

"The road ahead will still be difficult…harder for you and others who share the color of your skin…but you are not strapped to the same mast. You can break those bonds and join with others like Zack and his friends here, to set a new course…leading others of all colors, shapes, and sizes, of all genders, of all ethnicities, races, and cultures: all of them your true brothers and sisters. Only you can decide now which path to follow. This is your opportunity to rise up, where those before you had been so mercilessly beaten down, to make the changes that will help all future generations achieve the joy and happiness that is their birthright.

"The light is coming…become *it*."

The other members of the gang had become very anxious. They couldn't see what the leader saw, and Ooray's words confused them. They started yelling at Morningstar and the others.

The leader turned to them, and in a tired voice declared, "It's over." He turned and faced Zack. "Sorry."

Zack removed the gold cross from his ear, clenched it in his hand, and felt its temperature rise. He then handed it to him. "This brings great strength," he said, as the boy cupped it in his hand. "It holds the messages we have tried to show you. It's full power I don't even know myself, but I have been told to pass something on, something important to me. So, I give this to you, to protect you and help light your way. It is sacred. You must then pass something of yourself on to others. In this way its strength—your strength—can be transferred to others, and from them to even more. But remember, while this cross has the power to protect you, and in turn your gift help others correct the path they are on, it is the messages you pass on, not the objects, that what will eventually become the force that saves the world: the messages we showed you—of truth, compassion, connectedness, and love."

The boy's countenance softened. Zack continued. "If you need urgent help at any time, you can summon me by grasping the cross and thinking of me. I will get the message. And I will be there."

The boy bowed his head, then turned to Morningstar, Liyah, and Kai Li, nodding for each. He brought his eyes back to Zack, lingering briefly, looked at Ooray, then up at the moon. He turned and began walking away along the side of the school, his two friends tagging behind.

Ooray's essence rose up, blinking and flashing. "I am done here, for now. It is up to the four of you. But you know how to reach me. I will always be just a whisper away. Kai Li, Morningstar, Liyah . . . you know how to get home now. There is much to do. Farewell."

There was a brief whining sound, then a flash. Ooray was gone.

Liyah took Zack's hand and cupped hers around it. "I think we will be seeing each other often. Maybe the rest of our lives. I guess time will tell."

Kai Li gave Zack a high five. "See soon, huh?"

"I'm sure," Zack replied. "I'm sure we will."

Morningstar stepped closer. Tears made their way over her high cheeks. "I will miss you, my friend."

Zack grabbed her and hugged her hard, then took her by her shoulders and looked into her eyes. "Yes, friends it is. But no sadness. We are connected forever. Isn't that what you taught us? So, we will be *forever friends*. BFFs." He laughed.

After saying their goodbyes again, Liyah, Kai Li, and Morningstar folded their arms across their chests, holding on to their necklaces. They gazed up at the moon, drifting between the rain clouds, and imagined being where they were before their journey began.

Bright cones of light appeared above each of them, and one by one, seconds apart, they vanished into the night sky.

———

Feeling depleted, Zack decided not to continue on to Tommy's house and instead just head back home before the rain set in. He took his phone out and texted Tommy. *Still works,* he mused, placing it back in the pocket of his hoodie.

Moving alongside the basketball court, he once again looked up at the old backboard that bent down toward the cracked asphalt below, metal rim dangling. He slowed to a stop. *I wonder?*

Removing his right hand from the hoodie, he held it out, palm and fingers facing the backboard. He began concentrating on transferring the energy from the wristband. A warmth radiated through his entire body. Soon his hand began to vibrate gently. He looked down at it, then again to the backboard. He began to feel a connection between his hand and the board . . . like the pull in the force field of a magnet. It grew stronger, and he heard the creaking of metal. He imagined the backboard as it was when he used to play with his friends. The creaking grew louder. The board began to rise, and as it did, the metal rim rose up as well, twisting itself back into position.

He rested his mind, and the noise stopped. He stared at the backboard and rim, looking as they once did. *Damn! That is way cool.*

———

Zack climbed the stairs of the front porch, then, taking in a deep breath and releasing it, pushed open the front door. His mother heard the door squeak. She entered the hallway, surprised to see her son return home so soon.

"What's up, boy. Forget sumthin'?"

"No," Zack replied, "just decided I was tired."

"Where your coat at?"

Zack looked down at his chest, considering it for a moment. He had last seen it on Liyah. "Uh . . . must'a left it at Tommy's."

She studied him. "How's that? You ain't been gone that long."

"Uh, yeah, well, I don't know."

"Sometimes I think you don't know much at all," she quipped. "What's that band on your wrist? You look like a girl." She paused. "And where's your cross?"

"Jeez, Mom."

She checked him over again. "I jez don't know any more. You okay?"

"Jus' tired," he said quietly, then smiled at her.

"What you smilin' 'bout? You been gittin' in trouble?"

"No trouble, Mom."

She looked at him for a moment, shook her head, then returned to the kitchen.

Zack went up the stairs and into his room, closing the door behind him. As he lay down on his bed, staring up at the ceiling, he began to think about all that had happened when time had stopped. *That strange gap in time.* He closed his eyes. *How could it be?*

Within minutes he was fast asleep.

———

Kai Li stood on the street near the factory, looking around, gathering his thoughts. His green ginger ale can completed its spinning, finally coming to a rest against the curb. Twilight was ceding to early morning, but the neon sign above was still buzzing. He bent down and retrieved his phone, then picked up the can, crushed it, and stuck it in his pants pocket.

Traffic was growing on the quiet morning streets as the workers piled into Chi Sun Exports. Kai Li started down the street to the factory, thinking about what he had just been through. The sign sputtered again. He stopped and looked up, pointing his finger at it as if to tell it to be quiet. Suddenly a bolt of blue light flashed from his fingertip and hit the sign. The neon bulbs exploded into a million pieces, and sparks flew out over the street. Kai Li stepped back, stunned.

As the workers entering the factory turned to see what was happening, a small cloud of smoke rose above the building. Everything was silent again. They paused briefly then returned to funneling through the gate.

Kai Li blended in with the stream of workers as they neared the front doors. Just before entering, he turned and looked up at the sky again. The orange-yellow ball was rising slowly over the bay. He looked at the bracelet on his wrist and fiddled with the chain around his neck. How was he going to explain this to his mom?

———

"You okay?" Liyah heard a voice say, as she opened her eyes. A man was extending his hand to her to help her up; she held on and rose to her feet. The crowd was being dispersed by the police. She remembered why she was there: to retrieve Khalib.

"Thank you, sir."

"It's best to get out of here now, before more trouble happens," the man advised. "What's a nice dressed up young lady like you doing here, anyway?"

"Looking for my brother," Liyah replied. "But I guess he's gone home."

Liyah thanked the man again and headed up the street. Rays from the sun hit her bracelet as her arms swung to-and-fro. Her eyes caught the prisms of multicolored light. She gazed down, and all at once memories flooded her mind. She brought her hand up to her chest and found the Timeless Teardrop.

Allah, it's not a dream after all!

As she held the stone it began to throb in her hand. Strong emotions poured forth. She remembered the visions Ooray had shown her and her new friends. And suddenly Khalib's face appeared in a mist in front of her. His voice whispered, "Help me, Liyah." Liyah jerked her hand from the necklace as if it were on fire.

Liyah opened the front door to her home and went inside. Many of the guests had just arrived and there was the usual hustle and bustle of activity. Her mother entered the living room from the kitchen, greeting the guests. Looking across the room, she spotted Liyah and made her way over.

"Well," her mother said as she approached, "I was *wondering* when you were going to make it back."

"There was a lot of trouble in the square."

"So I heard. Everyone is talking about it. I hope this isn't going to escalate like the last time. I fear your father will have a heart attack over the business. Things are hard enough as it is." She looked down at Liyah's feet then scanned back up to her face. "What happened to those nice sandals?" she asked. "The straps are torn . . . and where did you get that jacket?"

"Jacket?" questioned Liyah.

"Yes. The denim one you are wearing."

"Oh . . ." Liyah responded, looking down at the long sleeves, surprised she hadn't even thought about it. "I . . . I . . . uh . . . Someone gave it to me."

"Gave it to you? Who? What for?"

"Oh, just someone. I, uh, must have looked cold."

"Cold? It's hot as the devil outside." She studied Liyah again. "Sometimes I wonder about you, child. You can't wear that now. Go take it off. Your father will have a fit . . . taking clothes from other people! You'll have to return it tomorrow."

Liyah turned to head to her room. "And what's that bracelet?" Her mother added. "I don't remember seeing that. It's pretty, though."

Liyah turned back around and began to stammer, but her mother interrupted her again. "And where is Khalib? Isn't he with you?"

"Khalib?" Liyah replied, confused.

"Yes. You know . . . your brother . . . the one we sent you out to bring back," her mother said impatiently. "Honestly, Liyah."

"Khalib must be here, Mother. He left the square ahead of me."

"Well, he's not."

"He must be," Liyah repeated, then remembered the image she had just seen of his face.

Liyah's mother disappeared into the den where her father was talking to friends. She came back dragging him with her. Liyah explained what happened in the square and that he was running home the last she knew.

Her father became upset. "That boy needs a talking to," he growled. "He's been hanging around the wrong friends. Those boys are much older than him and are a bad influence. That's probably why he was at the square . . . throwing rocks with the rest of them."

"He wasn't with them when I saw him last, Father. He was running to get away from the crowd. He was running home."

"Well, he knew we were having this party and was to be home on time. He better get home soon if he knows what's good for him." Her father turned around and headed brusquely back to his guests.

Liyah was puzzled, but very glad she was finally home. At the same time, she knew there was no way she was going to say a word to anyone about the journey she had just been on. *Not just yet.*

———

Morningstar found herself perched on the concrete stoop, once again, exactly as she had been before she was taken away. She stared out at the horizon, remembering the storm of light that had taken her away. Suddenly the faces of her new friends flashed in her mind. She brought her hand up to the necklace, then looked down to her wrist at her bracelet. She smiled.

She played with the bracelet as she dug the toe of her moccasin into the dirt in front of the stoop. The dust settled at first but then began to swirl and rise up. It formed a tiny funnel, then sparkled with many colors.

The dust settled back down as a voice came from behind her. "Sarah? Sarah Morningstar?"

She spun her head around; it was a policeman. She looked up at him as he approached. "Yes, that's me."

"I'm sorry it took so long for us to get to you. The tornado went through late at night and levelled all the homes here. We don't know for sure how many people were killed or injured yet. We didn't get any messages until a plane flew over two hours ago and called in about your park. We stopped at several other places along the way and finally got here. I checked the records and you and your grandfather are listed as living here."

At the mention of her grandfather memories flooded into Morningstar's mind, forcing out everything else. Looking at the officer, tears welled up in her eyes. She suddenly felt alone in the world; her heart ached for him.

"I'm so sorry, Sarah. I didn't mean to upset you. You see, we found your grandfather on the edge of a field on our way into the park. He was badly hurt when the wind blew him into the field. But he's alive and has been taken to the hospital. I'm sure we'll know something more shortly. Headquarters radioed me to check this location for you."

Morningstar couldn't believe her ears. She stopped crying and stood up. "I need to go to him right away," she pleaded.

"First things first, Sarah. We need to find you a place to stay until we hear it's okay for you to visit him. Come with me, and I'll take you to the makeshift center at the school, where all the people without homes will be housed and fed. From there we can arrange for transportation for you to the hospital, which is a good distance away. But for now, I'll get someone to find you a bed and something to eat . . . you must be hungry."

"Not really," Morningstar replied, "I just ate a little while ago."

The officer looked puzzled. "Are you sure? What did you eat? The storm came through early."

"Well, I, uh. Maybe I didn't have anything now that I think of it."

"Come with me, young lady. How would you like a ride in my patrol car? I'll take you to the center myself. And when you hear about your grandfather, I'll bring you to the hospital."

The two headed off through the maze of twisted rubble, both looking straight ahead, watching their step. Morningstar's braids bobbed as they made their way across the field and down the hill toward his car.

"Everything's going to be all right, Sarah," the officer said, turning to address her.

She smiled up at him. "That's exactly what I was going to say to you."

———

Several days later, the doctor in charge of the emergency center finally notified Morningstar that her grandfather was better and able to see her. She hopped into the squad car sent to take her to the hospital.

Arriving at the front entrance, she followed the officer to the nurses' station, then into the room where her grandfather sat propped up, and bandaged up, but resting easy. Breaking free from her escorts, she flung herself at him.

"Lala! Lala! I missed you so. Are you okay?"

He hugged her tightly. "Yes, Sweetie. Everything is fine. A bit beat up, but pretty lucky I'd say."

Tears poured down her face. "I thought I'd lost you."

"Now, now. You know nothing could keep us apart. That storm was simply not big enough to defeat a warrior like me . . . or you . . . it appears."

"I know," she replied. "I know."

He took her hands in his. "So, you have to fill me in on what happened to you and what you've been doing the last few days. But first, tell me what that light is, the one blinking on your bracelet." He brought his eyes down toward her wrist. "Don't think I've seen that before. Is that some sort of hospital messaging thing?"

"What? What do you mean?" She glanced down at the bracelet.

The Teardrop was flashing its ruby-red light. *Liyah needs me.*

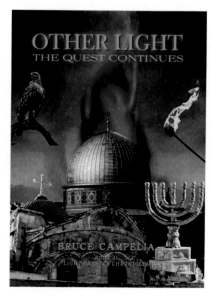

Pre-order Other Light
Book II
Light Passers Chronicles
[Release planned for the fall]

Follow Morningstar, Liyah, Zack and Kai Li in OtherLight, Book II in the Light Passers Chronicles series, as Liyah attempts to rescue her brother, Khalib, abducted by a terrorist organization in Palestine and held in an unknown location. The story takes place in and near Jerusalem, considered the holiest of all cities, as the four attempt to follow the clues to obtain Khalib's release. However, renewed conflict in the region, flaring up between cultural and religious factions, not only places them in grave danger but threatens the entire mission. What starts out as a planned short intervention transforms into an international powder keg, threatening to bring our heroes, and the region, to an explosive end.

lightpasserschronicles.com

Turn the page for a sneak peek...

ONE

TWO DAYS PASSED and still Khalib had not returned home. Liyah's parents notified the authorities on the second day, but there had been no progress of any kind.

In the early afternoon of the sixth day, when Liyah was at the market buying vegetables for dinner, she was approached by one of her brother's friends. He told her that when her father questioned him and some of Khalib's other friends, they hadn't seen Khalib or been with him that day, even though they were supposed to meet up. He says this was the truth, but what he didn't tell her father was that he and his activist friends knew of other young boys and men who had been kidnapped over the past few months by a terrorist group.

Liyah, visibly upset, asked him what else he knew.

He told her that people inside the police organization had information that this group is not from Palestine, but a terrorist organization from another country. He explained to her that the terrorists were indoctrinating and training their captives at some unknown location, then sending them out on suicide missions around the world.

The boy gave Liyah a small, folded piece of paper with a name and address on it and told her that his older brother was a new police recruit and obtained the name from someone within the department but wouldn't disclose who. He said the man on the paper may have more information about her brother. He made her promise not to tell anyone, or he would be in danger. . .and then he left.

The next day, Liyah was in town again on an errand. She went to the address on the piece of paper; it is a mosque in the oldest part of the city. She enters, falls to her knees, and prays. She remained there and thinking of her brother. She began to cry but dried her tears and rose to her feet. A man who witnessed her sadness approached her. He was dressed simply. "What is the problem my child?" he asks Liyah. "Certainly, it is a shame to be unhappy on such a beautiful day that Allah has provided for us."

"I am looking for a man," she told him and handed him the piece of paper. He looked at it and gave it back to her with no change in his expression.

"And what do you want with this man?"

"He may know where my brother is."

"Is your brother lost?"

"No. But he is missing. . .since the day of the trouble in the square."

"And what makes you think this person can help you?"

"I was told by a friend he might be able to help. My brother is sometimes an angry young boy. And he is impulsive. But he has a good heart. . .He loves his country. I fear he can be influenced by bad teachings, and that those who have taken him will turn him into something he is not. "

"And who is the one who knows this man?"

"I cannot tell you. . .for his safety."

"If you find this man will you keep his safety in mind too?"

"I will not tell anyone. It is my brother I wish to help. I will do anything to find him. I won't tell a soul, as Allah is my witness. Please, can you help me?"

The man looked deeply into Liyah's eyes. "I am the Imam, here."

Liyah's eyes immediately turned downward and she bowed her head.

"Oh, I am so sorry. I did not know, my Imam. I should have known. You are dressed differently. Please forgive me."

The man reached his hand out and raised her chin back up until her eyes meet his again. "And what is your name, my child?"

"Liyah. . .Liyah Al-Rahim."

"Ah, yes. I know of your father. . .and your brother. Your father is a businessman of some repute. He is a good man. Your brother has been throwing stones, so I hear."

"He doesn't mean it. He is a good boy," Liyah protested to him.

The Imam smiled. "Yes, I know this. I did not say his heart is bad. I just said he has been throwing stones." He smiled again.

"Can you help me find this man? Do you know who he is? Why would this paper send me here. . .to a mosque?" Liyah asked.

"So many questions." The Imam laughed. "Yes. I believe I can, my young lady. For it is I. I am that man."

Liyah was stunned. How could this kind Imam be a man who would know about the kidnapping of her brother?

"Well," he continued, "I have your assurances that all that transpires between us and all that is said will end here. . .yes?"

Liyah, still caught in her amazement, hesitated for a moment then in an anxious and hurried voice replied, "Oh. . .yes. . .yes of course. I have said that, haven't I? Yes. . .above all. . .you can trust me. . .I have pledged to Allah."

"I see you have. But I am not sure I can help you at this time. I am aware of the recent kidnappings in Beit Lahia, but I am not directly connected to them. However, I do know many people, as you might guess from my position in the community, and some of these people are involved in the various sides of the political and religious. . .shall we say. . .*discussions* that are taking place these days in our country. I can only promise you that I will look into it. I can guarantee nothing. Can you come back here in two days, at this same time?"

"Yes, certainly," Liyah replied. "I appreciate any information you can provide."

The Imam extended his hand, and upon receiving hers, cupped his other hand on top of both. "All right then. . .to be continued." He smiled, let go of her hand, and walked back to his chamber in the mosque.

Two days later, after making an excuse to her mother to go to visit one of her girlfriends, Liyah returned to the mosque. She walked through the main doors and stood where she had met the Imam. She waited there patiently for a while, but the Imam didn't show. Disappointed, she returned through the main doors and made her way across the small plaza that led from the mosque to the street. As she was about to step back onto the street, the Imam appeared in front of her at the stone pillar marking the street entrance to the mosque.

"I bet you thought I had forsaken you?"

"I would have come back again," Liyah responded confidently.

"I see. I'm sure you would. Good for you."

"Do you have any news? I'm so worried. And time is going by."

"Yes. And I am here, outside the mosque, for a reason. There are few new faces at the mosque at this moment. It would not be wise to speak there, where the sound bounces about the marble walls. I left by way of a rear door when I saw you come in."

Liyah could not contain her anticipation. "What did you find? Do you know where he is?"

The Imam spoke quietly and slowly. "There is a terrorist organization from Iran which a few people I know refer to as Nuqi al-Islam. They have at times teamed with Al Qaeda, the terrorist group that originated in Saudi Arabia. Their mission is to destroy Israel. . .at all costs.

"Nuqi al-Islam originated in Iran but have splinter groups now in many countries. They take innocent people from their homes, mostly those who already have hate in their hearts, and those, like your brother, who are young and can be molded to their wishes. They bring them to different places, sometimes in different countries. . .training camps in Africa, Asia, and Iran. There they are brainwashed and taught elements of terrorism, like making bombs of all kinds, using automatic weapons, infiltrating communities, starting riots and unrest, and other hateful and evil things.

"It is believed that Nuqi al-Islam are the ones behind the kidnappings in Palestine, mostly here in the Gaza Strip, where the Israeli's have stirred a lot of anger with their actions over recent years. They came here to Beit Lahia after the bombings several years ago but have only recently set up the connections of how to get the kidnap victims out of Palestine, past the Israeli checkpoints."

Liyah was distraught. "How will I ever find Khalib, then?"

"I know a man in Jerusalem. He is an old friend of mine who has had strong ties to some of the radical groups in the past. He is a Muezzin, the one who calls people to prayer. He is at an ancient mosque in Jerusalem and has not been involved with these people ever since many of them turned to more extreme activity. He does not believe in the bombing of innocent people and children no matter what the cause, which is how these terrorist's fight. But if anyone could find Khalib, he is the one."

"I will go to him," Liyah replied emphatically.

"It is difficult for a woman, let alone a girl, to travel by herself throughout Palestine without an escort. And it could be dangerous as well if you run into some of these people. Besides, what will you do if you find out where he is? You will not be able to help him by yourself, and I cannot risk involvement from my side. No one must find out who I am or what my connection to these affairs is, here in Beit Lahia."

Liyah thought about his words for a moment, then it came to her. "Don't worry, my Imam, I will keep your name out of this," she assured him again. "I have friends. . .they will come. I know they will help me and protect me. I will need the name of your friend and how to find him. Can you do this for me?"

The Imam studied her with concern, and then spoke. "You are a good sister, my young friend, and a brave one. I can see you love your brother very much. I am worried for you. . .but yes, I will do that. Do you have something to write on?"

Liyah separated the wooden latch of her woven handbag and reached in. "Yes. I came prepared, hoping you could give me some information." She took out a pen and small piece of paper and handed it to him. The Imam wrote the name of the man and the mosque in East Jerusalem on the paper, then handed it back to her. "You can use my name with him but no one else. Yes?"

"Yes, I understand. I don't know how to thank you."

"Just bring your brother home safely. These are troubled times. May Allah go with you."

Do You Want to Make an Impact?

NOW Publishing will help you build your book and deliver your message in a powerful, impactful way.

Everyone has a story to tell and NOW Publishing is here to help them bring those stories to life. Whether you have already written a book and need a marketing partner to promote your story, or have an idea for a book that can change lives and inspire others, we are here to help you turn that into something memorable and marketable.

Download your free copy of the 90-Day Author!

THE
90-DAY
AUTHOR

8 Simple
Steps to Create and Publish a
Powerful Book

SHIRLEY JUMP
Wall Street Journal & New York Times
Bestselling Author

Litz Marie Garcia | Maureen Fanunno | Michael Kawula

Ask about our
90-Day Idea-to-Author Program!

EMAIL US!
publish@nowscpress.com

NOW
PUBLISHING

VISIT US!
www.PublishWithNOW.com

About the Author

Bruce Campelia was born in Boston, Massachusetts and now resides in St. Paul, Minnesota. He holds degrees in engineering, business, and health, and has traveled extensively throughout America and the world over the years. He is the father of three girls, loves music, and is an avid hiker. This is his first novel of The Light Passers Chronicles.